Praise for Leslie LaFoy

The Perfect Seduction

"Intelligent [and] sexy . . . you won't be able to resist
The Perfect Seduction."
—Kasey Michaels, *New York Times* bestselling author

"*The Perfect Seduction* is incredibly delectable and satisfying!"
—Celeste Bradley, author of *The Spy*

"Romance, emotion, marvelous characters—no one does it
better than Leslie LaFoy!"
—Maggie Osborne, award-winning author of *Shotgun Wedding*

"*The Perfect Seduction* is a perfect blend of heart
and soul and wit."
—Mary McBride, author of *My Hero*

"I was seduced by the first page."
—Marianne Willman, author of *Mistress of Rossmor*

"The lures of LaFoy's writing are not just great characters,
fantastic storytelling and heightened sexual tension, but also
the subtle ways she plays on your emotions."
—*RT Bookclub* (4½ stars, Top Pick)

"LaFoy's remarkable characters utterly seduce the reader."
—*Booklist*

St. Martin's Paperbacks Titles
By Leslie LaFoy

The
Perfect
Desire

Leslie LaFoy

St. Martin's Paperbacks

THE PERFECT DESIRE

Copyright © 2005 by Leslie LaFoy.

Cover photo © Melody Cassen.

ISBN: 0-312-98765-X
EAN: 80312-98765-7

Printed in the United States of America

St. Martin's Paperbacks edition / January 2005

St. Martin's Paperbacks are published by St. Martin's Press, 175 Fifth Avenue, New York, NY 10010.

10 9 8 7 6 5 4 3 2 1

In memory of Richard LaFoy
husband, father, citizen soldier, businessman

Prologue

If it wasn't one thing, it was your mother. And the things one was willing to do for the sake of family peace . . . Barrett Stanbridge sighed, propped his shoulder against a marble column, and watched the people move toward the theater doors and the lines of waiting carriages outside. Somewhere in the dignified melee were his parents; his mother no doubt striking up conversations with every unattached woman within ten meters and his father just as certainly craning his neck to see where their errant son had fled this time.

Barrett scowled down at the floor in front of his feet, deliberately hiding his face so that they couldn't easily find him. He'd lost count of how many perfectly proper young women had been shoved in front of him over the last two months. His mother had presented three for his consideration this evening alone. If he had to endure even one more round of inane small talk with a breathless and skittish woman, he'd pull his hair out.

He moved nonchalantly around the marble column, putting it between himself and both the tide of swaying skirts and his parents' determination to see him permanently attached to one of them. There was nothing wrong with being married, he knew. His mother and father had been happily wed for almost forty years. His friends certainly seemed delighted with their marriages. But he didn't feel any particular compunction to fling himself on the altar of Holy Matrimony just for the sake of flinging, for the sake of being like everyone else, or for the sole purpose of making his parents happy.

His mother had tearfully declared his resistance selfish in the extreme. She wanted grandchildren to dote upon and brag about in her feminine circles. His father had been much more pragmatic but no less forceful. He wanted to be sure that the considerable family fortune would pass to Stanbridges in perpetuity. All of which required Barrett to find an acceptable woman, marry her, and produce a litter of little Stanbridges. Preferably male. And definitely without wasting any more time than he already had.

"You're thirty-one," his father had barked yesterday afternoon. "If it weren't for your flagrant dalliances with unacceptable women, people would think you're unnatural. You have obligations and, by God, it's time you stepped up to them."

For the sake of ending his father's tirade and stemming his mother's tears, he'd agreed to attend a play with them tonight and make yet another effort to sort through the marital possibilities. He'd honored his word, but this evening hadn't been any different from all those he'd spent at parties, balls, and galas for the last two months; he'd hated every single minute of it and couldn't wait for it to be over.

Barrett lifted his gaze from the floor, mindful that he needed to sweep out with the crowd if he had any hopes of avoiding his parents and another painful introduction. The tide was thinning, he noted. Coming toward the doors now were the ones who always brought up the rear of any mass exodus—the elderly couples and the doddering dowagers with their plain-faced attendants.

But there was one who wasn't plain faced. Not at all. Very well dressed. Not too tall, not too short. Voluptuously curved. French maybe, he thought as he considered her. And from what he could tell by her movements, she didn't seem to be attached to anyone in particular. Old or young. Male or female.

She turned her head and met his gaze. Barrett instantly recognized the possibilities and smiled. She was the perfect companion. Cool. Direct. Openly sexual. Temporary. There wouldn't be much conversation with her, inane or otherwise.

She glided over, her gaze certain and knowing, his loins tightening.

"Might I persuade you to have dinner with me?" he asked as she came to a halt in front of him.

"Might I persuade you," she replied, smiling up at him, her voice an exotic mixture of French and something else, "to forgo such unnecessary formalities?"

He went hard as he grinned and presented his arm. "I'm the soul of accommodation. Your residence or mine?"

"I am traveling," she said, slipping her arm around his and pressing her breast against his elbow. "With my maid."

He happily took his cue and led her off toward the doors saying, "Mine it is, then."

Out on the walkway, his parents scowled in disapproval but he studiously pretended that he didn't see them and led the delightful morsel off, thinking that playing the dutiful son had more than earned him the all-night, utterly wanton feast the Frenchwoman promised to be.

Chapter One

❦

Dead women didn't care what happened to their wardrobes. Well, Mignon might, but there was nothing she could do about it except stomp around heaven, waving her arms and screaming. Not that it was even remotely possible that Mignon had gone to heaven, Isabella Dandaneau reminded herself, staring out the window of the rented hack.

She exhaled long and hard, brought her gaze down to her lap, and then worked at smoothing a wrinkle in Mignon's skirt. *My* skirt, Isabella silently corrected. And sensibilities—hers *and* Mignon's—aside, desperate situations didn't allow for squeamishness. She needed clothing and Mignon didn't. Not anymore. The constables had turned it all over to her, and sending it back to Louisiana would have been nothing more than an exercise in foolish pride. What she couldn't easily alter to fit her more meager attributes, she'd sell. It'd be nice to have enough money to buy food for a while. Knowing that the bounty had come—albeit indirectly—from Mignon might make swallowing it a bit difficult, but she'd manage.

The cab rolled out of traffic and slowed to a stop before a dark gray granite building. The gold-lettered sign plate beside the heavy door was the right one and she let herself out of the carriage. Her heart racing, Isabella considered the five stone steps that led up to the door. Desperate situations didn't allow for cowardice, either, she sternly reminded herself. Still, it took a deep breath and every measure of her self-discipline to gather her skirts and march upward and into the offices of the man the authorities considered Mignon's killer.

The secretary looked up from his desk and only reluctantly rose to his feet to say, "Good morning, madam. How may I help you?"

Isabella took another slow, deep breath and committed herself to seeing it through. "I'd like to speak with Mr. Barrett Stanbridge, please."

"I'm afraid that is not possible, madam," the little man replied, his nose tilted at a disdainful angle. "Mr. Stanbridge has canceled all of his appointments for the foreseeable future."

Of course he has, Isabella thought. *Defending oneself against murder charges would be rather time-consuming.* "Please tell him," she said firmly, unable to let the man's concerns override her needs, "that I am here regarding the woman killed the night before last."

The secretary's eyes narrowed. "Regarding in what manner?"

Hoping that she held all the cards for the next few moments, Isabella smiled and politely, quietly replied, "What I intend to say to Mr. Stanbridge, I intend to say in private. I'll wait here while you deliver my request."

He assessed her, clearly weighing his hope against his employer's instructions. After a long moment, he tugged the hem of his coat and stepped around his desk, saying, "Your name, madam?"

She hesitated, then decided there was a slight advantage in taking Barrett Stanbridge by surprise. "It's not necessary that you know it."

The man hesitated again, but finally knocked on the door, opened it just wide enough to slide through sideways and then instantly closed it, leaving her alone in the anteroom. Isabella sagged and rubbed her sweating palms along the side seams of her skirt. God, this would be so much easier if she had even the slightest bit of experience at parlor intrigues. Mignon had been one of the best at it and she was dead. What did that suggest about the odds of *her* succeeding?

Closing her eyes, Isabella held her breath and lifted her chin. There was no going back. There was nothing to go back to. She'd simply have to assess the man when she met him and make reasonable judgments as matters went along. The trick would be to tell him no more than she had to, before she had to. And if her instincts even so much as whispered for her to run, she would. Dignity and poise be damned. Staying alive was what mattered.

The twisting of the doorknob warned her of the secretary's return in time for her to slip the mask of cool composure back into place. The door opened wide and the slight man stepped back into the anteroom, moved to the side of the doorway and gestured to the opening, saying regally, "Madam."

Both relief and trepidation washed over her in a single wave. Not trusting her voice, she nodded her thanks and swept forward, bracing herself and hoping her bold plan didn't turn to disaster. Or suicide.

Resolve and fortitude took her across the threshold and halfway to the desk before wavering. Momentum alone provided two additional steps and then she found herself standing on the Persian carpet, her heart racing and her mind careening through a tumble of observations.

He was a massively shouldered, incredibly long-legged man. Dark eyes, dark hair, a wonderfully hard chiseled jaw. Wickedly handsome. Of course Mignon had noticed him in a theater crowd. Every woman had. And at any other moment—when he wasn't strangling on curses as he was now—he'd be rakishly smooth and confident. The perfect ladies' man. Which was why Mignon had chosen him.

He blinked, took a deep breath. As he was swallowing, Isabella seized what there was of an advantage. "No, you're not seeing a ghost, Mr. Stanbridge," she said, putting on a soft smile and forcing her feet to carry her forward again.

He'd cocked a brow and begun to openly assess her by the time she reached the edge of his desk, stopped, and added, "My name is Isabella Dandaneau. Mignon Richard was my cousin. Our mothers were sisters. There is—or rather *was*—a strong family resemblance."

He nodded ever so slightly. "Are you here for vengeance?"

Good God, the man's voice had the most delicious rumble to it. If his hands were just half as efficient at caressing . . . She started, appalled by the direction of her thoughts and stunned by the ease in which they'd not only escaped her control, but also set her heart skittering with a ridiculous kind of feminine anticipation.

"Well, in the first place," she replied as her stomach twisted into a knot, "I never liked Mignon well enough to go through all the effort of avenging her. In the second place, the only thing surprising about her death is that it didn't happen long before now. And in the third . . ." She considered him and listened to her instincts. "You're not the one who killed her."

"And why do you think that?"

Cool and calm and analytical. The advantage of surprise was gone. "If you don't mind my saying so," Isabella countered, trying to affect a manner matching his, "that's a rather odd response from a man who stands a good chance of being charged with murder before sunset tonight."

"What did you expect me to say?"

"Something approximating 'Thank God! You must tell the constables that I'm innocent!' " she replied honestly. "The last part of that would have been while you had your hand wrapped around my arm and were dragging me out of here and to the nearest officer of the law."

One corner of his mouth lifted in a decidedly cynical smile. "I'd like to know what you're going to say before I hear you say it to the crown's investigators. So I'll ask the question again. How do you know that I didn't kill your cousin?"

She liked his direct manner; it spoke of a disciplined, somewhat wary curiosity. And she most certainly understood the need to proceed cautiously. "According to the accounts I've read in the papers," she offered, "everyone is of the opinion that beating a woman to death simply isn't in your nature."

"The crown's men haven't been the least impressed by the testimonials."

"Understandably, I suppose," she countered. "It's their job to be suspicious. Although I personally think there's much to be said for the fact that, without exception, people have nothing but good things to say about you. Mignon couldn't have reasonably expected the same from those who knew her."

"Why?"

If he and Mignon had had any sort of sustained relationship, he wouldn't have had to ask. Oddly, the realization instantly settled her stomach. With considerably more confidence than she'd possessed since the entire fiasco had begun, she replied, "I gather that your acquaintance with her was both brief and casual."

"It was brief." He paused to clear his throat before quietly adding, "But intimate."

A gentleman? Mignon had chosen a gentleman? Poor Barrett Stanbridge. "Intimate only in a physical sense, I'm sure. My cousin never took her heart into a bed," Isabella supplied. "In fact, if I were of a mind to wager, I'd bet that you didn't know her name until the constables battered down your door and began asking their unpleasant questions. I'd also bet that if you told her your name, she didn't bother to remember it."

He hesitated, studying her, his head tilted slightly to the side. "We'll never know the answer to the latter," he finally ventured.

"No, we won't," she agreed, impressed with his effort at diplomacy. She grinned. "But I am right about the former, aren't I? Mignon didn't slow down enough for even the most basic of conversations, did she?"

He sighed and gave her a rueful smile. "My mother has always told me that one shouldn't speak ill of the dead."

"It's a nice custom if you can afford the luxury of it," Isabella instantly countered. "In the case of Mignon . . . The truth, as dark as it may be, would serve us both better."

"Us?" he said, folding his arms across his chest. "As I've heard it, I'm the only one under suspicion."

"Well, the truth, Mr. Stanbridge, is that if they didn't have you, they'd suspect me."

A dark brow shot upward. "Oh? Do you make a habit of beating women to death in alleyways?"

No, she didn't. But in dealing with her cousin in recent months, she'd been sorely tempted—several times—to suspend her adherence to law-abiding conduct.

"Why have you come here, Miss Dandaneau?"

She didn't know whether he was referring to her presence in his office or the larger purpose that had brought her to London. But she was keenly aware that they were approaching the point where she was going to have to make a decision. Could she trust him with the entire story? He seemed to be an honorable man; not at all the sort that Mignon usually chose.

"It's Mrs. Dandaneau," she corrected, deliberately delaying an honest answer as she mentally sorted through and organized her impressions of him. "I'm a widow."

"My condolences, madam," he replied crisply and with a small dip of his chin. "And now that we've dispensed with that bit of edification, evasion, and civility, perhaps you'll answer my question. Why are you here?"

She wasn't at all sure that she liked the fact that he'd seen through her ploy so easily. "You're an innocent man under suspicion," she offered, wondering if his intelligence would make him a dangerous ally in the end. "You could very well end up on the gallows for a crime you didn't commit."

"I'm well aware of that," he countered dryly. "Do you have any evidence to support the claim that someone else killed Mignon Richard?"

"Not that would be acceptable in court."

"Then," he drawled, unfolding his arms and coming around to her side of the desk, "while I appreciate your moral support in the present situation, I really—"

"What I have is a story to tell you," she interjected before he could actually gesture to the door and ask her to leave.

"A story."

He was more irritated than he was interested. But she'd committed herself to trusting him for the moment and there was nothing to do now but plow ahead and hope he was gentleman enough to listen and desperate enough to offer his assistance. "Tell me, Mr. Stanbridge," she began, "have you ever heard the name Jean Lafitte?"

With a sigh of obviously strained patience, he sat on the

corner of his desk, refolded his arms and answered, "He was a pirate, as I recall. Turn of the century. That's the sum total of my recollection. History was not one of my favorite subjects in school."

"He was a Baratarian pirate," Isabella clarified. "A reformed one, depending on who's telling the story. What do you know of the 1814 Battle of New Orleans?"

Shrugging, he supplied simply, "It was a slaughter of British troops. A needless one since the war had ended some days earlier."

His lack of interest in the topic didn't, unfortunately, make it any less vital to the explanation she had to give him. "Yes, the news didn't reach America in time to prevent it," Isabella said, trudging on. "Andrew Jackson was the commander of the American army in New Orleans. Such as it was. If accolades are to be awarded for the victory, they rightly go to Jean Lafitte. It was his men and his knowledge of the terrain that tipped the advantage to the American side."

He cocked a brow and sighed, not bothering to make it politely quiet. "And the point of this history lesson?"

She bristled at his tone, but deliberately set her irritation aside to continue. "Andrew Jackson not only became a national hero as a result of that battle, but also our seventh president."

"So you're a Yank."

"Yankees are Northerners," she corrected, trying, and failing, to sound unruffled. It took considerable effort, but she summoned a smile and a softer tone of voice to add, "I am a Southerner, Mr. Stanbridge. A Louisianian of Acadian descent."

"My apologies," he offered with a strained smile. "The insult was unintentional, a consequence of English ignorance. Please continue."

Despite his obvious hope that she wouldn't, Isabella did,

saying, "Jackson may have had a good number of faults, but he was loyal to those he considered friends. And he reportedly counted Jean Lafitte as a member of that small group. He is also reported to have believed it quite appropriate to use his influence to reward his friends handsomely for their respective services to him and their country."

In the pause she took for a breath, he asked dryly, "What does all this have to do with your cousin?"

"I'm working my way in that direction," she retorted, months of worry and frustration bubbling to the surface. She tamped down her irritation to add, "Please try to have just a bit of patience. The foundation of the past must be carefully laid or the present circumstances won't make any sort of sense at all."

He nodded and eased off the desk. Gesturing at the chair beside her, he asked, "Would you care for a cup of coffee?"

"I'd love one," she admitted, gratefully dropping down onto the upholstered seat. "Thank you," she added, more for the fact that he'd at least resigned himself to hearing her out than anything else.

Barrett watched her out of the corner of his eye as he made his way to the sideboard and the silver coffee service. He had thought, in the first moments she'd walked in, that he was seeing a ghost, but, after that initial shock had passed, the differences had been more apparent than the similarities. She was more slightly built than her cousin had been. And definitely more talkative.

Unfortunately, she was every bit as physically appealing and he couldn't seem to keep his mind fully engaged in what she was saying to him. It kept wandering back in his recent memories and wondering if Isabella Dandaneau was anywhere near the skillful lover her cousin had been. Oddly, and most disconcertingly, part of him rather hoped she wasn't.

Not that he was ever going to know one way or the other, he reminded himself. The encounter with Mignon had been a memorable one from a physical standpoint, but he was going to be put through the proverbial mill for the pleasure. The last thing he needed now was to complicate his existence even one whit more. The fact that she'd walked into his office . . . Jesus.

He had to give her credit for the sheer courage it must have taken, though. Courage and, no doubt, a sense of desperation. Try as she might to appear cool and calm, he could hear the slight hesitations in her speech, see the indecision in her dark eyes, could feel her constant assessment. She wanted something from him and was slowly working up to the point of asking for it. It was a sure bet, however, that she wouldn't ask him to bed her. The woman's fires were well banked. Thank God.

Pouring out two cups of coffee, he asked, "Cream or sugar?"

"Plain, please."

He carried them back to the desk, handed her one, and then took up his position on the corner. As he expected, she thanked him politely and immediately launched back into what she called her "story."

"Mignon's and my grandmother was . . ." She made a little face that suggested she was trying to find a delicate way of putting an indelicate truth. "Well, the family has always referred to her relationship with Lafitte as a 'special friendship.' "

"They were lovers," he supplied bluntly and then took a sip of his coffee.

"I think so," she admitted. "And, judging by the look that always came to my grandmama's face whenever anyone mentioned Lafitte, it must have ended badly."

"The affair that ends without hard feelings is the rarest of exceptions."

She nodded as though she had some experience at such things and then added, "In fairness to Grandmama, though, it was before she met and married Grandpapa. Who was, in his own right, something of a pirate himself. He and Grandmama had two daughters, Juliana, my mother, and Michelle, Mignon's mother.

"Three months ago a package was delivered to the law firm that has represented our family for four generations. It was addressed to Grandmama. Since Mignon and I were her only living descendants, we were summoned to the office for the opening of the package."

"Let me guess," he said, at last seeing the pattern of her discourse. "It was from Jean Lafitte."

"In a manner of speaking." She sipped her coffee before explaining, "Apparently he died some years ago and under circumstances which aren't quite clear. His last will and testament was only recently discovered and the package was an attempt to see that it was, at last, executed."

God, the woman took forever to get to the crux of a matter. Hoping to move her along in the telling, he prompted, "And what did he bequeath your grandmama?"

"That's where things become a bit of a mystery."

"A mystery," he repeated, a dull ache beginning to bloom in the back of his head.

"There have always been rumors that Jean Lafitte buried a great treasure."

"As any self-respecting pirate does," he quipped, struggling against the urge to roar in frustration.

"Part of it is assumed to be the proceeds of his pirating days and part of it the reward given for services rendered to his country. It's rumored to be worth millions of dollars."

"Of course," he observed tightly. "What would be the point of burying a few shillings? Keeping its location a secret wouldn't be worth the lead and powder to kill the poor bastards who helped you dig the hole."

She gazed up at him with big, dark eyes. Big dark eyes that were bright with irritation. "You're not taking this seriously, Mr. Stanbridge."

"My apologies," he offered, sincere only in his intent to get the tale told before he was an old man. "Please continue. Three months ago you and your cousin were informed that you'd inherited buried pirate treasure."

With a nod, she added another bit to the slowly emerging picture, saying "Either Jean Lafitte was a deeply suspicious man or he enjoyed games. It's not possible to tell which from the will. What is clear is that to claim the treasure, one has to follow a trail of clues to find it."

"You're joking," he accused before he could think better of it. The fire in her eyes instantly prompted him to add, "All right, you're not. I gather the first clue is what brought you and Mignon to London."

Fixing her gaze on the center of his chest, she crisply went on. "As I said, the law firm in New Orleans has represented the family for generations. They know all the family secrets. As well as what's common knowledge. Most notably, they know the kind of people we are. In what he no doubt considered an act worthy of Solomon, the family lawyer gave half the map to Mignon and half to me."

"A map," he repeated, wondering how a seemingly rational woman could tell such a penny-dreadful tale with not only a straight face, but with apparent utter sincerity. "Does X mark the spot?"

"Yes," she replied, her voice tight, her eyes shooting daggers in the general vicinity of his heart. "Of the next clue."

God help him; he had to ask. "And the map is of London?"

"I have no idea." She paused to take a slow and dainty sip of her coffee. "Apparently Mignon thought so. She bolted with her half of the map. I had no choice but to chase after her, hoping to find and convince her that we stood a better chance of finding it if we worked together."

His mind clicked furiously along several strings of possibility. "And what did she say when you caught up to her and presented your argument?"

Her complete attention shifted to the cup and saucer in her hands. Twisting the cup ever so slowly back and forth in the saucer's indentation, she said quietly, "That she didn't need me."

"Well," Barrett drawled, "I must say that being denied buried treasure worth millions would be an excellent motive for murder."

She nodded, but didn't look up. "It's certainly a far better one than any they can fabricate for you."

Yes, indeed, it was. When the authorities finally got around to posing the right questions to the right people . . . "You're in trouble, Mrs. Dandaneau."

Her gaze snapped up to his. The fire was gone, replaced by the glint of steely resolve. "No deeper than you are, Mr. Stanbridge."

"But eventually my name is going to be cleared," he pointed out. "Especially when the authorities learn the reason for your cousin's presence in London. And yours."

One delicately shaped brow inched upward. "Do you think they'll believe—any more than you do—a story of a scavenger hunt for buried pirate treasure?"

"Probably not," he admitted, lifting his cup and saluting her with it. "Until they find Mignon's half of the map."

"True," she admitted as he sipped. "Which is going to be very interesting since you're the one who has it."

Hot coffee and cold realization caught hard midway down his throat. If she was right . . .

Isabella concluded that his coughing fit wasn't life-threatening and waited for him to recover. Timing, she decided, was everything with Barrett Stanbridge. His coolly analytical—and slightly cynical—manner was fairly easy to knock off kilter if she tossed the right information at him at just the right moment. He didn't strike her, however, as the sort of man who would let her get away with the tactic indefinitely. Intelligent and quick-witted, he'd soon come to anticipate the surprises. Which meant that she needed to use them while she could.

"I have half the map?" he said, his voice a bit strained. He cleared his throat before adding more firmly, "What makes you think that?"

"Mignon liked to appear important," Isabella supplied, relaxing as she headed into the end of the tale, certain that she'd made the right choice in sharing it with him. "Within hours of being handed our respective halves of the map, all of New Orleans and half of Louisiana knew of it. There were two attempts to steal my half of the map. Three to steal Mignon's."

He hesitated, slowly cocking a brow. "Do you have any idea by whom?"

"The list of possible thieves is endless." She finished her coffee and set the cup and saucer on his desk. Settling back in the chair, she folded her hands in her lap and met his gaze squarely. "It has, however, been narrowed to someone with the financial resources required to follow us here. After I identified Mignon's body yesterday evening, I went to her lodgings. They'd been ransacked. Whoever attempted to steal her half of the map in New Orleans attempted it again here."

"How do you know they didn't find it?"

Something in his manner suggested that he already knew the answer and that the question was more a test of her reasoning abilities than anything else. "Mignon was killed the night before last," she replied confidently. "I went by her lodgings yesterday morning and the landlady let me in to wait. The room and her belongings were in typical Mignon disarray when I arrived and when I left. It was after her death and after my departure that someone tore things to shreds."

"They could have found it."

She shook her head and smiled. "Mignon wouldn't have left it in such an obvious place. And it's just as apparent that she didn't have it on her when she was accosted and beaten or it wouldn't have been necessary to search her lodgings after she died. Which makes it likely that she hid it somewhere, intending to keep it safe for the time being and come back for it later. According to the landlady, the only time she left her rooms the day she died was to dine all three meals in public establishments and to attend a play in the evening."

He slowly nodded but didn't say anything.

"And," Isabella went on, "according to the constables, witnesses report that she left the play on your arm, climbed into your carriage, and wasn't seen again until her bludgeoned body was found in the alleyway behind your house yesterday morning."

"Do you have any idea of where she dined that last day?"

Isabella shook her head. "But it doesn't matter," she clarified. "Mignon wouldn't have hidden the map in a public place. The risk that it might be accidentally lost or discovered would be too great. No. She hid it during the time she spent with you, Mr. Stanbridge. It's somewhere in your carriage, your house, or on your property."

He finished his own coffee and set the cup and saucer aside, saying quietly, "Are you aware that, as a holder of half of the map, you're in the same grave danger your cousin was?"

Of course she did and she found it interesting that his mind was tracking along that course. Was it based in something approximating chivalry? Or was it more a natural consequence of his occupation? Private investigators probably focused on the potential danger more than others did. Not that the answer mattered, she reminded herself. By nightfall, he'd be nothing more than another person she'd met along the way and would never encounter again.

Isabella nodded. "I also know that my best chance of staying alive is to find Mignon's half as soon as possible so that I stay well ahead of whoever it is that killed her."

He folded his arms across his chest and crossed his ankles. "Did you come here thinking to hire me to protect you?"

He did that sort of thing? The possibility had never crossed her mind. "No, Mr. Stanbridge," she assured him, chuckling darkly. "Until I find Lafitte's treasure, I can barely afford one meal a day. I came here this morning because I need your permission and assistance to search your private property. If you'll give it, if you'll assist me in this one small way, I'll tell the authorities the entire story and clear your name."

The cynical smile lifted one corner of his mouth. "And make yourself the principal suspect in Mignon's murder?"

It was a small price to pay for invaluable—no, absolutely essential—help. And one she'd concluded was worth the risk before she'd walked in the door. "I'll be well gone before they open the letter. Let them try to find me."

Barrett stared down at the carpet, his mind racing. How long had Mignon Richard been in London before she'd met him in the theater lobby? he wondered. Was he the only man with whom she'd spent time? Was his the only property she might have used to hide her half of the map? They were important questions, he knew. But not absolutely vital. Not unless a thorough search of his house and carriage failed to produce results. At that point, he'd have no choice but to find the answers.

But if, on the other hand, the map was where Isabella

Dandaneau thought it was . . . It wasn't going to solve his problems as easily as she believed. Her vouching for his innocence wasn't going to carry all that much weight with the authorities. Especially when they couldn't find her or another suspect to haul into the dock for a grisly murder.

The decision of what to do in the long run could wait, he decided. At the moment, it was in his best interests to help her find the missing half of the map. Hopefully, she was right and they'd discover it tucked somewhere in his carriage or his house. The prospect of having to trace every move Mignon had made while in London was too daunting to even contemplate. And spending hours and hours with Isabella at the task . . . God, he wished she didn't look quite so much like her cousin had. His eyes seemed to be linked to his memory and his memory to his loins. All by the shortest of cords.

Unfolding, he pushed himself off the desk and strode across the office. "Quincy," he said, pulling open the door. "Have the carriage brought around, please."

He was taking his greatcoat from the rack in the corner when she rose from her seat saying, "Thank you, Mr. Stanbridge. I appreciate your trust and accommodation."

"Those are noble reasons," he replied, shrugging into the wool garment. "I'm going along with this strictly in the interest of self-preservation."

"I do understand the importance of that."

Barrett considered her. Her initial nervousness had subsided in the course of their exchange and the woman who now met his gaze from across the room was absolutely certain of the direction in which she was setting them. And beneath that confidence lay a steely resolve every bit the equal of that her cousin had displayed during her time with him.

But there was more to Isabella. Or maybe less, depending on how he looked at it. Mignon had been the kind of woman who moved through every moment like a chess player; each action, each breath, calculated for effect and strategically planned well in advance. But while Isabella knew just as well where she wanted to go and what she wanted to accomplish, she didn't seem to employ cold manipulation to get there. She danced along the edge, trusting instincts to keep her balance from one moment to the next.

All in all, he decided as he motioned for her to precede him out of the office, she was a much more dangerous woman than Mignon had ever been. Isabella was comfortable with behaving in largely unpredictable ways. The sooner she was gone from his life, the better.

Chapter Two

"Is this the seat Mignon occupied during the trip to your house?"

Barrett's chest tightened as an unpleasant certainty settled in his brain: the particulars of his time with Mignon couldn't remain private. Not given the realities of why she'd left the theater with him and why Isabella Dandaneau had marched into his life in her cousin's wake. Expelling a long, slow breath, Barrett resolved to handle the circumstances with as much dignity and decorum as possible. "Initially, yes," he replied tautly.

The arch of her brow and the cynical shadow to her smile told him that she knew exactly what had transpired the instant he'd closed the carriage door that night. Precisely why he was embarrassed by that . . .

"Still, it bears searching," she announced jauntily, turning on the seat and skimming her fingers along the seam where the bottom cushion met the back one. "She could have hidden the map in the moments before putting you on your back."

Barrett watched her as yet another realization took up

residence in his brain. He had two choices: he could either focus on the trampling of his sense of propriety and wiggle in acute discomfort, or he could ignore all that and concentrate on understanding the spiderweb in which he'd become ensnared. Since the latter of the two courses actually offered him a glimmer of hope for influencing the outcome of the disaster, he concluded that there really wasn't much of a choice at all. And given that, he needed to gather as much information as he could. Mignon and the map were the keys, Isabella the logical—the only—source of what could be learned.

"You truly didn't like your cousin, did you?" he asked, beginning his quest.

Shifting about to continue her exploration, she replied, "I can't tell you the number of times I've been mistaken for her and been groped, mauled, and all but raped." She moved her search to the space where the lower cushion met the walls. "And as you might well imagine from that bit of information and your own experience with her, her behavior wasn't exactly a sterling contribution to the family reputation."

He could have surmised that much on his own. But the fault didn't lie in Isabella's answer; it lay in the question and his approach to the matter. Frowning, he silently cursed the mush his brain had become since the constables had appeared at his door. In a great many respects, it felt as though the better, more capable part of it had packed its bags and departed with the detectives.

She'd finished examining the seams of the lower cushion and was almost done with her inspection of the seam between the upper cushion and the back wall when he temporarily abandoned the attempt to chart a sounder course and drawled, "Find anything?"

"No," she admitted, turning back to sit squarely facing him. "I'd like to search your seat, if you wouldn't mind."

She was thorough; he had to give her credit for that. And apparently, judging by the direction of her thoughts, she wasn't the least bit priggish either. Shrugging his assent, Barrett moved to her side of the carriage, easing her hoops and skirt aside to avoid crushing them as he did. Oddly, the courtesy seemed to fluster her. Her gasp was tiny and quickly strangled, but he heard it nonetheless. The sound prompted him to glance at her just in time to catch a glimpse of widened eyes and slightly parted lips.

Even as he was thinking about how delectable she looked, she slipped the mask of cool composure back into place and gracefully, ever so nonchalantly, transferred herself to the seat he'd just vacated. Barrett watched as she began a systematic search of the cushions and added *persistent* to her list of more favorable qualities.

Not, he had to admit, that he'd seen anything in her so far that he'd consider to be a glaring character flaw. Judging by her behavior in his office, she did seem to have a tendency to act first and think later, to make judgments and decisions on instinct and at the spur of the moment. But, he reminded himself, that wasn't something terribly uncommon in women. At least with most of the women of his experience. His mother had always maintained that women were gifted with highly developed senses of intuition. And while he'd always considered it a rather flimsy excuse for the lack of cool logic and well-planned actions, he'd learned that efforts to make them think more like men were not only hopeless, but exceedingly frustrating. They were happily what they were and there was no changing them.

On the more positive side of the ledger, Isabella Dandaneau didn't seem to have even a sliver of false pride; she'd outright and easily admitted to poverty. And the fact that she'd come to him asking for help certainly implied that she had an uncommon amount of pragmatism; that she understood the importance of putting success before any notions of personal independence.

And, thanks to the combination of her moving around on the seat and a rather pathetic set of hoops, he could see that she also had a most wonderfully curved waist, hip, and backside.

Barrett reined in his smile and forced his gaze to the floor. God, he really needed to see that she found what she was looking for and was on her way as soon as humanly possible. The longer her departure was delayed, the greater the chance that he would do or say something he'd later regret. Although, he had to admit, it was going to be hard to do anything that turned out more regrettable than having taken Mignon home.

Leaning down, he trailed his fingertips over the seams joining the seat bench to the floorboard. It was tight and he knew even as he made his search that he wasn't going to find anything in the course of it.

"The floor as well?"

Hearing the amusement in her voice, he leaned forward and checked the other side, replying, "I'm not going to provide you with the specific details."

"I should hope not," she countered, the distinct sound of laughter edging her words. "Not that I can't very well surmise them on my own, you understand."

"Oh?"

Isabella struggled to keep her smile suppressed as he straightened and met her gaze. "I'm well acquainted with the carnal possibilities in even the shortest carriage ride," she assured him.

"Really."

Oh, Lord help her; the way he cocked his brow and the dry, almost sardonic edge to his drawl were so . . . so . . . Appealing. If the one time in her life when she'd listened to the little voice of temptation hadn't turned out so very badly . . . She swallowed down her suddenly skittering heart and somehow managed to blithely retort, "Of course. I simply haven't made it quite the habit or the art form that Mignon did."

His brow rose another degree. "But since you are a widow, those days—and possibilities—are past you now."

She couldn't decide if it was a backhanded invitation or an observation that she was, fundamentally and to his general disappointment, a woman with obvious moral standards. "They were past me while I was still a wife," she admitted and then abruptly, firmly, took the subject in a less personal direction, saying, "I gather that you didn't find anything in searching the floor? She might have folded it quite small."

"Nothing."

"Damn," she muttered on a sigh, looking down at her lap. "Despite knowing better, I had hoped this might be relatively easy."

He snorted quietly and said, "I know my acquaintance with your cousin was limited, but it was sufficient to form the distinct impression that Mignon never did anything in an 'easy' fashion."

"No, sadly, she didn't," Isabella supplied, absently smoothing the persistent wrinkle in her skirt. "Her life would have been much happier—and longer—if she had. In a great many respects, she seemed to go through her days trying to make as many enemies as she possibly could. In my kinder moments I often felt very sorry for her."

Barrett pursed his lips and considered the woman in the opposite seat. What would Mignon have said about her? he wondered. That she was naïve and altogether too honest and trusting? That she was, despite her moments of bravado and resolve, too sentimental and kindhearted for her own good? That Isabella Dandaneau stupidly put being a good person ahead of self-interest?

The carriage slowed and maneuvered to the side of the roadway, signaling the end of their ride and his pointless musing. As they were drawing to a halt, he leaned forward and grasped the door handle, sternly reminding himself that there was no reason to know any more about this woman in a personal sense than he had her cousin. Once Isabella got her hands on the missing half of the map, she was going to be nothing more than a flash of disappearing skirts.

No, he amended, as he vaulted down onto the walkway in front of his house, that wasn't entirely true. Or honest. She'd promised, in exchange for his help, to write the authorities a letter exonerating him in Mignon's death and her actions so far suggested that she was, above all else, an honorable woman. She'd write that letter.

And be gone within the same instant as she handed it to him, his more cynical side added darkly. If the authorities didn't believe a word of what she wrote . . . If they had questions he couldn't answer . . . If she turned up dead after leaving him . . . His stomach a tight and frigid pit, his mind numbly staring at the crumbling edge of the abyss, Barrett managed to summon a polite and courtly smile as he handed her down onto the public walkway.

Gesturing up the walk that led to his front door, he let her lead the way and desperately tried to marshal his wits as he followed in her wake. No matter how he looked at it, he was buggered six ways to Sunday. If he let her walk away to pursue Lafitte's treasure on her own, he stood a damn good chance of quickly regretting it. If he tagged along with her in the quest, he was going to regret that, too.

She was trouble. A different kind of trouble than Mignon was, certainly, but trouble nonetheless. Just what exactly she'd end up doing to him, putting him through, he couldn't even begin to imagine. But the heavy sense of dread and doom was undeniable. It was much like the feeling that came with looking out over a river gorge and knowing deep inside that it wasn't meant to be bridged, that you were pitting yourself against the will of God.

Isabella slid a quick glance up at him as he reached around her and opened the door of his home. His brows were knitted, his lips compressed, and his jaw a hard granite line. The light in his dark eyes wasn't angry, though. No, more troubled and pensive, she decided as she stepped into the foyer. Not knowing what to do from there, she stopped and openly surveyed the portions of the house visible from the entry.

"You have a lovely home," she ventured. "It's so English. I like it."

Gesturing for her to unbutton her redingote, he then set about removing his own wrap and took up his end of polite conversation, asking, "Are your homes so different in Louisiana?"

"I've noticed that English houses, no matter how large, tend to have a very structured and tight feeling to them. Ours, on the other hand, tend to sprawl in a rather indolent manner and blur the lines between indoors and out."

"My friend Carden is an architect," he replied, taking the light coat from her shoulders. Hanging it on a wall peg beside his, he added, "I've seen illustrations of your homes in one of his books. As I recall, there seems to be a fondness for what the author called verandahs."

"My own house had two of them," she provided, trying—and failing—to keep the sadness from tightening her throat. She swallowed and forced herself to smile. "One on the main level and one on the second. Both wrapped the entire house."

"This way, please," he said, indicating the stairs that led to the upper floor.

Isabella gathered her skirts and started up, acutely aware that he was following on her heels, his hand not touching her, but hovering protectively near the small of her back. It had been such a long time since any man had made even the smallest effort at gallantry. Those who had made it the cornerstone of their lives were all gone. Those who were left—

"You used the past tense just a moment ago," he observed, gently interrupting her thoughts. "I gather you no longer own that house?"

The tone of his question implied that it had been sold and she'd moved on of her own volition. "It was burned to the ground by the Union Army," she supplied as the horrible memories of that night played through her mind. Reny. Nigel. Bartholomew. Their desperate insistence that she leave first. The three shots as the flames had leaped high and the bluebellies stood in the yard and laughed. Isabella took a deep breath and shook her head to dispel the memory. "The land on which it once stood is still mine," she added, forcing herself, yet again, to move on. "Until they take it for unpaid taxes, of course."

Barrett winced at the stoic resolve evident in her voice and regretted his part in stirring what were obviously painful memories. The Americans and their war. It had been over for the better part of a year now, but he should have remembered it and known that Isabella Dandaneau was likely to have suffered in the course of it. Feeling the need to say something comforting and apologetic, he offered, "I know that words are of very little consolation," as they reached the top of the stairs. "But I'm sincerely sorry for your loss."

"What's done is done," she said tightly—almost as though by rote. "What's lost is lost. You can't dwell on what was."

"A healthy attitude."

"Well," she replied, looking up at him and arching a dark brow, "it's either find a way to go on or lie down and cry yourself to death. And since I've seen quite enough of death in the last six years, it's really not a difficult decision to make."

Not for the strong, he knew. The weak never saw the choice and the cowards pretended there was only one. *An interesting woman, this Isabella Dandaneau,* he thought as he gestured absently in the direction of his bedroom door. He watched her move off. *She has secrets. Dark secrets.*

Her abrupt halt, her gasp, instantly brought him from his musings. Turning his head to see what had alarmed her, he found the door to his room standing wide open. Beyond it, the contents lay in complete shambles. He quickly put himself between her and the room while drawing the pistol from the small of his back, and then strode forward to the threshold.

No one was there; whoever had ransacked the place was apparently long gone. But to have gotten in to do their damage . . . His heart in his throat, he turned on his heel and raced to the staircase and started down, yelling, "Mrs. Wallace! Cook!"

He was aware of both Isabella following on his heels and of the unnatural stillness of his house. He should have noticed it the instant he walked in. Jesus! If something had happened to the two women . . . Older. Trusting. Defenseless. He'd find and kill the son of a bitch. "Mrs. Wallace!" he bellowed as he scrambled into the kitchen. "Cook!"

Isabella's hand was already on the pantry doorknob when he, too, heard the thumping sound. "No," he whispered harshly, catching her wrist and drawing her back. "I'll go first. Stand aside."

She nodded once, crisply, and took two small steps back. It wasn't as far as he would have preferred, but it was far enough to be out of his and immediate harm's way. He flung the door wide, instantly vaulting into the dimly lit space with the muzzle of his pistol sweeping across it.

The shelves were in perfect order and his housekeeper and cook were neatly wrapped in sheets, bound, gagged, and lying in the center of the floor. And apparently, judging by the way they were kicking the base of the cabinets, relatively unharmed.

"Thank God," he murmured, tucking the gun away and dropping to one knee beside Mrs. Wallace. At the edge of his vision he saw Isabella kneel beside his cook. Reaching up his sleeve, Barrett withdrew his knife and slashed the gag and then the cording that encircled his housekeeper's arms and legs.

"Here," he said, blindly extending the knife toward Isabella, "use this."

"Thank you, but no," she replied quickly, quietly. "I carry my own."

Stunned, he looked over just in time to see her slip a stiletto into the side seam of her skirt. Deliberately setting aside his wonder and all the questions that came with it, he put his own knife back up his sleeve and then set about helping Mrs. Wallace free herself from the linen wrapper.

"Who did this?" he asked as he helped her roll onto her back and then rise to a sitting position. "Can you describe him?"

"There were two, sir," she supplied, shoving her disheveled gray hair off her forehead. "Judging by the sounds, one was tying up Cook when the other dragged me in here."

"Came in through the back door, they did," Cook added as Isabella helped right her. "Said they had a delivery of ice. The lying dogs."

"What did they look like?" he pressed.

"Can't say that I saw their faces clear enough, sir," Cook replied. "I wasn't wearing my spectacles since I was doing the laundry and that tends to fog them over."

"The one who surprised me dropped a sheet over my

head from behind when I was in the parlor," Mrs. Wallace contributed, still working on repairing her coiffure. "I had no idea he was there until that moment. I'm sorry, sir. Have they stolen everything?"

Barrett rose to his feet and extended his hands. "I have no idea and, frankly, don't care if they did. Have you been harmed in any way?"

"Aside from the fright of it all, no, sir," she provided, accepting his assistance and gaining her feet. "They were quite careful in how they tied us."

Watching Isabella competently get his cook on her feet, he continued his questioning, asking, "What did they sound like? English? French? American?"

"The one that said they were here with ice was English," Cook answered. "Not a man of quality, though. I never heard the other one speak so I can't rightly say what he was."

"Neither did I, sir."

Barrett sighed in frustration and moved on to his next concern. "Did you hear them leave?"

"Yes, sir," Cook hastily assured him. "Some time ago. They weren't here for long. They went directly upstairs, banged about, and then left straightaway, going out the same way they came in."

Isabella inched backward to better take in the scene before her. The two women were physically rumpled, but otherwise quite composed. If any one of the three other people in the room was visibly shaken from the ordeal, it was, surprisingly, Barrett Stanbridge. He raked his fingers through his hair, utterly destroying the style, and then expelled a long hard breath and squared his shoulders.

"It's not safe for you to remain in the house, ladies," he said firmly, motioning them all to precede him out of the pantry and into the kitchen proper. As they complied, he went on, saying, "I want you both to pack a bag for an extended stay away. If you have someplace you'd prefer to go other than a comfortable inn—with family, perhaps—please let James know and he'll take you there. When I believe the danger's past, I'll send for you. Consider this a paid, well-earned holiday."

"Yes, sir," Mrs. Wallace replied, dropping a quick curtsy. "We'll see to it immediately." And, true to her word, she started for the servants' stairs, calling back over her shoulder, "Come along, Edna."

Cook—Edna, apparently—gave Barrett a curtsy of her own and obediently followed after her, leaving Isabella alone with him in the warm and humid room.

His gaze dropped to the side of her skirt for a second and then came back up to meet hers as he said, "I'm going out to the carriage house to speak with my driver. I'll be back shortly. Don't leave this house."

"I wouldn't dream of it," she assured him. "I'll be upstairs when you return."

She couldn't clearly define the light that came into his eyes as he nodded his acceptance. There was an element of wariness to it. And perhaps a bit of curiosity too, she thought. But there was something else as well. Something . . . Well, "menacing" wasn't quite the right word. Neither was foreboding. But her stomach was tight and it was hard to breathe as he walked away. And she most definitely had the sense that, unless she were very careful, in the end she was going to add Barrett Stanbridge to the long list of reasons she hated Mignon.

"I'm destined to live long," she reminded herself, turning and heading back through the house. "Madame Tanay said so."

Chapter Three

Barrett took the stairs two at time, wishing that it didn't require quite so much effort to keep his thoughts coherent. Getting his staff on their way to their respective destinations had been accomplished in a relatively painless process that had owed much to their ability to think for themselves once he'd managed to set them in motion.

Damn Mignon. If it weren't for her, he'd be tucked away at his club, drinking whisky with Carden and Aiden and letting them bore him to tears with their stories of children, pets, and marital bliss. His life would still be well ordered and his only goddamned problem would be finding a wife to make his parents happy. His bedroom wouldn't be a shambles. His staff wouldn't be fleeing for their safety. And he sure as hell wouldn't have one foot on the gallows steps.

He stopped on the threshold of his room. And, if it weren't for Mignon Richard's deviousness, he'd have never known that Isabella Dandaneau existed. Unless he saw her at a play. Or on a public walk. Or at someone's party. Damn if she wasn't every bit the beauty her cousin had been. Maybe even more so for lacking Mignon's obvious carnality. There was something inherently appealing about innocence and goodness. And where Mignon had spent her time in his room doing her best to tear the sheets from the feather mattress, Isabella was using hers to put them back on.

He leaned his shoulder against the doorjamb, stunned by her domesticity and all that she'd accomplished in just the few minutes she'd had. His clothes were back in the armoire, the doors and drawers pushed neatly closed. She'd righted the night tables on either side of the headboard and rolled up the oil-soaked, glass-encrusted rugs that had run the length of the bed. The books were still lying on the floor at the base of the shelves and she hadn't gotten his sitting area put back to rights yet, but, given her efficiency, it wouldn't be long before his room was completely habitable again.

She smoothed the top sheet and moved toward the comforter lying on the floor at the footboard. Then her gaze moved past it to his feet and slowly up the length of his body. He tried to stifle the warmth that her perusal sparked and failed miserably. Having no greater success in finding some pithy comment with which to open a conversation, he crossed his arms over his chest and cast himself on her mercy.

"Well, looking on the bright side," she said softly, blindly gathering the comforter from the floor and holding it in front of her like a fluffy shield, "it's obvious that they didn't find the map when they searched Mignon's rooms."

He nodded and pushed himself off the jamb. Making his way to the far side of the bed, he observed, "But looking on the other side, we don't know whether they found it in searching mine."

Dropping the comforter on the bed, she began searching for the corners of it while saying, "They certainly upended things well enough." As he collected the ends for his side of the cover and pulled the lower one into place, she added, "And I'm afraid that they broke your night lamps and crushed in one side of the center drawer on your desk."

"Things can be replaced or repaired," he replied with a shrug as they drew their respective sides of the comforter to the top of the bed.

Scooping the pillows from the floor at her feet, she tossed them into place, fluffed them, and then stepped back to put her hands on her hips and survey the rest of the room. "Can you tell if they missed looking anywhere?"

Barrett, too, looked around the room. Despite her efforts to tidy it, he could well remember what it had looked like when he'd first seen it in the aftermath of the rough search. "They appear to have been quite thorough," he admitted. "At least in searching this room."

Isabella blinked as realization struck. "Mignon had to pass through others to get to this one, didn't she?"

Something akin to a chagrined smile lifted one corner of his mouth as he nodded. "It took us quite a while to get this far, actually."

And this was the only room the intruders had thought to rifle. The obvious place for Mignon to have hidden the map. But Mignon never chose the obvious course. Never. "You can spare me the details," Isabella declared, her hope renewed. "Just show me the general path you took."

He started for the door, motioning with his head for her to follow. She obediently fell into step behind him, her heart racing in anticipation. In a matter of mere moments she could have the map in hand. All she had to do was think like Mignon, to see the opportunities as she had.

And to keep up with Barrett Stanbridge's long strides, she reminded herself as he reached the base of the stairs and headed for the rear portion of the house. She hiked the hems of her skirts, silently cursed the tightness of her corset, and trotted to catch up to him. She was winded by the time he reached the back side of the kitchen and stopped.

"We came in the back door there," he said, pointing to the doorway leading outside, his gaze distant, obviously fixed on the memories of that evening. "It's closest to the carriage house."

The stitch in her side easing, Isabella stepped around him to move to the door. Once there, she turned and stood looking into the room, trying to see it as Mignon had. It was approaching noon now, though, and the room was flooded with light. Isabella squinted in an effort to dim the room and blur the edges as the night would have. A central worktable. A dry sink, counters, cupboards, and cabinets. There were a thousand possible hiding places. *If* Mignon had had the time and the freedom to get to them.

"Did you leave her alone in here?" she asked. "Did you turn away for a little while? Perhaps just long enough to light a lamp?"

"We didn't need a light," he answered. He swallowed and expelled a hard breath. "And, no, I never left her or turned my back on her."

The edge to his manner reminded her of his uneasiness while she'd searched his carriage. She arched a brow. "Did you pass directly through here or did you . . . pause?"

"Paused," he admitted tightly, his chin lowering and his brows drawing down. "Your cousin was a woman with a ferocious appetite."

"So I've heard," she quipped, finding his discomfiture rather endearing. The poor man; there simply wasn't going to be any way to spare him. "As much as I am loath to ask, I must," she began, eyeing the kitchen table. "Where, precisely, did you pause with her?"

"Take one step back."

Ignoring the tautness of the command, she did as he

instructed. The impact was unexpected and she couldn't help but look back over her shoulder to be sure. "I'm against the wall," she announced, perplexed.

"So was she," he practically growled.

Understanding came on a sudden, vivid image. Only it wasn't Mignon pinned against the wall in the darkness, her skirts rucked up to her waist, her legs wrapped around Barrett Stanbridge's lean hips. No, it wasn't Mignon at all. Isabella dragged a shaky breath into her lungs and locked her knees. She had to moisten her parched lower lip before she could find the wherewithal to admonish, "I told you that I didn't need the details."

"Well," he snapped, his dark eyes flashing indignantly, defiantly, "how am I supposed to tell you where the hell she might have hidden a scrap of paper without telling you precisely where she was at any given moment and what she was doing at the time?"

That would teach her to find someone else's embarrassment amusing. "You have a point," she conceded.

"Thank you."

She knew that he wasn't the least bit grateful. "I know this must be difficult for you."

"You have no idea just how difficult."

She suspected that she did, but she wasn't willing to argue with him. Admitting to a too vivid imagination, a throbbing pulse, and weak knees wasn't a good idea at all. Isabella drew another deep breath and looked around, surveying what would have been within Mignon's reach during those moments. Only Barrett, she concluded. Which, as tactile sensations went, couldn't have been at all disappointing.

"Perhaps if we move along?" she blurted, disturbed by the physical impact of her visualization. "Where did you go from here?"

"The dining room," he supplied, turning and walking away. "And, before you ask, *yes,* we *paused* there, too."

Sweet Jesus, Joseph, and Mary, she thought as she once again trailed after him. Standing just inside the dining room, she gazed absently around it. She'd always heard the whispers but really hadn't believed them. But apparently Mignon had indeed been insatiable. The carriage, the kitchen, the dining room . . . Barrett was undoubtedly an inspiration and perfectly capable of fueling intense desire, but . . . Good God, even rabbits needed time to recoup their strength.

"I fail to see," he snarled from off on her left, "what might be the least bit humorous about any of this, Mrs. Dandaneau."

And I'm not about to tell you, she silently replied. "Please call me Belle," she offered, trying desperately to gain control of her smile. "Given the nature of our general conversation—and our task—any sort of formality is a complete farce. Don't you agree?"

"Formality," he replied, folding his arms across his chest, "is the only thing standing between me and complete mortification."

He wasn't making self-control easy for her. Still, she tried yet again to rein in her smile. "You don't strike me as the sort of man who would be easily mortified."

"I'm not," he admitted, meeting her gaze squarely. "Is there any hope that I could persuade you to have a seat in the parlor and allow me to conduct the search on my own?"

She shook her head as her amusement and its attendant smile faded. "No. You haven't the slightest idea of how Mignon's mind worked. You can't see things as she did. I can."

"With all due respect," he retorted, "from what I can tell, the family resemblance went only skin deep. You're nothing at all like your cousin."

She knew that he hadn't meant it as a compliment, but

she took it as one nonetheless; the years of living in Mignon's shadow had taken their toll. "Why, thank you, Barrett," she exclaimed. "I think that's one of the nicest things anyone's ever said to me. If I knew you just a tad bit better, I'd be tempted to give you a little peck on the cheek."

He closed his eyes and quietly groaned.

Lord, he was the most intriguing man; so very much like a bear. Teeth and claws and snarling bad temper one moment, shy and adorable and practically cuddly in the next. Which side had Mignon seen? she wondered.

Isabella shook her head and sighed, reminding herself that she had a task to complete and that the bear would be ever so much happier when it was done. "Where in here did you happen to pause?" she asked.

"On the table," he supplied, opening his eyes to fix his gaze on the ceiling. "And under it." She'd barely arched a brow in silent comment when he added with a sigh, "Then on the floor over by the buffet."

"Well," Isabella observed blithely, "if she even half tried, she died a satisfied woman. I don't know what more she could have wanted."

"Christ," he half groaned, half choked.

Oh, he would no doubt—at some point very soon—exact retribution for it, but she simply couldn't resist the temptation. "Why, Barrett. I do believe you're blushing. Again."

"I'll look under the table," he growled, all but diving for the cover it afforded.

Isabella grinned and set about examining the large tabletop. A vase of flowers sat in the center, a finely crocheted doily protecting the flawlessly finished mahogany from scratches. The water and flowers were fresh, telling her that it hadn't been there the night before last. The doily hid nothing, not even the grain of the wood under it. Isabella focused her attention on the only other possibility. The long expanse was composed of four distinct sections with the leaves providing three narrow slits running across the width.

Leaning forward, half standing, half lying on the table, she ran a fingertip lightly along the nearest of the seams. Just off from center, she felt a slight change in the width of the space. "Aha!" she cried, slipping her fingernail into the space and using it to catch the slip of paper.

"Did you find it?"

The too small piece of paper, she realized as she freed it. "Damn," she whispered, taking the ragged-edged piece into her hands.

"I'll take that as a no."

"She tore her half of the map," Isabella explained, studying the lines arcing across the scrap. "Judging by the size of this piece, into eighths."

"That inconvenience aside," he offered from somewhere under the table, "it's obvious that you were correct in thinking that she came here with me just to hide her half of the map."

Yes, but Mignon had been both self-serving and self-destructive when it came to her choices in men. She'd always attached herself to the wrong ones and never appreciated the right ones. If she'd had an ounce of good sense, she'd have understood that going with Barrett to hide the map hadn't been at all necessary. If, instead of using him, she'd told him of her fears, of her need for protection . . . Had Mignon known a good man when she met one, she'd still be alive.

"One down, seven to go," she murmured with a sigh, tucking the paper into her pocket.

"Two," he amended, rolling out from under the table and handing her another piece of paper. "I'll go look by the buffet."

Isabella stared down at the scrap he'd found and her heart skittered. The upper edge was smooth, the right and lower edges matching the same rough pattern on the piece she'd found in the table. The left edge, though, was torn in a different, very familiar fashion. She read the words and knew precisely where they fit into the puzzle.

Park and Hyde
Gentle Bride

Park and Hyde. Hyde Park? Is that what had brought Mignon all the way across the Atlantic? A twisted reference that might or might not refer to a London park? Her blood went cold and her stomach sank to the soles of her feet. Oh, dear God in heaven. Surely there had to be more of a reason. Surely Mignon hadn't come all this way on that clue alone.

"Three and four."

She forced her gaze up. Barrett Stanbridge stood there with his arm extended, two scraps of paper neatly pinched between his thumb and forefinger. "Thank you," she murmured numbly, taking them from him with a trembling hand.

"Is something wrong?" he asked, tipping his head slightly to the side to study her.

Without answering, she looked down at the newest puzzle pieces, hoping, praying that one of them would have the other half of the missing text. One piece, obviously a corner, had a single line running diagonally across it. The other greatly resembled the one she'd found.

"It's a shame Mignon's dead," she said, blinking back tears. "Because I'd really like to kill her."

Barrett clenched his teeth and shoved his hands into his trouser pockets. As impulses went, the one to wrap her in his arms and console her had to be among the five worst he'd ever had. But, Jesus, if he had to stand there and watch her cry . . .

"There's my study yet to search," he offered, deliberately adding a note of grim resignation to his tone. "And then the parlor."

She looked up at him incredulously and the corner of her mouth twitched upward.

"I'm sure we'll find the other four pieces by the time we're done," he went on, relieved at the apparent success of his tactic. They wouldn't find anything in the parlor, of course. Unless Mignon had slipped in there while he slept. But if thinking of him as some sort of satyr kept Isabella from dissolving in tears and him from doing something incredibly stupid . . . All things considered, being thought of as an inexhaustible rake really wasn't that bad. People had certainly said worse things about him.

"Shall we?" he asked, motioning for her to precede him out of the dining room and down the hall.

She was fighting that delightfully broad and knowing smile of hers as she walked away. Barrett fell in behind her, yet another realization slowly worming its way into his awareness. Whoever wanted the map desperately enough to have beaten the life out of Mignon would do the same to Isabella. And while standing between her and harm was a matter of conscience, honor, and decency, it was also selfishly practical; nothing would clear his name more efficiently than handing the authorities the real killer. Looking at it that way . . . He had to go the course with her. It was the only sane and rational thing to do. He'd just have to keep his wits about him and tamp down the sparks she seemed so easily capable of igniting.

Isabella had the distinct feeling that she was being manipulated. Artfully, subtly, ever so kindly, and since the moment they'd walked in to search his study. Not that she was overly concerned about it or the slightest bit resentful. She had six of the eight map pieces and was about to sit down to a hot meal that she didn't have to buy with what few coins she had. That Barrett Stanbridge seemed to have ulterior motives for helping and feeding her didn't matter. Food was food. And there were two more scraps of the map to be found; one of them the missing text. Which had damn well better have the word "London" in it, she silently groused as she carried the platter of fried potatoes from the stove to the kitchen worktable.

Placing it between the two plates of ham and eggs, she smiled at Barrett and let him assist her into her seat. Food, a significant part of the map, *and* gallantry. If that was all she allowed herself to look at, today stood as one of the best days she'd had in years.

"I'm curious about something," Barrett said as he took his own seat on the opposite side of the table.

And so we begin. "Oh?" Isabella placed her napkin across her lap and picked up her knife and fork. "Curious about what?"

"Why do you carry a knife?"

He might well be wondering about that, but she suspected that he was using it largely as a conversational prelude. "As a woman traveling alone," she provided, "I want to be able to protect myself and thought it wise to have a weapon with a bit more heft than your average hatpin."

"A derringer," he countered, helping himself to the potatoes, "would be a more commanding and equalizing choice."

"I couldn't agree with you more, but I can't cut ropes with it."

He froze, the spoon suspended over his plate. "Are you telling me that you also carry a gun?"

"Such as it is," Isabella admitted, delighting in having

surprised him. "A Colt revolver is my firearm of preference, but it's far too bulky to carry around in a skirt pocket."

He dumped the potatoes on his plate, returned the spoon to the platter, and then sat there, his forearms resting on the edge of the table as he openly studied her.

She ate a bite, took a sip of her tea, and then, grinning, ventured, "You're still curious, aren't you?"

One corner of his mouth quirked upward as he nodded. "How does a seemingly genteel young woman like yourself happen to become a walking arsenal?"

She's determined to survive, she silently answered. Unwilling to be that honest with a man who was largely a stranger, she opted for evasion. "Ah, *seemingly* is the key word. And I'm not really all that young. I'm twenty-seven."

"And you haven't answered the question."

A persistent stranger. "New Orleans fell to the Union early in the war," she supplied with a shrug as she sliced off another bite of ham. "We were an occupied city for a full three years. Even before then, my husband was gone, serving in the army, and I was left alone to fend for myself. It was easier to do so armed."

"But the war ended."

"Formal hostilities, yes. But not the military occupation. And I was still alone."

"And still armed."

She met his gaze across the table and decided that there was no harm in giving him a fundamental, most unfeminine truth. "I doubt that I'll ever be without a weapon of one sort or another at hand. Some people may find their comfort in the biblical rod and staff, but mine comes from my knife and derringer."

"Have you ever had to use them?"

He'd crossed a line. He saw her flinch and knew that her reaching for a helping of potatoes was meant to both disguise it and give her time to decide how she wanted to answer. He picked up his fork and ate a bit of potato as he waited.

"More times than I care to remember, actually," she replied, her tone too light, too casual. Her chuckle was entirely too breathless and forced as she added, "And certainly more often than I hope anyone will ever discover."

"Self-defense," he pointed out gently but firmly, "is always an acceptable reason for committing violence."

"So they say." She forked up a bit of egg and stabbed a sliver of ham. Looking at it, she arched a brow and smiled wryly. "But, given the widely differing views of what constitutes self-defense, I'd rather not take the chance."

"There's a far greater leeway in defining acts of war," he ventured, watching her carefully.

She nodded, crisply said, "I've heard that mentioned a time or two," and then popped the bite of food in her mouth.

If she thought that response would squelch his curiosity, she'd badly miscalculated. "Were you a spy, Isabella?"

"Your food is getting cold."

He grinned, for some unfathomable reason inordinately pleased. "You were, weren't you?"

She met his gaze and arched a delicate brow. "I couldn't help but notice that you carry a knife and a gun," she said coolly, calmly. "Were you a spy at one time in your life?"

"I was an engineer in Her Majesty's Army," he countered, enjoying the game, fascinated by her complexity. "I built bridges and train trestles. And defended them when necessary."

"Necessity does make for interesting habits, doesn't it?" She speared a chunk of potato and popped it in her mouth.

"You're not going to give me a straight answer, are you?"

She grimaced and made a production of shuddering. "I'm afraid that the potatoes need more salt."

His suspicions largely confirmed by the determination of her evasion, Barrett accepted her change of subject, offering, "They're perfect as they are. You're a good cook."

"Thank you. I'm afraid that I learned the hard way and by my own devices. My husband suffered greatly in the process."

"But I'm sure that he appreciated the fact that you were making the attempt."

"No, not really," she admitted, her eyes sparkling mischievously. "But then I didn't much care. He deserved to suffer."

Another little mystery. Barrett grinned and took up the dangling thread. "I gather your union wasn't a happy one."

"Well," she drawled, "if there's one good thing that can be said about the Union Army, it's that they spared me the trouble of putting a bullet in him myself."

"You couldn't have simply said 'Damn the scandal' and divorced him?"

She snorted in a most unladylike and delightfully honest way. "Henri was very Catholic. I was forced to convert to marry him."

"You make it sound as though they actually held a gun to your head."

"Henri's and the priest's, too," she replied, nodding emphatically. "None of us went to the altar willingly. If I had it to do over again, I'd do a good many things differently."

"Such as?"

"To start with," she said readily, having apparently given the matter a great deal of previous thought, "I wouldn't try to be Mignon and flirt with a man renowned for his lack of self-control. And I certainly wouldn't climb into his carriage thinking he truly intended to see me safely home."

"Ooh," he murmured, understanding. "Compromised."

"Not actually, but the appearance of it was quite sufficient for my father. He hauled out his hunting rifle and declared me formally engaged."

Henri could have done worse for a wife. It could have been Mignon's father pointing the muzzle at him. "How old were you?"

"Seventeen. I thought I was terribly grown-up then. A truly worldly woman." She rolled her eyes and then shook her head with a sigh. "Did you do anything particularly shortsighted and foolish at that age?"

"Yes," he admitted, remembering. "And again at eighteen. Twice at nineteen as I recall." The disaster at twenty-four flashed through his mind's eye, but he firmly set it aside and went on, saying, "And now, at thirty-one, there's Mignon. That one's shaping up to be one of my more memorable mistakes in judgment."

She waved her fork dismissively. "I don't see how you could have reasonably known that she'd be killed after leaving your company. If she hadn't, you'd likely consider her to be one of the better things to have happened to you this year."

It was the perfect opening and he seized it. "Which brings me to a matter I've been mulling for the last hour or so."

She sat back, a tiny little shadow of a smile playing at the corners of her mouth, and arched a brow in silent question.

"I'm not prepared to let you go off in search of your treasure alone," he said bluntly, firmly.

Isabella could clearly see the track of his thinking and what he was proposing. Part of her was sorely tempted to accept the offer right then and there. Another part, the one that remembered the bitter costs of partnerships, was vehemently opposed to even considering the notion. "It's not your decision to make," she rejoined quietly, mentally trying to weigh her concerns.

"Granted. And I'll admit that my motives are purely personal and extremely selfish. But I'm in considerable trouble because your cousin was killed in her quest for Lafitte's millions. If you're killed, too . . ."

"I assure you that I have absolutely no intention of ending as Mignon did."

"I should hope not," he countered dryly. "But murderers seldom put our intentions ahead of their own." He sighed and gave her a softly apologetic smile as he added, "I don't give a fig about the treasure, Belle. Truth be told, I don't believe it exists. But I understand your need to pursue the possibility. All that I'm asking is that you try to understand my need to see that you stay alive."

He was right about the dangers, of course. And she'd be a fool to refuse his protection. Still . . . Her heart racing, her stomach churning, she swallowed down her trepidation and said, "I can't afford to pay you for your time. Not until I find the treasure, anyway."

"I don't need or care about money," he instantly countered. "My primary concern is keeping you alive and my neck out of the hangman's noose."

"It would be a purely investigator-client relationship?"

"Absolutely," Barrett assured her despite the prickling of his conscience. "Strictly professional."

"Would your assistance be limited to protecting me or would you actively assist me in the search?"

"That depends entirely on how much you feel you can trust me. If you want my help in the actual search, I'm willing to give it."

She looked away, fixing her gaze on the window that overlooked the rear yard and the alleyway where Mignon's battered body had been found. Her cousin had shamelessly used Barrett Stanbridge's body, his good nature, and his home for her own ends. That he was willing to look past all of that and offer *her* his assistance . . . Yes, she wasn't Mignon. Thank God. And yes, he stood to gain by it if all went well. But if anything went wrong, the gallows was a certain end for him. What did it say that he was willing to take the chance?

More importantly, what did it say about her that she was inclined to accept his help? It would be one thing if she believed that their relationship could remain purely professional. But she knew better. He was handsome and capable and he stirred fantasies that warmed her in the most delicious ways. It had been so long since she'd felt the deep tug of wanting, the quick spark of carnal hunger. To learn that part of her hadn't been reduced to ash was disconcerting and yet wildly exhilarating. The thrill of it was telling; it was only a matter of time before she reached for him, before she closed her eyes and let desire run its course. And in surrendering to passion, she'd be putting herself on the edge of the precipice again.

Did she have the strength to endure another tumble into hell? Did she really care whether she did or not? Living long was one thing. Living happily was another. Living for the moment at least offered a hope for pleasure, however fleeting it might be. Would Barrett mind overly much if she used him every bit as deliberately as Mignon had?

After a long moment, Isabella lifted her chin and turned back to solemnly meet his gaze. Reaching into her pocket, she withdrew the tattered portions of her cousin's half of the treasure map, silently laid them on the table between them, and accepted whatever fate would bring.

Chapter Four

There was the common-sense thing to do, Isabella admitted as they moved into Barrett's study. And then there was the only thing to be done. In the case of enlisting Barrett Stanbridge's help, the two rational courses were one and the same. He was right; whoever had killed Mignon was likely to come after her next, and if she faced the encounter alone, she didn't stand any better chance of survival than her cousin had. Added to that was the reality that she didn't know London, and Barrett did. If indeed Mignon had come to the right place, then Barrett's knowledge of the city would be invaluable in hunting down the treasure.

It didn't matter, she reminded herself as she watched him arrange the paper rectangles on his desktop, that every feminine bone in her body had misgivings. After all, their partnership was decidedly temporary even if it didn't turn out to be strictly business in nature. Once they'd accomplished their task, she'd go her way, he'd go his, and they'd never see each other again. In the meantime, everything would be fine as long as she kept that reality in the forefront of her mind.

Which was damned difficult to do, she mentally groused. Practicality was being shoved aside by the realization of how broad and thick his shoulders were, how nimble his fingers were for a man with such large hands, how full and soft his lips looked, and how his dark hair practically begged to be ruffled.

"All right," he said, intruding on her self-censure. "Come take a look at this and tell me how it relates to your half of the map."

He didn't move so much as an inch as she joined him at the desk. As if he'd deliberately decided to challenge her resolve, he stood squarely in front of the reconstructed map, his feet firmly planted and his hands braced on either side of it, giving her a choice between standing a proper distance off to the side where she couldn't really see anything, or sidling up beside him and trying to pretend that she wasn't at all aware of him. One course was patently ridiculous, the other only foolhardy.

She stepped up beside him, reached past his arm, and laid a fingertip on the uppermost center piece. "If you put my half up against what we have here, the full line would read 'Lies to Cross, Park and Hyde.'" She shifted her finger down to indicate the lower line. "The full second is 'Lion's Paw and Gentle Bride.'"

He slowly nodded and she drew back, resisting the brazen urge to step closer to the warmth of him, slip her arms around his narrow waist, and fit her hips against his.

"What abuts these two missing pieces?" he asked, indicating the two obvious holes in the puzzle.

"In the center, squiggles that look remarkably like these." Reaching past him again, she tapped the empty space at the bottom. "There are another two lines of text right in here. The first half of the first line is 'Setting sun on . . .' The first half to the last one is 'Fifteen paces to . . .'"

"That's it?" he asked in a tone that was both incredulous and frustrated.

Light-headed, she expelled the breath she'd been holding and leaned down to rest her forearms on the desktop. "Just please tell me you see something that would suggest the treasure's here in London. I really need to hear that Mignon didn't take off on a wild-goose chase."

Roses. She smelled like roses; soft and warm and not too sweet. And the nape of her neck, with the little curling tendrils of dark honey hair . . . Jesus, it would be so easy, so deliciously rewarding, to lean down and slowly take a taste. Barrett straightened, crossed his arms over his chest, and forced himself to swallow.

" 'Park' and 'Hyde' are all that imply London to me," he admitted, narrowing his eyes so that the map was all he could see. "But that's a reach. There are probably at least a hundred British cities and towns with streets named Park and Hyde."

"So you think that these lines represent streets?"

"It's purely an assumption," he conceded, watching her nudge one of the pieces into a better fit. She had graceful hands. Swallowing again and shifting his gaze to the wall on the back side of his desk, he shrugged and added, "But they could be rivers or streams for all I know. Do you have any idea of when the map was drawn? How old it is?"

"That's a subject of considerable speculation."

"Wills are generally dated."

"Yes," she allowed, straightening to stand squarely beside him. "The one delivered to the family lawyers was dated January 1823. Some people say that Lafitte died off the coast of Galveston in the early 1830s. Other people claim that Jean Lafitte became a respectable businessman in St. Louis, lived to be quite old, and passed only in the last ten years or so. In the final analysis, no one seems to be absolutely certain when, where, and how he actually died."

He should have expected as much; so far not one single aspect of this mess had been clear-cut and easy. And a will some forty years old? If he'd lived some time after that, Lafitte could very well have changed his mind and written another will that superseded it. Isabella Dandaneau could well be chasing after a treasure the man had decided to give to someone else.

Mentioning the possibility seemed a cruel thing to do, though, and so he focused his attention on other, less troubling, aspects of the mystery. "Do the stories ever have him traveling to London?"

With a heavy sigh, she rubbed her fingertips over her brow and replied, "According to the tales, there isn't a country in the world that he didn't visit. Whether or not any of the stories are true . . ." She shook her head and shrugged.

"And there are no labels on any of the lines on your half of the map?"

"None. And no directional markers, either."

"Why would Mignon have thought the map was of London?" he wondered aloud.

"I honestly don't know. I was hoping you might be able to tell me."

Her hope was entirely groundless but he knew there wasn't any reason to point out that fact; it was patently obvious to both of them. "The only thing I can think to do is to find old maps of the city and compare yours against them."

"And hope that we're incredibly fortunate," she added, sounding as though she might be on the verge of tears.

His heart twisted. One set of instincts urged him to wrap his arms around her and assure her that everything would turn out well. Another set fairly screamed in warning. He was caught up in this web because he hadn't had the good sense to resist the carnal promise of a beautiful woman. Surrendering to the temptation of comforting a sweetly needy one wasn't going to get him out of it.

Barrett softly cleared the lump from his throat and forced his mind back to his desk. "I'm certainly willing to entertain any other suggestions you might have."

The only ideas consistently presenting themselves for consideration were those that, in all likelihood, Mignon had suggested before her. Irritated with her lack of self-control, Isabella frowned, turned, and started toward the windows overlooking the street, saying softly, "Lies to Cross, Park and Hyde. Lion's Paw and Gentle Bride."

Once a fair distance from the distraction of him, her mind relaxed and a possibility glimmered. "Could they be the names of pubs?" she posed, staring blindly at her reflection in the rippled window glass.

"They might be. But where? London? Liverpool? New York? Are they still standing? How many times have the names changed since the map was drawn?"

And how would they even begin to make a search for the answers? she wondered. "We need to find the two missing pieces. There must be something on them that made Mignon think it was a map of London. Why would she have come all this way otherwise?"

"Maybe she was on her way to somewhere else and was simply passing through the city. Lafitte was obviously of French descent. Paris could have been her ultimate destination."

Isabella turned the notion over in her mind, knowing it was a logical one but sensing a flaw in it. "No," she ventured after a long moment. "Mignon didn't take rooms at an inn. She took them at a boardinghouse. She intended to stay in London."

"Or," he instantly countered, "it could be that, knowing

she'd been followed, she took the boardinghouse rooms so that she'd be more difficult to find."

"*If* she knew she was being followed. If I were worried about the possibility, I wouldn't dine out three times a day and then attend a play in the evening."

"A good point," he conceded. "But then, you probably wouldn't have left the theater with a perfect stranger, either. And you wouldn't have torn your map into pieces, hidden them around his house, and then left them behind when you slipped away in the morning."

"No, I wouldn't have. So why did she?"

"I don't know. She was your cousin. Why would she do those sorts of things?"

There was no rational reason to protect Mignon's reputation. Aside from the fact Mignon hadn't cared overly much about it while living, she was now past caring at all. And Barrett Stanbridge had to have had some realistic notion of the kind of woman Mignon was before he'd propositioned her at the theater.

"The dining out and the going to the theater . . ." Isabella supplied. "That was the way Mignon lived. So was spending the night with men she didn't know."

"And here I was thinking that I inspired her to embark on a brave new adventure," he drawled. "I'm crushed, you know."

Isabella grinned. Oh, yes, she could almost hear the devastation in his voice. Almost. Sobering, she considered the one part of the puzzle for which she had no ready answers. "But she had to have known she was in danger or she wouldn't have hidden the map. So why didn't she hide herself instead? Why was she willing to be such a public presence? It doesn't make any sense. Not even for Mignon."

"Well," he said ruefully, "I must admit that—from the very beginning—she struck me as a woman who didn't so much as breathe without having a larger plan for it."

She looked over her shoulder to find him leaning against the edge of his desk and watching her, his arms still folded across his chest. "You're very astute," she offered.

His dark eyes sparkled as one corner of his mouth quirked up and he replied, "It's an occupational skill. Most of the time I use it purely for show. It tends to impress the clients."

Yes, she could see how people would feel confident in handing their problems to him. Nothing really seemed to deeply ruffle his composure and he had the most delightfully distracting smile. When he grinned like that . . .

Isabella freed her gaze and returned it to the calm haven of the window glass. Her mind slowly followed suit, allowing her to once again focus on the riddle Mignon had left for them to solve. "She was working with her half of the map. Which is why she didn't put it in a bank vault as I have my half. The next logical question is why she chose to hide it here."

"Perhaps it was a matter of first opportunity," he posed. "Maybe no other man had made her an offer in the course of the day."

Isabella couldn't tell whether he was tossing out possibilities as a sort of devil's advocate or because he truly thought the idea had genuine merit. "Mignon didn't believe in being passive about invitations," she explained as diplomatically as she could. "If she needed an opportunity, she created one. And I assure you that very few men ever declined to oblige her."

"Then something or someone at the theater must have alarmed her."

"Someone she recognized," Isabella offered, thinking aloud. "Someone she wouldn't have expected to see and whose presence could only be explained by the fact that he'd followed her from home, that he was the one who had tried to steal the map before." She nodded slowly, accepting the fit of the pieces. It was right; the only way all of Mignon's actions made any sort of sense. "Seeing him there made hiding the map an immediate necessity."

And made him the marked man, Barrett wryly, silently added. He should have questioned his good fortune; he'd known just by looking at her that she was the scheming sort. But he hadn't thought twice. No, he'd blithely offered her his arm, considered himself lucky in escaping his parents' plans, and let himself be used. If she hadn't been killed the next morning, no great harm would have come from his shortsightedness. But she had to have known that she'd be in danger the second she struck out on her own. If only she'd asked him to protect her. If only he'd looked past lust and . . . *If, if, if.*

Barrett raked his fingers through his hair, shoved himself off the edge of his desk, and headed toward the credenza and the decanter set. "Would you care for a sherry?" he asked as he reached for a glass and the scotch.

"I'd prefer bourbon if you have any."

Bourbon? He grinned as he filled his glass. Part of him was utterly stunned that she'd so casually asked for hard liquor. Another part wasn't the least bit surprised. "Whisky and gin are your only other choices," he declared, getting her a glass. "Which poison will it be?"

"Whisky, please. Neat."

Damn, a woman who not only consumed spirits, but didn't want them watered down to do so. What a rarity. He filled her glass to the level of his own, wondering if she played cards, too. As a betting man, he'd wager that she did. And well. She'd be an unpredictable player, her mind running at full tilt as she chatted and smiled and bluffed her opponent down to his unmentionables.

Her game was poker, he decided as he met her at the

midpoint of the room and handed her her glass. Barrett lifted his own in salute, saying, "To luck."

"Wagonloads of it," she countered, clinking her rim lightly against his. "We're going to need it."

He wasn't quite so sure of that, but he kept his opinion to himself and took a sip of his drink. She seemed to have considerably more common sense and a much stronger commitment to self-preservation than her cousin had had. And there was nothing wrong with Belle's intellect or the quality and speed of her thinking. She'd very quickly grasped the danger of her situation and swallowed her pride to accept protection. And once she'd made that decision and accorded him the role of her partner . . . She was open and honest and impressively capable of using logic. In a way, though, that seemed to take rather inexplicable jumps from point to point and back again. To his way of thinking, all of it boded well for their eventual success.

The pulling in his loins whenever he looked at her—hell, whenever he so much as thought about her—suggested that there might well be a few complications along the way, though. He took a long sip of his drink and watched her do the same, knowing better than to make promises he couldn't keep. Especially to himself.

She had a wonderful smile. Sometimes soft and tentative, sometimes childlike in the purity of its happiness. And sometimes it was so deliciously wicked that his blood scorched his veins. The way she sipped whisky and used the tip of her tongue to catch a drop on her lower lip didn't help to cool it, either. Adding in the creaminess of her skin, the flawless, delicate lines of her face, the sweet scent of roses, and the inviting curves . . . He was going to be hard-pressed to behave himself, to maintain the strict protocols of the investigator-client relationship.

It would have been ever so much easier to do if the circumstances were different and he could put some hours and a few miles of city streets between them every now and again. But since he didn't have that luxury, he was simply going to have to make the best of it and hope she did her part in keeping him from doing something utterly pleasurable.

His course charted and his resolve set as firmly as it could reasonably be, he cleared his throat, smiled, and said, "What do you say to finishing our drinks, putting what we have of the map in the wall safe, and then going to collect your belongings?"

"And Mignon's," she added, nodding her assent. "The authorities turned it all over to me yesterday evening."

How typically Belle, he thought, throwing the last of his drink down his throat. No hesitation, no pausing to mentally sort through the reasoning, the implications, or the possible consequences. She understood and accepted in the blink of an eye. "Have you had a chance to go through her things for clues?"

"It's how I spent last night. I didn't find anything." She grinned sheepishly. "Well, aside from some clothing I could use and a couple of very good pieces of . . ." She blinked and her smile faded as her brows knitted. "Chocolate," she finished slowly.

"I gather that's suddenly meaningful?"

"Mignon couldn't eat chocolate. It gave her horrible hives."

"Interesting," he drawled, seeing what had intrigued her. "It certainly begs the question of why she had it and where she got it."

Her smile was weak as she looked up at him. "We're doing extremely well at asking questions, aren't we?"

"The answers will come," he assured her, his conviction firm. "They always do. It's simply a matter of being patient and resourceful."

Shaking her head, she finished her drink and then extended her free hand in a silent offer to take his empty glass. He surrendered it with a nod of thanks and then took a slow, deep breath of roses as she moved past him to the credenza, saying, "I feel compelled to admit that while I am fairly resourceful, I've never been particularly good at patience."

That didn't bode well for the maintenance of protocol. "Neither have I," he admitted, crossing to his desk to gather up the pieces of the map.

Isabella took one step across the threshold of her room and froze.

"Is something wrong?" Barrett asked from behind her, the low rumble of his voice instantly taking the sharpest edge off her alarm.

"Someone's been in here," she replied, slowly moving forward while sweeping her gaze over the room a second time. "The bed was smooth when I left this morning, my valise was sitting square to the wall, and I never leave my hand mirror face up. Never. My mother once did and the sunlight came in through the window, struck it and bounced off to focus on the headboard. It caught fire, and if she hadn't come in when she did, we would have lost our house. I'm very careful about that."

"So is my mother," he supplied, closing the door and stepping to her side. "For much the same reason, I think." He glanced around and gave her a weak smile. "At least our searcher didn't feel the same sense of desperation he did when visiting my room."

"And Mignon's." She nodded to the end of the bed. "That's her trunk."

Looking over first one shoulder and then the other, he asked, "Where's yours?"

"I don't have one," she admitted, setting herself in motion, suddenly wanting to be gone from there in a most desperate way. "The valise is sufficient for my things."

"You travel lightly."

"Largely because I live lightly." She dropped the heavy fabric bag on the bed, pulled it open, and then retrieved her possessions from the rickety bureau drawer, adding, "Henri fancied himself a wonderful gambler. Unfortunately, there was a great deal of difference between his self-opinion and reality. I never bought anything that I really liked or didn't know who would buy it from me when I needed the money."

While he seemed to ponder that, she dropped her clothing into the bag, then cleared her few toiletries from the vanity top and packed them away. "I'm ready to go," she announced, pulling the valise closed and fastening the latch. "What shall we do about Mignon's trunk?"

"You said that there were things in it that you wanted. We'll take it with us. I assume that you have the key to it?"

"Yes, the investigators found it slipped into the seam of her garter." With her valise in hand, she moved toward the door, adding, "I'll get the driver to help you with the trunk."

"No need," he countered. "I can manage it on my own as far as the front door. I'll let him help me with it from there."

Isabella turned back, her hand on the doorknob, wondering just how he intended to haul the heavy, bulky thing on his own. In silence, she watched him take a handkerchief from his pocket, drop it on the hardwood floor and then take one of the trunk handles, lift up the end, and use his foot to slide the linen square under a corner. Returning that end to the floor, he stepped to the other, lifted it and then neatly rolled the entire trunk so that its weight was balanced on the one corner and the small white square of cloth pinned beneath it.

She smiled in appreciation as he drew it effortlessly and soundlessly toward her. "I'm so very impressed," she admitted, opening the door and preceding him into the hall leading to the front door of the boardinghouse. "You're amazing."

"Oh, I hardly think so," he replied with that charmingly quirked grin of his. "Basically, I'm just lazy. If you're looking for rippling brawn or stunning brains, you'd be far better off looking elsewhere."

It occurred to Isabella that while their partnership was temporary, it would go ever so much more smoothly if they were clear about their personal expectations. But while dragging a trunk past her curious landlady didn't seem to be the appropriate time to have the necessary conversation. Making a mental note to pick up the thread as soon as they were alone, Isabella stepped off to the side and let Barrett move out the front door with his burden in tow.

Turning to her landlady, she smiled and explained, "Circumstances require me to be gone for a few days, Mrs. Brown. My rent having been paid through the end of the week, I hope there isn't a problem with allowing the room to sit unoccupied in my absence."

Mrs. Brown shook her head. "You will send next week's rent by the end of this week if you intend to keep it?"

"Of course," Isabella assured her, understanding the widow's need to have a paying tenant in the space. "It's a lovely room and perfect for me in every way," she added, backing toward the door. "I won't let it go unless I simply have no other choice. And I will let you know my decision, one way or the other."

"Fair enough."

Satisfied that she'd met the requirements of both common courtesy and prudent planning, she turned and skipped down the front steps.

Barrett met her at the door of the rented hack and opened it for her as the driver climbed up into the box. Mindful of where they'd left the conversation and the need to finish it, she waited until he dropped into the rear-facing seat and then began, saying, "As I recall, you were telling me that if I were looking for certain qualities in a man, I wouldn't find them in you."

He cocked a brow and one corner of his mouth twitched, but she didn't let his apparent amusement deter her. With a deep breath, she plunged into the heart of the matter. "I think I should make it very clear that I'm not looking to attach myself to a man in any permanent way, Barrett. Regardless of what sterling qualities he might have to offer. I've discovered that there are very distinct advantages to living alone. Doing as I please, when I please, being foremost."

His nod and shrug eloquently, if silently, said, "I can appreciate that." Then he leaned back into the corner, knitted his brows and asked, "Being on your own . . . How do you deal with the ugly necessity of money? Obviously Henri didn't leave you any. And I'm guessing that your parents didn't, either. Not if you're missing meals on a regular basis."

True, and all of it compounded by the ugly consequences of war and enemy occupation. And all of it entirely too depressing to discuss in any sort of honest way. "Since my father and my husband died deeply in debt, money has been something of a quandary for quite some time," she admitted. "But finding a pirate's treasure should generally resolve that little concern, don't you think?"

"And if you don't find it? What are you going to do?"

Go on as I have for years, she silently answered. *From day to day, coin to coin.* Unwilling to open a discussion of her past, she smiled and countered, "I'll cross that bridge when I come to it."

His grin was instant and wide and brilliantly bright. "Well, I'll give you credit for pluck. I can't think of any other woman I've ever known who would have set off across the Atlantic on hope alone. How did you pay for your passage?"

Rolling her eyes at the memory, she retorted, "Don't ask."

He blinked and his grin faded as his eyes widened. "You didn't."

Was he thinking that she'd— Dear God! "Of course not!" Isabella hastened to assure him, shuddering at the very idea of so compromising her principles. "I cooked and cleaned for my way across."

She could have sworn that he muttered a "phew!" under his breath but the speed with which his grin returned sent her heart skittering again. "And, if you're agreeable," she went on, struggling against the impulse to wiggle onto the seat beside him, "that's how I'd like to pay for my keep in the present circumstances. Until I find the treasure, of course. When that happens, I'll pay you in hard currency."

The way he tilted his head and the amused shadow to his smile suggested that he knew what effect he had on her, that she was trying to ignore it, and that he'd allow her to get away with it. "I thought we covered this subject already," he countered. "I'm not interested in payment. Clearing my name in your cousin's murder is sufficient recompense."

"You're being a gentleman about it." Summoning what she could of a confident smile, she added, "And while I don't have money, I do still have a few shreds of pride. I can't live on the charity and kindness of others. Especially that of men. It makes me too much like Mignon to be tolerable."

"She lived on charity?" he asked, his amusement unabated.

"Mignon married well and divorced well. Twice," she supplied. "After the second occasion, she dispensed with the legalities and became the mistress of a wealthy, much older man."

"Who remembered her kindly in his will."

"Precisely. And whose friends were willing—each in their turn and in the last days of their time—to comfort and care for her in her grief and loneliness."

He chuckled softly and his eyes sparkled with devilment. "Did they draw straws at the funerals?"

"Rumor was that the high card won the right of first proposal."

Barrett couldn't keep from grinning at the absolute outrageousness of it, at the delightful way Belle could paint the mental pictures for him. Lord Almighty, he could see the whole thing in his mind's eye. And yet there was a niggling sense of something important wrapped up in the story. Deliberately setting aside his enjoyment, he turned the salient facts over in his brain. It didn't take long at all to find it. "As Mignon's only surviving kinsman," he ventured, "wouldn't you inherit her wealth?"

"She would have left it to anyone but me," she countered with a dismissive and dainty snort. "I'm sure there's a will somewhere saying so in the bluntest of terms." Suddenly she started and looked at him, concern darkening her eyes. "Do you think I'll have to give her half of the treasure to her heirs?"

He doubted there were any heirs. In the first place, the Mignons of the world expected to live forever and, in the second, they found the idea of giving their money away to be utterly abhorrent; rather than think of heirs, they spent their earthly days looking for ways to take it all with them.

But opening that barrel of possibilities wasn't something he wanted to do in that moment. Why, he didn't know. It was enough to know for himself that, in all likelihood,

Isabella Dandaneau wasn't as destitute as she thought she was. He'd put his solicitor on the task of discovering the particulars and when the treasure hunt was over and Mignon's killer hauled into the dock, he'd hand her into the care of his legal man. As ends went, it would be neat and tidy and his conscience wouldn't be the least troubled as he walked away.

"Why don't we worry about that bridge when we come to it?" he suggested, immensely pleased with his plan.

She laughed quietly, a mischievous sparkle in her eyes. "You build and defend bridges. I've always believed it was easier to simply blow them up. One way or the other, I don't see that we're going to have any problems getting to the other side. Do you?"

Not if attitude counted for anything along the way. "Has anyone ever mentioned that you're an incredible optimist?"

"It's certainly better than crying in your grits."

Grits? "Your what?"

"Grits," she repeated more clearly—as though proper pronunciation would help. "I especially like them made with cheese and lots of butter and cream."

Clearly they were something to eat, but beyond that he didn't have so much as an inkling. But he nodded anyway and offered diplomatically, "They sound delicious. Perhaps you'll prepare some for me in the days ahead."

"Oh, I'd love to," she offered, seeming to be genuinely thrilled by the prospect. "And gumbo. Have you ever had gumbo?"

"If I have, it apparently didn't make much of an impression."

"And cornbread," she went on, fairly bouncing on her seat in excitement. "You have to have cornbread with gumbo. And a praline cake for dessert. Or maybe a pecan pie. Yes, pecan pie would be the better choice. Then for another meal we could have red beans and rice and—"

"Are you hungry?" he asked, chuckling.

"Famished, actually. It's all this talk of good food." She shrugged and her smile took on a chagrined edge. "Well, that and meals have been few and far between lately. It makes you truly appreciate and savor food when you have some in front of you."

"How long is 'lately'?"

"The last three or four years," she blithely supplied. "War tends to make every part of life somewhat unpredictable."

And apparently it also made people quite immune to the everyday hardships. Which was a decidedly sobering realization. At least he could make sure her stomach was full during the time they'd be together.

"I wish I could offer to take you out to dine," he began apologetically as the carriage eased to the side of the road. As it slowed, he reached for the door handle and continued, saying, "But it's not a wise course. Not given that whoever searched your room today is likely to be the same one who searched mine and killed Mignon. The less you're out and about, the safer you are."

"Oh, please don't feel bad about that," she said as he pushed open the door and vaulted out. Accepting his hand and assistance down onto the walkway, she added, "I really don't mind cooking. Honestly, I could probably do it in my sleep. And I am so hungry for good old-fashioned, familiar food."

It might be familiar to her, but with the exception of beans and rice, all of it was quite foreign to him. But, in the belief that life should be lived as an adventure, he was willing to take a chance or two. Nothing made with cheese and cream could be totally inedible.

"Did you happen to take note of the kitchen stores earlier?" he asked as the driver helped him pull Mignon's trunk from the rack. "Is there enough there to prepare a decent meal this evening or do we need to put these things inside and then make a furtive trip to market?"

She appeared to be mentally sorting through the pantry as she followed them up the walk. They'd reached the front door and were carrying the trunk inside when she finally answered, "I think we can make do well enough for to-night. It won't be anything fancy, of course. Tomorrow, though . . . We'll have no choice but to make a list and go shopping."

A movement in the street beyond him caught his attention. "Damnation," he muttered, nodding his thanks to the driver and dismissing him.

"You were just being nice in offering to go to market?" she laughingly asked from behind him. "You don't *have* to go with me, you know. I'm perfectly capable of buying shrimp and pecans on my own."

"Not that," he growled, his stomach twisting. "My parents have just pulled up."

Chapter Five

Tamping down the urge to slam the door closed and use Isabella's trunk to barricade themselves inside, Barrett watched his father hand his mother out of their carriage.

"I assume from the look on your face that it's not a welcome visit."

"You don't know the half of it." And he didn't have anywhere near sufficient time to even make a start at explaining it.

"I'll be polite. I promise," she offered quietly as his parents started up the walk toward them.

Bless her heart for wanting to try. "If only it'd make a difference," he muttered darkly, knowing that his only hope lay in keeping them all together. His parents were far too polite to bring up any sort of unpleasantness in the presence of a stranger. If one of them managed to get him alone, though, there'd be no holding back the tide.

"Hello, Mother. Father," he began, dredging up a civil smile as they reached his doorway. Edging backward, he gestured to the foyer and continued the farce, saying, "What a wonderful surprise to have you call. Won't you come in?"

Neither of them said a word; their attentions were riveted just past his right arm, on Isabella. And judging by the way his mother's lips were pursed and the way his father's eyebrows were knitted at the bridge of his nose, they weren't the least bit pleased to see her there. Did they know who she was? he wondered. Or was their obvious displeasure rooted in finding him with company of any sort?

Reaching back and taking Belle by the elbow, he drew her forward and to his side, saying, "May I present my client, Mrs. Isabella Dandaneau? Isabella, my parents, Mr. and Mrs. Cecil Stanbridge."

"It's a pleasure to make your acquaintance," she offered on cue and in perfectly genteel tones. Despite the tension he could feel in the muscles of her arm, her smile was easy and unruffled.

"Charmed," his mother replied tightly, her own smile clearly a painful effort.

"Mrs. Dandaneau," his father offered with a crisp dip of his chin even as he brought his gaze squarely to Barrett's. "Might I have word with you privately?" he asked in the same breath.

God, how he wanted to say no. Barrett swallowed down the rising knot of his stomach and shrugged. "Of course. My study?"

Without another word, his father started across the foyer, his back ramrod-straight, his stride long and angry. Reluctantly turning to follow, Barrett flashed a weak smile at Belle, silently passing his mother into her care and hoping for a miracle he knew he wasn't the least bit likely to get.

"Would you care for a cup of tea, Mrs. Stanbridge?" he heard her ask in the wake of his departure. "It won't take but a moment to put the kettle on."

"Thank you," his mother answered after a long pause. "That would be lovely."

It was going to be anything but, Barrett knew. The fact that Isabella was quick-witted enough to handle the situation was a double-edged sword. On the one hand, she'd graciously handle all of his mother's inevitable questions. On the other, she'd easily read between the lines of what his mother offered in the way of stilted conversation and emerge from the encounter with questions he'd give his right arm to avoid answering. And to think that he'd actually thought—mere hours ago—that his life couldn't get any more complicated than it already was.

Swearing under his breath and knowing that he didn't have any choice except to make the best of a bad situation, he closed the door of his study behind himself and eyed the decanters on the credenza. He was about to offer his father a drink when the opportunity was snatched from him.

"Jesus F. Christ, son. Have you lost your mind?"

And so it begins. As always, he darkly, silently groused. And, as always, he knew better than to let himself be sucked into his father's emotional vortex. Slipping his hands into the pockets of his suit coat, Barrett slowly rocked between his toes and heels as he calmly replied, "If you could define the specific cause of today's outrage, I'd be most appreciative."

"That woman with your mother!" his father practically bellowed, gesturing wildly toward the front of the house.

Barrett slowly shook his head and held his ground. "You didn't know Isabella was here until your carriage pulled up to the curb. Why don't we start with what prompted you to make the trip in the first place?"

For a second his father seemed to puff up to half again his normal size and then, as though he'd been stuck with a pin, he deflated in one swift *whoosh*. Raking his fingers through his white mane, he admitted, "I've spoken this morning with Chief Inspector Larson about the investigation."

Barrett considered the likely facets of his father's concern and managed a smile as he addressed the first of the two, asking "And how is your good friend Michael these days?"

"Heartsick. He's not going to have any choice but to arrest you for the murder of that American woman. The public clamor for justice is too loud to avoid the course. He's being pressured by his superiors to bring the matter to a quick and neat resolution."

Never mind about a just one. "Arrest me on what evidence?" Barrett pressed, crossing to the credenza.

"You were the last person to have seen her alive."

"No," Barrett countered, pouring himself a Scotch. "The person who accosted her in the alley was. What Larson has against me is nothing more than pure, blind assumption. There's not so much as a shred of evidence to support it."

"There's no proof that there was someone else, Barrett," his father countered, the raw notes of burgeoning panic edging his words. "God, I've always been afraid that you'd come to this sort of end someday. The business with Su—"

"Would you care for a drink?" Barrett offered, cutting him off.

"No!"

"Take one anyway," Barrett insisted through clenched teeth, thrusting the glass into his father's hand. "It'll settle your nerves."

"There are times when it's entirely appropriate to be frazzled. This is one of them."

Barrett filled another glass and took a healthy swig of it before he had the wherewithal to calmly reply, "Father, I didn't kill Mignon Richard. She was alive and well when I fell asleep. It may take a while, but eventually I'll prove who *did* bludgeon her to death and hand him over to the authorities."

"You have twenty-four hours to accomplish it. That's the most Michael thinks he'll be able to delay the process."

Justice by the sweep of the hour hand. So much for the scales of truth. "Twenty-four isn't likely to be long enough," he posed aloud. "Isabella—"

"Is she the dead woman's sister?"

Barrett took another sip of his scotch, his mind sorting through the options he had. "First cousin," he supplied absently.

"And you're moving her in with you? Have you no self-control at all? Don't you care how that might look to others?"

Barrett knew better than to be honest and confess that the opinions of others had never crossed his mind. It was an aspect of his character that his parents had never understood or accepted. Deliberately choosing to avoid the pitfall, he gave his father another truth instead, explaining, "Isabella walked into my office this morning and by the time she was done telling me her and Mignon's story, I was fairly well boxed into a corner. Whoever killed Mignon is going to come after Isabella. A second woman dying after being in my company would be even harder to explain than the first one. She's here so that I can protect her."

"And capture the brigand when he comes to harm her."

His father's tone clearly said that while he could see the logic, he didn't believe a word of it. Ignoring the wholly expected skepticism, Barrett lifted his glass in salute and managed a half-smile. "If you decide to give up the glittering world of the financier, you'd make a fairly good investigator."

"Well, answer me this," his father went on, as always undaunted by anything he said. "How are you going to protect her when you're behind bars? Have you given that any thought at all? Are you perhaps planning to move her into your cell?"

Resisting the urge to bang his head against the nearest wall, Barrett stared at the scotch in his glass and tightly replied, "I'll post a bond and be released on my honor. It won't take any more than a couple of hours at the most. I'll see that Carden and Aiden watch over her in the interim."

"And if the authorities don't allow you to post bond?" his father countered acerbically. "How are you going to protect this Isabella woman and catch the real killer if they insist upon holding you until the trial? Are you going to pass those tasks to your friends as well?"

As much as he hated to admit it, his father had a most valid point. Telling him so, however . . . "I'm sure I'll figure something out."

"While you're about it, I hope you can find the time and summon the effort to find a way to spare your mother the embarrassment of yet another horrendous scandal. She's been in constant tears since yesterday morning and has had to cancel every single one of her social commitments."

And now they were, ever so predictably, on to the second facet of his parents' concerns. "I'm sorry," he offered dutifully while thinking his parents would be far happier people if they didn't live their lives according to the opinions of others.

"Being sorry doesn't make the slightest bit of difference, Barrett. Even if you're eventually exonerated for this hideous crime, no acceptable young woman in her right mind is going to entertain a proposal from you."

He was going to be arrested and charged with a gruesome murder within the next twenty-four hours and his parents were worried about the effect that would have on finding a wife? God love them both. They had the strangest perspectives and priorities. "Well," Barrett drawled, "look on the bright side of all this. If I'm convicted, you won't have to worry about the embarrassment of my choosing an unacceptable woman."

"And the public hanging of my son would be ever so much more endurable?"

"I don't know," he admitted with a shrug, suddenly tired of the whole exchange, of trying to be someone he wasn't. "I don't spend a great deal of time thinking about the gossip mill. How do you think the two possibilities weigh out? There is the sympathy factor to be considered in having to bury me."

His father looked at him as though he were a complete stranger. His brows knitted, his head tilted to the side, he said quietly, "Barrett, this is not a situation to take lightly. You're in very serious trouble."

"I'm well aware of that." Just as he was aware that, under all the hard-edged blustering and interminable lecturing, his father deeply cared and was, in his own way, trying to make things better. As if that were within the realm of possibility.

"Your mother and I discussed the situation," his father said, intruding on his thoughts. "And we've decided that it would be best if you disappeared until this matter is resolved." From the inner pocket of his suit coat he removed two thick stacks of currency. Laying them on the desk, he added, "We thought Paris might be an appropriate place for you to go. Or perhaps Vienna, if you'd prefer."

Barrett considered the money and shook his head. "If I were interested in running, I wouldn't need money from you to do it."

"This is not the time to put pride before common sense, son. Take the money and buy yourself passage on the next vessel heading across the Channel. Michael can't arrest you if you're not here."

"And I can't find the real killer if I leave."

Raking his fingers through his hair again, his father sighed and looked toward the front of the house. After a long moment, he countered, "Take this Isabella woman with you, then. If someone truly wants to kill her, they'll follow you to the Continent and you can deal with them there."

"Logistically, it would be much more complicated."

"It's not going to be simple here. Not if you're incarcerated."

"I'll think about it," he promised vaguely, his instincts telling him that bolting across the Channel would be the worst thing he could do. While he didn't care for meeting social expectations, legal ones were another matter entirely. Innocent men didn't flee the country.

"Your mother needs to be reassured, Barrett. I want to be able to climb back into our carriage and tell her that her son's going to do the sensible thing."

"For a change," he finished.

"I didn't say that."

Because I said it for you, Barrett silently countered. He polished off his scotch and held up the empty glass, asking, "Another drink?"

"Barrett, I'm your father and I've lived considerably more years than you have. I think you'd do well to listen to . . ."

Barrett poured himself another drink as his mind drifted away on the notes of the too familiar litany. God, he hoped Belle was having an easier time of it with his mother. Not, he suspected, that there was much chance of it. Where his father was predictably persistent and direct, his mother was predictably persistent and oblique. But Belle was intelligent; she'd know an insult when she heard one, no matter how vaguely couched. It remained to be seen just how patient and gracious she could be in the face of it.

There was nothing more to be done, not another single thing with which she could putter in the hope of disguising the absolute absence of conversation. Isabella adjusted the position of the cookie plate one last time, then smoothed her skirts and sat in the seat opposite Barrett Stanbridge's mother. She was readying the strainer when the other woman finally decided to break the awkward silence.

"If I might ask . . . Does my son's staff have the day out?"

A simple "yes" would have sufficed, but Isabella wasn't willing to risk the consequences of such a terse reply. "They left earlier today for an extended holiday," she explained, hoping the additional, unnecessary information would prompt her companion to ask another question or offer a comment on which they could build something approximating a cordial exchange.

"I can certainly understand why they'd wish to go."

Isabella poured the first cup of tea while puzzling the remark. Unless Mrs. Stanbridge had crossed paths with Barrett's housekeeper and cook on their way out of town, there was no reasonable way she could understand the reason for their departure. So how—

"And I'd be most surprised if Mrs. Wallace chooses to return," Barrett's mother elaborated. "Truth be told, I was stunned when she accepted the post in the first place. She's a good Christian woman and considering the debacle with Mrs. King—"

Barrett's mother started, seeming to suddenly realize that she'd said too much or perhaps something she shouldn't have said at all. "Well," she added too breezily, "there's no point in going into all of that, now is there? Water under the bridge and all of that."

Isabella smiled and handed the cup across the cart, asking, "Would you care for cream or sugar?"

"Both, please. Your accent . . . It's not British."

"I'm from Louisiana," Isabella supplied, placing the sugar shell and the creamer within the woman's easy reach.

"Oh," she said dryly, knowingly, as she splashed cream into her cup. "You're an American."

Isabella poured herself a cup of tea, pondering the woman's tone and wondering what assumptions lay beneath it. Clearly Mrs. Stanbridge didn't think too highly of Americans in general. Would there be any point to sharing the regional distinctions they made among themselves? Would Barrett's mother care that there was a great deal of difference between Northern Americans, Southern Americans, and those who came from the Western part of the country?

"You're quite a long way from home," the other woman observed, effectively putting an end to Isabella's musing. "Surely you didn't come all this way just to hire my son."

Well, she had to give the woman credit for the incredible politeness of the query. "No, I came to London in pursuit of my cousin. Unfortunately, she refused to listen to reason and Barrett and I have become entangled in the consequences."

The other woman ladled two heaping spoonfuls of sugar into her tea, picked up her spoon and stirred it all together. Only as she lifted her cup and saucer did she ask, "Your cousin is the young woman who . . . left the theater with my son?"

"Yes. Mignon."

The woman nodded and took a sip of her tea. Setting down the cup to add a third measure of sugar, she arched a pale brow and casually inquired, "And did your husband accompany you on your jaunt to our side of the pond?"

Oh, she was so very smooth. The Yankee generals could have taken interrogation lessons from Mrs. Cecil Stanbridge. "My husband is deceased," Isabella provided. "He was a casualty of war."

Mrs. Stanbridge made a little sound; not exactly a gasp of regret for having inadvertently opened sad memories and not quite a whimper of sympathy, either. No, Isabella decided, it sounded more like a groan of disappointment combined with a half-strangled growl of frustration.

"How very unfortunate," Mrs. Stanbridge offered blandly. "It must be exceedingly difficult for you to carry on without him."

"I'm trudging along," she replied with what she hoped passed for a stoic smile. Then deliberately closing the door on the more personal aspects of their conversation, Isabella picked up the plate of cookies, saying brightly, "Would you care for one? Cook made them this morning before she left. The little butter crisps are especially good."

Mrs. Stanbridge didn't even look at the cookies. "Thank you, but no." Then, just barely pausing to draw a breath, she asked, "May I be frank with you, Mrs. Dandaneau?"

Cursing the requirements of civility and the woman's deliberate use of the expectation, Isabella set the plate aside and reluctantly smiled her assent.

Mrs. Stanbridge didn't waste another second. "You seem like a very nice young woman," she said kindly enough. "And it's apparent that you were raised with certain expectations of gentility. Barrett is my only child and, while I love him dearly, he is not without his faults. Most are relatively minor ones that a mother learns, over the years, to accept. However, his ability to consistently choose inappropriate female companions isn't one of them."

What, Isabella wondered, did her having been raised genteelly have to do with Barrett choosing inappropriate women? "I can understand," Isabella ventured diplomatically, unable to see how the two ideas connected, "why a mother would find that discouraging."

"He recently promised his father and me that he'd select a suitable girl and settle down. And we were making some progress in narrowing the selections."

Why on earth was Barrett's mother telling her all of

this? It wasn't information she needed to know and she couldn't see what it had to do with her and Barrett's association. "But?" she pressed, hoping that traveling just a bit farther down the path might reveal the reason of the journey.

"The consequences of his involvement with your cousin have fairly well dashed any chance that a respectable family would permit a daughter to marry him," his mother continued. "At least for the next year or so. The Suzanna King scandal took almost three years to fade from memories. This isn't quite as bad, of course, but one scandal tends to revive memories of the previous ones and . . ."

Isabella blinked and took another sip of her tea, stunned. As scandals went, being falsely accused of a grisly murder wasn't as bad? Good God, what had happened to Suzanna King?

In the other woman's silence, Isabella realized that she was now expected to make some sort of conversational contribution. Since she knew nothing whatsoever about Barrett's apparently checkered past, the only subject she felt capable of addressing was his future. "I'm rather hoping," she began, "that we can resolve the problem before Barrett faces any formal charges, Mrs. Stanbridge. He had absolutely nothing to do with Mignon's death and we intend to prove it. I'm sure that once we accomplish that, any hint of scandal will disappear and he can resume his search for a wife."

"I do so hope that you're not falsely raising my hopes."

It was a request for tangible proof if she'd ever heard one. Isabella wished she had some to lay on the cart between them for no other reason than to end the woman's exceedingly polite inquisition. And to think that Mrs. Stanbridge looked like everyone's favorite Aunt Midge. Short and round, with cherubic cheeks, sassy little blond pin curls and blue, blue eyes. But, unlike the Aunt Midges of the world, this woman had considerably more on her mind than dispensing homespun wisdom and pieces of sassafras candy.

"Are you hoping to someday remarry, Mrs. Dandaneau?"

Isabella hid her smile around the rim of her teacup, suddenly seeing how all the disparate points of their conversation came together. Mrs. Stanbridge was worried sick that all of her maternal efforts to find a good and virtuous daughter-in-law were going to be crushed in the swirling scandal Mignon's murder had created, and that, in the shadows of scandal, her son would fall prey to the matrimonial designs of an American hussy.

"No, ma'am," Isabella replied honestly. "Once was quite enough for me."

"Most women prefer to be married."

"I have very little in common with most women," she assured her, knowing even as she did that the words were falling on completely deaf ears.

True to form, Barrett's mother nodded and immediately asked, "How long do you plan to stay in London?"

With a silent prayer for patience, Isabella gave her the truth one more time. "I have business to attend. When it's completed, I'll likely return home. I wish I could tell you precisely when that will be, but I can't. I can assure you, however, that I won't dally once I'm free to go."

"In the meantime, you'll be residing in my son's home?"

Lord, Isabella silently groaned, her father's blueticks hadn't pursued raccoons with as much persistence. "It's a matter of necessity at this point," she explained, trying very hard to keep the frustration out of her voice. "But I've kept my rented room so that I can move back there at the first opportunity. I don't like imposing on the kindness and hospitality of others."

"Appearances are so very important, you know," the other woman countered. "It has such a direct effect on one's reputation." She took a sip of her tea and then added, "At least here in England. I have no idea how you view such matters on your side of the Atlantic."

Isabella bit her tongue and sternly reminded herself that no protest, assurance, or explanation would make the slightest bit of difference in the woman's concerns and opinions. Barrett's mother was going to believe as she wanted to believe. Which, in this particular situation, was obviously the worst. There was nothing to be done about it. Except, she amended, feel a bit sorry for Barrett. And a great deal sorry for the poor woman he eventually talked into marrying him.

"Melanie, dear, it's time for us to be on our way."

Isabella couldn't tell which of them—her or Barrett's mother—was more relieved to hear the pronouncement from the parlor doorway. Both of them sagged in the same instant and to much the same degree. Isabella, however, managed to recover before the other woman did. Summoning a polite smile, she rose from her seat and turned to face Barrett's father, saying, "I hope you had a pleasant visit."

"It was typical," he replied with the tightest of smiles and without meeting her gaze. "Melanie?"

Melanie Stanbridge rose, said, "Thank you for the refreshments, Mrs. Dandaneau," and then proceeded across the parlor, past her husband, into the hall and toward the front door.

"Mrs. Dandaneau," Barrett's father offered crisply just before turning on his heel and following in his wife's regal wake.

Isabella stood there staring after them, shaking her head in wonder. It certainly qualified as one of the most interesting afternoons she'd had in quite some time. Being all but formally declared morally bankrupt and socially unacceptable was a decidedly new experience. Although, she admitted, smiling, there was something rather exciting about the notion of being so utterly, irredeemably wicked. Being so wanton left no room for reservations and hesitations, not to mention trepidation and fear. Why, being so bad could make a woman positively bold.

Grinning, she headed down the hallway, intending to find Barrett and thinking that perhaps she might get him to tell her the torrid, horribly scandalous story of his relationship with Suzanna King.

Or perhaps not, she amended from the doorway of his study. He sat in the chair behind his desk, his feet propped up on the blotter, his booted ankles crossed. She might have considered him relaxed were it not for the depth and darkness of his frown and the white-knuckled grip he had on his empty glass.

His gaze slowly slid from the distance to connect with hers and she summoned a smile for him as she advanced, observing, "You look as though you've been dragged through a knothole backwards."

"Oh, it's a thrice-annual ordeal," he replied, barely shrugging one shoulder. "I've become accustomed to it. I trust that my mother was her ever gracious self?"

Isabella dropped into the leather-upholstered chair on her side of the desk. "She reminds me a great deal of my dearly departed grandmama."

"Is that good or bad?"

"Good," she admitted, "in that you know exactly where you stand with her."

"Lord," he groaned. "What did she say?" He'd barely gotten the words out before he raised his hand to stay her answer and hastily added, "No, wait. Let me rephrase that. I know my mother. What did she ever so clearly *imply*?"

Ah, he did know her well. "Barrett, darlin'," she drawled, deliberately thickening her accent, "I sincerely regret havin' to tell you this ... I know your heart's set ... But your mother would *kill* you if you married me."

His jaw dropped.

"And she'll kill *me*," Isabella went on, "if I do anything that lessens your chances of eventually snaring a good woman."

It took him several long seconds to recover enough to blink, swallow, and clear his throat. "You are a good woman."

"Not nearly good enough," she countered, waving her hand dismissively. "Evidenced by the fact that I'm an American and that I've taken up residence with you. I formed the distinct impression that in your mother's mind the former directly accounts for my willingness to do the latter. And no, I didn't try to explain the circumstances to her. I didn't think it would make any difference."

He set his glass on the desk and scrubbed his hands over his face. "I know that you don't have any particular reason to believe me, but she really is a nice person."

"Oh, I doubt that she has even one malicious bone in her body. But, as I said, your mother reminds me of my grandmama. The unpleasant side of that is that no matter who you choose to marry, your mother will always think that you could have done better. Papa and Tio Jasper paid dearly for handing their hearts to Grandmama's daughters."

"Damned if I do," he said on a sigh. "Damned if I don't."

"That seems to be a fair summation."

One corner of his mouth quirked up. "If you were in my shoes, what course would you take?"

"I'd marry whomever I pleased and then move far, far away."

He nodded and seemed to be giving the idea serious consideration. After several moments he slid his gaze back to hers. Devilment sparkled in the depths of his eyes as he asked, "Do you know if it's difficult to learn to speak Chinese?"

"I think it would be well worth the effort."

He laughed outright and she decided that kindness lay in not dampening his humor with questions about the past. And that wisdom lay in putting some distance between herself and a handsome man whose twinkling eyes warmed her body and soul.

"How do ham croquettes with a horseradish sauce sound for dinner?" she asked, pushing herself up out of the chair and heading for the door. "With peas and little pearl onions—or carrots—on the side. Rolls and butter, of course. And maybe apple dumplings for dessert. With whipped cream."

Barrett watched her walk away, wondering if she even noticed that he hadn't answered. Jesus, she was a fascinating thing. Sweet syrup and moonlight one minute, wicked irreverence in the next. And then blushing, skittish innocence in the moment after that.

Lord, he could only hope that she decided to leave the whipped cream off the dumplings. As fantasies went, he really didn't want to resist that one.

Chapter Six

Full, warm, and satisfied, Barrett leaned back in his chair and stretched his legs out under the kitchen table. "That was absolutely delicious," he offered, smiling at his empty dinner plate. "Don't tell Cook, but it's one of the best meals I've had in ages."

"Thank you. Would you care for more peas and carrots?"

"It depends," he drawled, sliding his gaze over to hers as he smiled. "Did you make apple dumplings?"

She nodded, her eyes bright. "Whipping the cream is all that's left to do. It won't take but a minute. The crock's already chilled."

"Then I'll decline the more healthy course and go straight for decadence," he declared, thinking that the statement summed up his approach to life in general. It also, he realized as she rose from her seat, fairly well expressed his inclinations regarding Isabella Dandaneau. Intelligent, companionable, a damned fine cook. And beautiful, he added, watching her move toward the larder. Perfectly curved in all the right places and owing precious little to either a corset or padding. At least from what he could tell so far.

So far? Barrett shook his head and forced himself out of his own chair. No, he told himself as he carried their dishes to the sink, Belle was a sweet indulgence he should resist. A delicacy he wanted, yes. Hell, a man would have to be long dead to not want her. But in the wake of Mignon . . . Rolling back the cuffs of his shirtsleeves, he shook his head again. It had been only a matter of days. He didn't have all that many standards and few of those were carved in stone, but the very notion of casually, deliberately setting out to seduce Belle so soon . . . It seemed low in the extreme.

The subject of his musing returned to the kitchen table with a gray stone crock, a bottle of cream, and a rotary eggbeater. "Leave the dishes, Barrett," she admonished. "I'll get to them in just a bit."

"No." He tossed some soap flakes into the washing pan and stepped to the stove for the hot water pot, adding, "You cooked, I'll clean."

"Do you make a habit of helping in the kitchen?"

"I went without household staff for the first two years after I left Her Majesty's Army," he explained, filling the wash pans and keenly aware that she was watching him. "When I didn't dine out, I made my own meals. I eventually concluded that the cleaning nymph wasn't going to flit through in my absence and that if I didn't want to make myself sick, I was going to have to wash some dishes."

"Necessity might well be the mother of invention, but what no one ever mentions is that drudgery is her stepchild."

He chuckled, amused by her perspective, and plunged the dishes into the hot, soapy water.

"You'd best put on an apron," she said a moment later, taking a frilly, bibbed affair off the wall peg beside the larder door. "You don't want to ruin your clothes."

"There are limits to my domesticity," he protested as she came at him with the hideous thing. Scrubbing an already clean plate so that he looked too diligently occupied to interrupt, he added, "A man has to maintain some standards, you know."

"So does a woman," she countered, standing beside him at the sink, the scent of roses enveloping him. "And while I'm perfectly willing to cook, I loathe doing laundry." Gently, she took his upper arm and drew him around to face her. "Please accommodate me."

Accommodate her? Oh, Lord, as invitations went . . . His pulse hammering, his blood heating, he tried and failed to rein in a wicked smile as he looked down at her. The blush across the high arc of her cheekbones, the way her gaze darted away from his told him that her thoughts had arrowed along the very same path as his own. And he couldn't resist the temptation.

"Do you always live so dangerously?" he teased, holding out his arms, giving her a choice between stepping into them or sliding the apron over them.

She swallowed and fixed her gaze on the center of his chest. "Not as a general rule," she replied, the color in her cheeks deepening as she carefully, almost hesitantly slipped the apron over his hands and forearms. "Sometimes the words just spill out before I can think better of them."

"It's an endearing quality."

"Oh, yes," she countered, laughing softly as she leaned closer to lay the shoulder straps into place. "Especially when it's not humiliating."

"Do you know that you're blushing?" he asked as he considered wrapping his arms around her.

"Yes," she admitted, her gaze coming up to meet his while she stepped back and took the decision away from him. She grinned and arched a brow, then moved behind him, adding, "But I was hoping you'd be gentleman enough to refrain from pointing it out."

"Just when, precisely," he posed, trying, unsuccessfully, to see her over his shoulder, "did you conclude that I was a gentleman?"

The apron pulled snugly around his waist as she tied the strings and answered, "This morning. You were decidedly uncomfortable in talking about the time you spent with Mignon. That's the hallmark of a true gentleman."

His conscience prickled. "I'm really not, Belle. Not down deep. You need to know that."

"Consider it duly noted," she declared, moving back to the table. "Not believed, mind you," she added, looking over her shoulder at him, her smile wicked and her dark eyes sparkling mischievously, "but noted."

Oh, he was going to hell anyway. It was too late for self-denial to make one whit of difference. Just when, he wondered, turning back to the sink, would it be all right to actively pursue her? A week? A fortnight? They were going to be together only for as long as it took to find the treasure. Once they did, Isabella would be on her way. It could be only days. At which point, he silently groused, the entire matter of appropriate timing would be moot. The more optimistic side of his thinking suggested there was also a distinct possibility that they might never find the treasure; theoretically, they could be together forever. Despite the heat of the dishwater, his blood chilled.

"I've been thinking about who our murderer might be," he lied, deliberately directing his thoughts down a less troubling path. "How long did it take you to discover that Mignon had left New Orleans and then go after her?"

Over the clinking of stone and glass, she supplied, "Two days to hear that she was gone and then another two to put my affairs in order and negotiate passage. Why?"

"Did anyone else leave town in that time?"

"New Orleans is a big city, Barrett. Not as large as London, of course, but it's certainly not so small that you see everyone every day. Added to that, and as you might have surmised, I didn't socialize in the same circles as Mignon."

He nodded, his hands working as his brain turned the puzzle pieces over and over. "Someone made several attempts to steal both halves of the map in New Orleans, correct? From both you and Mignon."

"Yes."

Collecting the pots and pans from the stovetop, Barrett continued, saying, "So that tells us that someone knew that it had been torn in two. Who knew that?"

"Me, Mignon, the lawyer who actually tore it, and whoever Mignon told about it. That latter number could well be in the thousands once the story rippled from person to person."

"And would everyone who heard about it believe in buried pirate treasure?"

"In New Orleans?" She laughed. "Yes."

"But would they believe deeply enough to make genuine, repeated efforts to get their hands on the map?"

A few seconds passed and the amusement had left her voice when she replied, "What you're saying is that someone tried to steal the map because they know—for sure and certain—that there really is a treasure and that it's worth the risk."

He nodded, his mind racing through the tangle of possibility. "Let's assume for the moment that the last part of Mignon's half of the text doesn't say *London*."

"I'd really rather not. It's too depressing."

Smiling and ignoring her uncharacteristic pessimism, he placed the last pot in the drying rack. "From what you've told me," he countered, reaching for a towel to dry his hands, "the family attorney sounds like a man who wanted to be as fair as he possibly could." Turning, he leaned back against the edge of the sink and watched her set to work with the beater. "Would he have given either one of you the advantage of knowing the treasure was in a specific city?"

"No."

"So my assumption stands a good chance of being a valid one. And if the text doesn't say *London*, then the question becomes why she came here to look for it."

"I've asked myself that question many a time. If you come up with an answer, I'm going to be slightly piqued."

"No you won't. You'll be hugely impressed," he countered, grinning and tossing the towel atop the dishes. Stripping off the apron, he asked, "Who, other than Lafitte, would know that the treasure hunt was in London?"

"We don't know that it is, Barrett."

"Look at the situation from the perspective of whoever tried to steal the map in New Orleans," he posed, dropping the apron atop the towel and moving back to the table. Turning his chair, he straddled it, folding his arms across the back.

"They failed and the repeated attempts put both you and Mignon on guard, making further attempts that much more difficult and even less likely to succeed. So what to do? Why not go for the easier course and give one of you a hint as to the general location and then follow along and snatch the treasure from you when you find it? Let you do all the work so they can reap the reward without expending much effort."

Her brows knitted, her hands pausing, she slowly nodded and said, "They knew that the place was London, but not where in London. Mignon and I, between us, knew the details of where to look, but didn't know in what city. Mignon would have been the logical one of us to nudge. She had the money to travel quickly."

"And the greed that would have made her jump at the chance to get to the treasure as fast as she could," Barrett added. "Before you had a chance to catch up to her and demand your half of it."

"She would have been so busy moving forward that she

wouldn't have bothered to look back for me or to question too closely the motives of whoever pointed her this way."

"Exactly. And it would have been a perfect plan except that Mignon saw them—most likely by accident at the theater—and realized that she'd been manipulated. She hid the map, and when they confronted her, trying to repair the breach in their plan . . . I doubt they intended to kill her. Dead people can't talk, can't tell you what you want to know. I think the interrogation simply went out of control and couldn't be reined in."

"It's plausible," she conceded with a shrug.

"It's more than plausible."

She sighed and removed the beater. Propping it carefully against the inner edge of the stone crock, she reached for the sugar shell, saying, "All right, as farfetched as it seems, I'll allow that the chain of circumstances suggest that London is where we're supposed to be."

"Then we're back to the question of who—other than Lafitte—would know that. Would any of Mignon's circle of gentleman friends have known Lafitte well enough to have been privy to his secrets?"

She rolled her eyes and softly snorted as she sprinkled sugar over the cream. "You can't swing a dead cat in New Orleans without hitting an old man who claims to have been one of Lafitte's pirates. If you added them all together, he would have had a force larger than the British Navy. Some of them might have actually served with him, but separating the real pirates from those simply claiming the glory . . . I don't know that it can be done without Jean himself doing the actual sorting."

"Well, I don't see that we have any real choice except to have something of a go at it ourselves. They're the most logical suspects."

"They're the only suspects," she countered dryly, setting aside the sugar.

"Start with the man most likely a former pirate and with the financial resources to travel."

"That would be Neville Martinez." Gently stirring the sugar in with a spoon, she continued. "I doubt he's our murderer, though. He's been confined to a wheeled chair for the last eight years. A riding accident. The horse cleared the hedge. Neville didn't."

"Next on the list."

"I'd put Jacques de Granvieux second if he weren't dead."

Barrett grinned. "That does tend to limit his opportunities for mayhem."

"Then there's Emil Caribe. He was Mignon's current lover. Of course, he's the one who told me she'd sailed for England."

An interesting possibility. Caribe certainly had more potential than a cripple and a dead man. "Might he have sailed after that conversation and before you did?"

"His wife is understanding, but not that understanding," she replied, shaking her head. "And she's considerably bigger and meaner than Emil is."

"Any others?"

She pursed her lips and after a long moment shrugged. "The Choteau brothers, Etan and Pierre. The story is that they went to Galveston with Lafitte in the early twenties and then came back to New Orleans when the Mexicans asked Jean to move elsewhere. They were named as responsible parties in Mignon's first divorce."

"Both of them?" he asked, the mental image instant and sufficiently lascivious to utterly overwhelm his better judgment.

"I'm not telling you the details," she declared, grinning at him.

"I don't think there's any need." Damn, the kind of conversation he seemed to have with Belle on a regular basis . . . He didn't know whether it was her or the nature of the circumstances in which they found themselves, but it was most decidedly a novel experience. And not in an uncomfortable way, either, he realized.

Although, he amended as she lightly dipped her pinky into the crock. His loins tightening and his breath caught hard in the center of his chest, Barrett willed her to offer him the taste. She defied him, but there was only a shadow of disappointment in his low groan as he watched her slowly, contemplatively suckle her fingertip.

The impulse was too powerful to resist. He cleared his throat and ever so nonchalantly asked, "Does it need more sugar?"

To his everlasting delight and reward, she brightened, said, "I can't decide," swiped her index finger through the whipped cream and held out the generous dollop for him to sample. "You tell me," she instructed half a heartbeat before she blinked in startled realization.

Grinning, he caught her wrist before she could pull it back. Holding her lightly, feeling her pulse dancing beneath his fingertips, he half rose from his chair. Leaning forward, watching her boldly, openly, he ever so slowly licked the cream from the very tip of her finger. Her breathing stopped, her pulse skittered, and the light in her eyes begged him to continue. He obliged her, opening his mouth and taking all of her finger inside. Suckling gently, swirling his tongue languidly about the length, he released his prize by exquisitely unhurried degrees.

She was swaying on her feet, leaning forward into his seduction, when he lightly nipped the end of her finger, whispered, "Perfect for my tastes," and then slowly surrendered his hold.

"So very good," she murmured, shaking her head. Then she started, blinked, and quickly turned away.

Barrett watched as she bent over to take the dumplings

from the warming oven. Jesus Christ. A week would be an eternity. If he had to wait a fortnight, he'd explode. Hell, if he didn't put his mind back into safer subjects, the dumplings would be stone cold before they got back to them. He forced his gaze to the table in front of him, but the sight of the whipped cream didn't do anything to bring his desires under control. Finally, he settled his attention on the window overlooking the rear yard and the carriage house.

"Do any of Mignon's friends strike you as being the perfect suspect?" she asked, bringing two bowls to the table with hotpads.

"It depends," he hedged as she put generous dollops of whipped cream atop each one. "Are any of them having financial difficulties? Were any of them noticeably resentful of you and Mignon having inherited the treasure map? Or maybe someone was overly curious?"

"I don't know about anyone's finances except in a most general way. And I didn't live in Mignon's pocket. If anyone was jealous or too curious, I didn't hear about it." She smiled weakly and sat down across the table from him. "I'm not much help, am I?" she ventured, picking up her spoon and beginning a dainty assault on her dessert.

Barrett shrugged, poked a hole in the top of his dumpling, and absently watched the steam pour out through the vent. "As with most investigations, this one is a matter of asking the right questions and then collecting the right information. We need to figure out who would know that there's a treasure, that it's in London, be in a position to provide Mignon that information, and then have the resources to follow her here."

"Well, I think we can exclude the Choteaus," she offered, her loaded spoon resting on the edge of the bowl. "Pierre owns a popular gambling establishment and Etan owns a pleasure house that operates on the upper floors of it. I can't see that either one of them would be willing to go off and leave their enterprises to be run by others. As treasures go, they have very profitable ones already."

It was logical. Not necessarily irrefutable, but logical. "And you're sure Emil's wife would draw the line and he'd respect it?"

"His money is from her family. She says jump and he asks how high and to where."

Barrett nodded, thinking that those kind of pathetic men seemed to be scattered all over the world. "Are you sure Henri is dead?" She started at the suggestion and he quickly explained, "My friend Carden's wife thought her first husband was dead. It turned out that he wasn't." He smiled thinly and added, "Well, not soon enough, anyway."

Curiosity, plain and obvious, lit her dark eyes, but she didn't press him for the story. Instead, she blew on her bit of dumpling and then admitted, "I never saw the body. The official reports said that Henri was killed at Gettysburg and buried there. Still, on the off chance that a mistake was made and he's alive, I haven't seen or heard of him. I don't see how he could have learned of the map."

"And you're sure that Jacques is dead?" Barrett went on, systematically gathering information.

She nodded and consumed the cooled bite of dessert before replying, "Absolutely certain. He clutched his chest and dropped dead on a public street. The battle between the family and Mignon over the will began the day after the funeral. It was not only very public, it was brutal."

"Who won?"

"Guess," she challenged, her grin wide.

Mignon, of course. As motives for murder went . . . And, now that he thought about it, there really wasn't any tangible proof that she'd been killed for the map. It might well have been a matter of a wronged heir having finally tracked her down. It wasn't likely, but it was a possibility. He'd seen stranger coincidences. "Who comprises the family? Any brothers? Sons?"

"His wife and two daughters. His sons were off in the war." She blew gently on another bite. "And before you ask, no, they didn't come home."

"Not too many did, did they?"

She shook her head sadly. "Pretty much all we have left are old men and young boys. And widows. We have lots of widows. Until just the last few months, the only fabrics you could buy were black bombazine, black crepe, and black tulle."

"Unless you were Mignon," he guessed.

A soft smile tipped up one corner of her mouth. "She did live by her own rules. You have to admire her for that."

Barrett suspected that Belle lived by her own rules, too. They simply weren't as outrageous or predatory as Mignon's had been. Nor did she go about flaunting them as her cousin had. Belle struck him as being more self-contained, more instinctively reserved than her cousin had been. But no less independent in her thinking.

And thinking overly much about her was going to get him into trouble, he silently reminded himself. Forcing his mind back to the puzzle of the map, of the murder, he searched for the point he'd reached before being distracted. "What about the man who was injured in the riding accident?"

"Neville Martinez?" She considered the idea for a few moments. "I suppose," she finally drawled, "that if he were willing to hire someone to be his legs and his fists . . ."

"He'd be a possibility?"

She nodded and ate a bite of dumpling and cream. "He's a banker. Rumor has it that he's always been heavily involved in smuggling and, more recently, in offering protection to businesses. Both of which I tend to believe. He's always—even in the deepest, darkest days after the war—had money. And those businesses who bank with him—the Choteau brothers for example—are never raided by the authorities."

Barrett ate several bites of his dessert, momentarily losing his larger train of thought in the wonder of what Belle could do with a simple piece of fruit, sugar, flour, butter, and cinnamon. "My compliments," he offered, spooning up another. "It's heavenly."

At her radiant smile, he again sought refuge in their puzzle. "Did Mignon know Neville well? Would she have accepted any information he gave her?"

"Emil's wife occasionally snaps her fingers and forces him to dance attendance on her. And Mignon wasn't the sort to sit at home alone. There were wagers being made—at Pierre's—that she'd throw Emil over for Neville before the year was out."

"Why would he want the treasure?" Barrett mused aloud, eating and pondering all the pieces he'd acquired. "He's a wealthy man already."

"Why did Mignon want it?" Belle posed in return. "She didn't need it any more than Neville Martinez does."

She was right, of course. Greed wasn't a rational thing; it simply existed, driving people to take otherwise inexplicable actions. "It's a relatively easy matter to hire thugs. Controlling them is another issue entirely. You need to be about to supervise them."

"Obviously matters weren't supervised in the alleyway or Mignon would still be alive."

"True," he allowed, thinking that a wheelchair-bound American with a Southern accent wouldn't be all that difficult to find. Especially a wealthy one; the man would consider most of London's corners to be unacceptable for a person of his status.

"Did you see anyone at the theater in a wheeled chair?"

"No," Barrett admitted, bringing his attention back to the moment. "That doesn't mean he wasn't there, of course."

"Some investigator you are," she teased, her eyes sparkling, her smile broad and easy.

"I had other things on my mind that night," he protested good-naturedly. "I was trying to keep my parents from marrying me off in the lobby."

"And then you noticed Mignon," she countered, scraping her bowl clean. "After that moment, like most men, you couldn't see anything else."

She was right yet again. Not that he was going to openly admit it. There was something particularly embarrassing about being as blind and stupid as every other man on the street. He finished off his dumpling while thinking back to that evening and the events that had been set in motion. "I wish it had been you at the theater instead," he ventured. "Things would have gone very differently."

"You wouldn't have noticed me."

"Oh, yes I would have," he assured her. "You're every bit the beauty your cousin was. Without the sharp edge of calculation."

A sweep of pink colored her cheeks and her smile was soft and shy as she pointed out, "But I wouldn't have left there with you, Barrett. Most certainly not to come here and . . . pause."

He laughed and laid his arms along the back of the chair. "That would have been all right. I'd have found a way to see you again."

"Your mother wouldn't have been at all pleased by that."

"I'm not overly restricted by my mother's opinion."

"Says the man," she countered, chuckling, "who's contemplating the moving of his life to China."

"Now that I've had some time to think about it, India might be better," he offered, enjoying their easy banter. "My friend Aiden's wife is the daughter of a raja. I'm sure

I could beg a favor or two out of her. They do speak English there, having been a British colony and all. Life would be considerably simpler than in China."

Leaning forward, she propped her elbows on the table and cradled her chin in her hands. "You have interesting friends. One whose wife wasn't a widow as she thought and another whose wife is Indian royalty."

"You'll like them."

"The wives or the husbands?"

"Both," he said. "As much as they'll like you," he added, recognizing the truth of it. "I think we'll go see Carden and Seraphina tomorrow. We need to compare the treasure map against those of London, and Carden, being an architect, has a collection of them."

She nodded her acceptance and he grinned. "I feel I should give fair warning, though. Their household tends to be something of a zoo. Between dogs and cats and children, it's always on the verge of complete chaos."

"It sounds perfectly lovely to me. It's probably because I didn't have any brothers or sisters, but I've always wanted a home filled with noise and life. I always thought that twelve would be the perfect number of children."

Hearing the wistful notes in her voice, he replied, "Twenty-seven is too young to give up hope for it. It's still attainable. Well, maybe not twelve. But six is easily possible."

"Oh, yes," she scoffed, chuckling. "And if wishes were horses, beggars would ride."

"Perhaps in Louisiana. But not here in London," Barrett countered in all seriousness. "When all is said and done . . . You could stay in London, whirl through the social glitter for a season or two, and find yourself a nicely suitable husband."

"But I don't want a husband. I enjoy my independence. Remember?"

"As I said, a nicely *suitable* husband."

She arched a brow and gave him a wide smile. "And you think *I'm* an optimist?"

"I think you're underestimating yourself."

"Ha!" Rising to her feet and lifting his bowl, she asked, "Another dumpling?"

He considered it and decided that he should at least try to develop some skill at resisting temptation. A second dumpling was a fairly easy place to begin. "I'll save it for a midnight repast," he announced, pushing himself to his feet. "As a reward for making yet another search for the two missing map pieces."

Carrying the bowls to the sink, she sighed and admitted, "I'm beginning to think she must have hidden them somewhere other than here."

"It's a possibility," he conceded. "If we don't find them with the next pass through the house, we'll search the gardens at first light. There aren't too many places she could have tucked them and been sure that they'd be safe from the wind and the damp."

Belle gazed out the kitchen window and into the darkened yard, trying to imagine her cousin being willing to even consider such a hiding place. Aside from the obvious uncertainties of the weather, Mignon had never been the sort to put her hands at the slightest risk from either soil or an accidental nick or abrasion. No, the missing pieces were somewhere dry and clean. It was a certainty. If not in the house itself . . . She shifted her gaze to the carriage house.

Letting herself into a stable was something Mignon would have never considered under normal circumstances, but since the situation had been obviously dire . . . Deciding that she'd mention it if their other searches didn't turn up the missing pieces, Isabella turned away from the window.

Barrett stood beside the table, casually rolling down his shirtsleeve. The pang of regret was instant and she shook her head, disappointed in herself for having a preference in how he wore his shirt. It really shouldn't make any difference to her at all; a man was a man and a shirt was a shirt.

But, the softer side of her countered, Barrett wasn't just any man. He had a keen mind and a wonderful sense of humor. He treated her, not as most men did women—like some fragile china doll or a dockside whore—but as an equal. It was most unusual, most unexpected. And so wonderfully gratifying.

Yes, Barrett was different; delightfully so. She liked him, liked being with him, liked how he made her feel. It had been such a long time since she'd felt as wildly alive as she had when he'd captured her hand over the table. And when he'd sucked the whipped cream from her fingertip her thighs had ached. And they were still aching.

When Mignon wasn't quite as much of a presence between them . . . No one would ever know. And if she consciously chose to sample temptation—just in passing—it really couldn't be considered a surrender. No, it wouldn't be a surrender at all. In fact, under the right sort of light, it might be seen as a rather healthy testament to her willingness to live fully again.

Not that Barrett needed to know that, of course. The less he knew about her past, the better, actually. The idea of being tumbled down out of pity or for restorative purposes didn't appeal to her at all. And, truth be told, she couldn't see Barrett being amorous under those circumstances. No, Barrett was undoubtedly the sort of man who liked his women without complications of any kind. She could hide them from him for as long as necessary. She was very good at hiding. And they wouldn't be together all that long, anyway.

"Belle?" she heard him call softly. "Are you troubled by something?"

Just who I am, she silently answered. *Where I've been and what I've done.* She drew a deep breath and summoned a smile as she met his gaze. "Not at all," she assured him. "I'm a bit tired. It's been a very long day."

"It has, hasn't it?" he replied, openly considering her. "Perhaps we could postpone another search until daylight and call our efforts for today sufficient. If you're agreeable, I'll show you to your room."

What would he do, what would he think, she wondered, if she told him that she'd prefer to sleep with him? Not that she could be bold enough to put the inclination into actual words. But if she could? If, for once in her life, she dared to be the aggressor in a seduction? Would he lay her down on the kitchen table and make love to her right there? Or would he sweep her into his arms and carry her up to his room to thoroughly ravage her on a silk comforter and feather mattress? In the throes of his passion, would he murmur her name or Mignon's?

Her heart fell like leaden ballast into her stomach. Acutely aware of the heat fanning across her cheeks, Isabella turned away and snatched up the now cooled pan of dumplings. "Let me put these in the larder," she said, bustling off, "and then we can retire to our separate quarters."

Barrett smiled as she darted into the shadows of the keeping room. Separate quarters? She'd felt a need to specify? Apparently he'd accurately interpreted the inviting sparkle in her eyes; she had been delighting in pleasurable possibilities. The prospect of which considerably delighted him. Lord, what he would have given for her wanton impulses to have held until they'd reached the upstairs hall.

Just over twelve hours into their acquaintance was a bit soon. Well, sooner than he would have thought at the beginning, but he wasn't of a mind to let the unexpectedness of her interest be a deterrent. Nor was he the least put off by her blush and obvious effort to squelch her fantasies. Not any more. Besides, only a saint could resist the temptation of teasing out the willing wanton. And he wasn't a saint, not by the longest stretch of any imagination.

Yes, there was—most definitely—still hope, he assured himself as she emerged from the larder, her eyes deliberately averted and her hands busily smoothing her skirts. Given her tendency to act before fully thinking, his experience in such matters, and the time it would take them to reach the guest room and a decision . . .

Barrett retrieved the oil lamp from the table and moved to the door. Pausing on the threshold of the dining room, he half turned back and extended his free hand. He held his breath as she considered it, then exhaled in sweet relief as she closed her eyes and placed her hand in his.

Barrett led her through the dining room to the front hall, conscious of how small and delicate her hand was compared to his own, how tentative was her acceptance of being shepherded. At the base of the stairs he shifted his hold on her, gently lacing his fingers through hers and holding her more firmly as he slowly drew her up the flight of carpeted steps. Her pulse was racing; it skittered through his flesh and bones and called his own heart to match the cadence.

He was almost light-headed by the time he drew her into the guest room and placed the lamp on the bureau by the door. But he wasn't so out of his awareness that he couldn't feel the tension vibrating through her, couldn't see the shallowness of her breath and the difficulty she had in swallowing. She looked up at him, her dark eyes huge and searching. Drawing her hand up to hold it against his chest, he smiled down at her. Anticipation whispered that he could obliterate—in mere seconds—every shadow of her doubts. His conscience cringed and then whimpered about being a decent man.

"Shall I light a fire for you?" he asked softly, hoping she would accept his oblique invitation and save him from his better half. "It would take only a moment and I wouldn't mind at all."

Her smile so soft, so gently appreciative. So knowing. "It's not necessary," she replied, her eyes twinkling brightly. "But you're most kind to offer."

It had to be one of the most endearing rebuffs he'd ever been served. And he knew her well enough that his hope wasn't the least bit dashed. Quite to the contrary, actually. While her current impulse might be to spend the night alone, she could just as well have an altogether different one before she drifted off into slumber. Lifting her hand to his lips, Barrett brushed a lingering kiss across her knuckles.

"Then I'll wish you pleasant dreams," he whispered as he released her and stepped away. "If you wake and need me, I'm but a few steps across the hall."

Isabella considered him and the scant difference between needing and wanting. "Good night, Barrett," she whispered, taking temptation and the edge of the door in hand. "I'll see you in the morning."

His smile as she closed the door suggested that he sensed her conflict and wouldn't chastise her should she decide to change her course in the hours between now and dawn. Belle closed her eyes and leaned her forehead against the cool wooden panel. She was genuinely bone-deep tired; the consequence of an exceedingly long and stressful day at the end of several truly grueling weeks. She'd be able to sleep without nightmares, without waking to wander the past and agonize over what she could have done differently.

But if she did . . . Belle half smiled and stepped away from the door, strengthened by the knowledge that if she wanted to be distracted, Barrett would be most willing to draw her under his sheets and thoroughly oblige her.

Chapter Seven

A flood of reality came in the first second of wakefulness. Barrett was there, fully dressed, one knee on the bed beside her, one hand cupped lightly over her mouth, the other curled firmly over the hand under the pillow. It was barely light and their breath hung in silver clouds between them.

"We have company," he announced quietly, releasing her hand and sliding off the bed.

Her heart racing, her body quivering and acutely aware of the cold, Isabella checked to make sure the revolver was still in place and then sat up, reaching for her wrapper and asking, "Who?"

"Chief Inspector Larson and five of his men are on the front step," he supplied, peering through the slit in the bedroom draperies without touching them. "They're pounding on the door, no doubt hoping I'll open it and calmly allow them in to arrest me."

Arrest him? Her heart turned over in her chest and she scrambled from the warm nest of her bed. "What are we going to do?"

"What any red-blooded, innocent Briton would do . . . Run," he answered, his smile tight and thin. Striding across the room, he said, "Kindly dress, gather up what you'll need for a few days, and then take the servants' stairs down to meet me in the study," and then disappeared into the hallway without a backward glance.

Isabella stared after him for a single heartbeat and then launched herself into concerted action. With her valise open on the bed and her clothing piled beside it, she stripped away her wrapper and night rail. Hurriedly pulling on her undergarments, she considered the fashionable shoes she'd worn the day before. Heaven only knew where she and Barrett were going and how they were going to get there. If they had to walk any distance . . . If he was genuinely serious about the need to run . . . Isabella dug to the bottom of her valise and extracted her riding boots.

And since she was forgoing feminine for the sake of practical . . . Isabella stuffed her corset and petticoat into the valise along with the night rail and the wrapper. There was no dispensing with the blasted hoops, though; not if she didn't want her hems pooling around her ankles.

If only, she silently grumbled, tying the contraption around her waist, she'd foreseen the necessity of bringing Mignon's trunk upstairs last night instead of deferring the task for today. A fresh dress—one a bit less fashionably noticeable—would have been nice. Under the circumstances, standing out in the crowd wasn't something she really wanted to do. There wasn't any hope of hiding it, either; her redingote and shawl were hanging on the coat tree in the foyer—right beside Mignon's trunk and within plain view of anyone standing on the front step and peering in through the sidelights.

Fashionably outstanding and shivering from the cold. This wasn't starting out well at all. Once she'd buttoned the front of the gown, it took less than ten seconds to pin up her hair, toss her hat and the last of her essential belongings into the valise, and head for the door.

He was just closing the wall safe when she entered the study. Glancing up, he swept her from hair to booted feet, and then snapped his valise closed, observing, "That was quick."

"It's a skill of war," she admitted, nodding toward the bookshelf that was clearly more. "A secret passage?"

"It's a priest's pocket. Most of the older homes have them."

She'd heard stories and knew that the passage was designed to allow a priest to hide within the home and to escape it if necessary. Bless the English and their devoted aversion to Catholicism. It was going to save Barrett this morning. She crossed the carpet and slipped through the opening and into cavelike damp and gloom.

"Don't move," Barrett instructed as he filled the narrow shaft of pale light and sidled into the space. "The stairs are right behind you. Let me get the lamp lit."

She stood perfectly still, feeling, hearing, the furious thumping of her heart, her body chilling beneath the heat of her racing blood. Barrett was a bold silhouette, his expression indistinguishable in the darkness, but his movements certain and deliberate. The distinct sound of sanded paper broke the silence and Isabella covered her nose and mouth with her free hand, knowing what was coming.

The scrape was fast, the flare instant, the smell as obnoxious and nauseating as always. In the light, she saw the oil lamp sitting on the wall shelf high and between them. Beyond Barrett's shoulder was the opening into the study. If the constables broke down the door and quickly made their way into the room . . . As he lifted the globe on the lamp, she eased past him, grabbed the iron ring in the back side of the bookcase and pulled it to, confining the stench of burning phosphorus and lamp oil to the tiny space in which they stood.

He looked at her and then the wall, nodded crisply, silently placed the lamp in the same hand in which he carried his valise, and offered her his other. Belle took it without hesitation, grateful for the warmth and strength of it, and let him lead her down the narrow stone stairs.

Their progress was careful and slowed even more by the necessity of having to stop every few feet to clear cobwebs from their path. As Barrett released her hand for the third time to sweep aside a sticky curtain, she glanced past him and into the stairwell ahead. The lamplight was meager and bounced palely back from the next whitish, wispy wall that lay ahead of them.

"Apparently it's been a while since you've used this way out," she observed as he wiped his hand clean on his trouser leg.

He grinned over his shoulder at her. "You're not afraid of spiders, are you?"

"Not overly," she admitted, putting her hand back in the warmth of his. "But if a grasshopper comes out of the shadows at me, you could go through the rest of your life deaf."

He chuckled, said, "I think grasshoppers may be the one problem we don't have," and led her on down the stairs.

Isabella went, letting him clear the way, thankful that she wasn't having to negotiate the passageway on her own, and realizing that the edges of her fears had blunted the instant Barrett had stepped into the passageway with her. It was most odd. Especially given that she had no idea where they were going—other than seemingly down to the center of the earth. That she was blindly following him, trusting him implicitly . . .

She shook her head, surprised by how quickly and completely she'd taken apparent leave of her senses. Logically, she should have let him flee on his own. The authorities didn't suspect her of any wrongdoing, and living as a fugitive would make finding the treasure all that more difficult. Evading Mignon's killer qualified as a pressing concern, but she did have some experience at disappearing into the shadows. And she was a very good shot.

No, all things considered, she didn't absolutely *need* Barrett Stanbridge. There was no denying, however, that her instincts were very clearly propelling her to follow in his wake. On his heels, actually, she amended as she brought herself up short to keep from stepping on them. She blinked and deliberately pushed her awareness beyond her thoughts and the broad expanse of Barrett's back. And blinked again, stunned to realize that she hadn't been aware of the distance they'd covered while her thoughts had been elsewhere. Chastising herself for inattentiveness, reminding herself of the danger in doing so, she watched as Barrett cleared the cobwebs from the doorway, ducked under the header, then took all of two steps to place his valise on the bare mattress and the lamp on the small side table. She went after him, noting that, like the space on the back side of the bookcase, the room was tiny and damp.

"Are you frozen yet?" Barrett asked as she dropped her belongings beside his on the bed.

"I'm a bit chilled, but I'll live," she supplied, thinking that England had to be the coldest, most miserably damp country on the face of the earth. March, and it was like the inside of an icebox. At home the tulips, jonquils, and daffodils were up and blooming, the wisteria and bougainvillea were wildly leafing, and the cherry trees were budding. God, when she got back there she was never again going to—

"I'm going back up to get our coats," Barrett said, interrupting her silent diatribe.

"Mine is right beside the front door," she explained,

shaking her head. "You can't retrieve it without the risk of being seen. Given that, I can certainly live without it."

"Not comfortably," he countered, extracting a wad of folded money from his pocket and tossing it down beside the lamp. "I intend to come right back down. But if I don't, take the lamp, go out the other door, and follow the pathway up and out. You'll emerge on the back side of the carriage house. Go several blocks in any direction before you hail a cab. Have him take you to the Blue Elephant store in Bloomsbury. Tell Aiden and Alex what's happened. Alex will take you in and Aiden will handle everything else." Without waiting for her assent, he turned to leave, adding, "I'll see you again by nightfall at the latest."

"It won't be necessary," she firmly rejoined. "I'll see you in a few minutes."

"Optimist," he laughingly charged as he disappeared into the blackness of the stairwell.

Alone, deep in the ground beneath the house, Isabella shuddered, turned up the wick on the lamp, and reminded herself that she'd been alone before, that she was perfectly capable of making her own way. There was absolutely no reason for the butterflies swirling around in her stomach. She didn't need Barrett. She didn't need him the least little bit.

It was hard to judge the passage of time without either a clock or natural light, but Isabella suspected that a man could be reasonably expected to retrieve two coats in the time it took for a woman to pace a tiny room twenty-five times. Staring up at the rafters, she strained to hear noises from above, not at all certain how long she should wait. She'd forgotten to ask and Barrett hadn't said. Next time, she'd be clearer on the expectations. If there was a next time, she morosely reminded herself.

What if the police had burst into the house, surprised them, and arrested him? Would she have heard the commotion? What if he'd tried to escape and they'd shot him? Would she have heard the gunshot? Barrett could be seriously injured or even—God forbid!—dead. Damn Mignon for having placed him in danger. Of all the men her cousin could have picked at the theater, she'd chosen what had to be the most decent one of the bunch, the one who least deserved to have hell visited upon him.

Deciding that pacing and worrying weren't accomplishing anything, Belle made her way to the door of the escape passage. It opened on creaking hinges and she flung it wide to make quick work of the task and the telltale noise. The light from the lamp beside the bed illuminated only the first foot or two, but it was enough for her to see that it was nothing more than a smallish, roughly chiseled tunnel. The air rolling over her was cool and damp, but delightfully fresh.

Even as she looked back over her shoulder, wondering how much longer she should wait, she heard the footsteps on the stairs. A single set, moving quickly and surely. Barrett, she knew, her knees trembling as the tension flooded out of her.

She met him at the base, saying as he ducked inside, "See? I told you it would be all right."

"But you didn't really believe it," he countered, smiling broadly. "You look like you could melt with relief."

"Only because I was dreading the thought of striking up conversations with strangers. I've never been very good at it," she offered quickly, trying to salvage what she could of her bravado as she followed him to the bedside table.

"You're not very good at lying, either," he observed, chuckling, separating the coats. His own he tossed onto the bed beside their bags. Hers he righted and held out so that she could slip her arms into the sleeves.

"How did you manage this without being seen?" she asked as he settled the light woolen garment over her shoulders.

Leaning around her to retrieve his valise, he supplied obliquely, "A little diversion."

"Involving?"

"An oil lamp," he supplied, setting his bag on the desk, "an open window, and the perfect pitch into a small, old woodpile in the side yard."

"Subtle, but effective."

"I'm so glad you approve," he teased, removing a small, portable writing set from his valise. He placed it on the table, flipped it open, and immediately uncapped the ink, saying, "Now that we don't have an immediate crisis, you can avoid throwing yourself on the mercy of strangers."

"Oh?"

"Eventually, Larson is going to pound on Aiden's and Carden's doors looking for me," he explained, scribbling. "And I won't put them and their families in the position of actively hiding us."

"There's my room at the boardinghouse. The rent's paid through the end of the week. We can go there," she offered, knowing even as she did that he'd turn it down.

"It's too public." He sanded the paper and then carefully poured it back into the pot as he continued, saying, "Carden bought an older town house a few weeks ago. His idea is to refurbish it for the day when his eldest niece marries and needs her own home. At the moment, it's unoccupied. As a rat hole for us, it will do perfectly. No one will think to look for us there. And no one will think it the least odd if Carden and Aiden are seen coming and going."

"And you're sending them a note to let them know that's where we're going?"

Barrett nodded and waited for the next question.

"What if the constables intercept it?"

What a wonderful mind inside that lovely body, he silently observed. "Even if they do, it won't mean anything to them," he assured her. Placing the paper on the table, he used the edge to tear off the lower third of it. Straightening, folding both the larger and smaller pieces into neat squares, he smiled at her. "I'll explain the rest of the plan once we're in the cab and on our way to the train station. Are you ready to go?"

"Yes," she replied crisply, hefting her valise as he slipped the papers into the inside pocket of his suit coat.

He pulled on his greatcoat, took up his own bag and the lamp, noting that she'd turned up the wick in his absence. It was an unexpected thing for her to do, he mused, moving toward the open door. She'd understandably started when he'd so suddenly awakened her, but she hadn't squealed when he'd told her of the threat on the front steps. And she hadn't dithered a single second when he'd laid down instructions. Not in her room, not when he'd left her alone in the room now behind them. And the way she'd moved to close the bookcase behind them to keep the odors from invading the study and giving them away . . .

The revolver under her pillow had puzzled him at first, but the soundness of her sleep had told him that it wasn't there out of fear. No, Isabella Dandaneau wasn't the sort of woman to be afraid of shadows or of being alone in them. And being armed had little to do with it. Exactly how she'd come by such stalwart traits intrigued him. As did the reasons they'd faltered in his absence.

Reaching the last, flat part of the tunnel, Barrett set aside his musings and blew out the lamp. Through the iron grate some three feet ahead and above them, a column of light, pale and gray, passed straight down and through the floor grate that let the rain and snow melt flow into the sewer. God help them, he silently growled, if one of the constables was wandering along the alley, wondering if the drainage line led to somewhere other than the Thames. After placing the lamp on the narrow ledge carved in the dirt wall, he half turned to his companion and pointed to the opening and then to his ear.

It was only as she nodded in understanding that he realized he'd instinctively fallen into the habits of his military years. His pulse racing, Barrett pointed to himself, the ladder leading up to the grate, opened his hand and splayed his fingers, then pointed to her and the grate. Again she nodded. And then bent down and snagged the handle of his valise.

He turned and strode to the base of the iron ladder, his heart hammering. God, the resolute look in her eyes, the set of her delicate jaw . . . He knew to the center of his bones that she'd done this sort of thing before—the skulking about in faint light, the need for silent, deliberate, coordinated movement. The realization surprised him. He'd suspected from the beginning that she'd been a spy during the war, but he'd assumed that she'd expended her efforts in parlors and on ballroom floors. Clearly, he'd presumed incorrectly. What, precisely, she'd done in the name of her country was one of the most intriguing puzzles he'd ever encountered. If the need to escape weren't so pressing . . .

Climbing up the ladder, he glanced down to note that she'd stayed well enough back to allow him to drop and scramble out of sight. Oh, yes, she knew what she was doing. Which was more than could be said for him, he silently grumbled. If he didn't stop marveling at her and put his attention where it needed to be, all of her skills would be for naught. Expelling a long, hard, steadying breath, Barrett willed her out of his immediate awareness and focused on the world beyond the grate above his head.

A faint whiff of wood smoke. And voices in the direction from which it was drifting. There was only silence in the alleyway before him and off in either direction. Again he listened to the sounds at the side of his house. Deciding that the constables weren't moving much beyond the confines of where he'd wanted them, he placed his shoulders flat against the grate and quickly shoved himself, and it, upward. The grating gave with a tiny cascade of dirt and gravel and rotting leaves, but no great betraying sound.

Lifting it off his shoulders, Barrett laid it aside even as he quickly surveyed the alley. It was empty and silent and still and the shadows were deepest on the west side of the town house directly across the service way. Placing his hands on either side of the opening, he pulled himself up and out, then turned to squat and peer back down. Isabella stood on the lower grating, his valise sitting on the palms of her hands. She arched her head to the side in silent question and he nodded in reply. A second later, his bag came sailing upward. He caught it neatly by the handle, set it beside him, then turned back to catch hers just as expeditiously.

He'd barely set it aside when she started up the ladder. With a tight but appreciative smile, he scrambled to his feet, noting with ungentlemanly openness that she'd hiked her hems to her waist and shoved her hoops to the back to keep them all from hampering her ascent. She was wearing boots. Tall ones. And damn, if they didn't mold around a pair of nice legs. Long and lean and apparently quite accustomed to scurrying up ladders. No hesitant, one-rung-at-a-time approach to things for his Belle. Not at all.

He knew what she'd do the moment her head poked out of the opening and she didn't disappoint him. In the time it took for him to lean down and offer her his hands, her gaze swept the alley and settled on the same shadows, the same path he'd chosen.

His smile widening, he clasped her wrists, waited until she'd done the same to his and then hauled her straight up and out. Dropping her on her feet beside him, he released

her as he jerked his head in the direction of the town
house. She nodded once, stooped to catch the handles of
both valises, cast one quick glance over her shoulder toward the house and then bolted at a dead run across the alley.

She was good. Very good, Barrett silently acknowledged
as he dropped the grating back into place and quickly
scuffed dirt and debris along the edges. Why the hell he
found it so intensely stimulating, he didn't know. And
didn't much care, he admitted, checking the back of the
house before sprinting after her. He wanted her and understanding the why of it wasn't going to change how he felt
one whit.

He found her just where he knew she'd be, in the deepest
of the deep shadows, standing motionless, blending with
them, a bag clutched in each hand and watching his approach.

"I have a few questions for you later," he warned in a
whisper, pausing just long enough to take the bags from her.
"When we have the luxury of time for leisurely conversation."

"Would you give me a hint?" she asked, falling in beside him as they made their way through the side yard toward the street. "I truly dislike being unprepared."

"I know. That's one of the things I'm curious about," he
admitted, glancing over at her and giving her a quick,
quirked smile. "Right now, though, we're going to stroll
out onto the walk and go along in a casual way, looking
like your typical couple leaving home for a brief holiday.
I'll hail the first cab we see."

"Sounds like a perfectly sensible plan," she allowed, her
smile appropriately serene, her gaze warily sweeping the
walk ahead of them.

Had she been just a spy during the war? he wondered.
Given the range of her abilities, she could have been a

courier, too. Curiosity was about to get the better of him when a hansom cab leisurely turned the corner and rolled toward them. Deliberately focusing on the more important tasks at hand, he hailed it, handed Belle inside, and instructed the driver to take them to Victoria Station.

Once inside, settled on the rear-facing seat, he resolutely kept his earlier word. Reaching into his jacket pocket, he removed the larger of the folded pieces of paper. "When we get to the station," he began, "we're going to go our separate ways to the same destination."

"That being your friend's town house."

He nodded. "Whoever killed Mignon didn't accidentally meet her in the alley behind my house. They were waiting for her to come out. And given that they didn't find the map on her or in searching our various rooms, you can wager the Crown Jewels that they're still actively trying to find it."

"Which means they're—in all likelihood—still watching the house," she added for him. "And us."

"And as a consequence, our only real choice is to divide and confuse them in the hope of losing them," he went on, handing her the paper. "You're going into the station and out the other side. Once you do, you're going to these markets, make some quick purchases at each one with the money I gave you in the priest's room, and then disappear into the crowd to catch another cab. After the third market you're going to instruct the driver to bring you to the alley entrance of the address at the bottom of the page. I'll be waiting there for you."

After a quick glance at her itinerary, she slipped the paper into her pocket and observed with a small, knowing smile, "You seem to think I can do all this with some degree of panache."

"As partners go," he drawled, "I couldn't ask for a more levelheaded and capable one."

"And while you may be curious as to why I'm the way I am," she countered, openly studying him, "for the moment you're willing to simply accept it as a reality to be used to our benefit."

Skilled in moving stealthily, unflappable, keenly intelligent. The odds, he decided as the cab drew to a halt in front of the station, were in favor of her having been a courier. "In case no one's ever told you so, Belle," he said, reaching for the door handle, "you have an excellent mind. With you in the pocket, I can't imagine how the South lost the war."

"We lost because we lacked heavy industry," she supplied as he helped her out, "and couldn't import enough to adequately supply the army. What we could get proved impossible to move because we lack the roads they have in the North. It was a doomed effort from the start. Unfortunately, Southern men have never been known for putting practical realities before honor and principle."

"A slight bit of shortsightedness," he observed, retrieving their bags from the floor of the rented hack.

"With largely ugly consequences." Her gaze sweeping the line of carriages rolling past them, she asked, "You'll be careful?"

He nodded. "Keep watch over your shoulder, don't take any chances, and I'll see you shortly."

"If anything goes wrong," she said, slowly backing away from him and toward the main door of the station, "I'll either go to the Blue Elephant or send word there. You'll do the same?"

She'd seen the possibility of disaster and thought to accommodate for it before he had. The generals would have been fools not to use her. Damn fools. "We're going to talk before the afternoon's out, Belle."

Her smile was soft and confident and somehow sweetly defiant. His blood singed through his veins as he struggled with the impulse to close the distance between them and plant a parting kiss on her deliciously taunting lips. It wasn't either strength of will or greatness of character that saved him from making a complete ass of himself. It was Belle turning on her heel and walking away without even so much as a hitch of hesitation or a backward glance.

Barrett stood on the walkway, the tide of travelers swirling around him, and watched her disappear into the crowd. The cool voice of reason told him there was no reason to worry about her. He could see that no one was following her. She was smarter by half than her cousin had been. Belle could take care of herself. She'd be quite all right off on her own for a short while.

Reason and certainty didn't make any difference, though. His chest was tight and his stomach was twisted into a cold coil of apprehension. If anything happened to her, he'd blame himself and regret the course for the rest of his life.

Ramming the fingers of his free hand through his hair, he exhaled a hard breath and forced his mind to consider the situation from a more practical angle. Turning, he stepped to the outside edge of the stream of pedestrians and then moved along with them, keeping himself decidedly visible and making it easy for Mignon's murderer to choose him as the immediate prey.

Chapter Eight

Wiggling her cold, wet toes inside her boots, Isabella watched the back sides of the town houses roll past and promised herself—yet again—that when she got back to Louisiana she was never again going to leave it. At least the rain there had the gumption to be rain. And it was warm, too. Not at all like this cold, heavy English mist that clung and eventually, insidiously, penetrated every nook and cranny of the world and everyone and everything in it.

The hack slowed and she hefted the new basket and its load of foodstuffs from the seat beside her. With it resting on her lap, she craned forward to look along the high stone wall separating the service road from the backyard of a particularly dilapidated-looking two-story house. The gate was wooden and sagging on its hinges, but it opened as the cab eased to a halt beside it.

Barrett, his dark hair plastered to his head and water running in tiny rivulets off the shoulders of his greatcoat, stepped through the opening to seize the hack's door handle, smile at her through the open window and say, "I was getting worried."

"What you're getting is drenched," she countered, accepting his hand out. Mud instantly squished up around the soles of her boots and the carriage rolled away, flinging clumps of sodden roadway in its wake.

Barrett quickly drew her out of the splatter and through the gate. Using his shoulder to shove it closed behind them, he asked, "Did you have any problems?"

"I never noticed anyone following me," she answered, smiling at the short path newly worn in the grass along the wall. "I was rather hoping that I would see someone and that I'd recognize them," she added, as he took the basket in one hand and her elbow in the other. "It would have answered all of our questions."

He shook his head and started toward the rear of the house, saying, "I'd rather not take the risks at this point in the game."

"We're going to have to take them sometime," she pointed out. "If we don't, we're not going to be able to name the real killer and clear you of suspicion."

"It's another of those bridges of ours. First things have to come first. Which, at this particular moment, is to get ourselves into some dry clothes. Carden should be here within the hour."

She stepped into the house and paused, surveying what had passed at one time for a serviceable kitchen. What few cabinet doors remained hung at odd angles from the frames. A water pump came up through a lower cabinet, unhampered by a countertop. The flooring had been tile once. Now it was largely gouged wood and chipped glue. Barrett placed the basket on a board that had been laid across another cabinet missing its top.

"The cellar would be my first choice as a hiding place, but it's too wet," Barrett said, drawing her forward and out into the main hall. "A problem Carden is most definitely going to have to address. There's only one room upstairs that has curtains left on the windows so it will have to do."

Isabella nodded, noting the dining room on her right as they passed, moving along the mahogany-paneled stairwell toward the base of the staircase. The front door—a thick, windowless, unadorned slab of mahogany—was straight ahead, the formal parlor to the immediate right of it, the sitting room to the left. Not surprisingly, the stairs creaked horridly beneath their feet as they made their way to the upper story. At least, Belle consoled herself as she winced, no one would sneak up on them in the night.

There were five rooms overlooking the stairwell. One straight off the small landing at the top, two on either side, fronted by a narrow strip of wood floor bounded by a painted, spindled balustrade. Belle considered the meager space, the thinness of the railing, the precipitous incline of the stairs, and made a mental note to not wander about in the dark. One wrong step and a person could find themselves— in a matter of mere seconds—slamming rather forcefully into the front door.

The room to which Barrett led her was on the front and right side of the house. Over the parlor, she noted, stepping into the darkened space. It was bare except for the faded green damask curtains hanging limply over each of the four windows. A hearth, framed by a simple mahogany mantel and surround, was centered on the outside wall. Ashes from a good many fires spilled out onto the simple flagstone hearth.

All in all, she decided, she'd slept in worse places. At least the ceiling seemed intact; there weren't any water spots and certainly no gaping holes. And all the windowpanes seemed to be there. The air was cool and damp but it wasn't moving through the curtains and across the room to stir the thick layer of dust that covered it from wooden floor to crown moldings. Mercifully, and more important than anything else, there wasn't the slightest evidence of rodent tracks.

"It can be made habitable," she offered, turning a slow circle. Her valise sat on the window seat that, were she brave enough to touch the dusty curtains, would overlook the street at the front of the house.

"With a lot of work and no small amount of money," Barrett added, moving to the door that connected the room with the one behind it. "You change in here and I'll do the same in this one."

She stood where she was, noting that while he'd stepped out of sight, he'd left the door open. The hem of her dress was sodden, weighed a ton, and really needed to be laundered. Her boots were equally wet. As were her stockings and the lower edge of her hoops. To be out of them, warm and dry, for just a little while would be heavenly. Discarding the discomfort even temporarily posed a significant problem, though. She had two choices in dry clothing, neither of which was a particularly good one. There was her nightgown and wrapper or there were her night clothes. The latter, aside from being shockingly form fitting, would look utterly ridiculous with either her dress shoes or her mules.

With a sigh, she resigned herself to the lesser of the two fashion offenses and began working open the buttons down the front of her dress. "Was anyone following you?" she called out, wandering toward the window seat where Barrett had placed her valise.

"Not that I noticed."

He was just inside the other room and to the left of the doorway, she noted, shrugging her arms out of her sleeves and letting the dress pool around her feet. "Maybe your house isn't being watched after all."

"It's more likely that they weren't positioned so they could see the back of the carriage house."

Logical. She undid the tie at the small of her back and let the hoops fall away. Dropping down on the seat, she used the toe of one booted foot to pry the muddy, wet leather from the other as she asked, "Do you think the constables will be watching it now?"

"Larson has to think that I'm smart enough not to go back there. I'm fairly sure that he wouldn't waste the time and manpower for a surveillance."

"But we do have to go back, Barrett," she protested, shifting about to use the base molding of the seat to remove the other boot. "We're still missing two pieces of Mignon's half of the map. One of them is absolutely essential."

"Yes, but Larson doesn't know any of that. And there's no *we* to it. I'll go back alone and search."

So he thought, she silently challenged, stripping off her stockings and tossing them onto the pile in front of her. Clad only in her chemise and pantaloons, she rose to her feet and pulled her nightgown, wrapper, mules, and a clean pair of stockings from the valise. "You're going to leave me here unprotected?" she taunted, dropping the nightgown over her head.

"Are you decent?"

"Not quite," she called out, letting the hem of the gown fall to her ankles on its own and snatching up the wrapper. "Give me just a minute more."

"No," he declared, stepping into the doorway with bare feet visible under the hems of his dark trousers, his shoes and socks in hand, his shirt collar open and his sleeves rolled back to his elbows.

"In the first place," he went on, advancing toward her as she swallowed down her flip-flopping heart and rammed her arms into the sleeves of the long, lightweight robe, "I wouldn't leave you here alone. I'd have Carden or Aiden stay with you. And in the second place, I strongly suspect that you're more capable of protecting yourself than any woman I've ever known."

"Ah," she said warily, yanking the waist sash into place and easing down on the seat so that the hem of her night-gown covered her bare feet. "We're to the I-have-some-questions conversation you warned me about."

"We are." He came around the pile of her wet clothing, dropped unceremoniously onto the window seat beside her, and began to put on his socks.

"Well?" she pressed, wondering what he'd do if she were to hike her hem, wiggle her bare toes, and start rolling a stocking up her leg. She had perfectly shaped feet, too. And it wasn't terribly fair that she was the only one struggling to maintain the illusion of decorum, the only one whose blood was warmed and who was battling tempta-tion's urge to touch.

Without looking at her, he pulled on a short boot and answered, "Why don't you spare me the necessity of ask-ing and just tell me about yourself?"

Because there's quite a bit I don't want you to ever know, she silently rejoined, watching him pull on his other boot. Knowing better than to be so provocatively honest, she summoned a smile and offered instead, "I have no idea what it is that has you curious."

He turned on the seat to face her, one foot on the floor, the other on the seat, and his arm resting casually atop his drawn-up knee. Temptation didn't whisper, it practically growled for her to slide over and curl into the space be-tween his thighs, to lean against his chest and let him wrap his arms around her. And his hair, so invitingly tousled from his having made an effort to dry it . . .

"You carry a knife and a derringer in the seams of your skirt," she heard him say through the thundering beat of her heart. "You sleep with a Colt repeater under your pil-low. When and why did you develop those most unfemi-nine little habits?"

His eyes were so dark, so intensely focused on her, that

she couldn't draw a full breath. Looking away, she moistened her lower lip and tried to stem the chattering chaos of her thoughts. "After Henri left for the war and because I was living alone and felt vulnerable," she answered, pleasantly surprised by how even and calm her voice sounded. "We've had this conversation already."

At the edge of her vision she saw him lean his head back against the window frame. He considered her for a long moment in silence, his gaze still intent, one corner of his mouth moving ever so slightly upward. "When we came up out of the tunnel," he said slowly, thoughtfully, "you looked around and instantly saw the darkest of the shadows. I didn't have to tell you where we were going. You knew. And you read my hand signals without so much as a second's hesitation. How does a sweet little widow from New Orleans develop those kinds of instincts and skills?"

He didn't give her time to answer before quietly adding, "And don't tell me it comes from having to evade men who thought you were Mignon. I'm not going to believe it, Belle. I know the look of a hunter when I see it."

Silently swearing, angry at having so blithely and inadvertently given herself away, she absently plucked up a stocking and drew it through her hand. God, what could she tell him that would be even remotely believable?

"You also recognized the need to have a secondary plan for our rendezvous and came up with a solid one on your own. While it might be logical to explain it as the sort of skill one develops in trying to keep track of a servant while out shopping, the look in your eyes said it was born of more than that."

"Was it the look of the hunter?" she asked, staring down at the stocking twisted around her hands, desperately hoping to find a way to salvage the illusion. Six years and no one had ever suspected. A single day with Barrett Stanbridge . . .

"It was the look of someone who was quite used to being the prey," he answered gently. "You didn't so much as bat an eyelash when I laid out the plan for you. I've seen soldiers who don't have the kind of field confidence you do."

What was the point of keeping the secret? her exhausted mind asked. What Barrett thought of her as a woman didn't matter. Who would he tell? Lord, of all the times for tears to crawl up her throat.

"How did you come by such skills, Belle?"

There was no evading it, no lying about it. He wasn't going to let her and she was too worn down to fight him. "The hard way," she answered, lifting her chin, resolved to make the best of it.

His smile was soft, growing by slow degrees. "That doesn't surprise me. Could I persuade you to elaborate?"

She suspected that he could persuade any woman to do just about anything when he smiled like that. Expelling a long, hard breath, she fixed her gaze on the far wall. "Remember," she began, "when I said that while you built and defended bridges, I was more comfortable with blowing them up?"

At the edge of her vision she saw him blink, saw his smile falter a tiny bit. "Yes."

She turned on the seat to face him squarely and took a fortifying breath. "I was speaking literally."

Barrett stared at her, his thoughts wildly tumbling over several courses at once. "You spent the war as a saboteur?"

"I was a very good one, actually."

One part of his mind reeled and struggled to imagine the woman sitting before him setting explosive charges. Without the hoops, without the wide shoulders of a gown, she was so small. The wet, golden ringlets framing her face, cascading over her flawless nape . . . Soft, dark eyes, so innocent, so warily defiant. Isabella, an angel of destruction?

Another part of his mind believed and calmly accepted it as the only truth that made sense. Yet another remembered the battles for the bridges he'd helped build. Imagining Belle in that bloody, screaming, bullet-raining hell . . . His heart slamming against the wall of his chest, his breath caught hard and low, he forced himself to swallow, to keep from reaching out and snatching her into his arms.

"It was really much easier than being a spy," she said softly, shrugging her shoulders and drawing him from his waking nightmare. "I tried that. Once. And . . ." With a fleeting wince and a nervous smile, she added, "While it didn't bother Mignon to seduce men for a larger purpose, it bothered me a great deal and so I looked about and found another way to help."

Her smile disappeared and then, a fraction of a heartbeat later, bloomed wide and full. "Not that they wanted it at first, you understand. Eventually, though, they decided that since I was determined, they'd be better off having me under some sort of control."

"You could have gotten yourself killed," he managed to choke out. "In a most grisly, lonely way."

She sobered and moistened her lower lip with the tip of her tongue. Her gaze drifted away and her voice came as a whisper. "It was a war, Barrett. Dying was a distinct possibility no matter what I did. Death was everywhere and came from every quarter. The market. A garden. On the road. At home. Sometimes it stalked, deliberately and slowly. They could see it coming, but couldn't get away. Other times it came swiftly and out of the blue. More usually, the dark. And the candle was snuffed in a single instant. I've buried so many people. Women and children. There are so many, many ways to die. All of them lonely. All of them grisly in one way or another."

Her chin came up and she took a deep breath as her gaze snapped back to his. "I decided," she said, her voice once again strong and vibrant, "that I'd rather die on my own terms than cowering in the corner of my house and letting someone else set them for me."

He was numb, body and soul. Awed by her strength, humbled by her resiliency.

"I was an only child," she went on, brightly filling the silence between them. "My father wanted a son and had to make do with what he'd been given. I grew up hunting and riding. I know the woods and the bayous better than most men." She chuckled and a chagrined shadow stole over her smile. "I wish I could say that I'm as comfortable in parlors and ballrooms, but I can't. Lord knows my mother tried to fashion me into a lady. But the plain simple truth is that I don't have the instincts for it."

"I haven't noticed any shortcomings," he managed to say, feeling suddenly, wildly flaring through every fiber of his being.

"I've been trying very hard to put my best feminine foot forward," she laughingly countered, looking down to unwrap the stocking she'd twisted around her hands. "And if I'd been playing the part well, you never would have even suspected there was more to me than that. I'm just ever so glad that none of the Yankees were as perceptive as you are."

So was he. "One more question, Belle," he began, wanting—needing—to know for sure. "Did you do it out of devotion to the great and glorious Southern cause or because you simply liked the danger?"

Arching a brow, she looked down at her feet, seeming to give the matter some thought. After a moment, she replied softly, "I knew the cause was doomed. From the very start. But there comes a point when you need a purpose so that living with death is endurable." She looked up at him and in an instant her face brightened with an unholy smile as the light in her eyes danced, wicked and wild. "And danger does have a way of making you feel very much alive."

"That it does," he admitted as compelling heat surged through his loins. "That it does."

He understood the appeal of it; Isabella knew it to the center of her bones. Just as she knew that if she reached for him, he'd meet her halfway. There was a desperate kind of restraint in his breathing, a hunger in his eyes. And more. A depth and a darkness that were both promise and threat and pulled at her in a way she wouldn't deny, couldn't resist. Making love with him would be no gentle, tender affair. It would be steel and fire and gloriously fierce. And dangerously intoxicating. No man had ever done what Barrett could so easily do to her. If she dared to let him. If she was brave enough to fling herself into the flames.

The tension in his body shifted abruptly and she blinked, startled by the sense of tumbling that came in the loss of his full attention. Desire still glimmered in his eyes, but it was overlaid with a resignation that tore at her heart.

"Carden's here."

She looked away, acutely aware of the edge and how close she'd come to blithely dancing over it. And, God forgive and save her, how very deeply she resented a man who had come only to help them.

"Aiden's with him."

She nodded, hearing nothing beyond the frantic thumping of her heartbeat. As Barrett shoved himself off the seat and turned to leave, she began rolling the stocking to the toe, saying far too breathlessly, "I'll be down in a few minutes. Once I've put my dress back on and done something about my hair. It wouldn't do to meet gentlemen looking this way."

He turned around and stepped back, slowly lifting his hand. Her heart skittered and her breath caught as he gently placed his fingertips beneath her chin and tilted her face up until she met his solemn gaze.

Trailing the pad of his thumb over her lower lip, he whispered, "You're perfect just the way you are, Belle."

She stared up at him, mesmerized and desperately wanting to believe him, desperately wanting more. As though he could read her mind, he bent down and, as her eyes drifted closed and her heart pounded, brushed his lips ever so gently over hers.

"Absolutely, stunningly perfect," he whispered as he slowly drew back. Then, with a long, hard exhale, he shook his head, turned and left her alone, her senses reeling.

Perfect? Barrett thought she was perfect? She smiled ruefully and quickly brushed away the welling tears. Men, she reminded herself as she placed her toes in the stocking, would say anything in the pursuit of women. And, every now and then, they managed to say just the right words, just the words a woman craved to hear. A virtuous woman kept her wits about her, realized the ploy for what it was, and didn't let it affect her good judgment. A less than virtuous woman recognized the ploy, admitted that she didn't care about the motives behind it, and marched boldly on into the seduction.

It had been ten years since someone had considered her worth the work of seducing. And she'd been ever so virtuous in the years before and since that one day. Well, except for the one time when she'd mistakenly thought she might have the wherewithal to follow in Mignon's spying footsteps. But since she hadn't had the courage to see it through, it probably didn't count against her.

Barrett Stanbridge would count, though. And there wouldn't be any flirting with the notion of bedding him, then changing her mind and clinging to virtue at the last minute. If she stepped into his arms it had to be with a clear understanding of just what she was doing. There would be no love in making love with Barrett. It would be solely for the physical satisfaction in it. And, honesty compelled her to admit, for the thrill of boldly meeting the challenge of a dangerous man. But there would be nothing more than that. There would be no commitments. No obligations. No expectations. No forever.

It would be, she realized, tying her garter, her idea of the perfect marriage. Blazing, breathtaking, and mercifully brief.

Chapter Nine

Barrett stood at the top of the stairs and took a settling breath. On the floor below, Carden and Aiden—judging by the sounds of their voices—had stepped into the parlor to wait for him. And wait they would; of that he was absolutely certain. Their rakehell days were well over, but they remembered the rules and would play by them.

Ahead of him, off to the right, clearly visible on the other side of the open doorway, Belle was rolling a stocking up a beautifully shaped, delightfully long leg. He deliberately looked away, allowing her privacy, trying to slow the frantic rhythm of his heartbeat.

A saboteur. Not for the love of country. Not for the glory. But because she liked the feeling of danger flooding through her veins. Because it made her feel alive as nothing else did. Because, in the moments when her heart thundered and her mind chattered, she couldn't hear the relentless whisper of death.

In the darkest days of his life he'd raced along the same fragile edges, courted the same fate and dared it to take him. For the very same reasons. He'd known at the time why he was doing it. Just as she had. In the years since . . . He'd always looked back on that time in a largely detached, shrugging sort of way. But looking at Belle and knowing . . .

With one hand on the newel post to steady himself and scrubbing the other over the stubbled lower half of his face, Barrett exhaled long and hard. She'd taken the same risks he had. It had been her choice and he fully understood the why of her decision. Logically, what she'd done shouldn't affect him in the least. But it did. Greatly. That it was all in the past didn't seem to make one iota of difference, either. The center of his chest was hot and tight, his limbs chilled and his skin prickling. Jesus. It was one thing for him to knowingly put his life in jeopardy. It was entirely another for Belle to do the same.

And, he silently growled, it was ridiculous in the extreme to stand at the top of the stairs and let himself be consumed by imaginary, absolutely pointless fear. The solution was as simple as it was obvious. If, in their time together, there came an instance when real danger threatened, he'd draw the line. Firmly. And make damn sure that Belle stayed on the safe side of it.

Resolved, he propelled himself forward and down the squealing flight of stairs. Given the obnoxious warning of his approach, it was no surprise to find his friends turned and waiting for his arrival in the parlor.

Ignoring their obvious curiosity for the moment, he strode forward, offering his hand to each in turn. "Card," he said, quickly gripping his friend's hand before releasing it to take the other's. "Aiden. Thank you for dropping your lives for me this morning."

Aiden half smiled and shrugged dismissively while Carden cocked a brow and said, "Your note arrived roughly five minutes ahead of your father."

Larson had moved fast. Cecil Stanbridge even faster.

And both of them ever so predictably. "You didn't tell him about it, did you?"

A conspiratorial smile slowly turned up the corners of Carden's mouth. "He said you were on your way to Paris. And I let him continue thinking so. He asked me to pass that information on to the constables if they came to make inquiries. I said I would."

"Thank you," Barrett offered, his mind clicking through the likely course. Larson would be led down the primrose path and call off his surveillance. Which was exactly what Barrett needed the man to do. So far, it was all going according to plan. Such as the plan was, he silently amended.

"Your father also thinks that you're traveling with a . . ."

Raising a brow, Barrett considered Carden and waited, knowing what was coming by the tone of his friend's voice and the devilish, expectant spark in Aiden's eyes.

"Client."

"I'm sure he didn't put it quite so diplomatically," Barrett countered acerbically, irritated not only by his parents' presumption to judge, but also by Carden's and Aiden's amusement and open curiosity. He tamped it down, reminding himself that, given his proclivities, his friends were making only reasonable assumptions. They didn't know Belle, didn't know that she was a world apart from the women who typically passed through his life. How to tell them that, though? Without sounding defensive. Or worse yet, like some blindly besotted fool.

The creak of the uppermost stair tread brought him a smile and no small sense of relief. He wasn't going to have to explain.

"Wait right here," he instructed, turning away. They'd see for themselves in just a moment or two. Belle would set them straight in an instant, would wipe the rakish, knowing smirks off their faces. Despite her protests otherwise, she was a lady. More a lady than Mignon—with her fine wardrobe and public airs—had ever been. How the hell his parents hadn't been able to see that . . .

Isabella stopped as Barrett filled the space three steps below her. The hard line to his jaw, the determined glint in his eyes . . . And then his tension was gone, seemingly erased in the instant it took for his gaze to sweep down the length of her.

"You changed your clothes," he said softly.

She waited until his gaze came up to meet hers. "I've lived with pretenses too long to comfortably abandon them in a single morning."

He nodded in acceptance and reached out, offering his hand. As she took it and let him assist her down the remaining stairs, he leaned close to whisper, "Thank you for not taming your curls. I like them."

It was silly to warm at such a simple compliment. And the butterflies swirling around her stomach were an absolute embarrassment. Hopefully, no one would know they were there, wreaking havoc. And, with any luck at all, they'd think that the blush fanning across her cheeks was the consequence of meeting strangers under what anyone had to recognize as strained circumstances.

She saw his friends the instant he turned her toward the parlor doorway. Both of them blinked before snapping to attention, looking between her and Barrett, and then passing a quick look between themselves. The obviously older of the two, the one who looked enough like Barrett to be his brother, tilted his head to the side and worked hard to rein in a smile as he watched them advance. The other man, the younger, sandy-haired one with brilliant green eyes, either didn't try to contain his smile or lost the battle almost instantly. She hadn't the slightest inkling as to what so plainly delighted Barrett's friends, but since there wasn't any tension in the hand wrapped around hers, she calmly let him lead her to the spot directly in front of them.

"Isabella," he began, ever so slowly releasing her hand. "May I present my friends, Carden Reeves, the seventh Earl of Lansdown, and Mr. John Aiden Terrell? Gentlemen, my client, Mrs. Isabella Dandaneau."

All of her mother's lessons in graciousness tumbled through her mind at once. Not a word of it clear enough to save her. Was it Lord Lansdown? Or Lord Reeves? Mr. Reeves? My lord? Oh, Lord. The butterflies in her stomach swelled to the size of turkey buzzards.

Barrett felt her hesitation and started in realization. He'd forgotten that she was American, that she wouldn't know the proper terms of address. He'd barely opened his mouth to save her, to redeem himself, when she plunged ahead on her own.

"It's a pleasure to meet you, your lordship," she said, extending her hand toward Carden.

Barrett silently sighed in relief even as Carden rolled his eyes, shook his head, and gallantly took her hand in his. Bending over it, he grinned and said smoothly, "The pleasure is entirely mine, Mrs. Dandaneau. And *please,* call me *Carden.*"

"Belle," she countered as he released his claim to her hand. Without the slightest pause, she offered it to Aiden, saying sweetly, "Mr. Terrell, it's a pleasure to meet you, as well."

"Truly charmed," he replied, his eyes twinkling as he bent. "And *Aiden* will do for me," he added, straightening and seeming, to Barrett's way of thinking, just a tad too slow in relinquishing her hand.

Barrett softly cleared his throat, but it was Carden who broke the silence with words.

"All right," his friend drawled, folding his arms across his chest, "now that we've dispensed with civility, would you care to tell us why we're skulking around and meeting in secret?"

Isabella watched as Barrett folded his arms in a similar fashion. As Aiden Terrell did the same. She was tempted, purely for the devilment of it, to make it a foursome. Resisting the urge, she instead slipped her hands into the side seam pockets of her dress.

"Michael Larson," Barrett explained blithely, "and his merry band of constables arrived on my doorstep this morning to arrest me for the murder."

Aiden rocked back on his heels as his brows shot upward. "And you bolted? Jesus, Barrett!"

"You could have made bond," Carden offered with considerably more calm but no less apparent concern. "We would have had you out of there by noon."

Barrett barely shrugged. "You're assuming they would have let me post one. I'll admit to having entertained the same notion yesterday. However, a conversation with my father changed my thinking on it." He gave them a quick, weak smile and added, "As much as I'm loath to admit it, I had to accept that he was probably right. Given the circumstances of the crime and the brutality of it, they very well could have denied the petition. I couldn't take that chance."

Both Aiden and Carden instantly looked at Belle and she nodded. "Yes, because of me," she admitted. "Mignon Richard was my cousin. To make a very long story as short as possible, we shared in an inheritance that requires us to find a buried pirate treasure. The hunt brought Mignon to London and I followed. Someone else obviously did, as well."

"And that someone," Barrett supplied, "is the person responsible for her death in the alleyway behind my house."

"After she'd hidden her half of the map in various places inside it," Isabella added. "We've recovered all but two of the pieces."

Barrett nodded and seamlessly picked up the explanation.

"We have several tasks to accomplish. The first is to find the rest of the map. We've searched the house from top to bottom and haven't had any luck. We're down to thinking that she must have hidden them somewhere on the property as she was leaving the next morning."

Aiden nodded, his gaze pinned on the floor at his feet. "Which means you have to go back to the house sooner or later."

"Preferably sooner," Barrett clarified.

"Our second task is to find the treasure itself," Isabella interjected, continuing the explanation. "There are no location references on the portions of the map we have and we doubt that there are any on the two missing pieces. But we've concluded that there's reason to believe that the treasure is somewhere in London."

"Which," Barrett drawled with a smile, "is where you come in, Carden. We need city maps for—roughly—the last forty years. Comparing the treasure map to them is a long shot, but it's the only one we've got."

"All right," he said, barely nodding, his jaw set. "I can get them easily enough."

"Our third task is to find Mignon's killer," Isabella went on. "Then turn him over to the authorities and clear Barrett's name. We've yet to work out a strategy for accomplishing that, though."

"And all of that has to be done," Barrett added crisply, "while keeping whoever killed Mignon from finding Belle and killing her for her half of the map."

Isabella resisted the urge to smile as both Carden and Aiden looked at her expectantly. "And keeping Barrett out of jail at the same time," she provided, not wanting to disappoint them.

"Christ Almighty," Carden said on a sigh, shaking his head and looking back at Barrett. "You two certainly know how to pick your challenges, don't you?"

"If you help us, you'll be guilty of aiding and abetting a fugitive," Barrett pointed out quietly. "If you don't want to be involved in that, I'll understand completely. You both have families to consider."

"Which we wouldn't have," Aiden observed firmly, "if you hadn't helped us when we needed it. We're in. And grateful for the chance to help."

Carden Reeves nodded. "Aside from getting you the city maps, what else can we do?"

"Do you want us to search the grounds for you?" Aiden asked, his eyes sparkling at the prospect. "Find the missing map pieces?"

Barrett slowly shook his head. "I appreciate the offer, but it would be better if you stayed away from the house. If it's being watched, they could follow you back to us."

"Or to your own homes," Isabella felt compelled to add. "The constables may not be the only ones watching Barrett's." Carden's brow shot up and he turned his full attention to her as she went on. "In killing Mignon, they proved themselves to be both dangerous and desperate. If they were to follow you home, hoping to force information out of you . . . It would place your families in danger. Very needlessly. We'll go back to the house and make the search ourselves."

Barrett's gaze snapped to hers so unrelentingly that her heart skipped a full beat. "We've yet to work out the particulars of the foray," he said quietly but firmly. His manner noticeably, instantly eased as he looked between his friends to add, "When we do, I'll let you know your respective parts. Mostly what we need from you two is logistical support. We're safe here, but only if we can manage to stay out of sight. Which obviously restricts us to moving under the cover of darkness. And markets aren't open at night."

"Speaking of which," Isabella ventured, unsettled by

the fleeting hardness in Barrett's manner and suddenly feeling a sudden, acute need to escape the intensity of the all-male company. "I picked up some things on my sweep through them this morning." Easing away from Barrett's side, she added with deliberate brightness, "If you don't need me for anything, I think I'll go fix us something to eat."

Barrett's smile was gentle and appreciative. Not even a shadow remained of the granite that had been there only seconds before. "I am a bit on the hungry side. And I'd kill for a cup of coffee."

Coffee would be divine, she had to admit. Nothing cleared the cobwebs from one's mind quite like a cup of steaming black magic. Unfortunately, they didn't have coffee beans. Or a grinder. Or so much as a pot to cook in. "I'll do the best I can," she promised over her shoulder as she left them.

Once out of sight, she knitted her brows and considered the ebb and flow of the exchange just past. Carden Reeves was much like Barrett in outward temperament; serious and businesslike, direct and practical. Aiden was a much more open person, clearly given to more genuine and immediate displays of his feelings. At least on the surface. Her father had always maintained that still waters weren't the only ones that ran deep and she suspected that Aiden Terrell was the sort of man he'd been talking about.

Barrett . . . Barrett was an intriguing bundle of contradictions. Cool and analytically detached on one level and yet, on another, in the very same heartbeat . . . He wasn't what she'd call volatile; she'd seen nothing to suggest that he might have even the slightest tendency for uncontrolled violence. And Lord knew that he wasn't excitable in the sense that people commonly used the expression. Still, there was a definite current of emotion surging just beneath the smooth veneer he presented to the world. And sometimes, for just a second or two, it broke through in defiance of his determination to keep it hidden away.

How openly stunned and worried he'd been when she'd confessed her wartime penchant for explosives. And good Lord, the intensity of his desire, the absolute certainty of his unspoken carnal promise. For as long as she lived . . .

Shaking her head, she deliberately shattered the enchantment, reminding herself that there was more to Barrett than hard-edged physical hunger. His emotions could be breathtakingly gentle, too; like those that had stolen over him when he'd looked up at her on the stairs. Or lushly tender as when he'd tilted her face up, kissed her, and declared her perfect just as she was. They could also be flinty and unbrookable, she added, remembering the look in his eyes and the tone of his voice when she'd mentioned the need to search the grounds of his house.

Something about the notion bothered him. Once Aiden and Carden left, she'd step up to the bridge and, if she had to, force her way across it. Whatever fears possessed him, she'd lay to rest. She'd blithely slipped around Billy Yanks and sweetly plowed her way past Johnny Rebs. Barrett Stanbridge, English gentleman, didn't stand a chance.

Barrett looked between his friends, not liking their Cheshire grins. "What?" he demanded.

Aiden had the good sense to sober, but his hastily murmured, "Nothing," wasn't the least bit convincing.

Carden, not so much as bothering to look even marginally chagrined, wandered over to drop down on the window seat and ask, "How did you find her?"

Jesus. There was no way around it; he was going to have to answer their questions and play his expected part. As bad as it was going to be, they'd put him through worse if he refused. "She found me, actually," he replied, trying to sound casual as he made his way over to the wall and propped his shoulder against it. "Yesterday morning. Just walked into my office and ever so blithely and thoroughly backed me into a corner. I didn't have any choice but to fall in with her."

Carden's smile widened. "I must say that you don't look too terribly pained by that part of the situation."

If they thought he was going to provide provocative details . . . Not that there were any of the sort Carden and Aiden expected. Barrett chose the middle course and a neutral tone. "I may be desperate, but I'm not blind or stupid. I can see the one positive aspect in it all."

Carden considered him for a few moments, and then, apparently having come to some measure of his good sense, let his smile fade away. "Where's she from?"

Aiden meandered toward the fireplace, saying, "I hear a slight whisper of the Caribbean in her voice."

"You're close," he allowed. "New Orleans. She's a war widow."

"She certainly seems intelligent," the younger man offered, leaning against the mantel. "And quick."

"She is," Barrett admitted, sensing that they were dancing around a more central issue, but not having the slightest notion of what it might be.

"She's different, too," Carden drawled, looking at the doorway through which Belle had disappeared minutes before. "I can't tell you what it is about her, precisely, but I can feel it."

That she'd spent years blowing up buildings and bridges for the sheer joy in it? That she had more grit than most of the men with whom they'd soldiered? Yes, Belle was decidedly different. But her past was hers and that she'd shared it with him didn't give him leave to pass it on to anyone who happened to inquire.

"It doesn't matter how old you live to be," he observed,

trying to walk the fine line between honesty and respect, "you'll never meet another woman quite like Isabella Dandaneau."

"You seem rather taken with her."

There it was; the central issue to which they'd been working along. The what-feelings-do-you-have-for-her-and-how-should-we-treat-her? question. Obliquely stated, of course. As always. He'd asked much the same question of both of them once. In much the same way. As it had turned out in the end, they'd lied to him. Not intentionally, but more out of having been—at that moment in time—as blind as bats and as stubborn as mules.

How to answer *them* was something of a dilemma, though. On the one hand, he could simply toss out the standard response and not worry about the accuracy of it all between now and the end. How it all ended was what mattered and he knew that there wasn't any sort of forever for him and Belle. She'd made it perfectly clear that she wasn't interested in marrying again and he'd all but legally resigned his choice in the matter to his parents. And while Mignon had found being a mistress quite acceptable, Isabella Dandaneau wouldn't even consider it. Ever. No, all they had was the time between now and when they found Lafitte's treasure. The end was a given and admitting it would be honest on the whole.

On the other hand, he'd be damned hard-pressed to pretend an indifference about her in the time they had together. She was, without doubt or dispute, the most interesting female who had ever crossed his path. And tempting, too. God Almighty, she was tempting. And never more so than when she abandoned any deliberate effort to be feminine. He sure as hell didn't understand why he felt such an acute attraction to her in those moments, but that didn't have anything to do with accepting it as reality.

But having to explain it all . . . Having to explain any of

it . . . Barrett shrugged and met Carden's gaze squarely. "I don't exactly have any other immediate prospects. Considering the present circumstances and all. As they say, a bird in the hand . . ."

Carden nodded, but his eyes and the edges of his smile said that he didn't believe a word of it.

From the other side of the room, Aiden laughed quietly and then quipped, "Well, if you don't mind my saying so, your choice of a love nest leaves a lot to be desired."

"As I recall from my inspection," Carden added, his grin widening, "there isn't even a bed."

As if a bed were all that mattered. Christ. "We'll make do," Barrett coolly assured them, hoping to close the subject. "We're fairly resourceful."

To his relief, Card's smile disappeared. "You're going to have to be to get yourselves out of this mess."

"Maybe you ought to turn yourself in," Aiden suggested earnestly from the other side of the room. "If your own friendships in the constabulary aren't enough to ensure they let you post bond, then your father's would be. Either way, you wouldn't be trying to unravel this snarl as a fugitive."

"I'll pay the bond," Carden offered quietly.

"And I'll stay with Belle until it's posted and you've been released."

Barrett looked between the two of them, knowing they were sincere in their concerns and their offered solutions. He also knew that sincerity didn't make it the right course. "Thank you, but no," he replied, shaking his head. "My instincts tell me that we're safer this way. My moving about freely would put Belle in danger. Sooner or later they'd get past me. I can't take that chance. Two women dead after being in my company would land me on the gallows for sure."

"Who is this mysterious 'they'?" Carden asked.

"It has to be someone from New Orleans," he supplied, pleased to be moving forward and on a topic not intimately related to Belle. "Someone Mignon knew and trusted. Someone who knows there's a treasure worth finding and that it's in London."

"And Belle can't think of anyone who meets all the requirements?" Aiden asked.

"She came up with four possibilities."

"Four? You're joking."

"One of them more likely than the other three," Barrett admitted. "In the end, though, she's making nothing more than educated guesses." He turned to meet Carden's gaze. "Card, you offered to do what needed to be done. And, at the moment, I need O'Brien put to work on finding our man. I want you to give him the list of possibilities and tell him I want them run to ground as quickly as possible."

"I'm ready to write," Aiden declared, pulling a little book and a pencil from the inside breast pocket of his coat.

"Neville Martinez," Barrett began, watching Aiden scribble. "He's supposedly confined to a wheeled chair. Emil Caribe. Apparently he's something of a sop." He paused, waiting until Aiden looked up and nodded. "Etan Choteau," he went on. "O'Brien's likely to find him with the shady ladies. His brother, Pierre, is a gambler. Any American named de Granvieux. And last, but not least, Henri Dandaneau."

"Who's Henri?" Carden asked as Aiden continued to make his notes.

"Belle's supposedly dead husband. Jacques de Granvieux is definitely dead. His sons are in the same column as Henri, though. I'm not eliminating them as suspects on the basis of an assumption grounded on a wartime report."

"Can't blame you," he replied with a decidedly rueful smile. "Will Quincy know how to find O'Brien?"

"If he doesn't, tell him he's fired."

Aiden tore the page out of his book and brought it across the room to hand it to Carden. And with that, Barrett mentally noted, they were largely done. All that remained was to remind them to bring food with them next time, walk them to the door, and close it behind them. Barrett stared down at the toes of his boots, wondering when he'd begun the slide into the mental attitude of a hermit. An ungrateful hermit at that.

"Breakfast, such as it is, is served."

As Carden vaulted to his feet and Aiden grinned, Barrett turned to find Belle standing in the doorway, a fairly wide, if broken, board in her hands. Atop it was a wrinkled piece of paper on which she'd placed slices of hard sausage, a couple of cheese wedges, and some crusty rolls. All of which surrounded a bottle of red wine.

"We don't have any coffee or a way to fix it even if we did," she explained with a smile as she moved past him and toward the window seat. "We don't have any wine glasses, either, but I decided to let you solve that particular problem."

He could carve them shallow bowls in under an hour. With a week and suitable chunks of wood, they could have proper goblets. Or, he decided, meeting Aiden's gaze, they could have glassware delivered later in the day.

"If our task is logistical support," Carden said, moving out of her way, "it's time to begin work on this place. Or at least make a show of doing so." Slipping the list into his pocket, he asked, "Can you two make yourselves invisible in here this afternoon?"

Barrett nodded crisply and his friend went on, saying, "Good. Aiden will get started on putting together the things you'll need to be marginally comfortable in this rat hole. I'll find O'Brien and then the maps you want. Aiden, how soon do you think you can have a rudimentary household crated and ready to deliver?"

He pulled his watch from its pocket on his vest and flipped open the cover. "Let's say three o'clock today. Alex is aces at this sort of thing."

"Then we'll be back here by late afternoon," Carden announced as Aiden put the timepiece away. "We'll have the carters dump everything in this room, so kindly be somewhere else in this beast. The fewer people who know you're here, the better. If any of the neighbors make inquiries about you, we'll tell them that you're the caretakers."

"Sounds fine to me," Barrett allowed, his mind racing through the opportunities the pretense afforded them. At the very front of the list stood a crackling fire—with hot food, coffee, light, and warmth following immediately behind.

"Then, considering all that has to be done," Aiden announced as he moved purposefully toward the door, "we'll see ourselves out and leave you two to your breakfast."

"And for God's sake," Carden admonished dryly as he trailed after him, "don't further complicate your situation while we're gone. It's sufficiently awful already."

Barrett watched them go, thinking that the circumstances didn't look all that horrible from his side of things. He and Belle were safe. They had a clearly delineated set of tasks and a rudimentary plan for accomplishing it all. They were dry and they had food and a bottle of wine. All in all, matters had much improved since daybreak.

"So," he began, stepping up beside Belle and snagging the bottle of wine from the makeshift tray, "how do you propose we spend the next five or six hours?"

She shrugged and pulled the knife from her pocket. Slicing off a chunk of the cheese, she answered brightly, "I found an old bucket in the kitchen closet and the well pump works. I'm not sure that I'd drink the water that comes out of it for a while, but it's perfectly fine for cleaning."

"Cleaning?" he repeated, the bottle stopped halfway to his lips. "Cleaning what?"

"The kitchen to start," she retorted, giving him a look that said she thought the answer should have been obvious. "And then the room with the curtains."

Well, it wasn't obvious to him. They were hiding, not setting up a real house together. "Why?" he asked before taking a healthy drink of the wine.

"Aside from the fact that they're very dusty, there's nothing else to do." She grinned and extended her hand. As he passed the bottle to her, she arched a brow and added, "Unless, of course, you have a suggestion of your own."

A bottle of wine . . . A gorgeous, adventurous woman with incredibly kissable lips . . . Five or six guaranteed uninterrupted hours . . . And no bed. He was resourceful, yes, but there were certain, very basic standards. Standards Belle deserved to have met . . . and exceeded.

"Have a swig of wine," he said on a sigh, "while I give it some thought."

Chapter Ten

Unfortunately, the only thought that occurred to him was that he'd never seen a woman sip wine from a bottle before. He wouldn't have thought that such a thing could be so damn provocative, but how she held the bottle, the bare angle at which she tipped it, the way the green glass rim barely kissed her lower lip . . .

"I don't think I've ever had wine for breakfast," she said, grinning and handing the bottle back to him. He saw the memory dart through her awareness just before her smile faded and she added, "Although I did have champagne the morning after the wedding. I suppose that counts, doesn't it?"

"Only if it wasn't left over from the night before," Barrett countered as she settled down on the window seat and reached for a hard roll. "Without the bubbles, it's nothing more than expensive grape juice."

She instantly brightened. "Then this is a first."

Henri hadn't thought to have a fresh bottle of spirits for the morning after? He hadn't thought enough of his bride to make the first morning of their life together a special one for her? She should have rolled out of the bed and left the boorish son of a bitch right then and there. Any man who thought hours-old champagne acceptable had to have been a thoughtless, inconsiderate lover. If he'd been the only man with whom Belle had ever lain, then—

"What?" she asked, her brow cocked.

Barrett sucked in his cheeks and listened to the shaky voice of good judgment. "An observation I don't have any business making."

"And that's going to stop you?"

"Yes. Yes, it is." *For the moment,* he silently added, assuaging the part of himself that was outraged by the way her husband had treated her.

"Coward," she accused with twinkling eyes, handing him a bit of cheese and sausage between two slivers of bread.

Lord, she had beautiful eyes. The kind that a man could happily search for an eternity and never become bored. And that smile of hers could melt an old monk's resolve. Mercifully, she turned her attention back to the food. Barrett took a huge gulp of the wine to distract his mind and, as the inexpensive alcohol singed a path down his throat, marshal his stumbling wits. "Haven't you ever heard the saying 'Discretion is the better part of valor'?"

"I seem to vaguely recall it. My mother's favorite credo was 'Idle hands are the devil's playthings.'"

That was generally true. And the devil always had a damned good time. He took another drink. "What was your father's favorite?"

"'Don't tell your mother,'" she replied, grinning at the sandwich she was making.

Barrett laughed outright, imagining Belle as a child looking up at her father, grinning impishly and nodding until her curls bounced.

"What were your parents' favorite admonishments when you were young?"

The amusing vision was gone, instantly replaced by a long string of shadowed memories. He unclenched his jaw and took another drink, reminding himself that he was the one who had broached the subject and was, therefore, obliged to provide an answer. "Mother's was—still is, actually—'Actions speak louder than words and are heard by all.' Father's has always been 'Wealth brings responsibility.' I wouldn't be at all surprised if they were his last earthly words."

"What kind of responsibility?" she asked warily, her little sandwich seemingly forgotten as she looked up at him. "Does he ever say?"

He snorted and drank again. With a blitheness that he most definitely didn't feel, he explained, "Oh, there are all sorts of them. To give to charity. Preferably at a large ceremony with important people and newspapermen in attendance. To invest wisely. Meaning profitably, of course. To studiously respect and maintain the lines of social class. To never spend a pound when a pence will do. To serve Queen and Country in a dignified but publicly noticeable way."

"Then they had to have been very proud of you when you enlisted in the army."

She was trying to find the silver lining; he could hear it in her voice. The nice thing about cheap wine, he mused, taking another drink, was that it hit fast and hard. And effectively. He smiled, appreciating the dulling edges. "I'd guess that they tried to make my service look as altruistic as they possibly could."

She made a little scoffing sound. "How could it be considered even remotely selfish, Barrett?"

"I enlisted," he replied, lifting the bottle in a toast to his stupidity, "because I was hoping to get myself killed."

One golden brow shot up. "That's not a very good reason."

"Yes," he agreed, knowing that his smile was a bit lopsided and not caring overly much, "but it would have been damned expedient if it had actually worked. It obviously didn't, though. Despite my best efforts. Then I met Carden and he rather roughly took me by the scruff of the neck and shook some sense into me."

He thought she said something about that being a good thing, but his awareness was flooding with the past. The thrill, the sweet hope. The horror. And the granite mountain of guilt and regret that had come down on his shoulders. Bless the wine; it made it all seem like someone else's misery.

"I fell in love and it turned out badly."

He started at the sound of his voice, stunned and appalled that he'd actually spoken the thought. He closed his eyes and silently swore, angry with himself for having inadvertently opened the door of what had always been his very private hell. How to close it again without being an absolute ass about it?

"I'm sorry," Belle said softly. "You must have loved her very much."

"In hindsight," he offered aloud, "I can see how I should have done things differently, but at the time . . ." He shrugged and took another drink. "You can't change the past," he reminded himself. "All you can do is learn to live with your mistakes and keep from making them again."

"That's very true," she allowed, nodding and smiling gently. "I learned to never again surrender my good judgment. No matter how handsome he is, no matter how big the gun is, no matter how horrific the scandal."

God love her; she'd offered him an out, a change in the direction of the conversation. And for some unfathomable reason—the wine, he suspected—he wasn't willing to take the generous gift. Instead, he sucked in a deep breath and countered, "I learned that men of God are just men. And that falling in love with a woman can be her death sentence."

"Barrett, talking about this is obviously distressing for you. Perhaps—"

"I know my mother," he interjected, shaking his head. He stopped abruptly and waited for the world to quit moving before adding, "She couldn't keep from mentioning the greatest of my scandals. As a ploy for discouraging females with what she sees as social-climbing aspirations, it works every time."

He winced as the shadings of his words penetrated his alcohol-hazed brain. But if Belle saw the backhanded insult in them, she didn't take obvious offense. Her voice was soft, her gaze tender as she looked up at him and said, "She didn't mention the details, Barrett. And there's no need for me to know them."

Yes, but as inexplicable as it was, he felt a need to share them with her. And, most oddly, that was the full extent of his feelings on it all. "Her name was Suzanna," he provided, "and she was the bishop's unhappy wife. He blew her brains out right in front of me on a dance floor. Then turned the gun on himself."

"Oh, God."

"I didn't see it coming, Belle," he went on. "Not until a second too late. The letter he left behind was brutal. Honest, but brutal. And it was made public at the inquest."

She looked down at the sandwich in her hand and then deliberately set it aside as she summarized, "You were devastated at the loss and your parents were mortified by your involvement."

"Mortified" was a good choice of words; at least it was the one that came closest to describing the aftermath from his parents' side of the debacle.

"How long ago did all this happen?"

"Six—almost seven—years." A time that, at the moment, felt like an eternity. "One good thing came of it, though," he offered, relieved to have the telling done.

"What was that?"

He smiled and offered her the nearly empty bottle. "It was at that point that I largely stopped living my life trying to please them. Life's been considerably simpler since."

As she took a smallish sip, he added, "And life stayed simple until I had that damned weak moment and agreed to get on with finding a wife so they could have blasted grandchildren. I should have just gone to an orphanage, bought a handful, and had them delivered with bows."

She grinned, set the bottle on the seat beside her, and retrieved her sandwich. "It's not too late to do that, you know. How many do your parents want?"

Remembering the sandwich he held in his own hand, Barrett took a bite while he tried to decide. "A good dozen or two would probably suffice."

"That would be terribly expensive, I should think. Do you suppose they'd be satisfied with eight or so? That many would be much more affordable."

"I make a very good living as an investigator and they know it," he countered ruefully as she ate. "I don't want to be accused of scrimping. I'm guilty of enough sins already."

She washed down the bite with another sip of the wine and then handed the bottle to him, saying, "I've always thought that sins, like beauty, are in the eye of the beholder. You certainly don't seem overly sinful to me, Barrett Stanbridge."

He stood there with a half-eaten sandwich in one hand, a mostly empty bottle of wine in the other, and the most delicious bit of sweet temptation sitting in front of him. Sparkling eyes, a luscious smile, darling ringlets framing a flawless face . . . She didn't have the slightest notion of what sin was. Oh, the delights he could show her . . . He exhaled long and hard and wondrously asked, "Just how did you come out of a war with your naïveté intact?"

She laughed and took the bottle back from him. "I'm not naïve," she alleged just before taking another sip.

"Belle, darling," he drawled, "in some ways you're as innocent as the proverbial lamb."

"It's an illusion," she countered, beaming. "A part of my concerted efforts to make everyone think I'm something of a lady."

He understood illusions. And their frailty. "I'm going to move while I still can," he announced, turning away and heading for the door.

"Did you ever think of something we could do to pass the time?" she called after him.

"No," he lied, telling himself he was a better man for it. "I'll see if I can find some cleaning rags in the cellar."

Oh, for the want of a bed and the absence of a conscience . . .

Rain pelting the windowpanes at her back, Isabella leaned into the corner of the window seat and surveyed the room. The curtains had been shaken out, the ashes removed from the hearth, and the layer of dust had been hauled away in one manner or another. The space certainly wasn't pristine, but with the makeshift broom, the equally cobbled together mop, and a good five hours of concerted work, they'd at least made it habitable. All it needed to be cozy, she mused, was furniture. Most notably a tall bedstead with a thick down mattress that would let her drown in sleep. God, she silently groaned, stifling a yawn, she was so tired.

And there was so much yet to do, she reminded herself in the same breath. Judging by how long the crashing and banging and swearing had been going on downstairs, the carters were hauling in an outrageous number of crates. To her mind, "rudimentary" would have been a couple of blankets, two place settings, a couple of pots, a few coffee beans, and a simple little coffee grinder. What Aiden and his wife considered to be basic household goods seemed— by the sounds of it—to be considerably more than that. And it all had to be unpacked and put somewhere.

But Barrett could be counted on to help with the task, she reminded herself, sliding her gaze to the other end of the window seat. He leaned back into his corner, his arms crossed over his chest, his long legs stretched out, his head tipped back and his eyes closed. How much younger he looked when sleeping. The beginnings of a dark beard shadowed his jaw and the tiniest of smiles curved his lips upward. His hair was still deliciously tousled and the thick fringe of lashes lying on the chiseled planes of his cheek-bones . . .

The center of her chest tightened and deep within her a warmth pulsed and spread. There was no denying the truth of what it was and she didn't try. There would come a time when he purposefully reached for her. When he did, she would willingly, happily step into his arms. Just as count-less numbers of other women before her had. And just like them, she'd be released and expected to go her own way. How many of them, she wondered, had ached at the thought of having to do that?

She tore her gaze away, fastening it on the cold hearth. It was beyond foolish to dream, however softly, of any sort of forever with Barrett. He'd marry, not out of love or for his own happiness, but appropriately and only to meet his parents' expectations. He had no hope for more than that, no willingness to risk his heart again. She understood how he'd come to that point, but the certain emptiness of his life . . .

Quietly clearing her throat and blinking back the tears, Isabella lifted her chin and deliberately listened to the sounds below. Were those feminine voices? She leaned slightly forward, tilting her head to better gather the higher pitched sounds. Yes, she decided, sitting back abruptly. She looked down at her gown and silently groaned. It was as filthy as the room had once been, the hem was stained from her forays through soggy markets that morning, and the damn wrinkle was still there. God. And her hair! Instinctively, she reached up in the hope that by some miracle she'd find the unruly curls—for once in her life—tamed.

But even as she considered making quick repairs, the stairs squeaked. Barrett bolted upright in the same second, his hand instantly going to the small of his back.

"I think it's Alex and Sera," she offered in quick assurance, gently grasping his arm to stay his motion. "I heard female voices a minute ago."

He blinked, held his breath, and went motionless as he listened to their guests' progress up the stairs. "Damn," he muttered, sagging and bringing his hand forward. "I could do without having to be charming."

She laughed and patted his arm, saying, "Maybe, if you're not, they won't stay long."

"There's that optimism again," he countered, smiling and shaking his head as he pushed himself to his feet.

He'd barely gained them when two large dogs bounded into the room, followed by two equally exuberant young ladies. The older one was dark haired and tanned. The younger looked very much like a blond china doll.

"Uncle Barrett!" they exclaimed as they and the dogs galloped en masse toward him.

Belle remained where she was, watching and enjoying the bubbling enthusiasm.

"Well, hello," Barrett said, gently shoving the dogs aside with his knee so that he could hug each of the girls in turn. When they'd both stepped back and he'd given each of the dogs a quick ear rubbing, he straightened and began the formalities. "I'd like you to meet my friend Mrs. Dandaneau. Belle, these delightful young ladies are Carden's nieces, Miss Beatrice," he said, indicating the older one, "and Miss Camille."

The girls nodded and smiled at her and she nodded and smiled at them, noting the mischievous sparkle in their eyes, their barely contained excitement. Wondering what they were about, she scratched the necks of both dogs and said, "It's a pleasure to meet you. And who are your friends here?"

"Lucy and Belize," the younger one happily supplied. "We brought them along today because baby Elise keeps pulling their whiskers out and Aunt Sera says that they deserve to escape the torture for a while."

"Poor things," Barrett said, rubbing their ears again as he looked past them to the doorway. "Where's Amanda? Downstairs yet?"

"She's at home," Camille answered, her grin going from ear to ear. "She's under house arrest."

Barrett tilted his head to the side and cocked a brow. "What?"

"She's calling it unjust imprisonment," Beatrice added, her approach seeming far more controlled but no less designing. "And behaving very badly about it all."

And just as Belle knew the sisters hoped, Barrett asked, "What did she do?"

It was Beatrice who answered. "She had her nipples pierced."

"Oh," he half breathed, half gurgled, his eyes wide and his stance suddenly faltering. "Oh."

Isabella held her breath and resisted the urge to intervene, to declare the conversation unseemly. Theirs was a relationship that had existed long before her arrival in Barrett's life; it wasn't her place to attempt to shape it in any way. That Barrett was being deliberately shocked to his toes was somewhat bothersome—until she realized that his discomfort stemmed from nothing more than the thought of a female assuming the prerogatives normally reserved for rakes.

"She did it without permission," Camille contributed before Barrett could regain his sense of equanimity.

Beatrice took her turn, adding, "Which no one would have given her and why she did it on the sly. And no one would have known she had it done if one of them hadn't festered."

The color drained from his face and he made a strangling sound. Afraid that he might actually faint, Belle took him by the hand and gently but firmly drew him back and down. He landed on the seat beside her, managing to groan, "This is truly far more information than I require."

"It's the fashion rage, you know, Uncle Barrett," Beatrice went on. "All the girls are doing it."

He gulped and then gasped a ragged breath, looking at them in stunned horror.

Camille didn't give him any further chance to gather his wits. "She has pretty rings for them."

Beatrice grinned and added, "I saw them in her jewelry chest. They're ruby dangles. Three golden chains with a stone on each end."

"Oh." He closed his eyes and then quickly opened them again, shaking his head. "Jesus."

"Uncle Carden's furious," Camille mercilessly supplied. "He said she wasn't coming out of her room until hell froze over. Aunt Sera's not having much luck in getting him to be understanding about it all."

Scrubbing his hand roughly over the stubble of his beard, he seemed to rally a bit. "Well . . ." he said strongly enough. And then ran out of steam.

"Would you be angry if one of your nieces did that, Uncle Barrett?" Camille asked, the perfect picture of innocent curiosity. "Would you consider it something really horrible and worth being locked away for?"

The inquiry was apparently sufficiently pointed to nudge his sensibilities back into place. His brows came together and there was actually a slight edge of outrage in his voice when he declared, "One of my nieces has done it."

Beatrice immediately fired another salvo. "Do you think piercing one's nipples is such a horrible thing?"

"I . . . uh . . ." He paused to swallow and take a breath before weakly continuing, "I have to wonder what the point of it is. I mean . . . Who's going to see them other than Amanda?"

"The doctor who came to the house to treat the infection," Camille offered brightly.

"And her beaus," Beatrice tossed out blithely, innocently.

Barrett started, blinked, and then fairly growled, "Only if Amanda doesn't mind them being drawn and quartered for the privilege."

With her hands on her hips, Camille looked at him with eyes widened in obviously feigned surprise and disappointment. "You don't approve any more than Uncle Carden does, do you?"

"I completely understand why he's locked her in her room."

Isabella looked between the two girls, knowing that they weren't done with him quite yet. He'd gotten his equilibrium back to a certain degree and that wasn't part of their plan. Which of them would take the point next? she wondered. So far, Camille seemed to be the one who made the first, slightly stunning jab and Beatrice the one who followed to quickly deliver the roundhouse on their dazed victim.

True to form and expectation, it was Camille who said,

"Amanda says that that sort of thinking is old fogy."

"Really," Barrett replied dryly, his calm seeming to deepen with every heartbeat.

The girls shifted slightly on their feet. Beatrice softly cleared her throat and Camille obeyed the command.

"She says she's going to find herself a modern-thinking man."

A dark brow shot up. "And she believes that a modern-thinking man would approve of such . . . such . . . ?"

"Adornment, Uncle Barrett," Beatrice supplied with a well-practiced sigh of strained patience. "The word's 'adornment.' "

"Hardly," he snorted.

"Uh-huh," Camille shot back, nodding so emphatically that a strand of blond hair slipped loose from her ribbon headband. She shoved it away from her eyes. "I've seen the rings, too, Uncle Barrett. They're beautiful."

He was about to offer another retort when Beatrice sweetly announced, "I've ordered myself a set just like them. Well, except not in rubies. I prefer emeralds. But most definitely the dangle style."

They'd succeeded yet again; his jaw went slack and the color faded from his face. For a second he stared at Beatrice, stammered and sputtered, and then he turned to Isabella. "Help me," he choked out. "Please."

The hopeful desperation on his face . . . The wary hopefulness on the girls' . . . Part of her enjoyed seeing the rake being set back so neatly on his heels. Another part winced at the deliberate manipulation. Torn, Belle quickly weighed her choices. The easy way out would be to claim the entire conversation unseemly and beneath her participation. But it was way too late for that ploy; propriety had been blown to bits from almost the start. Lord, was there a middle ground?

"I never would have guessed, Barrett," she ventured

carefully, "that you're so traditional in your thinking."

Beatrice and Camille recognized the ploy for what it was and maintained their wary assessment. Barrett, however, rocked back with widened eyes. "Would you consider . . . such . . . such . . . ?"

"Adornment," Beatrice supplied with exaggerated weariness.

"Belle, you can't seriously . . ."

Definitely not, she had to admit. But the ability to rattle a rogue to his core was a delightful temptation. "Beautiful rings are beautiful rings," she admitted, shrugging her shoulders, knowing that she was going to have to eventually set matters straight and then spend the rest of the day making it up to him. "Personally, I've always had a weakness for sapphires."

The girls grinned and Barrett . . . He blinked, struggled to swallow, and sounded as though he were using his last breath to say, "I'm going downstairs."

All three of them watched as he managed a swift but fairly decorous retreat. When he disappeared down the stairs, Isabella looked back at the girls and grinned. "Did your sister really have her nipples pierced?"

Beatrice arched a brow and nodded. "And Uncle Carden threatened us with imprisonment if we told anyone about it. But watching Uncle Barrett squirm was worth the price we're going to pay."

"Thank you for playing along," Camille offered, her smile wide. "You're very good."

That assessment depended, she knew, on which side of the game a person was standing. When Barrett stopped long enough to think about what had happened, he wasn't going to be pleased with her having fallen in with Carden's nieces. "You two are a very bad influence."

"If you think we're bad," Beatrice remarked, "wait until

you see what Aunt Alex sent over. Aunt Sera sent us to the Blue Elephant to help her pack it."

Apparently Miss Beatrice and Miss Camille had learned their lessons at the knees of experts. "Do I get any hints?" Isabella asked, finding some comfort in the fact that Barrett had undoubtedly been through this sort of ordeal before.

Camille shook her head and again shoved aside her tumbling hair. "It would ruin the fun of watching Uncle Barrett unpack."

"Which we should see to," Beatrice said, casting a look at the stairs, "before he has a chance to let Uncle Carden in on what we've done."

So much for being willing to gladly accept the consequences of their game, Belle thought. She deliberately took her time to gain her feet and then took several long moments to make an utterly futile effort to smooth her skirts and tuck her hair back under its pins. When she'd given Barrett all the time she reasonably could, she smiled and said, "Then we should be about it, don't you think?"

Carden was standing amid a maze of wooden crates in the parlor when Barrett reached the bottom of the stairs. "You have my deepest, most abiding sympathies," he offered, striding into the room.

He looked puzzled and asked, "Why would . . . ?" And then the puzzlement was gone, replaced in rapid succession by realization, horror, and outrage. "They told you!" Glaring past Barrett's shoulder at the stairs, he growled, "They'll be thirty before they set foot out of the house again."

Barrett leaned his forearms on the top of a crate and shook his head in bewilderment. "What was Amanda thinking?"

"I haven't the foggiest notion," the other railed. "You'd think that with all the females in my household, I'd have some idea of how their minds work. But every time I think I've got some inkling of the process, one of them goes off into the realm of outrageousness and leaves me standing there gaping and gasping and flopping around like a fish on the bank."

He paused just long enough to suck in a hard breath and then went on, "Take my hard-earned advice, Bare . . . Do *not* get married. Don't do this to yourself. Run. Run far and run fast."

The high-pitched creaking of the stairs made any sort of response unnecessary. At the first sound, Carden started forward, quickly threading his way through the crates.

"You!" he called from the doorway as their hems came into sight and the dogs bounded past and toward the rear of the house. "Both of you! Out to the carriage!"

"But we have to help unpack," Camille asserted as she danced down the remaining stairs.

Bea came on her heels, jauntily adding, "It wouldn't be fair to bring all this and then let Uncle Barrett and Mrs. Dandaneau deal with it all by themselves."

Belle joined them at the foot of the stairs, a knowing smile flirting at the corners of her mouth.

Carden didn't so much as glance her way. Instead, he looked between his nieces, pointed toward the rear of the house and practically bellowed, "You should have thought of that before you sang like birds. Out!"

They went, Bea saying as they passed, "Uncle Carden, you're positively stodgy."

"I'm positively furious!" he clarified to their backs. Watching them, he lowered his voice to add, "The maps you wanted are in the tube on the window seat."

"O'Brien?"

"He's on the task and said to tell you that he'll come by

here as soon as he has a report. He's guessing that it will take maybe a day. Two at the most. He has everyone working on it."

"Thank you. And Aiden? Will he be here shortly?"

"I wouldn't look for him," Carden admitted, finally bringing his gaze back to the room. "The girls said that he was called down to the docks this afternoon. Some problem with the repairs being done on the *Rana* that he had to address." He glanced at the crates and said, "I hate to leave you with all of this, but . . ."

"Understood," Barrett assured him. "Good luck."

"Remember what I said," Carden instructed as he left. "Don't do it! Save yourself!"

"What aren't you supposed to do?" Belle asked quietly as the back door slammed.

"Get married," he replied, smiling and turning to lean back against the crate. "Although I don't think marriage is as much his frustration as having children is. He inherited his nieces with the title. And then he and Sera have three little ones of their own. Six girls in total. Some days he's a tad overwhelmed by it all."

She came to stand beside him. Looking at the crates, she softly asked, "How old is Amanda?"

"Seventeen." The same age, he realized, that Belle had been when she'd been marched to the altar.

"Ah," she said, nodding slowly. "A particularly dangerous point in life. Old enough to get yourself into serious trouble and too young to know how to get yourself out of it."

And, he knew, some women never got any better at making decisions. Women like Mignon Richard. Others, though . . . Women like Belle learned the hard lessons quickly and never made the mistake again. "So, tell me," he drawled. "What do you really think of Amanda having herself pierced?"

"I know that her behavior's appalling by the standards of genteel society, but young women have always been prone to pushing the limits of tolerance. It's how we learn what's truly important and what's not."

"That's not the kind of answer I was looking for."

"No," she countered, smiling up at him, her eyes sparkling. "What you want to know is whether I'd really consider doing it myself."

"Well?"

Mischief danced in the depths of her eyes. "I think that some things should remain mysteries."

She wouldn't, he assured himself as she wandered off into the maze. Belle didn't strike him as the sort of woman who fantasized about leading a secret life as a light-skirt. And piercing was the kind of tawdry thing those sorts of women did. But . . . He folded his arms across his chest and stared down at his feet. There was something about her . . . The way she enjoyed risk . . . God, he just didn't know for sure what she'd do. And for some reason not knowing made his blood run faster and decidedly warmer.

Expelling a long, hard breath, he shook his head and reminded himself that whether she would or wouldn't didn't matter. There was work to be done. And when all the falderal was put away, there were the maps to consider and a mystery to be solved—a mystery, he sternly reminded himself, that actually mattered.

Chapter Eleven

※

What Alex had sent, Barrett decided as he stood in the doorway and surveyed the newly furnished surroundings, was basically a harem room in a box. Although "boxes" was the more accurate term. Twelve to be exact. Each of them labeled with grease pencil as to their ultimate destination. There hadn't been any need for Aiden's wife to indicate her intent. That had been obvious the moment he'd pried open one of the crates marked "domestics" and seen the huge copper bathing tub.

The tub over which Belle had exclaimed in delight and immediately hauled off to the kitchen. The tub in which she was currently soaking. Barrett glanced back over his shoulder and down the stairwell, listening to the soft notes of her song. Smiling, he leaned his shoulder against the doorjamb and went back to studying the room he'd put together while Belle had toiled at composing a functional kitchen and preparing a meal for them.

A fire was blazing in the hearth and a stack of splintered crating sat waiting to keep it going through the night. Alex had sent six three-stem silver candelabra and a sufficient number of sandalwood tapers to burn into the next century. He'd lit eighteen of them. The scent was heady and heavenly and the softly flickering light glowed over the silk bedding. Belle's pallet was white, heavily embroidered with trailing green vines and bright pink flowers of some sort. His was a deep maroon, starkly plain and masculine.

He'd placed the beds on either side of the hearth and then built them a nest in front of it. Bless Alex and her sense of the necessary, he mused, grinning. A huge, thick rug, at least three dozen brightly colored, fringed and tasseled pillows, a low and beautifully carved little table . . . At the moment it held two place settings of fine china and a pair of crystal goblets. The copper-clad brazier was on the hearth, the silver coffee urn on a little carved barrel off to the side.

He hoped Belle liked the arrangement. Actually, he amended, he hoped that she heard the same seductive whisper he did when looking at it all. He'd be willing to surrender gentlemanly restraint if she asked him to. Hell, he admitted, shaking his head, he'd hand it up if she even looked like she might be about to hint at it. There was something incredibly erotic about a woman who delighted in even the smallest things, who laughed over copper tubs and reveled at the prospect of peeling carrots and potatoes.

He'd spent the better part of the evening marveling at that discovery, alternating between deliberately triggering her joy and resisting the urge to slip his arms around her and see if her delight extended to him. In short, Barrett realized, chuckling darkly and shoving himself squarely onto his feet, he'd spent the last several hours torturing himself.

The rest of the evening would go as it would go, he warned himself as he made his way down the stairs. The rain that had been mist that morning and a light patter against the panes that afternoon was now a full-blown storm. As messages from Mother Nature went, it was plain: Tonight wasn't meant to be spent in searching his yard for missing map pieces. And as heartfelt suggestions from mere mortals went . . . The next time he saw Alexandra Terrell she was going to get a hug and a grateful kiss.

Yes, he decided, making his way into the parlor and toward the window seat, if he simply exercised some patience and didn't overtly press . . . If he unrolled the maps on the little table and invited Belle to sidle up beside him to study them . . . They didn't have anywhere to be before tomorrow night. There weren't any pressing domestic chores to attend to between now and then, either. They could well afford to spend all of the night twisting silk sheets and the next day in blissful, sated slumber.

He was halfway back to the doorway when Belle stepped into it. He grinned, taking in the heavily laced wrapper cinched around her waist as he made his way to stand in front of her. And her hair . . . Obviously she'd gathered it up and haphazardly pinned it atop her head just to get it out of her way. Curling strands framed her face and trailed down her back. Never in his life had he seen a style that so begged to be touched, that so bordered between circumspect and wildly wanton. God, she should wear it like that all the time. It was so quintessentially Belle.

"Your timing is impeccable," she said, smiling up at him in the darkened hall.

"I've been told that on a number of occasions."

She laughed softly and moved past him toward the stairs. "I put fresh water in the tub and the basket of clothing Alex sent for you is behind the dressing screen."

He offered his thanks as she started up the stairs. Bending down, she smiled at him through the space between the handrail and the stairwall. "Supper's ready whenever you're done with your bathing. I'll be down in the next few minutes to bring it up. I promise not to peek at you."

He bit off the quip, but there wasn't anything he could do about reining in the roguish smile that went with it.

Laughing, she went on, leaving him standing there, hardening as he envisioned the tub accommodating two. Christ, he growled, making his way toward the kitchen, patience was a vastly overrated virtue. If Belle didn't have some mercy on him before the night was over, he was going to explode.

Isabella froze in the doorway, vaguely aware that she was gaping. The room had been divided into halves. And the half obviously hers was ... well, positively *bridal*.

She moved forward, her mind staggering as it tried to take in the myriad details. New curtains hung at the windows. Dark green damask from the looks of them. Fluffy pillows filled the window seats. And there were rugs everywhere. She stopped at the foot of her bed, slipped off her mules, and curled her toes into the thick pile. Sandalwood candles, silver candelabra, carved tables, bejeweled mirrors ... To think that it was possible to have heaven delivered in a crate ... Lord, before she left London she was going to have to find Alexandra Terrell and thank her. Profusely.

Barrett, too, she reminded herself, her gaze wandering to the center of the room. He really was the most amazing man. Henri had never made a bed in all the time she'd known him, had never made so much as the slightest effort to make their home more commodious. And if he'd ever once noticed her efforts in that direction, he'd kept the observation to himself. Henri had been very much like her father in that respect: utterly oblivious. Barrett was obviously cut from an entirely different bolt of cloth than any other man she'd ever known. He not only knew how to arrange furnishings, he knew how to do it well. He understood the need for function to be comfortable and pleasing to the eye.

He understood, she realized, grinning, how to go about properly seducing a woman. Oh, yes, that was most definitely what he'd been about. The crackling fire, the piles of pillows, the bottle of wine, uncorked, breathing, waiting to be poured into the crystal glasses. A realization niggled into her awareness and she looked back over her shoulder. Yes, he'd placed every single mirror so that it reflected the bed. Oh, the man was a rake to his very core.

And, as insane as it was, she deeply appreciated his willingness to be open and honest about his intentions. There was no subterfuge with Barrett Stanbridge, no false promises, no devious deceptions. He was what he was without excuses. He wanted what he wanted without apologies. The world would be a far better place if more men were like him.

Her life, she knew, had certainly taken a turn for the better in having crossed the path of his. Even though it was only temporary, it was a respite her soul had needed so very desperately. She was warm and dry. Her stomach was full and she was all but wallowing in luxury. She had a partner who trusted her judgment and who would do everything in his power to keep her safe. What more could a woman want?

Love.

She started and instinctively took a step back. The attempt to escape was pointless, she realized in the same fraction of a heartbeat; the answer had come from within. Rolling her eyes, disgusted with the persistence of fairy-tale hope, she lifted her hems and made her way to the table.

Barrett leaned back in the tub, cocked a brow, and listened to the creaking of the stairs. He was staring blindly up at the ceiling and enjoying yet another impossible fantasy when the glass of wine appeared from over his left shoulder.

"I'm not peeking," she promised, laughter edging her voice as he took the glass from her.

Ignoring the little whisper of polite convention—and the fact that the water was too soapy to see anything anyway—he grinned and replied, "I wouldn't mind at all if you did."

She laughed softly and moved toward the stove behind him, saying, "I like what you've done with the room upstairs. It's lovely."

Lovely? Barrett sighed and took a sip of the wine. "That isn't precisely the feeling I was hoping to elicit."

"How about breathtaking?"

She was toying with him. He could hear the amusement in her voice. "That's closer," he allowed, leaning back and grinning up at the tin ceiling.

"Cozy?"

"That sounds like a little old lady's parlor."

"Heavenly."

"It makes you think of harps and cherubs and hovering saints?"

"Lord, no. It's not at all wholesome."

His grin broadened another degree. "Good."

"It's a bit decadent. In a refined sort of way."

There wasn't anything the least bit refined about his decadent motives, but he knew that admitting it outright wouldn't help his cause. "Refined decadence," he said instead, "is the British way of life."

"It's sultry too," she ventured, the amusement gone, replaced by softly enticing notes that strummed wildly over his senses. "And inviting."

"Inviting what?" he asked as casually as he could, his heart hammering. "Have you any ideas on that?"

"Quite a few, actually." He was fumbling to catch his wine glass when she added, "I'm going to take dinner upstairs. I'll put it in the brazier to keep it warm so there's no need for you to hurry your bath. Take your time and enjoy it."

Every impulse urged him to bolt to his feet and dash after her. Dignity suggested, rather dryly, that unbridled enthusiasm was all well and good, but didn't amount to anything positive if his wet feet went out from under him.

A naked, soggy, winded mass skidding face first over the floor wasn't all that seductive. And the possibility of splinters in certain portions of his anatomy . . . God, he didn't even want to contemplate it. Asking her to help remove them would most decidedly ruin any sort of romantic aura the room created. No, running after her, while keenly tempting, was a very bad idea.

His hand shaking as he brought the rim of his glass to his lips, Barrett willed himself to stay right where he was, to find whatever it took to proceed with a bit of decorum. He wasn't a boy anymore, he reminded himself; this wasn't his first foray into the sheets. There was absolutely no reason to be breathless with anticipation. Absolutely none. Or nervous, either. He'd taken women to bed God only knew how many times. This wasn't going to be any different from all the trysts that had gone before and all that would follow it. He'd make her gasp in delight, sate them both, and then ever so kindly but firmly go along his blithe and merry way.

The trick was going to be keeping all of that in the forefront of his brain until Belle made it perfectly clear that she'd reached the end of her patience. He sipped again and leaned back in the tub, resolved to letting her set the pace, determined to soak away the ridiculous tension vibrating through every fiber of his body.

Either she had an infinite reserve of patience, he silently grumbled, rolling out the maps on their after-dinner table, or she was trying to see just how deep his own well was. Whatever the case, push was about to encounter shove. Let her wiggle up beside him to study the map and try to ignore him.

Which she happily proceeded to do, much to his frustration. Kneeling beside him, she propped her elbows on the table and cradled her chin in her hands as she poured her attention onto the map. He tried to concentrate on the lines spreading across the vellum sheet, but it was exceedingly difficult to focus on them for any length of time. The warmth of her body beside his seemed to pull him off balance and the curves accentuated by the wrapper were far more captivating than any the mapmaker had drawn. He gave studying it a try, though. Albeit a short and not necessarily wholehearted one.

"I don't see anything that looks even remotely like the lines on Lafitte's map. Do you?"

She straightened and sighed. "There's another way," she said softly and then, without further explanation, rose to her feet. "I'll be right back," she declared as she stepped over the pillows and headed in the direction of her bed.

He sat back on his heels and watched her take a pair of tapers from the box. She scooped her stiletto up from the night table and neatly severed the wick, separating the pair into singles. Tossing the knife and one of the candles into the coverlet, she headed back to him, the candle and her nightgown fisted in her hands.

"Don't scoff, Barrett," she said, dropping down beside him again.

He didn't say anything. Largely because he was too busy wondering what she was about to think of anything particularly pithy. She held the candle up over the map, the wick pinched between her thumb and finger, then slowly moved it along, keeping a scant distance between the end of the candle and the vellum. Her gaze focused intently on the candle, she seemed to be holding her breath.

Since she didn't seem to think that any explanation was necessary, he was finally forced to ask, "What are you doing?"

"Divining."

"You've lost your mind."

"I have not," she quietly countered, her focus still very much fixed on the candle. "It actually works. I'm about to prove it to you."

"I thought they burned all the witches in America."

"Only in the North. We Southerners have an entirely different attitude about them."

"Which would be?"

"Everyone has at least one on retainer," she said as the candle ever so slightly swayed beneath her hand. "You never know when you'll need a spell or two cast."

It was almost as though the wick were bending. He leaned closer to see it, asking, "What kind of spells?"

She moved her hand in the direction the candle seemed to want to go and as the thick end of the taper began to make a tenuous circle, she replied, "Love spells are the most common, of course. Desperation being the powerful force that it is. Vengeance and retribution are also popular." The speed of the candle's circling increased and she smiled. "This is the way the witches help you find lost things. See?"

"See what?"

"How the end is circling," she declared, moving her hand ever so slightly so that the speed increased and the circumference decreased.

"Yes. So?"

"That's where the treasure is," she declared, wrapping her free hand around the candle, her gaze fixed now on the map.

"Where?"

"Right here on the map," she maintained, putting the candle aside. She placed her fingertip on the spot over which the candle had done its dance. "This spot. This is where the treasure is."

If not for the obvious earnestness of her conviction, he would have laughed. Reining in his smile, he leaned forward to see just exactly where in the city the trove could be found. "Belle, darling," he drawled, hoping she didn't take offense at his lack of faith, "that's a cemetery."

"Well, if you wanted to bury a treasure in London, tossing it in with someone's dearly departed certainly would be the easiest way to do it," she countered, clearly undaunted. "There would be no hole to dig, the dropping it in wouldn't attract undue attention, and there are fairly good odds that no one's going to think about digging it up any time soon."

They were all good points, he had to admit. "Lies to Cross, Park and Hyde," he offered, looking at the surrounding streets and not seeing a single one that matched the clues Belle had been given.

"All of them are surnames. One leads to the next."

All right, he silently conceded, that was plausible. "Lion's Paw and Gentle Bride?" he prompted.

"I don't know about here in London, but at home we put all sorts of statuary on the tombs, and when people hire the stone carver for the inscription, they tend to wax rather poetic over those inside."

"We do the same." Barrett considered the map and the strange way that she'd come to focus on that portion of it. "I don't know, Belle. It's a very long shot."

"It makes sense, though. Far more than do streets or pubs."

"Granted." It was the manner in which she'd come to the conclusion that he couldn't believe. It was simply too illogical, too unscientific, to be sound. To pin any real hope on it, much less make it the foundation of a physical search, was more than he could willingly do. He didn't want to hurt her feelings, but neither did he want to waste time and effort. "Do you have any idea of how many cemeteries there are in London?"

She tapped the map with her finger. "It's this one."

The weakness of his smile must have betrayed his skepticism.

"How do you think I found Mignon in a city as big as London?" she asked.

"Asked about?" he ventured. "She wasn't the sort of woman who passed without being noticed by everyone."

"Oh, you doubter," she laughingly challenged, picking up the candle. "Watch this."

"What are you—"

"Just hush and wait," she admonished, holding the candle over the map just as she had the other time.

Barrett sat back on his heels and crossed his arms over his chest, having no idea what she was looking for this time, but willing to be patient and kind in the debunking of her obviously heartfelt beliefs. Again the wick bent and then eventually circled over a spot on the map.

"This," she said, placing her finger on it, "is where your friend Carden lives."

He leaned forward. And blinked, stunned. "Damn."

"Am I right?"

"Yes. How the hell—"

"Would you like for me to find something else?"

"My parents' house," he suggested, not quite willing to accept it as possible, but—surprisingly—hoping she could convince him.

She succeeded, crushing his doubts before she could lay the candle down. "Do you have to have some sort of gift?" he asked, picking up the candle and carefully examining it. "Or can anyone do this?"

"Some people are better at it than others," she replied with a shrug, her grin wide. "But if it's attempted with an open mind, I think anyone could make it work."

If he could actually make it work, it would be a gold mine. He'd never be able to tell his clients how he came up with the solutions so quickly, but that wasn't something they needed to know anyway. "I want to try," he announced, taking the wick as he'd seen her do.

"Hold it just tight enough to keep it from falling," she instructed, taking his hand in hers and slightly adjusting the angle of his wrist. "Clear your mind of everything except what it is that you're looking for and then move the candle slowly over the map. When it starts to angle in a particular direction, go that way and let it find the spot. It will begin to circle when it does. The closer you get to the right place, the faster and tighter the circling becomes."

It took a few moments for the directions to filter through the heady sensations of her touch, her warmth, the caress of her voice. Only as she moved away from his side did her actual words reach the conscious part of his brain. He considered them for a moment and then blinked as another realization struck home.

Now? She'd chosen *now* to lie back and snuggle down invitingly into the pillows? Jesus Christ. He kept himself from looking back at her, kept his attention focused on the candle hanging from between his thumb and finger. He'd give the attempt a couple of minutes—just so that he didn't look desperate, just to give her time to become truly comfortable—then ask her for help. Odds were she'd tell him to abandon the effort for the time being and join her in the pillows. Nature would control the course from there.

Expelling a long, hard breath, Barrett stared at the candle and considered his choices. He had no idea what Neville Martinez looked like apart from a wheeled chair and a likely lap robe. Emil Caribe was probably a slight man with a tendency to look over his shoulder and cower. But the characteristics weren't specific enough to separate either one of them from a good number of other men in London. The Choteau brothers were a mystery aside from a vague sort of French look. And try as he might, he couldn't imagine Henri Dandaneau and Jacques de Granvieux as anything other than bodies laid out in coffins. No, finding any of their suspects through divining was going to fall to Belle.

He needed to look for someone he knew and could picture clearly in his mind's eye. Unfortunately, he knew where everyone was and thus might unconsciously influence the candle's choice, or those whose whereabouts he didn't know precisely—like O'Brien—were moving around at this wee hour of the night and could be anywhere. There was no immediate way to verify the accuracy of any homing the candle might do.

All in all, he decided, searching was going to be a waste. But the time spent thinking about it had been just long enough.

"It's not working," he announced, trying to sound a bit dejected about the failure. When she didn't reply, he called softly, "Belle?" and looked over his shoulder.

Oh, for the love of God. She was asleep. Dead to the world, beautifully, serenely sound asleep. He dropped the candle on the table and sat back on his heels, frustrated and disappointed. She was exhausted, his conscience offered in her defense. It had been an exceedingly long, labor-intensive day. Just three hours short of a full twenty-four. Scrubbing his hand over his jaw, he accepted that, truth be told, he was bone weary, too, and that the second he closed his eyes, he was going to be just as oblivious as she was.

Ruefully resigned to the circumstances, he used the table to steady himself as he gained his feet. Snuffing the candles one by one, he made his way around the room, ending at her bed. Placing her knife and the extra candle on the nightstand, he pulled the embroidered cover off and carried it back to the center of the room.

And stopped. The firelight cast an inviting glow over the rainbow of pillows, over the satin- and lace-clad woman sleeping in their midst. A gentleman would resist the temptation, see her covered, and then retreat to his bed. A rogue would gather her up in his arms, take her with him, and make sure the movement awakened both her and her passions.

The first course was a lonely one; the second low. Barrett stepped into the pile of pillows, choosing a middling way that he knew would satisfy neither the gentleman nor the rake. Gently lying down beside her, he arranged the cover over them both and then wiggled his shoulders into the pillows beneath him.

As he settled himself, she did as well, curling onto her side and closing the distance between them with a sleepy, heart-tugging murmur. It was the oddest, most unfamiliar kind of satisfaction that stole over him, but he was content and so chose not to examine it all that closely. Instead, he shifted again, sliding his arm under her head and drawing her into the circle of his arms.

A tiny smile tipped up the corners of her mouth as he pulled the pins from her hair and let it tumble down over her shoulders. And when he trailed his fingers through the riot of silken curls, she sighed the sweetest sigh he'd ever heard as she laid her arm over his chest and drew her leg across his.

The feel of her body pressed against his was rousing. And yet deeply soothing, too. He closed his eyes, trying to stave off sleep long enough to fathom the feelings eddying deep inside him. There was a rightness to being with her like this; a perfection that didn't come from anything he'd done or hoped to do. Lying with her, holding her . . . An innocent thing that satisfied a hunger he hadn't known existed.

Isabella. Angel of destruction, angel of divining, angel of sweet trust and peaceful rest.

Chapter Twelve

Belle started, away from the carnage and into light too sudden for her eyes. Her heart racing, her breathing ragged and too quick, she whimpered at the chaos of her thoughts and not knowing where to run.

"I'm here, angel."

The low rumble instantly silenced the chatter in her mind. Barrett. She was lying curled against Barrett. Wrapped in his arms. She was all right. Death wasn't coming for her. Not tonight.

"Go back to sleep," he murmured, feathering a kiss across her forehead.

She slumped against him, every muscle in her body aching as the fear drained away and tears of a myriad of emotions welled in her eyes. Blinking them back, she silently recited the litany of a thousand nights. What had happened, had happened and couldn't be changed. Where others had been marked to die, she'd been chosen to live. Why wasn't hers to know. What mattered was that she make the time she'd been given count for something, that she live as fully and as happily as she could.

And there was no doubt that being with Barrett Stanbridge made her happy. The warmth and comfort of being held so securely . . . She watched the slow rise and fall of his chest and set her own breathing to match the rhythm. And when it had settled into easy tandem, she closed her eyes and slipped her hand between the buttons of his shirt. The heat of his skin, the sprinkling of crisp hair, the steady, strong beat of his heart . . .

Drifting back into slumber, she smiled softly, thinking that Barrett was a very nice reward for having survived.

Isabella awakened again, this time by weighted degrees and feeling as though she were returning from somewhere far away. She smiled at the linen expanse on which she half sprawled and then eased her head out of the cradle of Barrett's shoulder to look up at his face.

His smile was lazy, the light in his eyes soft from a slumber every bit as recent as her own. "Good afternoon," he said quietly, brushing an errant curl off her brow.

Deep inside her a spark quickened. "What time is it?" she asked as her pulse roused and life flowed back into her limbs.

"I can't see the clock from here," he replied, his voice a luscious rumble beneath the palm of her hand, "but judging by the light coming in around the curtains, I'd guess it to be around teatime."

"We've slept half the night and all the day?"

"Well, in our defense, there wasn't much of the night left."

Just as there wasn't much of the day remaining. But, oh, the temptation to spend what was left of it right where she was . . . "I know I should, but I'm not sure that I can make myself move."

His smile widened and he shifted his shoulders under

her as he somewhat breathlessly admitted, "I haven't felt this leaden in years and years. And the last time was coming out of a five-day drunk. One of the hazards of being Carden's friend."

It took great effort and no small amount of will, but she managed to roll off him and onto her back. Languidly stretching sleep-stiffened muscles, she said, "Mine was two years ago and laudanum induced. One of the hazards of jumping off a bridge."

He rolled onto his side with enviable ease and propped his head in his hand. With a quirked smile, he said, "That rather begs an explanation, don't you think?"

"The fuse burned too fast," she supplied, a slow heat filling her core as she looked up at him. "There's no way to know that it will until you light it and then there isn't enough time to run."

His gaze holding hers, he took a tendril of her hair and twined it around his finger. "Now that the war's over . . . What do you do to keep yourself from being bored?"

She could tell him all manner of things, all of them true and none of them the least bit dangerous. "I sleep on the floor with men."

His brow shot up and his eyes sparkled as his grin turned wicked. "You make a habit of this?"

"I'm giving it very serious consideration. I like it."

The light in his eyes deepened as his smile faded away. "It has risks, you know," he said quietly, unwinding her hair and letting it fall.

Her heart racing, she reached up and trailed a fingertip along the line of his stubbled jaw. "I'm very much aware of that. Therein lies the attraction."

"There are consequences, too."

"Not permanent ones," she countered, tracing a line from the tip of his chin, down his neck and to the first button on his shirt.

Reaching up between them, he wrapped his hand around her own and then lifted it back to his lips. Feathering kisses over the backs of her fingertips, he said, "Only a cad would kiss a woman before offering her breakfast."

He was giving her a chance to change her mind? He was truly putting her comfort ahead of his desire? Or, the more realistic side of her suggested, it could well be that he was starving and was too kind to bluntly admit that wanting her wasn't nearly as important to him as filling the void in his stomach. Regretting her seductive inexperience and the need to ask, she managed what she hoped looked like a serene smile. "Are you hungry?"

His grin was slow and lazy and ever so sweetly inviting. "Not for food."

Delightful certainty flooded through her. "Neither am I."

"I find that hard to believe," he said, laughing softly. "You're always hungry."

"True, but at the moment, my attention is elsewhere."

"On what?"

On how handsome he was, how truly happy he seemed. And on how merely looking at him made her heart tight and her body tingle. "On wondering just how much more than a kiss you might want."

His eyes twinkled with devilment. "Quite a bit, actually. How do you feel about that?"

"Tempted."

One brow inched upward. "How much distance is there between being tempted and being willing to surrender?"

She lifted her free hand for him to see, holding her thumb and index finger a scant distance apart. "About this much."

"That's not very much at all."

Nodding, she examined the space herself and then slid her gaze over to meet his. "I think it's about the length of one kiss."

His grin was huge, his laughter rolling and full as he pressed her hand back into the pillows and leaned over her. *So happy,* she thought, grinning and reaching up to twine her free arm around his neck.

"Does it have," he whispered, his lips grazing the curve of her jaw, "to be a traditional kiss?" Her reply was lost in a sweet sigh as he gently nipped her earlobe. "Or," he went on, laying a slow trail down her neck to her shoulder, "might little kisses also lead to surrender?"

She laughed softly and turned her head to grant him free access. Nuzzling aside the edges of her wrapper and gown, he rewarded her with a long, lingering, delightful assault on just the right place. Belle softly, happily moaned as a wave of pure pleasure cascaded through her.

"It appears," she murmured, settling her hips closer to his, "that it doesn't make much difference at all."

"Really," he laughingly countered, kissing his way slowly down to the curve of her breast. "Are you sure?"

"Oh, Barrett," she said on a gasp of delight and keen anticipation, "I've never been more sure of—"

His start strangled the rest of her assurance. She instinctively snagged a quick, shallow breath even as his gaze snapped to the door and he snarled, "Goddammit!"

It took a long second for the sounds to make their way past the pounding of her pulse and the disappointed whimper of her heart. Someone was downstairs and calling their names. Carden, she decided the next time he raised his voice.

Barrett heaved a sigh and released her hand in the same smooth motion in which he rolled away, saying, "My apologies for my language."

"Which aren't necessary," she assured him, sitting up and pushing her hair back over her shoulders. If there were any apologies to be handed around, they were due from his friends. "I don't suppose that I could hope that you'll head them off so that I'm not caught in my nightclothes?"

Shoving his shirttail into the waistband of his trousers, he gave her a rueful smile. "Never let it be said that I'm a complete cad."

"I'll be down shortly to fix us something to eat."

"It will have to be a quick meal, Belle," he cautioned, heading for the door. "We're going back to the house to look for the missing map pieces as soon as the sun fully sets."

"Quick it will be then," she promised, gaining her feet and pulling the nightgown and wrapper into place. "Give me five minutes to get dressed."

"Be careful where you're walking. Your hairpins are somewhere in the pillows."

"Thank you," she called after him, bending to pick up one lying in plain sight.

"When you find them?"

She straightened to find him standing in the doorway, his smile quirked. "Yes?"

"Do me a favor and put them away in a box somewhere."

He didn't wait for her to either accede or protest, but turned away and disappeared momentarily from sight. Two seconds later he reappeared, making his way down the stairs. The look on his face took her aback. The happy man was gone. Absolutely gone; not a trace of him remained. She winced, feeling a tiny bit sorry for Carden and Aiden, and then set about searching for the other hairpins.

It didn't matter what she did with them at the moment, she knew. Her hair was going to be stuffed up under a hat for the next few hours. After that . . . She grinned. If Barrett wanted the riot tumbling all over the place, she'd be more than willing to oblige him. On that and anything else his heart desired.

Finding the last pin, she carried them all over to the bed and dropped them on the nightstand. Untying the sash on her wrapper, her gaze fell on her reflection in a mirror. Isabella slowly froze, not quite recognizing the woman staring back at her. The tumble of uncontrolled curls was familiar. As was the height and the general shape of the body. But that was all that remained of the Isabella Dandaneau who had climbed aboard a ship in New Orleans. The woman who stared back at her was flushed with the rosy heat of desire, her nipples hard points pressing against the silk of her gown. And her eyes . . .

Isabella moistened her lips with the tip of her tongue and drew a steadying breath. The effort didn't change the reality. There was a hunger in the depth of her eyes. And a glint of confidence and certainty, too. She'd seen the look before. In Mignon's eyes.

Suppressing a shudder, Belle turned away and took another deep breath as she resumed her disrobing. She wasn't like Mignon, she assured herself. She didn't make a habit of bedding men and then sauntering away to find another. Yes, she wanted Barrett Stanbridge, but he was a unique desire. There was no one before him—not even Henri—and there wasn't likely to be anyone after him, either. Barrett stood completely alone in her experience with men. He stirred her senses. He made her feel alive and beautiful and wanted. She liked how her heart raced when he was near, loved how her breath caught when he touched her, how her blood heated at the thought of making love with him.

Being with Barrett felt good. It felt right in a way nothing else ever had. And she was going to revel in that wonder for as long as she could. If that made her a wanton, then a wanton she was. An absolutely unapologetic one.

Barrett hesitated at the bottom of the stairs just long enough to meet their gazes and grunt in greeting before continuing on his way. Unfortunately, they didn't take his less than cordial welcome as a hint to leave. They followed him to the kitchen and took up perches on the cabinets to silently wait for him to take care of the most pressing of his ablutions.

He was blessing Belle's little organized heart and appreciating the water simmering on the back burner of the stove when Aiden ventured, "You seem a bit unsociable this evening."

Stoking the fire, he replied gruffly, "I'll be all right once I get some coffee in me."

He was taking the grinder down off the shelf when Carden made his attempt to start a decent conversation. "We thought that since the weather had cleared, you'd want to go look for the missing parts of the map."

He nodded, reminding himself that they were here out of friendship and that their sense of timing wasn't deliberate. "Which one of you wants to stay here with Belle?"

"John Aiden drew the short straw."

"And Carden wouldn't hear of a sporting two out of three."

He didn't have anything to say, he realized, cranking the grinder. They were his friends. They'd been through thick and thin and countless rounds of cards and bottles of whisky together. And he couldn't for the life of him think of anything he wanted or needed to say to them. Oddly, they felt like strangers who had come to roost. What was wrong with him? What had happened to change the ease of their camaraderie?

"Are you all right, Bare?"

So Carden sensed it, too. Barrett tossed the grounds in the boiling water and then stepped back from the stove. There was nothing to be done but throw himself on their mercy and hope they could draw him back from wherever it was he'd drifted.

"I can't remember the last time I slept that deeply, that

long," he confessed, remembering that he'd been perfectly himself as he'd lain down beside Belle. "I didn't so much as move for over fifteen hours."

Carden chuckled. "Braggart."

"Not that it's any of your business," he countered dryly, cocking a brow, "but it wasn't induced by a round of recreation."

Aiden looked genuinely puzzled. "Have you taken vows of some sort or another?"

No, I haven't, he silently retorted. *And I'd be thoroughly enjoying myself right this minute if you hadn't walked in when you did.*

"Sorry," Aiden said, wincing. "Forget that I inquired."

"I'm the one who's sorry," Barrett grumbled, raking his hands through his hair. "I can't seem to get my mind on center. It's not your fault."

"I always feel a bit off when Alex and I butt heads. Have you and Belle had a spat?"

"No." The stairs creaked and he moved back to the stove, pulled the pan off the fire, and then reached up to take two thick mugs down from the shelf. Not wanting to wait for the grounds to settle, he rummaged through a crock of utensils, searching for a strainer.

Behind him, Aiden made a strangling sound in the same instant that Carden offered a stunned, "Whoa."

Barrett looked over his shoulder and felt his jaw drop.

"Good afternoon, gentlemen," she said jauntily, striding toward the icebox by the back door.

She chattered on, but the words were nothing more than a dull patter to his ear. She was wearing trousers. He blinked and shook his head, certain that the effort would put his world back to rights. It didn't. Black trousers. Well tailored. And the boots she'd worn yesterday. All the way up to her knees. Perfectly molded.

His gaze skimmed upward. Then down and up again.

Dear God, he'd never seen such incredible lines and curves. She bent to retrieve something from the lower portion of the box and his blood turned to liquid fire as his mind reeled and staggered between two disparate thoughts: she was dressed scandalously and skirts were a hell of a lot easier to get out of the way.

His knees quaked and the threat of them buckling was sufficiently dire that he tore his gaze away from her to make an attempt to marshal his wits. When he had the first tattered shreds in hand, he forced himself to swallow and to breathe.

The ragged influx of oxygen cleared the haze from his vision—a not altogether pleasant thing. Not looking at Belle had put his gaze in the vicinity of Carden and Aiden. And neither one of them were making the slightest effort to recover from their shock. Their mouths were hanging open, their eyes were the size of dessert plates, and both of them were gripping the edge of the cabinets beneath them as though they were hanging on for dear life.

Which was a damn good idea, he decided, grabbing the top edge of the cabinet in front of him. His knees were just beginning to steady when Belle moved to the stove and the very edge of his vision.

"Oh, good. You have the coffee ready. I'm dying for a cup."

He was just flat-out dying. And coffee wasn't going to save him. He had to do something. *Now*. He dragged a desperate breath into his lungs and looked over his shoulder at his friends. It took every measure of what little control he had to firmly say, "If we could be alone . . ."

His words took a moment or two to penetrate the fog of their brains. Another couple passed as they gathered their wits and found the wherewithal to actually move. "We'll be outside," Carden announced, his gaze riveted on the back door as he made a beeline toward it.

"Take all the time you need," Aiden offered, shouldering past him to yank the door wide and vault out into the yard.

Well, Isabella thought as Barrett turned to her, on the positive side of things, he'd recovered from his shock. Unfortunately, he seemed to have moved rather quickly to furious. Perhaps if she gave him a few minutes, he'd reach a slightly less volatile state. She reached nonchalantly past him and took the strainer from the crock.

"What the bloody hell are you thinking?"

So much for giving him time; he didn't appear to want it. "That you seem somewhat appalled," she replied calmly, pouring a stream of steaming coffee through the strainer and into a mug.

"Jesus Christ, Belle! Trousers?"

Oh, for heaven's sake. For all their pride in cool logic, men so seldom employed it. "Blowing up bridges is a dangerous enough business, Barrett," she patiently pointed out, transferring the strainer to the second cup and pouring. "There's no need to add to it by trying to get it done while wearing hoops, a corset, crinolines, and a dress."

"Are you planning to blow up something tonight?"

"No," she admitted, setting the pan back onto the stove. Handing him a cup, she added, "I'm planning to scurry around in the dark—with great efficiency—and not be seen while I'm at it."

He blinked in one second. His jaw went granite-hard in the next. "You're staying right here. With Aiden."

"I am not," she instantly countered, indignant at his presumption to issue decrees. "It's my map and my cousin who hid it."

"I don't care," he shot back. "You're not going with us."

Oh! How *dare* he play the lord and master! "Then you'd best be about knocking me over the head and tying me up," she declared, her pulse hammering behind her eyes, her fists clenched at her sides. "Because that's the only way you're going to leave me behind. If there's anyone who has the right—no, the obligation!—to go out and find the missing pieces, it's me. And need I remind you that you're the one the constables are looking for? Not me. That you're the one taking the greatest risk in walking out that door? An absolutely needless and foolish risk, I might add."

He growled and slammed his coffee mug down on the stove, but she ignored both his display of temper and the hard glint in his eyes. "If anyone's to be left behind tonight, by all rights it should—"

The rest of the words were lost in her gasp as he took her by the shoulders and pulled her to him. A protest at the rough handling flickered and then was gone, swept away as he bent his head and covered her mouth with his own. The storm of sensation was fiercely instant; the fullness of her breasts skimming over the hard planes of his chest, the spicy scent of soap and heated skin, the silken caress of his tongue over the seam of her lips. And the incredible, undeniable hunger. It gathered low and hot deep inside her and then shot like lightning through every fiber of her being, through every corner of her soul. Instinct flared and the hunger became a need beyond reason. She surrendered to it, parting her lips and melting fully into the power and strength of his body.

His moan rippled through her, turning her core to liquid fire. Her arms slipped up to encircle his neck, to draw him closer, to offer everything she was and all he cared to take. Take he did, tasting her deeply, sliding his arms around her to fit her hard against his chest, against his hips and the hardened proof of his own need.

More, instinct desperately urged. *Closer*. She strained to obey, twining her fingers in the hair at his nape, stretching up. His breath caught and she felt the jolt of his heart along the full length of her body.

He pulled back, gasping for air, and gazed down at her,

the wonder and confusion in his eyes somehow a balm on the rawest edges of her need. But it wasn't enough; she didn't want to be soothed.

"Barrett," she whispered, willing to plead.

He closed his eyes and groaned as he lowered his head and captured her mouth again. But even as he did, she sensed the end in the beginning. She could feel it in the measure of his reserve and she strangled on a whimper of frustration.

For a quicksilver instant his control faltered and her hope blazed. She stretched up again, pressed closer, and then she was without him, choking back a cry of disappointment as he abruptly tore his lips away. One arm around her shoulders, he shifted the other to the back of her head and gently tucked her under his chin.

Beneath her cheek, his heartbeat thundered. She leaned against him, her breathing as uneven and labored as his own. Never. Never in all her life . . . God, how could she have lived this long without truly knowing how deeply and wildly desire could burn? Or how quickly it could consume all rational thought and reduce good judgment to cinders?

"Why did you do that?" she asked when the sharpest edges of wanting began to mercifully dull.

"Kiss you?" he asked on a ragged breath, gently easing her balance onto her own feet. "Or stop?"

She stepped out of the circle of his arms, now as suddenly desperate to be independent as she'd been needy in the moment before. Dragging a steadying breath into her lungs, she picked up her coffee mug and clung to its warmth with both hands. At the edge of her vision, through the kitchen window, she could see Carden and Aiden pacing around the yard. If they'd happened to have glanced toward the house at just the right moment, they'd have been provided quite the show. Barrett must have, at some level, realized that. Thank goodness his mind had been more aware of the world beyond them than her own had been.

"Why you kissed me," she answered.

He cleared his throat ever so quietly, then picked up his coffee and took a sip. "The first time because I couldn't think of any other way to shut down the torrent of words. The second time because I really liked the first." He stared into his cup for a moment and then looked up to meet her gaze squarely. "And when I kiss you again, it will be because I intend to make love to you."

Her pulse skittered and a sliver of lightning shot into the center of her soul. She tamped down the spark of hope it ignited and tried to sound amused as she countered, "Right then and there?"

"Yes."

There was no laughter in his voice at all. Nor in his eyes. No, the light shimmering in them was a breathtaking mixture of open desire and steely resolve. He was serving her formal notice, giving her fair warning and the chance to stomp away in a maidenly huff. "Are you always so honest?"

A brow slowly cocked and one corner of his mouth quirked upward. "Not with women."

"Why are you being so honest with me?"

"You're not like any other woman I've ever met. It rather suggests that a different approach is required with you."

He wasn't like any other man she'd ever met, either. It wasn't because he was English, though. Of that much she was certain. New Orleans was a major trading center; before the war Englishmen had passed through it frequently. And it wasn't because they were partners of a sort either. Only at the start of the war had she worked alone.

"When we come back here later," he said, quietly intruding on her thoughts, "I'm going to put an end to your illusions of me being a gentleman."

Another bolt of heavenly fire. Another flare of hope. "Is that a promise?"

He smiled ruefully. "If Carden and Aiden weren't waiting, I wouldn't be, either."

And neither would she. Buoyed, she deliberately focused her thoughts on the hours that lay between now and then. "You will be able to keep your mind on the task at hand, won't you? You won't let yourself be distracted?"

"I'll do my best," he offered, lifting his cup in salute before taking a sip.

"Just think of me as nothing more than a fellow soldier."

He swallowed hard. "Belle," he began, his tone ringing with the certain notes of opposition.

"I'm going," she declared, unwilling to yield on the point. "I can hold my own and you know it. You admitted as much yesterday." He considered her, clearly remembering, his decision faltering in the face of it. "Barrett, I'm not a china doll," she added gently, determined to make him understand. "If I fall, I won't break. You don't have to tuck me away on a shelf in the name of chivalry."

He blinked and looked away, took another sip of his coffee. "Is that what Henri did with you?" he asked after a long moment. "Did he tuck you away?"

His gaze was fixed blindly on the door that led to the front of the house, but she nodded anyway. "Not out of chivalry, but yes. And then, for the most part, forgot where he'd left me."

He'd heard her; she could tell by the hard line that came to his jaw. Sipping her coffee, she waited, watching him purse his lips, frown. Then he closed his eyes for a second and ever so slightly shook his head. Finally, with a slow sigh, he opened them and brought his gaze back to hers.

"Two things," he said quietly, firmly. "Just so that you're

aware. The first is that while I have very serious reservations about this, I won't be accused of being an overprotective and narrow-minded oaf. And the second . . ." His gaze slipped slowly down the length of her body, caressing every curve. "Her Majesty doesn't have any soldiers that look that damn delectable in a pair of trousers."

Heat flooded through her and she knew her cheeks had gone cherry red. Afraid that he might mistake her high color for embarrassment, she grinned and drawled, "Why, thank you for noticing, Mr. Stanbridge. And being appreciative enough to say so."

Chuckling, shaking his head yet again, he turned and headed toward the back door, coffee mug in hand and saying, "Please stay behind me so that I don't have to battle temptation the entire time."

It was a good thing that he didn't look back or wait for her assent. She knew better than to make promises she didn't intend to keep. If she'd learned one lesson in her years slipping through the dark of bayou nights, it was that plans seldom went as they'd been so carefully laid down.

Life, she observed, heading to the icebox, seemed to be all about learning. It never stopped. Not if you were paying the least bit of attention to what was happening to you. Barrett had just given her a most stunning lesson; one she hadn't expected at all.

He maintained that she'd emerged from a war with her naïveté intact. She'd argue differently until her dying day. But there were different kinds of innocence and in looking back . . .

It was really most amazing to think that she'd passed through a marriage without her presence of mind having ever once been shaken—much less overwhelmed. She'd assumed that was the way it was supposed to be; that it was perfectly commonplace to be able to make love with half your brain while making a list of chores with the other.

She'd had no idea desire could so easily and completely obliterate self-control.

That naïveté had just been destroyed. Utterly and forever. By mere kisses. Given the power of them, she realized, actually making love with Barrett would be far more dangerous than she'd thought. She'd be vulnerable, wholly at his mercy. Part of her recoiled at the notion of granting anyone that measure of trust, of deliberately and knowingly courting mortal embarrassment.

Another part of her thrilled at the prospect of taking such a risk. If she trusted him enough to willingly put her life in his hands, then surely he could be trusted with her mind and body too. And if the heated, breathless pleasure of kissing Barrett Stanbridge was any indication of the pleasure to be had in tumbling into a bed with him . . .

Good God Almighty. If she had any hope of fully savoring the magnificence of him, she needed to find a much longer, much, much slower fuse.

Chapter Thirteen

Ten blocks, Isabella silently marveled. Carden's town-house-turned-hideaway-lair was less than ten blocks from Barrett's house. She hadn't known and wouldn't have guessed the distance between them to be any more than a nice evening's stroll. Which, with all the markets and hopping between rented hacks she'd done the morning they'd fled, wasn't all that surprising. And since no one had battered down the door to arrest Barrett or attempt to steal the map, she had to admit that the distance didn't seem to be a dangerously narrow one.

Tonight it was the perfect distance. Just close enough to make their coming and going a silent footpad affair, just far enough that it would be quite possible to lose a pursuer in the dark warren of alleyways and yards that lay between.

As they'd agreed in the yard of the town house, Barrett and Carden led the way while she and John Aiden brought up the rear some ways back. The goal was to look like day laborers heading home for the night. She and Aiden were doing well with their parts, ambling along with their hands stuffed deep in their pockets and being companionably silent. The other two, though . . .

It certainly wasn't the cut of their clothing that betrayed them. All four of them were wearing simple black trousers, shirts, boots, and jackets. No, it was more a matter of manner and attitude. You could apparently take the man out of the military, but he strode purposefully forever. All Barrett and Carden were lacking was a brass band.

"At least he's not a pompous ass."

"I beg your pardon?"

She winced, realizing that she'd not only spoken aloud, but used a most unladylike expression. "I was thinking that Barrett and Carden walk like generals," she supplied, hoping that Aiden really hadn't heard clearly and that she had a chance to salvage the illusion of femininity. "And I concluded that it wasn't an entirely negative thing. Barrett's sense of himself isn't the least bit inflated."

He grinned. "The first way you said it was more entertaining."

It had been a flimsy illusion anyway, she consoled herself. The only thing to be done now was to apologize for it. "But certainly not very genteel."

"Genteel is boring." He hesitated, then added, "Barrett hates to be bored."

The hair on the back of her neck quivered. "Don't most people?" she asked, trying to focus their conversation on the topic in the most general way.

"Actually, no. Most have no idea of how dreadfully dull their lives are. Or at least that's my observation. Barrett's always worked very hard at avoiding the mundane. That's why he didn't follow his father into finance."

The hairs quivered a little faster, a little harder. "Why," she asked, resolved to deal with the issue and be done with it, "do I sense that you're trying very hard to tell me something in a roundabout sort of way?"

His gaze slid over to hers as he smiled and replied, "Probably because you're perceptive."

"And that something would be . . . ?"

"You're not at all like the women he tends to find for himself."

If she looked at his comment from just the right angle—and squinted—it passed for a compliment. "That's undoubtedly because I found him and for reasons quite apart from those that motivate his hunting."

"True," he allowed. "Which is just one of the ways you've managed to completely upend the order of his deliberately unconventional world. No small feat."

There wasn't the slightest hint of censure in his voice, but she felt under attack just the same. "It hasn't been intentional."

"That doesn't matter. The consequences, however, do." He cleared his throat and fixed his gaze on the pair ahead of them. "Look, Belle," he said quietly, "we're getting close to the house and running out of time so I'm going to say it straight-out. Barrett's my friend and I don't want to see him hurt. I can't tell just what his feelings for you are, but I do recognize an uncommon infatuation when I see one. If you don't have genuine feelings for him, you need to walk away before any more damage is done."

She stopped dead in her tracks, staring at his back as he ambled on, apparently oblivious to how he'd just all but poleaxed her. Was he saying that Barrett was falling in love with her? No, the rational part of her brain contended. Barrett was a man-about-town, a rake, a committed bachelor. Men like that didn't tumble head over heels. They were too smart, too experienced, and far too jaded to let themselves be swept off their feet.

Aiden stopped, looked over his shoulder, then turned and came back to her. He said nothing, though; just met her gaze and cocked a brow in silent question.

"I can't," she managed to stammer.

"Can't love him? Can't walk away? Can't what?"

Love him? Her heart skittered and panic shot through her veins. "Walk away," she declared, desperately seizing the safer possibility.

"Why?"

How John Aiden could be so calm . . . Her heart pounding frantically, Belle tried to draw a full breath. And failed. "I need him to help me find the treasure," she offered, snatching at the wholest of the notions careening through her mind. "And I can't just leave him to fend off murder charges on his own. I'm obligated to stay and see that his name is cleared."

"Why?"

Oh, God. The man was positively relentless. "He's in this mess because of Mignon and me. And because leaving would be selfish and he deserves better. He's a good, decent, and honorable man."

"Would his being a handsome devil happen to be a consideration, too?"

"A slight one," she admitted, grateful that he hadn't pressed any further on the nature of her feelings.

"Just slight?" he teased, his grin wide and knowing.

"All right, a significant one," she allowed, seeing no reason to maintain pretenses. "I'm not made of stone."

He sobered only slightly to admonish, "Just be honest with him, Belle. Please. If you owe him anything at all, it's that."

Her nod seemed to satisfy him and he turned away, motioning with his head for her to come along. Obediently, she fell in beside him, pushing her hands deeper into her pockets as her gaze skimmed over the pavers and her mind chattered.

Barrett deserved honesty, yes, but she thought that more than anything else, he deserved to be happy. He deserved to have every minute of his life filled with the kind of joy that had been in his eyes as he'd pressed her back into the pillows. And if Aiden was to be believed, the light in his eyes hadn't been from having found another willing woman in a long line of them. According to Aiden, *she* made Barrett happy. Being with her was different for him.

Which, she ruefully had to accept, was most definitely not within her realm of experience with men. There had been a time, long ago and for a very brief span, when she'd wanted to make Henri happy and had tried everything she knew to make him so. Nothing had achieved that end, however, and she'd abandoned the effort. In a single moment, she remembered, looking back. As she'd sat alone at the dinner table. She'd surrendered the entire campaign with a simple shrug and no great sense of having lost something important.

Making Barrett happy, on the other hand, didn't seem to require any conscious effort at all on her part. At least not any that she'd noticed herself making. It just seemed to happen on its own. They talked, they teased, Barrett's smile went wide. His eyes sparkled. And in those moments, he made her feel acutely, deliciously alive.

The feelings Barrett stirred in her were completely apart from those she'd ever experienced with Henri. Theirs had been a forced union, one neither of them had truly wanted. Initially it hadn't engendered much emotion beyond indifference. In time it had evolved to a true dislike and an abiding regret.

From the first moments with Barrett she'd been on unfamiliar ground. She'd been physically attracted to him from the start. There was no denying that; she had never even tried to evade his advances. But where was the line that separated physical desire from love? she wondered. Had she crossed it? How did you know that you loved someone? Was the realization supposed to spring up from nowhere, certain and full and blinding a person to all but the revelation? Her mother had maintained that a woman would simply *know* when she met the man of her heart.

Isabella lifted her gaze from the ground. The back side of the carriage house lay straight ahead. Carden had moved on to his assigned place and Barrett stood alone in the shadows, waiting for her and Aiden to arrive. What were her feelings for him? He certainly inspired confidence. A myriad of things could go wrong this evening, but she wasn't the least bit worried; Barrett could be counted on to handle his part of any disaster both competently and swiftly. The basic plan he'd laid down was solid and well conceived; there was no question as to his intelligence or his logic. Trusting him with life and limb didn't require any leap of faith. She knew that he'd watch her back just as carefully as she would watch his.

None of it, even combined, amounted to love and she knew it. She'd never carried explosives into the dark with men she didn't trust and respect. It was a fundamental requirement of self-preservation. Barrett wasn't any different in that than any one of a dozen men with whom she'd worked.

Why that realization saddened her, she couldn't fathom in a definitive way. She wanted him to be special, to be more. Largely, she supposed, because she knew to the center of her bones that he was. How precisely—beyond the physical appeal of him—was a mystery, though.

Beside her, John Aiden said quietly, "Two trills in quick succession."

She didn't bother to acknowledge the reminder, but let him walk away to take up his post. Barrett, she knew, ambling up to join him, wouldn't dream of questioning her ability to remember the warning signal.

He cocked his brow and tilted his head to the side and in

the expression she clearly heard his unspoken question. *Is there a problem?* She smiled up at him in reassurance as she reached to the small of her back and withdrew the revolver.

Barrett did the same, angling the muzzle toward the ground between their feet as he checked, yet again, the cylinder to be sure it was loaded. *Always certain,* she thought, grinning as she edged toward the corner of the carriage house.

The trill of a night bird came from the darkness to her left. Carden was in place and all was clear. She waited, aware of Barrett moving to the far side of the building. Another trill came; this one from Aiden on the right. Pausing just long enough to collect Barrett's quick nod of assent, she moved out of cover and slipped up the side of the outbuilding, keeping to the shadows.

He'd been right about Larson not posting constables to watch for his return. Now if only she could be equally right about where Mignon had stashed the remaining pieces of the map. The quicker work they made of the foray, the better. Barrett was just as likely to be right about the presence of Mignon's killers as he'd been the absence of Larson's men. Her skin prickled at the thought, but she reminded herself that if Barrett trusted Carden and Aiden to keep watch, then she could, too.

Reaching the front corner of the building, she poked her head around to check and, seeing Barrett moving swiftly and silently up the edge of the yard, quickly rounded it and moved to the stable door. It opened without a sound and she slipped inside. Pulling it barely closed behind her, she listened and let her eyes adjust to the darkness of the interior.

Hearing only the sound of her own breathing, she relaxed and let her heartbeat slow. Certain of Mignon's tendencies, Isabella swept her gaze around the structure and objects nearest the door and then set to work, one hand skimming over surfaces and along joints, the other firmly gripping the butt of the revolver. A search of the framework on either side of the door produced nothing. Reaching up, she poked her fingers into the left corner of the header.

"Seek and ye shall find," she whispered, carefully pulling the tattered strip from its hiding place. The light was dim at best, but sufficient for her to know in a single glance that she held the rest of the verse in her hand. The valuable piece, the piece that would allow them to put together all the rest of them and find Lafitte's treasure. It took everything she had to suppress a peal of laughter and even more to tamp down the urge to run out into the yard and call Barrett off his part of the search. Resolutely stuffing the slip into her pocket, she forced herself to continue to look for the last missing section of Mignon's half.

Careful examination of the other side of the header and of all the seams between the door and the windows on either side of it produced nothing. Isabella sighed and studied the ancient, obviously retired carriage parked in the far corner of the space, the stalls that lined both walls, and knew instinctively that Mignon wouldn't have gone that far.

Barrett might have been right, she admitted, making her way back to the door. Mignon might well have had only one piece left to hide by the time she actually reached the yard. She listened at the door for a few seconds and, hearing nothing, eased it open and peered out into the yard.

Her heart instantly slammed up into her throat. A horrible pain throbbing where it had torn free of its moorings in her chest, she swallowed hard and clenched her teeth. It was all the time and preparation she could allow herself. Adjusting her grip on the revolver, she slipped out of the stable, knowing what she had to do.

• • •

Barrett looked down at the muzzle pointed at his gut, at the bandaged hand wrapped around the grip, and then back up into eyes too old for a young man's body.

"Toss away the gun and give me the map, guv'nor."

Lifting his hand, Barrett deliberately eyed the newfound slip and then turned his attention back to his assailant. As he did, at the farthest edge of his focus, he caught sight of movement in the shadows of the carriage house. His blood turned to ice and his stomach clenched solid just before it plummeted to the soles of his feet. *Belle. Low and fast.*

Determined not to give her away, equally determined to cover her advance, he held up his gun hand so the other could see it without having to shift his gaze. Slowly loosening his hold on his weapon, Barrett let it roll free in the palm of his hand until it hung uselessly from his index finger. Where the hell were Carden and Aiden?

"Makes no difference to me whether you give it or I take it, mister," the young man said. "Either way, I'm havin' it. How's up to you."

She was three-quarters of the way across the yard. Just another five meters or so to go. "If you're thinking it's the whole of Mignon's half of the map," he countered, buying her time, keeping the other's attention fixed on him, "I'm afraid that you're going to be terribly disappointed."

"I'm not paid to think. Give it to me."

One meter. Barrett heaved a sigh and slowly stretched out his arm.

The man leaned forward, meeting him halfway to snatch it from his fingertips. Stepping back he laughed and sneered. "And they say that rich men's brains is in their—" The remaining portion of the taunt snagged in his throat and his eyes widened as his face went moon white with fear.

"Wallets," Belle finished for him sweetly, calmly. Standing behind him, she added, "I'll have the paper from you now. Slowly and over the left shoulder, please."

To the credit of his good sense, the man obeyed the command. As he carefully passed the paper over to Belle, Barrett flicked his own gun back into his hand and stripped the hapless fellow of his.

"Thank you," Belle offered politely, tucking the paper into the pocket of her trousers. "And since you're in such an accommodating mood, I have a few questions for you," she went on as Barrett grinned in appreciation of her aplomb. "We'll start with the most central one. Who's paying you to retrieve Mignon's half of the map?"

The man looked at him expectantly. What he was hoping he might do, Barrett could only guess. But if he thought it likely that he'd take control of the situation from Belle, he was going to be disappointed yet again tonight. "I wouldn't frustrate a woman who has a gun poked in my back, son," he drawled. "Answer the lady's question and she'll let you trot away unharmed."

The report pounded through the silence accompanied by the high-pitched, fleeting whine of a bullet. Barrett's heart jolted and his body instinctively recoiled as the yard instantly became a ballroom, the crumpling body that of a blue-eyed woman.

And then it was gone, the past swept away by the brutal reality of the present. Belle stood in front of him, the body lying at her feet, her horrified gaze riveted on the rear yard of the house to her left. *Tracking the path,* part of his mind supplied even as another part screamed, *Second shot!*

He lunged for her, sweeping her gun hand outward and burying his shoulder into her midriff to drive her back and down as the report boomed and echoed, as the bullet whined and thudded into the sodden dirt beside them.

A passing notice was all he gave it. Rolling onto his

side and then his feet, always keeping himself squarely between the shootist and Belle, he yanked her up and spun her about, snarling, "Run!"

How she had the breath and strength to comply he didn't know, but she did. In a second she was gone, racing full tilt for the darkest of the shadows. Trusting her to her instincts, he whirled, dropped to his knee, and made quick work of clearing the dead man's pockets. Shoving the contents into his own, he too darted for the shadows, his senses keenly aware of every sound, every change in the world around him.

Curtains were drawn back in the surrounding houses, window sashes were flying up and voices crying out. The shrill peal of the constable's whistle pierced the din of Carden and Aiden's crashing arrival into the rear yard. At the broad sweep of his arm, they both turned and sprinted toward the alley. He followed in their wake, his strides long and hard, his heart racing and his mind staggering before the onslaught of delayed realizations.

Head shot. Clean and precise. The first shot to prevent betrayal, the second so they could take the map from Belle's pocket. Cold, ruthless evil.

Belle. Oh, Jesus. The shots had been so close. Never again. If he had to, he'd clap her in irons.

The pavers flew by under his feet, his path back to the town house a compromise between prudent and expeditious. He came into the yard from over the back fence just as Aiden bounded into it from the neighbor's and as Carden laced his fingers behind his head and gulped air by the back steps.

Barrett came to a sliding stop beside him, asking, "Have you seen—"

"She was going in just as I got here."

His knees practically gave out. Locking them, he lifted his chin and took a long, deliberate breath. The staccato rhythm of his heartbeat eased and the pounding torrent of his thoughts slowed. "Christ Almighty," he murmured, returning the gun to the small of his back with hands that were embarrassingly unsteady.

Aiden trotted up, breathing hard and quietly demanding, "What the hell happened?"

He'd turned his back when he shouldn't have. He'd made a mistake. And Belle had saved him from his own damn stupidity. Clearing his throat, swallowing down his regret and relief, Barrett replied, "He was in the shrubbery to the right of the back door. I didn't see him until I came down off the stairs and he stepped out. Belle came up from behind, had him properly cornered, and then someone took him with a shot to the head."

"It's going to be goddamn difficult," Carden growled, "to explain a second body on your property."

"It might not be entirely a bad thing," Aiden quickly countered. "Larson thinks he's in Paris. It's damn hard to shoot a man from that far away. He'll have to look for someone other than Barrett."

It was a possibility, but not one that he was willing to waste time considering in any great detail. Larson was a minor consideration in the grand scheme of things at the moment. He stared at the back door of the house, knowing that Belle had had time to think, to fully realize what had happened. She was alone with it, doubtlessly struggling with the horror of it.

Carden's hand on his shoulder brought his awareness back to the yard. "I caught sight of her a time or two as I was making my way back here," his friend offered gently. "She was running like the blazes, Bare. She can't be hurt."

He nodded, accepting the assertion in part, knowing that the injury wasn't to her body, but rather to her mind. He'd give her a few minutes alone to grapple with it and then do whatever he could to make her as whole as possible.

"Are you all right?"

Uncertain which of them had asked the question, he looked between them both and nodded. "It was a little close to déjà vu to be comfortable," he admitted. Marshaling his wits, he resolved to deal with the practical aspects of the disaster as efficiently as he could. "Did either of you see the shooter?"

"I saw the muzzle flash of the second shot," Carden replied. "It was over the fence on my side of the house and he pulled back the instant afterward. I didn't see anything more definite than that."

"There was nothing, no one on my side," Aiden contributed. "If he had an accomplice, he was sticking close."

Barrett reminded himself that they'd escaped the debacle physically unscathed, that the gratitude for that should far outweigh the disappointment at having gained nothing else from it. Except . . . Before things had gone to hell, he'd found tucked in the back door trim, one of the missing pieces. He'd glanced at it just long enough to see that it was another portion of meaningless lines, but perhaps Belle had found the other, the one with the text.

"You two had best be getting home," he suggested, giving them both something approximating a confident smile. "It wouldn't do for you to not be there if Larson should haul a niggling suspicion to your front doors."

They nodded and moved toward the gate with Aiden asking as they went, "Do you need anything?"

Just time alone with Belle. "No, but thanks for offering."

In the name of friendship, he remained where he was and watched them depart. But as the gate closed silently behind them, he turned to face the kitchen door. And confronted the reality that simply pulling Belle into his arms and holding her tight wasn't going to be sufficient. He had to say something, offer her some words of comfort and reassurance.

Women expected that sort of thing in the aftermath of a crisis. And he wasn't about to deny Belle whatever she needed or wanted from him. She'd earned it.

Giving himself time to think of something more meaningful than the usual, largely empty platitudes, he reached into the breast pocket of his jacket and extracted the silver case containing his cheroots. He was two hard pulls into the smoke when another realization stole over him: There weren't any words. And of all the women in the world, he'd had the uncommon good fortune to find the only one who understood that.

Chapter Fourteen

Isabella inhaled sharply and shuddered as the icy water sluiced down over her cheeks. So cold, so cutting. She quickly scooped two more handfuls from the freshly filled bucket and doused her face a second time. She shuddered again and drew a long, steadying breath. So mercifully distracting. A reason to tremble and shake that had nothing whatsoever to do with fear and haunting memories.

Gripping the edge of the cabinet in front of her, she clenched her teeth and let the cold knife deep. The urge to run still pounded through her veins and she locked her knees as she tried to bring the desperate instinct under control. She was safe. So was Barrett. John Aiden and Carden, too. Someone was dead, yes. But not anyone she knew or cared even marginally about. Disaster had been averted. There was no reason to tremble, to cry. She couldn't let Barrett walk into the kitchen and find her so agitated. She didn't want him to know how scared she was, just how right his misgivings had been.

Not that he didn't already know that she'd been a detriment to the mission. Barrett had had to think—and act—for her. If he hadn't been there . . . She owed him her life. How she was ever going to repay the debt . . . Throwing herself into his arms wasn't toward that end. But it was what she wanted to do with every fiber of her quaking body and battered soul. God, she wanted the warmth of his arms around her so badly, wanted to feel the low rumble of his voice against her cheek. And she wanted with all her heart to hear him say that he didn't think any less of her for her having failed. She didn't deserve his acceptance, but that had nothing to do with the need for it. Tears welled in her eyes again.

The back door opened as they spilled, scalding hot, over her cheeks. She did the only thing she could think of to save herself complete embarrassment; she scooped up more of the icy water and flung it onto her face. The tears were obliterated in an instant, in a gasp and another shudder. Her eyes closed, she felt about and found the cotton dish towel. She expelled a hard breath into it and then squared her shoulders and opened her eyes, prepared to pay the piper.

He was leaning back against the cabinet, his arms crossed and a glowing cheroot clamped between his teeth. His gaze gently searched hers, and unable to bear the scrutiny, she looked away.

"Would you like to talk about what happened?"

The gentleness of his voice tripped her heart and melted some of the starch out of her backbone. "Not particularly," she admitted, carefully folding the towel and laying it aside. "But thank you for offering."

"It might help."

More likely it would make her cry. "It never has before," she replied, trying to sound unaffected. "I can't imagine it making a difference this time."

After a moment's hesitation, he nodded and then eased himself fully upright. She watched as he stripped off his jacket, tossed it aside, and then stepped around her to the pump. Recognizing his intent, she moved—just far enough to be out of his way while staying close enough that she could still feel the comforting heat of his body. The tip of the cheroot glowed bright as he drew on it and then handed it to her for temporary safekeeping.

It had been years. Considering how deep her failures had already gone that night, one more wouldn't matter. As Barrett splashed water over his face, she took a light pull on the tightly twisted tobacco. The heat was marvelous and instantly settling, the taste sweet and invigorating. And blowing the stream of smoke out into the darkness gave her a powerful, intensely gratifying sense of control. She took another pull, a harder one this time, savoring the sensations and feeling her world slowly sliding back to rights.

She was making another smoke stream when Barrett finished drying his face. At the edge of her vision she saw his brow shoot up. And one corner of his mouth.

"Don't you dare say a word," she challenged, turning the cheroot in her hand to flick the ash away.

Tossing the dish towel aside, his smile broadened. "A man who buggered the bishop's wife isn't in any position to criticize anyone for anything. Would you like one of your own?"

Shaking her head, she handed it back to him. "A little makes me strong. A whole one will make me wish I could die."

If he noticed her wince, he was kind enough not to mention it as he settled back against the cabinets beside her. Examining the fire on the cheroot, he quietly asked, "Are you sore? I hit you harder than I intended."

Isabella smiled, knowing that the ache in her chest had far more to do with standing beside him now than it did the shoulder he'd put into it earlier. "I'm probably a bit bruised," she allowed. "But I'll be all right." She took a deep breath and went on. "Thank you for taking me down.

I was too stunned to think of getting out of the way. Even as the little voice in the back of my head was telling me there'd be a second shot."

"It's been some time since you had to use those skills," he offered with far more diplomacy and kindness than the situation warranted. "You're out of practice. They'll come back to you in time."

"If I live long enough to rehone them," she countered drolly.

"For a second, I thought that chance had been snuffed out."

The softness of his words didn't blunt their impact. She started in horrible realization. Swallowing back a wave of tears, she turned to face him. "Oh, Barrett," she choked out. "I've been so wrapped up in my own memories of it that it never occurred to me how that must have looked to you. I'm so sorry."

His smile was patient. Accepting. "You're entitled."

No she wasn't. Not in the least. "Do you want to talk about it?"

"Not particularly." He looked over his shoulder, tossed the cheroot into the water bucket, and then brought his gaze to hers. "What I'd like to do is forget that the whole thing happened."

"How can I help you do that?"

He tilted his head to the side, openly considering her. She waited, her heart racing, willing to make amends in any way she could. Slowly, he reached up, took the brim of her hat in hand and eased it off her head. Her breath caught and her hair tumbled in free riot as he dropped the cap on the floor behind her.

Gently threading his fingers through the curls and drawing her toward him, he whispered, "Kiss me, Belle."

She stepped into him, knowing where it would take them, where they would end, knowing that she didn't deserve the wonder of him and accepting that she was too selfish to put honor before the promise of pleasure. Not tonight.

Twining her arms around his neck, she couldn't say whether she drew his lips down to hers or she offered hers up to him. And it didn't matter. The fire was instant and fierce, turning her core molten and reason to ash. She stretched up and pressed against the length of him, her body pulsing with an urgent need to be closer.

His fingers tightening in her hair, his desire hard against the pillow of her stomach, he deepened their kiss, possessing her mouth with a rapaciousness so slow, so deliberate that her breath caught and her entire body trembled in delight. He smiled, his joy rippling through her, as he kissed her deeper still and melted her bones. Releasing his hold on her hair, he slipped his arms around her just as her knees began to buckle.

His tender assault never faltered as he lifted her up and turned to deposit her on the edge of the makeshift cabinet top. Using his hip, he moved her legs apart, then drew her closer to settle himself in the space between her thighs. She gasped at the bold prelude of what was to come, whimpered at the barrier of their clothing and the reminder of what had to be discarded before the promise could be fulfilled.

As though driven by the same need, his hands slipped up between them and feverishly worked at the buttons of her shirt. Struggling for patience, she fumbled to open his, desperately craving the feel of heated skin against heated skin.

Fabric tore. A button rolled off somewhere into the darkness. His or hers, she didn't know, didn't care. Cold air on feverish skin sent a sharp shudder through her. The friction of crisp hair and hardened planes of muscle against her palms sent another, deeper, wider, and deliciously grounding. And then it was gone, obliterated in a brilliant bolt of sensation that arrowed, hot and piercing, from her nipples to her already molten core.

Barrett tore his lips from hers. Gasping for air, ignoring her cry of frustration, he took a step back, half turned, and caught her calf in his hands. She groaned in wordless assent and leaned back, bracing herself to ease his removal of her boots. The brazen thrust of her bare breasts nearly destroyed his sense of purpose. The boots landed in quick succession somewhere on the floor. He turned square to her and pressed his hands against her shoulders, holding her back, keeping her breasts offered up for his feasting.

Beautiful, full, and ripe. Begging to be tasted, to be savored. He leaned forward and touched the tip of his tongue to the underside curve. She gasped and arched up, pressing her hips hard against his own and sending a jolt of pure fire through his veins. He licked upward, deliberate and quick, to the hard bud of her nipple. Whispering his name, she arched higher, closer. He couldn't have resisted the offering even if he'd wanted to. Taking her into his mouth, he suckled her, teased her with his teeth and tongue. She moaned and rocked beneath him, straining against his hands, his hips, and fueling the blaze of his desire.

Belle gasped as his hands skimmed down off her shoulders, over already tantalized skin. God, what he was doing to her . . . Far more exquisite sensation than she could bear, so much less than she needed. She couldn't endure much longer; she had to move, had to climb. Something. It was there, drawing her up, daring her to reach and soar. Delight, exquisitely breathtaking, shot from her breasts to the center of her womb.

His fingers skimmed lower, over the sensitive expanse of her midriff and lower still, trailing luscious fire all the way to the swell of her belly and the waistband of her trousers. The buttons separated at his touch and she held her breath as he bent his head and laid feathering kisses along the still burning path his fingers had forged. Consumed with need, intoxicated by the promise, she arched up against his lips, against his hands, and begged him for deliverance.

Her plea penetrated the heat of his wanting and jolted his conscience. *Not here. Not like this. Not like Mignon.* He didn't want Belle looking back and comparing, thinking . . . He straightened abruptly and just as quickly swept her up into his arms.

"No," she protested, clinging to him as he carried her out of the kitchen and down the hall. "It's too far, Barrett."

It was only a matter of meters, of stairs, and a short bit of hall. It was just far enough to let his blood cool a necessary degree or two. There was a difference between making love and ravaging and he wanted her to remember him for knowing that and caring enough to take the time.

At the base of the stairs, she burrowed her cheek into the curve of his shoulder and nipped lightly at his neck. "Please don't make me wait."

"You deserve silk," he replied through clenched teeth, starting up. "And making love on stairs is a bitch."

She nipped him again, growled, "I don't care," and then arched her back, thrusting her breasts upward as she boldly trailed her tongue over his earlobe.

His blood sang and his breath caught. "But I do," he reminded himself, tightening his hold on her and quickening his pace.

Catching his lobe gently between her teeth, she whispered, "I hate you."

"No you don't," he countered, reaching the second floor and striding toward their room and the silk sheets he'd promised her. "What you hate is having to wait for your pleasure."

Easing back into the cradle of his arms, she looked up at him. "I don't want to lose it," she said, her eyes dark with a desperate honesty. "Barrett, please. I've never wanted like this. Don't deny me."

"As though I could," he admitted, dropping to his knees on the edge of her bed. She didn't give him a chance to lay her down; she rolled out of his arms, onto her back, and arched up, her hands pushing her trousers down over her hips.

And shattering his noble intentions. He leaned forward, neatly swept her feet up, grabbed her pant legs, pulled them off her and flung them away. Even as he did, she sat up and reached for him. His breath caught high and painfully hard as she deftly unbuttoned his trousers. He stopped breathing altogether when she slipped her hands around his shaft and freed it.

"Please, Barrett. Don't make me wait."

He couldn't. The friction was too exquisite, the promise too inviting. He shoved the fabric of his pants aside, took her wrists in his hands and forced her back, pinning her arms into the sheets over her head. She wiggled beneath him, drawing him into the cradle of her thighs. Damp curls brushed hardened heat and he sucked in a ragged breath as his body shuddered and he strained to savor the sharp edge of delight.

She arched up, moving her hips to deliberately caress the full length of him and strip restraint from his grasp. Locking his gaze with Belle's in silent warning, he mated them in a single sure stroke. Conscious thought reeled beneath the wave of breathtaking sensation. For a heartbeat he froze, struggling to salvage control, trying to bear up to the wonder of their fit, the heat of her welcome, the urgency of his need. And then Belle moaned his name and shifted her hips to deepen their union. Undone, he closed his eyes and surrendered to primal instinct.

Arching, meeting his thrusts, Belle strained to ride the swiftly building crest. It was heaven. And it was hell. A wave of pleasure higher and deeper than she could embrace and fully know. She gasped in awe, wanting to possess it forever, and then gasped again as it was swept away by another even more intense, more demanding, more unfathomable. Even more unkeepable. Soaring higher than she'd ever been before, she desperately strained to reach higher still. She was going to die when she reached the top, die a thousand deaths if she didn't.

The pleasure rolled through her ever faster, ever harder and deeper until it was all that there was. The spark ignited in her core in a single second, narrowing her reality to its breathtaking promise, to its exquisitely slow explosion. Pleasure, pure and brilliant, rolled outward from her center—to her breasts, to her thighs, to her toes and out the top of her head—and flung her, quaking and gasping, into the tumbling stars.

She drifted down too soon, too weak, too gloriously satisfied to struggle against it.

"Belle."

A lush whisper against her lips that sweetly caressed her soul. His kiss was gentle and she sighed, her contentment complete. His own sigh mingled with hers and he drew slowly back to release her wrists and collect her into his arms.

When he rolled onto his side and drew her with him, she smiled. It had been as she'd always known it would be; fierce and wild and perfectly right. They were well suited, their needs and their sense of time, one. Even now his breathing was every bit as labored as hers, his body just as relaxed and spent, his satisfaction seemingly every bit as deep.

"Barrett?"

He made a low humming sound and gathered her closer. "I wish," he whispered, slowly feathering kisses along her brow, "I could have made that go on longer."

"I'd have cried if you had," she confessed, running her fingers through the sprinkle of coarse hairs on his chest. "Thank you for having mercy on me." She smiled and added, "Finally."

His laughter was quiet, but Isabella felt it all the way to her soul. "Do you think," he drawled, "that you might have the strength to do it again? Perhaps, between us, we might try to go slowly enough next time to actually savor it a bit."

"I'm more than willing whenever you're ready. As for the going slowly . . ." She gave him the truth. "I'm not sure I'm capable of restraint. Not where you're concerned."

"So you don't really hate me?"

Never. "I was being petulant. Most unpleasantly so."

Catching her chin between his thumb and finger, he tilted her face up until her gaze met his. His grin was wicked. "Don't ever apologize for wanting, angel."

"I wasn't going to go quite that far."

He laughed again and gave her a quick kiss before easing his arm out from under her head and sitting up. Lying curled on her side, she watched him tug off a boot and throw it aside. The second was halfway off when he froze and muttered darkly, "Damn."

She arched a brow. "What is it?"

His shoulders rose as he took a deep breath. "I didn't think of putting on a sheath. It never crossed my mind."

Ever the responsible gentleman. Grinning, she sat up, pleased by the fact that he'd been too involved to think of protection, to make a list of chores to be attended. "Don't feel guilty," she offered. "It didn't occur to me, either."

"Belle, this is serious," he admonished, yanking off the boot. It sailed across the room as he growled, "Christ. I never forget. *Never.*"

"It's another bridge," she observed, watching as he stripped away his shirt and flung it after his boots. "And a most unlikely one. Henri and I tried for several years and I never conceived. The doctor said that it probably wasn't possible for me to ever have children."

She stretched out her legs and wiggled her toes as he lay back, divested himself of his trousers, and asked, "What if the doctor's wrong?"

"The midwife told me the same thing. And they always know more than the doctors do."

For a long moment he frowned up at the ceiling and then he rolled onto his side, saying, "I don't suppose that it ever—" Whatever else he'd been about to say was abandoned as he reached out and gently traced the dark line that curved over the top of her calf. "I know a bullet scar when I see one."

Isabella grinned, glad that he'd found something else to occupy his mind. "That one hurt. And it took forever to heal."

His gaze snapped up to hers. "*That* one?" he repeated, his brow cocked. "There are others?"

Nodding, she unbuttoned the cuffs of her shirt. Baring first her right arm, she turned so that he could see the scar that ran diagonally across the top of her shoulder. "This one eliminated the possibility of ever wearing another fashionable ball gown."

He was trying to swallow when she freed her left arm and dropped the shirt beside the bed. "This is from a piece of debris," she explained, tracing the line that ran down the inside from her elbow to midway above her wrist. "I wasn't quite far enough away when the charge went off. It means I always wear long sleeves. This one," she said, half rolling onto her side to show him the uppermost curve of her backside, "was, as you can tell, just a graze."

His fingers slowly skimmed over the wide scar. "You didn't have this one stitched up."

"I wasn't about to drop my trousers," she supplied, her blood warming again, her pulse quickening. "Even for a doctor. It would have been entirely too humiliating."

"You dropped them for me."

Actually, she'd all but torn them off for him. Most decidedly a first for her. But then, with Barrett everything was different than it had ever been. She'd certainly never let any other man unbutton her—

"Trousers!" she exclaimed, remembering the contents of the pockets and flopping onto her stomach to reach past the bedding and retrieve them. She had a pant leg in hand when the pleasure came, lusciously slow and intensely compelling. "Oh, sweet Mother of Pearl," she moaned as he laid another lingering kiss on the inside of her thigh.

"You're not going to be needing them anytime soon, sweet angel."

No, she wouldn't. She didn't need anything other than Barrett Stanbridge.

As soon as he could feel anything beyond satisfaction, it was likely going to be acute embarrassment. Apparently, neither one of them was particularly good at exercising restraint. With what energy he had left, Barrett smiled. They'd simply have to keep working toward that end. Practice, after all, did eventually make perfect. And exceedingly, delightfully, wondrously satisfied along the way.

Belle slipped down to lie against his side and drape her arm around his neck.

"Was that a sigh of contentment?" he asked, settling her head into the crook of his shoulder, her body into the circle of his arms.

"I have never in my life been this bone-deep satisfied." She sighed again and languidly drew her leg over his. "I am so glad Mignon picked you out of the crowd."

Mignon. Barrett stared up at the ceiling, remembering. There had been a satisfaction with her. But it wasn't at all like the kind he felt now. With her it had been a sense of accomplishment, a knowing that he'd given a grand physical performance and acquitted himself well as an experienced lover. His body and his mind had been equally exhausted from the strain of it. And it had been nothing more than that.

But with Belle . . . God, he had no idea what he'd done in any specific, technical sense; sensation and desire had overloaded the conscious portion of his brain. Both times. But he was most definitely satisfied. Yes, bone deep. And well beyond. Satisfaction thrummed through every fiber of his body and resonated softly in the very center of his soul.

It had ended badly with Mignon. His neck could end up in a noose for the shallow pleasure of that night. But he was glad she'd picked him out of the crowd, too. If she hadn't, he'd have never met Belle. He'd have never known that making love with a woman could feel this blissfully good. And it was nice to know that at thirty-one there were still some delightful discoveries to be made in life. It made waking up in the morning something to look forward to.

Waking up was especially nice with Belle beside him. He gathered her closer and lightly pressed a kiss to the top of her head. He hoped they didn't find Lafitte's treasure too soon. Not until the wonder had faded away and he was ready to let her go. He smiled, closed his eyes, and let himself drift off into sated slumber.

He didn't know how long he'd dozed, but he knew Belle was sliding out of his arms. His sweet, impetuous, persistent Belle. He let her go. "Are you going after those trousers again?" he asked, already knowing the answer. And that she'd come back to him.

"I have something to show you."

Opening his eyes, he found her sprawled out and dragging

her trousers back toward the bed. The effort gave him the most splendid view of her backside. "I like it."

"Not that," she laughingly admonished, flopping back to lie against him again, her hand rammed deep in the pocket of her rumpled pants. "This," she declared, dropping the trousers and holding up a strip of paper.

It wasn't the piece he'd found. This one had the lines of missing text.

" 'Lies to Cross, Park and Hyde,' " she said softly as she held it for them both to read. " 'Lion's Paw and Gentle Bride. Setting sun on Castle's Rise, fifteen paces to the prize.' "

His heart hammered wildly, his mind raced. They had the instructions. The hunt for the treasure could be over before daybreak. And Belle could be gone before breakfast.

Or perhaps not, the rational part of his brain quickly countered. The treasure hunt might involve a trail of clues. It could take days or weeks to follow it along to the end. And then there was the matter of discovering who had killed Mignon. That part of the puzzle wasn't going to be solved before breakfast. Not the next one, anyway.

She rolled half atop him, cradling her chin on her hands and smiling up at him. "I'm not really all that tired."

"I'm offended," he teased, slipping his arms around her, feeling more in control, understanding her excitement, her unwillingness to wait. Given all they had to accomplish, he could afford to be indulgent.

"I'll make amends when we come back."

Oh, such a thinly veiled offer. Such a delightful game to play. And as long as he was indulging *her* . . . "And you're absolutely convinced that it's the directions for making your way through a cemetery?" She gave him a look that said she preferred not to think of him as an idiot. He moved smoothly to the next gambit. "The sun's not setting."

"We'll squint and imagine it."

"What about your half of the map?" he posed. "It's in a bank vault."

She arched a brow and her eyes sparkled. "And you think I can't draw it from memory?"

"It's cold and damp," he countered next. "It would be a miserable hour to go out and about."

"It's always cold and damp in England. Where you are, what you're doing, and the hour of the day don't make the least bit of difference."

It wasn't *always* cold and damp, but he suspected that she'd have to personally experience a beautiful day to believe it; his word wasn't going to suffice on the subject. And the English weather wasn't worth debating at that particular moment, anyway. He had another topic altogether in mind. "You're not going to be put off, are you?"

"You know me so well."

Not really, but he was making quick progress on the front. "How well do you know me?"

"Well enough that I know you're being obstinate just for the sake of being obstinate." A mischievous edge came to her smile and she added, "And to exchange your compliance for promises of later favors."

She did know him; not that he'd been making any effort whatsoever to hide his objective. Lord, playing the game with her was fun. "What kind of favors are you willing to grant?"

Devilment sparkled in her eyes and in her smile. "Apple dumplings for dessert?"

He took a moment to pretend to give the offer a bit of consideration and then shook his head. "I'm afraid that's not quite the kind of reward I have in mind."

The amused light in her eyes was replaced by a slow, sultry heat that jolted his heart and caught his breath. "Whatever you want," she said softly, knowingly. "Name your pleasures and they're yours."

If her intent had been to rattle his sense of self-control, she'd succeeded beyond his wildest imagination. "That's quite a bit of leeway, angel."

"I'm very much aware of that."

Jesus. He'd had no idea she could be so damn deliberately seductive. "What if they're dark ones?"

"I'll take the chance."

She would; there wasn't a doubt in his mind. And she wouldn't flinch, wouldn't retreat regardless of what he asked of her.

"Can we go, Barrett? Now?"

If they didn't, odds were it would be a fortnight before he'd had enough of her to even think about climbing out of her bed. He nodded and closed his eyes as she laughingly rolled out of his arms and onto her feet.

God, she was the most incredible woman he'd ever known. She'd dance along the razor's edge with him, tumble over with him if that's where he wanted to take them. She'd give him whatever his heart desired and never once weigh the risks, never once think past the moment to what price she might have to pay or to what expensive gifts might come out of his gratitude.

No, Belle didn't think about such things. Ever. They didn't matter to her. She'd endured the hell of war, emerging from it physically scarred and with a remarkably simple approach to living. Belle lived to *live*. Each and every moment. Fully. Wondrously. Without apology or regret.

The kind of strength and courage it took to do that . . . His chest tightened and in that instant a truth swelled to fill his soul. Her happiness had brightened his world and her spirit made his own soar. He needed her—and had for long years before she'd walked so boldly into his life.

Christ on a crutch. How had it happened? When? He swore silently and reminded himself that how he'd gotten to this point wasn't nearly as important as deciding what the hell he was going to do about it.

"Are you planning to go naked? Not that I'd mind, you understand."

He opened his eyes to find her standing beside the bed already half-dressed, her hair a wild tangle of untamed curls, her smile wide, and her eyes bright with the anticipation of adventure. The wonder of her wasn't going to ebb away, he realized, his heart thundering. Not tomorrow. Not next month, not next year. He could think all he liked and until hell froze over, but the effort wasn't going to change anything. He loved her.

She tilted her head to the side, her smile fading by slow degrees as she searched his eyes. "Is something wrong, Barrett?"

"Not at all," he replied, managing a smile as he rolled off the bed. *If you love me. But if you don't* . . . Gathering up his clothes, he decided that it was pointless to spend any time worrying about it. She either loved him or she didn't. Once they'd found Lafitte's treasure, he'd offer her a bridge and give her a clear choice between crossing it with him or blowing it to bits. God Almighty, he didn't want to hope. But he did.

Chapter Fifteen

Sitting cross-legged on the rug, the portable writing desk balanced on her lap, Isabella drew her half of the map from memory and then copied the scraps of Mignon's half. When it was completed, she corked the ink bottle, laid aside the pen, and considered the design. "It almost looks like one of those knots the Irish make," she ventured, squinting. "If you took the four corner lines and pulled them tight."

"It looks to me," Barrett contributed, emptying the contents of his pockets on the bedside table, "like the web of a drunken spider."

She could see that, as well. Carefully folding the map in quarters, she handed it up to him and then set aside the desk and let him pull her to her feet. As he did, her gaze fell on the items he'd discarded. "Where did you get this?" she asked, plucking a bit of green and white waxed paper from the pile of odds and ends.

"Out of the dead man's pockets. Why?"

"It's the same kind of wrapper that was around the chocolates I found in Mignon's trunk." She turned it over in her hands, examining it. "This isn't creased in the same way, though."

He took it from her and sniffed it. "Peppermint," he declared, handing it back.

"Could we hope that it's a wrapper used by a little-known candy maker?"

"Sorry," he replied, sounding genuinely regretful for having to dash her fledgling optimism. "It's from Nickel's on St. James. And they sell thousands of kilos of sweets a year. The fact that Mignon and our dead man both had candy from them isn't likely to be the least bit important. If there's anything even mildly significant about it all, it's that Nickel's is expensive and not the kind of place the common man can afford to lay down his coins. That tells us that our dead man was being paid handsomely for his work."

And he'd paid dearly for the chance to buy a few peppermints. Frowning, Belle turned the paper over in her hands again. "I know I've asked the question before, but I can't stop wondering. Why would Mignon buy chocolate when she couldn't eat it?"

"I've been known to buy chocolates from time to time and not eat them."

Not eat them? She looked up to meet his gaze. "Good God, why?"

His smile was softly, deliciously roguish. "Nothing persuades or cajoles quite like fine chocolate."

"You're shameless."

"I'm good, too," he admitted with a wink. His smile faded, the end of it marked by a shrug. "Mignon might have bought them intending to give them to someone, but was killed before she could."

"It's far more likely that someone gave her the chocolates." The angle of his brow said that he needed an explanation and so she added, "Not to disparage the dead, but it's a well-known fact that Mignon firmly believed that it was far more blessed to receive than to give."

"Then it had to have been someone who didn't know her very well."

"Or someone who did," Belle countered, "and was hoping she'd give in to temptation and then break out in hives."

"There's a third possibility, you know. Our dead man might have dropped them while searching Mignon's trunk."

Yes, she had to admit, he very well could have. And if he had, she was truly wasting time and effort in trying to see a clue where none existed. "That's not a very interesting possibility," she grumbled, tossing the wrapper down on the tabletop.

"Sometimes they're not," he replied, sounding both rueful and amused. "In fact, most of the time detective work is damn boring."

"Then why," she asked, bending down to scoop her revolver from among the pillows, "do you do it?"

"It allows me to behave badly every now and then."

"Badly in what respect?" she pressed, tucking the gun into the waistband of her trousers at the small of her back.

"In the name of professional conduct," he supplied over his shoulder as he headed toward the door, "I get to visit the seamier haunts of London. Once or twice a year, on average, I get to threaten someone with violence."

Isabella quickly followed as he continued, "And then there are the parties my parents insist that I attend. You can't imagine how many secrets people don't really have and how they pale when they see me come through the door."

She'd never considered the social consequences—as obvious as they were—of his occupation. It was some consolation to realize that apparently his parents hadn't, either. If they had, they certainly wouldn't have put their fellow guests in such awkward positions. "And you enjoy having that power over people?" she asked as they made their way down the squeaking, groaning stairs.

"Of course," he admitted blithely, grabbing the newel post at the bottom and swinging off the stairs. "My father uses money as a means of maintaining social position. But money comes and it goes. Secrets, on the other hand, can be leveraged forever."

Isabella froze on the bottom step, her heart skittering and her throat tight. "You'd engage in blackmail?"

"Never," he solemnly replied, looking up at her. "But they don't know that. And I deliberately let them wonder. Out of their uncertainty comes a bit of fear and a sufficient amount of respect to make up for the slights of childhood." Giving her a quirked grin, he shrugged. "One really should have the maturity to set aside and forgive the taunts, but, quite frankly, I don't want to. It's petty and I know it and I don't care."

And she adored his honesty. "Why did they slight you?" she asked, coming down off the stairs.

Leading the way down the hall and toward the kitchen, he answered, "My father didn't inherit influence and power. He earned it through service to the crown. Financial service. Earned money and earned power are considered tainted by those born into both. And those not born into them consider the achievement the worst sort of class betrayal. You can't win for winning."

Always the child apart by circumstance. And the man apart by deliberate choice. She understood completely. Just as she realized how comforting it was to know that the experiences and choices weren't unique ones. "When I was younger," she began, "we had planters and merchants. The planters were something akin to your titled class, I suppose.

"My father was a merchant tradesman. He built, renovated, bought, and sold buildings. Homes, warehouses, factories—those sorts of things. Since he worked with his hands, I wasn't considered good enough to associate with the planters' daughters and I didn't mesh well with the daughters of the other tradesmen and merchants."

"Why?" he asked, stepping up to the stove and testing the heat of the pan of coffee they'd fixed earlier in the evening.

"Even as a little girl," Isabella supplied as he filled their mugs with the steaming brew, "I thought dolls were a ridiculous waste of time. And when I got older, I didn't care one whit what the ladies were wearing in London and Paris. I found more pleasure in gardening myself than in supervising the slaves—which we didn't have, anyway—and I didn't enjoy needlework the least little bit. Given that the other girls didn't care about construction, demolition, hunting, fishing, or riding, there simply wasn't anything for us to talk about."

"What about Henri? To which group did he belong?"

She lifted her mug and took a cautious sip. It was scalding hot and strong enough to peel paint. Wincing, she explained, "His family owned three sawmills. Not that Henri ever saw any part of them beyond the money they made. His older brothers were running the business by the time Henri and I were marched up the aisle. They didn't approve of me."

Propping his hip against the edge of the cabinets, he stared down into his mug and asked, "For any particular reason? Or was it simply on general principle?"

How interesting, she mused, taking another sip of the coffee, that in all the years since she'd married, this was the first time anyone had ever thought to ask her how she'd been treated by her husband's family. "I didn't stand in awe of their money," she answered honestly. "That and I refused to pretend that having acquired the Dandaneau name was the most wonderful thing that had ever happened to me.

Our relationship was always strained, and when Henri went off to serve in the army, they gave me a hundred dollars and wished me all the best."

"Did you take it?"

The gentleness of his inquiry warmed her in the strangest, nicest way. Marveling at the unexpected absence of pain in remembering, she nodded. "Not happily, mind you, but becoming an emaciated corpse lacks even more dignity than accepting charity."

"It had to have hurt, though."

"It did. But life has a way of coming to a balance," she announced, smiling and lifting her mug in salute. "The Dandaneaus refused to disable their mills when New Orleans fell to Farragut and, rather than let them produce lumber for the Union, the Resistance marked them for demolition."

"Did you personally light the fuses?" Before she could answer, he laughed and added, "Never mind. I already know. Did they ever find out?"

"I have no idea. They left New Orleans within days of the blasts."

"Where did they go?"

"I have no idea about that, either," she admitted, grinning as he took a sip of his coffee and grimaced. "Rumor said they were intending to make their way to England somehow."

He started, then tilted his head to the side and drawled, "And you didn't feel it necessary to mention them when we were compiling our list of suspects?"

"Well, firstly," she countered, "you have to understand that everyone who ever leaves New Orleans is supposedly on their way to London. Secondly, the only piracy ever committed by the Dandaneaus was in pricing their lumber. And while they might hate me for any number of reasons—most notably for blowing their mills to kingdom come—they were well and long gone before the news of inheriting Lafitte's treasure arrived. They wouldn't know about it, wouldn't know why Mignon was in London, or that I'd followed her. And I can't imagine that Mignon would have felt threatened enough at the sight of one of them to think it necessary to hide her half of the map.

"And, in addition to all of that," she went on, setting her coffee aside, "there's nothing to suggest that they actually made it to England. For all we know they could be in Baton Rouge or any one of a dozen Southern cities. Placing any of the Dandaneaus on our suspect list would be stretching plausibility beyond reason."

"You never give people the benefit of the doubt, Belle. Not when it comes to the pursuit of wealth or power."

"Or vengeance," she added, scooping her hat up off the floor. "But, in this case, the Dandaneaus simply can't be considered a real threat. The string of coincidences would have to be entirely too long."

"Are you ready to go?"

He wasn't quite willing to believe her; she could hear the reservation in his voice. Resigned to the fact that there was nothing more she could say that would convince him to abandon his suspicions, she clapped the hat on her head and replied, "I will be once I get my hair tucked up and put on my jacket."

He watched her for a few moments, then set aside his cup and came squarely onto his feet. Trailing his fingertips along the curve of her jaw, he looked down into her eyes and softly said, "Promise me something."

Anything. Everything. She slipped her hands to his waist, steadying herself as she savored the luscious warmth his touch sent rippling through her. "What?"

"After tonight, you'll save the trousers for the rarest of occasions. Getting past them takes just too damn much time and work."

She reminded herself that it was silly to be so thrilled by the admission of his desire, but her happiness couldn't be squelched by the admonishment. "I think I can be accommodating," she admitted, stretching up to brush a kiss over his lips. "Would you prefer I wear a dress or nothing at all?"

Swallowing a growl, he drew her into his arms and close against the length of his body. "How badly do you want to go treasure hunting tonight?"

Oh, Lord, he was so tempting. Why he ever felt the need to resort to offering chocolates . . . The more practical and rational part of her whispered that pleasure should be like dessert—a reward for having dutifully fulfilled the requirements of good sense. There was a treasure to be found, a murder to be solved. Once they were, once Barrett's name was cleared, they would have forever and a day to—

Her heart skittered and her mind chattered frantically. There was no forever with Barrett. She knew it. He knew it, too. All they had together was the time it took to accomplish their various, mutual goals. Beyond that . . . His parents wanted him to marry advantageously. She didn't want to marry again and didn't have the temperament to be a mistress. England was cold and damp and dreary. It wasn't home. And it was utterly ridiculous to feel like crying about it all.

She managed a smile that she hoped passed for composed as she stepped out of his loose embrace, saying, "Business should, I think, come before pleasure."

Maybe it was the flicker of disappointment that passed over his features. Or maybe it was the chill that washed over her body as she stood apart from him. In either case, she suddenly wanted—with all her heart—to step back into his arms and let the rest of the world career on without them. Practicality battled with desire. And barely won.

"But, if it's all right with you," she said, smiling up at him, "let's not spend one more moment at it than we have to."

His smile was bright. "An acceptable compromise. One I can live with for the next hour or so."

Yes, an hour or so, Belle thought, retrieving her jacket from the cabinet by the water pump. Just long enough to satisfy her conscience and the requirements of obligation and not so long that an awkwardness and hesitation could creep between them. Although, she had to admit, glancing around the kitchen before leaving, making love with Barrett wasn't at all like it had been with Henri. There had been no division of her mind with Barrett as there had always been with her husband. And the pleasure that came of that . . . Smiling, she went out the door, knowing deep in her bones that for as long as she lived there would never be a moment of awkwardness or even so much as a second's hesitation when it came to tumbling into bed with Barrett Stanbridge. She was absolutely shameless. And utterly, thoroughly happy.

Barrett watched appreciatively as she flipped herself over the top of the iron gate and dropped neatly to her feet beside him inside the cemetery. How long had it been, he wondered, since he'd had a partner like her? There had been a time, in the army, when Carden had gone along on the forays. But those had involved a great deal of drinking and no small amount of skirt chasing. And then they'd returned to London and their hunts had become more sophisticated and civilized. Not to mention largely boring. He and John Aiden had worked as partners, but it had been brief; just a single expedition that Aiden had led.

But neither Carden nor Aiden was remotely like Belle, Barrett mused as he handed her the map she'd drawn earlier. And the difference was far more than could be accounted for by a consideration of luscious breasts and delightful curves. He grinned. Not that those were unimportant attributes.

No, working with Belle was satisfying in a way that went beyond mere companionship and a shared quest. There was something deeply right about wandering dark streets with her, about climbing locked gates and poking around a graveyard with her at his side. It was certainly the most unconventional activity he'd ever undertaken with a woman and yet it didn't seem the least bit odd. In fact, if someone were to push him into explaining the feeling, he'd have to admit that it felt as though they were meant to work together, that he'd simply been biding his time, waiting for her to come into his life and step to his side.

"So where do we start?" he asked, watching her glance between the map and the field of gravestones sprawling out before them. "Any ideas beyond wandering about and hoping to stumble across someone named Lies?"

"There has to be some reason why all the lines were included. I keep trying to see if there's any resemblance between them and the paths."

"And?"

"I don't," she admitted, refolding the map and tucking it into her coat pocket. "Which way do you want to wander first?"

"People tend to favor their right."

She nodded and moved out of the shadows and into the moonlight to make her way along the path on their right. They were some twenty feet into the maze when she sighed and observed, "Judging by the dates I'm seeing on the stones, this is a very old cemetery. The odds of Lafitte tossing the treasure into an open grave aren't all that good."

"Frankly, I'm more than a little relieved. I wasn't looking forward to digging up some poor soul. I'm already accused of murder. Adding grave robbing to my crimes would send my mother into apoplexy."

"You'd think that, over the years, she'd have become accustomed to your dangerous behaviors."

He shrugged. "Mother lives in a world of illusions. Deep in her heart—and despite all the hard-edged realities—she still hopes that I'll marry a title."

"It would be a way of making up for the social disdain she's endured over the years."

Barrett started and frowned. He'd never considered the fact that his parents might have endured the same sorts of personal slights he had. Which didn't, he realized, reflect very well on his sense of empathy or compassion. But now that Belle had presented the truth, he could easily understand why his parents were so intent on his marrying well. He could also see that while Isabella Dandaneau was the perfect woman for him, she wasn't at all the daughter-in-law his parents were envisioning. An American. An impoverished widow. A woman with a decidedly strange upbringing, who delighted in turning structures into smoldering rubble.

Christ, it was going to be unpleasant. At first. But once there were grandchildren, they'd—

"Barrett, look. George Lies."

Pulling his mind to the present, he focused his gaze on the headstone in front of them. He glanced to the right. "And Robert Lies," he pointed out. He looked to the left. "And William Lies and Herbert Lies."

"You're being a pessimist," she blithely accused, turning a slow circle.

Actually just the opposite, he countered in silence, shoving his hands in his pockets. He'd been thinking of the more distant aspects of the future and figuring out how to navigate through the difficulties—without having given any thought to just how he was going to get to the point of having the problems to solve. He'd assumed that Belle loved him. He'd assumed that marrying her was the course he wanted to pursue. And somehow he'd simply set aside her repeated declarations otherwise and presumed that she would happily marry him if and when he asked her to.

"Cross."

He blinked and forced himself to take a settling breath. Belle was striding between the graves off to his left, obviously making her way toward a headstone capped with a large granite cross. "That's a bit too obvious, don't you think?" he wondered aloud as he followed after her.

"And who says this has to be difficult?"

"Well, why go through the trouble of making a map and writing cryptic clues if following them doesn't take any more acumen than that of the village idiot?"

"Perhaps the hard part was intended to be the finding of the graveyard."

Hard? Hell, Lafitte had made it almost impossible. They wouldn't be there if Belle hadn't waved a candlestick over a city map. As long shots went, it was one of the biggest he'd ever taken. Unless he measured it against falling in love with her. And then it paled. "You're being an optimist again," he countered as she swept a circle around the stone, examining the inscriptions.

"Humor me," she laughingly challenged.

"Do I have any other choice?" Just as he didn't have any choice in whether or not he loved her. Done was done and life was life. All he could do was ride it out and hope it came to a reasonably happy end.

"There's Park!" she exclaimed, quickly slipping between stones. "Joseph and Gloria Park. Oh," she added, her voice softening with melancholy. "She died a week after he did. Probably of a broken heart."

"More likely of whatever disease it was that killed him."

She threw him a quick look that wasn't nearly as chastising as it was amused. And then she was off again, sweeping another circle around the stone, apparently oblivious to the fact that she'd melted his heart another impossible degree.

"And here's Hyde! Walter Hyde." She barely paused before setting out in yet another ever-widening circle.

So sweetly relentless, he thought, so delightfully determined to follow the trail. And so absolutely certain that not only would she find the prize at the end of it, but that it would be worth the effort. She was a delight, a marvel. And if he could convince her to marry him, he'd be the luckiest damn man who ever lived.

"Do you see a lion anywhere?"

"So it's not easy," he murmured, trailing after her, resolving to move heaven and earth to keep her by his side.

"We're halfway there, Barrett. Now isn't the time to surrender to discouragement."

"Was I suggesting surrender?" he posed, smiling and knowing they were on two different conversational courses, knowing that he'd never be able to give her up. If she went back to America, he'd follow her. If she didn't want to marry him, he'd offer . . .

He didn't know precisely what he'd offer. Whatever, he supposed, it took for her to agree to be his companion. His partner. Yes, he wanted that, too. And if there were going to be any little Stanbridges in the world, they needed Isabella Dandaneau to be their mother. She could teach them how to endure, how to laugh and find the joys amid the challenges and sorrows of life. He'd have to draw the line at explosives, though. There were some things that—for the sake of domestic peace and tranquility—children really didn't need to know.

"Someone has to have a lion carved into the headstone itself. It's simply a matter of finding it."

Yes, it was. And he would find a way to get what he

wanted, what he needed. In the meantime, though . . . Setting aside his private musings, he put himself wholly into the search for the next headstone. Looking back over his shoulder, he visually charted the course that had brought them to Walter Hyde's graveside. It was a fairly consistent line and he stepped off in the direction it seemed to be leading. "Belle," he called after a few moments. "Over here."

Together they stood in front of the resting place of Lymon Jones, who had died after fifty years of faithful service to the crown. "Now," Belle said quietly, "for the gentle bride."

"It should be this way," he said, catching her hand in his and drawing her along. "He's moving us to the northeast."

It took them several minutes to discover Lafitte had changed the direction slightly, but eventually they stood before a tombstone capped by a bouquet of stone roses. " 'Lydia Nelson,' " Belle read, her voice soft. " 'Bertram's Beloved, Gentle Bride.' She was only sixteen."

"Well, ol' Bertram didn't pine for long," Barrett countered, nodding toward an adjoining grave. "Gloria, his second beloved, was dead just over a year after Lydia." Leaning to see around Belle, he scanned the tightly placed row of matching markers. "It looks as though he buried a total of three—no four—beloveds before he chocked up his own toes."

"He seems to have been a bit hard on wives. One would think there would have come a point when women would have been leery of his proposal."

"He must have been quite the charmer."

"Or wealthy enough to make the risk worth it."

Chuckling, Barrett observed, "An optimist with a cynical edge. You're unique, Belle."

"You've just now noticed?" she asked, grinning up at him.

"Actually, I knew that the instant you walked into my office."

She rolled her eyes. "And you were utterly fascinated."

"Yes, I was," he admitted, suddenly realizing just how early he'd begun to tumble head over heels. "I still am."

Belle gazed up at him, her soul aching at the gentleness of his smile, her heart straining to hear the faint whisper of words unspoken. She could feel them hanging in the damp air between them, could see them shimmering in his eyes. They were important words, she sensed; words she needed, words that she instinctively knew would change the whole of her world. That she yearned so desperately for them frightened her. That he withheld them hurt in a way that was unfathomable.

Quietly clearing the lump from her throat, she drew a steadying breath and managed a smile as she pulled her hand from his and said, "Well, we're almost done with the trail. The next part is 'Setting sun on Castle's Rise.'"

He nodded, breaking the spell, and visibly squared his shoulders as he looked around them. "Why," he asked as she moved past the line of beloved brides, "would Lafitte go to all this trouble?"

"To protect the treasure from those he didn't want to have it?"

"He could have placed it in a bank vault in some city in America and it would have been perfectly safe. All he would have had to do in his will was name the bank and provide either a key or a password."

"That's assuming," she replied, "that pirates trust bankers."

"You have a point. Grave robbers are generally a cut above." She was puzzling his comment when he called out, "To your right, Belle. The crenellated headstone."

It took her a moment to see it, shadowed as it was by a

granite mausoleum. She moved over the dampened grass to stand before it. The stone was old, the relief of the inscription worn by the years and the elements. " 'John Malcolm Castle,' " she said as Barrett moved to her side. " 'Who threatens to rise from the dead and wreck those who put him in his grave.' "

"Probably bankers."

She looked up at him, puzzled by his persistent return to the subject. "Your father's a banker, isn't he?"

"A financier, actually," he clarified, his hands stuffed into his pockets and his gaze skimming over the face of the mausoleum. "It's a fine distinction between the two, but one to which he holds quite religiously."

"And what's the difference?"

He looked back over his shoulder, answering, "My father's something of a master puppeteer. He plays people and their money, moving them here and there, putting them together for resounding applause and considerable profit." Turning his attention back to the grave marker, he added, "Bankers sit behind their desks and benefit from peoples' aspirations and desperations. They're not much better than common leeches."

It was a most decidedly odd topic of conversation— especially considering where they were and what they were doing. But he seemed to have a deliberate purpose for it and so she accepted it and asked, "If you have such a low view of bankers, where do you keep your money? In a tin buried in the rear yard?"

"My father's firm. In a large metal lockbox in a large steel vault. His clerks move money in and out of it as need be and at the end of every month I'm sent an accounting statement." He gave her a quirked smile. "Along with a note from my father suggesting investments."

"Do you ever follow his advice?"

"He does know how to make money."

"Apparently his son does, too," she laughingly quipped.

"I prefer to do it in a considerably less public fashion than he does. But yes, Belle, I'm a wealthy man."

She started, appalled. "I wasn't trying to—"

"I know," he calmly interrupted, his smile confident and satisfied. "And if I hadn't wanted you to know that about me, I wouldn't have told you."

Put another way, he'd manipulated both the conversation and her so that he could convey the information. Part of her was irritated that he'd felt the need to be less than bluntly honest about it all. A greater part, however, was curious. "And why," she ventured, "do you think I need to know that?"

"It's a bit complicated. Let's finish our search for the treasure and I'll have a go at explaining on our way back to the town house." He didn't give her a chance to accept or decline. "This is the point where we're to squint and imagine the sun setting on Mr. Castle's headstone."

He'd broached the subject of his wealth and then pointedly dropped it? Belle knew that she could ponder the logic and purpose of it all for the next month and still not arrive at an acceptable rationale on her own. Barrett would explain when Barrett wanted to and not one second before then. Whether that explanation made any sense remained to be seen. She sighed and deliberately set the matter aside. "I've lost my sense of direction," she admitted. "Which way is west?"

"Over our shoulders. We're facing the way we're supposed to be. Are you squinting?"

"There's no need to," she countered dryly. "I can see the mausoleum quite clearly."

Apparently undaunted by her lack of enthusiasm, he said, "With the sun setting, the top of the headstone would throw shadows over the face of it. Some of the letters of the inscription would be in sunlight, some in shadow."

"But which of them would change as the sun moved down?" she asked, her frustration intensifying. "And they'd be different from day to day as the seasons come and go. If Lafitte was trying to spell something, we'd have to know on what day and what time he intended for us to be standing here."

Barrett stepped to the back side of the headstone and she counted as he deliberately stepped off the distance between it and the padlocked door of the mausoleum. Fifteen paces. Exactly.

"This has to be it," he announced, taking a half-step back and removing a small, dark bundle from the inside pocket of his coat.

Her brows knitted, Belle closed the distance between them. He'd knelt and unrolled the bundle on the ground by the time she reached his side. "What are you doing?" she asked as he extracted a short, slender rod from the case with one hand and took the lock in the other.

"Just what it looks like I'm doing," he replied, grinning and inserting the pick in the keyhole. "I'm a man of many and varied talents."

Fascinated, she leaned close, barely daring to breathe as she watched him deftly work the pick and listened to the sound of the tumblers clicking. Only when he chuckled did she dare expel her held breath and ask, "Would you be willing to teach me how to do it?"

"If you want to learn," he replied, yanking the lock free from the hasp. He pulled the pick in the same smooth motion in which he snagged the case up from the ground and gained his feet.

"I am so very impressed."

His eyes sparkled as he grinned down at her and tucked the bundle back into his coat. "As I intended for you to be."

Oh, if he weren't so damn interesting and boyishly

charming, he'd be insufferable. Removing the lock from the door, she laughed softly. "I'll be even more impressed if you pull a lamp out of your pocket."

He produced his cheroot tin, opened it and shook a fair number of lucifer sticks into the palm of his other hand. "Not a lamp in the strictest sense of it," he said, his smile widening. "But hopefully close enough to earn me some small measure of your regard."

"Some very small," she allowed teasingly while pulling open the door and dropping the lock on the ground.

The hinges groaned in protest. A match flared and cast a flickering light over the narrow corridor inside as Barrett stepped past her. She followed on his heels, her gaze sweeping over the inscribed granite blocks that lined the sides from top to bottom. There seemed to be two allotted for each of the occupants; one over the other. The uppermost one was by far the largest and bore the name of the deceased along with their dates of birth and death. The lower, smaller one bore an expression of the survivors' grief.

They were halfway to the back wall when Barrett lit a second match off the first. In the brightness of the new flame, Isabella gasped in recognition.

"It's the pattern of the lines, Barrett!" she exclaimed, pointing to a twisted tangle of patinaed rods that protruded from one of the memorial blocks just above her head. She stepped back to see the name on the block above it.

" 'The sweet knots of life by death undone,' " he read aloud as her heart skittered. " 'The course of love and betrayal run. Regret and sorrow my masters be. Sleep pirate princess and dream of me.' "

"Louise Benoit was my grandmother's younger sister," she explained, feeling slightly queasy. "The family legend has it that she ran off with a sea captain when her father refused to let them marry. No one ever heard from her again."

Lighting another match, he asked, "How old was she at the time?"

"In her early twenties, I think," she supplied, trying to remember not only all that she'd ever heard of her great-aunt, but the nuances of the telling. "It was a year or so after the Battle of New Orleans and just months before my grandparents married."

"According to the dates here, she didn't live long after that."

"Pirate princess," Belle whispered. "She didn't run off with a sea captain. She ran off with Lafitte. With her sister's lover."

"Which would go a long way toward explaining why Lafitte left the treasure to your grandmother. It's nice to know that pirates can feel guilty." He handed her the cheroot holder and a newly lit match, saying, "If you'd be so kind as to hold all this for a minute."

She took them absently, her mind whirling through childhood memories, her eyes seeing them for the first time in understanding. The way her grandmother's lips had thinned every time someone sang the praises of Jean Lafitte . . . The way her eyes had misted the few times she'd ever spoken of the sister lost to forbidden love . . . The hard edge of her mother's tone when she'd warned her to abandon her curiosity about Great-aunt Louise's fate . . . There was no reason to search for the missing, her mother had declared. Louise had left by choice and had been given up by choice. There was no undoing the decisions that had been made so long ago.

The sound was raw and cold and Isabella started from the past. Two realizations struck in the same instant—that the web of metal rods was more than merely symbolic of

Lafitte's sentiment. And that the heat of the flame had reached the tip of her fingers. Tearing her attention from Barrett's effort, she lit another match just before she was forced to drop the other.

Stone grated against stone again and she held her breath, looking back to watch Barrett, his hands wrapped tightly around the ornate handle, coax the inscribed slab of granite from the wall. The world around her was beginning to narrow and gray and spin ever so slightly when it suddenly slid free. Her gasp of surprise steadied her and she stepped forward to peer into the opening as Barrett set the slab of stone at their feet.

It was a shallow recess; a stone box of sorts. And inside lay a single piece of folded parchment. With a trembling hand, she retrieved it, hoping and praying that it wasn't another map, another string of clues to be followed. Barrett straightened and wordlessly took the matches and cheroot box from her.

Swallowing down her heart, she unfolded the paper and skimmed the first lines. Vaguely aware that her jaw had dropped, she looked down at the bottom of the page. It was real. The seal was there. The signature. The signatures of officials and witnesses, too.

"What is it, Belle?"

"A land grant," she answered, looking back up to the first lines of the document. "From James Madison, President of the United States of America, to Mr. Jean Lafitte. Five hundred thousand acres of Western land in appreciation for his service to the United States during the New Orleans campaign of the Second American War for Independence."

Dragging a breath into her lungs and locking her knees, she looked up to meet his gaze. "A half million acres, Barrett."

His smile seemed brittle and forced as he said, "Welcome, Belle, to the world of the wealthy."

Yes, she was wealthy. Wealthier than she had ever imagined it possible to be. So why did she feel as though the world had just crashed in utter ruin around her?

Chapter Sixteen

The document tucked inside her jacket, Belle walked along at Barrett's side, her hands stuffed deep in her pockets and her mind not so much reeling as simply staggering. It was one thing, she knew, to hold title to large amounts of land and quite another to have actual possession. Making the land somehow pay was yet another monumental thing altogether.

Then there was the matter of getting back to America to begin the work of claiming the inheritance. She didn't have the money for passage. She didn't have money to live on while the lawyers filled out papers and argued among themselves. Barrett would doubtlessly loan her what she needed to travel and to survive in the interim, but the very idea of asking him for it made her stomach squirm and her chest tighten. The notion of accepting a freely made offer didn't sit one whit better.

And every aspect of her quandary was based on assumption, she realized, her heart skittering. The document could be a forgery. Or it might have been rescinded in the years since it had been issued. Lafitte hadn't been known as a sterling citizen; what the government had awarded for exemplary behavior, it might well have taken back for bad. Lafitte could well have sold, gambled, or traded it all away, too, and then forgotten that he'd done so. Such memory lapses were wont to happen as the mind aged and the soul tried to mend fences before passing to the world beyond. Lafitte certainly wouldn't be the first man to bequeath something that wasn't his to give. Or he might not have been able to get rid of it no matter how hard he'd tried. She'd read the journals of Lewis and Clark. She knew that there were vast stretches of utter wasteland in the West.

Then again, she admitted on a sigh, the document might be perfectly legal and still in force. When she walked in the door to claim it, the government lawyers might sag in relief and hand it over to her for nothing more than her signature. The land might be a gold mine of resources, sitting there pristine and waiting for her to unlock its potential. She could sell it. She could lease it. She could work it. She could build herself a fine house and rattle around inside its walls for the rest of her want-for-nothing life.

And do what other than pace about her palace? she wondered. Count her piles and piles of money? Fend off suitors who were more interested in her bank account than her hand? Even if one happened along who would do for a husband, there wouldn't be any children to fill the house with laughter and raucous noise. She'd never have to lie awake at night and wonder if her daughters had secretly had their nipples pierced.

Possibilities. Both good and bad. The only certainty was that she wasn't going to know the value of Lafitte's legacy until she made an effort to claim it. To do that, she was going to have to go home. To where it was warm, she reminded herself as a strange kind of numbness crept into her limbs. To where the flowers were blooming and the rain had a definite beginning and a definite end.

Barrett pushed open the gate at the rear of the house. Stepping aside to let her pass, he said softly, "You don't seem very pleased by your good fortune, Belle."

It crossed her mind to lie about it, to assure him that fatigue and relief were simply masking her incredible happiness. Chances were that he'd accept the assertion and not press. For the moment. But eventually he would; he wasn't the sort of man to pretend that he didn't see. As he closed the gate behind them, she shrugged and admitted, "I certainly don't feel as I expected I would."

"Why?"

Moving across the rear yard, she stared at the back door and replied, "Rubies and ropes of pearls would have been easier to convert into actual money, I suppose. A square of parchment doesn't have the same sort of immediate substance as jewels and gold doubloons."

"But land can be worth considerably more than sparkling baubles."

"If it's good land in a good place," she countered, thinking that he didn't sound all that enthused about her inheritance either. "And if someone else hasn't already made claim to it and settled on it."

"A good solicitor should be able to clear any misunderstandings as to proper ownership."

"True," she allowed as her stomach chilled and quivered. "And I'm sure most would be willing to undertake the work in exchange for a few thousand acres."

"Do you have any idea of where the land is in any specific sense?"

She didn't want to talk about it any more, didn't want to think about it. Doing so did the strangest, most inexplicable and unsettling things to her insides. Taking a deep breath in an attempt to calm her roiling stomach, flexing her fingers in an attempt to bring some feeling back into them, she replied, "No, but that Madison referred to it as

Western lands tells me that it's somewhere west of the Appalachian Mountains, east of the Rockies, north of the Gulf of Mexico, and south of the Dominion of Canada."

"As I recall the maps I've seen of the hemisphere, that's a fairly large bit of geography," he observed dryly as he held the door open and allowed her to pass inside.

She nodded, but said nothing as she stripped off her hat and shook out her curls.

"Belle, darling," he drawled from behind her. "What's really troubling you?"

Eventually had arrived. And not all that much sooner than she'd expected. "I don't know," she admitted on a long sigh, turning to face him. His tilted head and cocked brow prompted her to press her hands to her midsection and add, "Honestly, I don't, Barrett. I have this hollow, queasy feeling."

"Perhaps you're hungry?"

Her smile was tremulous and she knew it. She also knew that she couldn't muster a better one. "Surprisingly, no. In fact, the very thought of food makes it all that much worse." *And if you say one cross word,* she silently added, *I'll cry and never stop.*

He closed the distance between them and slipped his arms around her shoulders to draw her against the warmth and hard planes of his body. "Do you think it's there forever?" he asked softly. "Or might I be able to make it go away?"

His voice vibrated through her, instantly calming her stomach and settling her mind. Wrapping her arms around his waist and nestling her hips close against his, she smiled up at him. "I'm feeling better already. You're very good."

As in the cemetery, there was something he wanted to say and couldn't. Something important. She could see it in his eyes, could feel his tension, his hesitation, resonating through every fiber of her being. Her breath caught, her pulse quickened and heated, she leaned into him and waited, silently willing the words to tumble free.

As though he could hear her unspoken plea, he gave her a faint, apologetic smile and ever so slightly shook his head. Tears clawed their way up her throat, pushing a tiny, strangled cry of disappointment past her lips.

"It will be all right, Belle," he whispered, threading his fingers through her hair.

She wanted, with all her heart, to believe him. For the moment, though, it was enough to be in the strong circle of his arms, to let him sweep aside her worries and doubts and fears. Tomorrow would bring what it would and she'd do the best she could with it. Tonight . . .

Tonight, her soul whispered as he gently angled her head and lowered his mouth to hers, was for making love with Barrett Stanbridge, for pleasure and sated happiness, for pretending that it all would never end.

It occurred to him that smiling up at the ceiling was becoming something of a habit. One, he reminded himself, sobering, that he wasn't going to have a chance to develop any further if he kept tamping down the declaration of his feelings. Three simple words. I love you. Four, if he personalized the statement by adding Belle's name to the beginning or end of it. And it wasn't as though he'd never in his life uttered them. He'd tossed them around rather freely in his much younger days, when the women in his life were just as inexperienced as he was and likely to believe him. He'd said them, fully meaning them, only once before.

Barrett frowned as he poked about in the long-closed closet of his memories. He had loved Suzanna. Genuinely and passionately. And with a young man's fascination for the forbidden and the unshakable belief that love could surmount and conquer all the obstacles life could throw in its path. In hindsight and through older, wiser eyes . . .

They'd been physically well suited for each other. Just as he and Belle were now. The difference between the past and the present lay beyond the pleasure, though, in the moments they spent together upright, clothed, and outside the bedroom. With Suzanna there had always been the looming presence of her husband, the unhappiness of her marriage, her desperation to escape it, and her dependence on him to save her. And nothing else that he could remember all these years later. They'd existed in the moment, wallowing together in the unfairness of their situation and focusing entirely on taking the one single step that would set them free. They'd never talked of the steps that would come after that one, never talked about the distant future and the days when they were old and gray and helping each other up and out of parlor chairs.

Not that he and Belle had ever discussed those days, either, he allowed. But being with Belle was so very different than being with Suzanna had been. In every possible way. Belle looked back and honestly admitted to making the decisions that had, in the final analysis, turned out to be regrettable. And while she lived in the moment as Suzanna had, Belle didn't spend her waking moments focused on how life hadn't measured up to her expectations. No, Belle spent her moments wringing from them all the joy and laughter that she could. But even as she did, she had an eye on tomorrow and where she was going and what life would likely demand of her. Being with Belle was a complicated proposition that had nothing whatsoever to do with their circumstances and everything to do with who they were as people.

He probably wasn't the ideal man for her. He was used to going through his days and nights alone, never having to be truly accountable to anyone for anything. And, as his friends had often pointed out, he had a tendency to pry into others' thoughts and motives and then mightily resent their attempts to question his. All in all, he wasn't the most dependable or open and communicative man in the world. But if Belle would have him, he'd do his best to change what he could of himself, to be the husband she deserved.

But having her accept him required that he first screw up the courage to tell her that he loved her. Why he kept faltering at that was as much a mystery as who had killed Mignon. Three, maybe four, simple words and he couldn't seem to spit them out. It was, he supposed, a matter of the time and the situation never being quite right in the same moment. He wanted his declaration to be special, memorable in a sweeping, life-altering sort of way. Tossing out an "I love you" before making love to her had struck him as being too much like a caddish ploy. He'd choked it back in the aftermath, thinking that it would sound too much along the lines of a "thank you." Just casually tossing it out in the midst of a conversation would be to invite her to just as casually dismiss his suit. Bringing it up in a somber, resolute way . . . Hell, he wasn't buying a horse or a house. Handing her his heart—and asking for hers in return—wasn't a business transaction.

Although . . . Barrett considered the ceiling. Perhaps making a business proposition was the way to start. They worked very well together. They both knew it. And Belle didn't seem all that excited about the idea of owning land in western America. She could sell it through a solicitor.

Yes, if he couched it in just the right terms, in just the right tone, she might be willing to give serious considera-tion to staying in London and forming an investigative partnership. If he could keep her close, he could work his way slowly along, eventually overcoming her resistance to another marriage. His parents would have the time to learn more about her and come to appreciate how perfect for him she was.

It could work. It was a damn fine plan, actually. He grinned, thinking that having arrived at such a perfect solution deserved celebration with an expensive cheroot. Turning his head, he pressed a kiss to her forehead and then gently drew his arm from under her while softly saying, "I'm going downstairs for a smoke, angel."

She murmured in her sleep and gave him a sweet smile of assent. Gazing down at her, his heart overflowed. God, she was perfection; his every desire come to human form. Beauty and intellect, daring and honesty, sweetness and undauntable courage. There had never been, would never again be, another woman like her. For as long as he lived, she would own every measure of his heart and soul.

"I love you," he whispered, smoothing an errant curl off her cheek. Her smile softly deepened and the tiniest, most satisfied of sighs feathered across her still-kiss-swollen lips. His chest tightened, but he resisted the temptation to take her back into his arms, wake her, and whisper the words again. He had a solid plan already, he told himself, sliding off the bed and reaching for his clothes. And surrendering to ill-conceived impulse was the most certain way of mangling its chances for success.

He'd barely rounded the newel post at the base of the stairs when a man stepped into the darkened doorway of the kitchen. For a split second Barrett's heart lurched. Even as it did, even as he instinctively reached behind himself for his weapon, he recognized the silhouette.

"It's me, Mr. Stanbridge," the man said a bit tardily and unnecessarily. "O'Brien."

"You're damn lucky I didn't shoot you," Barrett countered, advancing and flipping open the cover of his cheroot case.

His man chuckled and turned back into the kitchen, saying over his shoulder, "No luck to it at all. You never take a blind shot. I wasn't sure this was the right house. Lord Lansdown gave me the number but I'll be damned if I could see any."

So, Barrett silently quipped, being the man O'Brien was, he'd simply let himself in to check. The constables called it breaking and entering. Or attempted burglary. O'Brien called it professional skill and harmless curiosity. However you looked at it, it was a combination of attitude and ability that had made the wiry, bowlegged Irishman eminently useful time after time. "I assume that you're here because you have a report for me," Barrett said, shaking out two of the tightly twisted little cigars.

Accepting one of them, Patrick O'Brien nodded crisply. "The boys have been busy. What do you want first? The bad news? Or the worse?"

Barrett struck the phosphorous stick, asking, "There's no good news at all?"

"Boss, you're packed in shit up to your eyeballs."

Well, he didn't pay O'Brien to gild lilies. Smiling wryly and drawing the flame into the end of the cheroot, he casually inquired, "Would that be the bad or the worse?"

"That's the part that's supposed to brace you for what's comin'," the other man replied, his teeth clamped around the end of his own smoke and leaning forward to share the flame.

As O'Brien drew, Barrett drawled, "I can hardly wait. When you're ready, start with the bad, O'Brien."

"That would be concernin' your list of suspects."

"Not a one of them's in London?" he guessed, tossing the match into the water bucket before leaning back against the cabinet and folding his arms across his chest.

"You should hope." O'Brien took the newly lit cheroot from his mouth, held it up in front of him and gave it an appreciative smile and nod before clamping it back into place and getting on with business. "You got an Emma and a Rose de Granvieux lodged on Queen's Gate in Kensington. Sisters, they say. And just between us, they ain't the most comely things I ever seen. Plain faced, which, bein' fair-minded men, we both know ain't an unforgivable sin all by itself. But these two looks like they's been suckin' lemons since they was in nappies."

Barrett reined in his smile. "The de Granvieux sisters, huh? They weren't the ones I'd picked to be the most logical suspects."

"And they might not be," O'Brien brightly offered. "They ain't here alone."

Yes, with O'Brien information always came in layers. Often layers within layers. "Oh? Who's with them?"

"Can't tell which one of them he's sweetest on, but Emil Caribe is dancin' attendance between 'em both most hours of the day. Little prancer, he is. 'Bout this tall," O'Brien went on, straightening to indicate a height just above his own shoulder. "And real fond of white kid gloves an' silver threads in his waistcoats. Does this," he added, picking an imaginary speck of lint off his coat sleeve and tossing it away with an exaggerated gesture of disdain. "Every other breath."

A fop. With a greedy, murderous streak. "Is he lodged with the sisters?"

O'Brien shook his head. "West End. On Shaftesbury."

The puzzle pieces fell together with an almost audible click. "Near Nickel's Sweet Shop."

"How'd you know that?"

"Candy wrappers," Barrett explained obliquely, his mind occupied by the other possibilities. "Who else is in town? The Choteau brothers? Neville Martinez? Anyone named Dandaneau?"

"If they is," O'Brien answered, flicking ash off the cheroot, "haven't heard or seen so much as a shadow or a whisper of 'em. Got our boys still lookin', though. Better sure than sorry in my book."

Barrett nodded, considering the odds of the conspiracy being any broader than it already was.

"You want the rest of it now?"

Deciding that the sisters and Caribe were likely the only players in the game, Barrett drew hard on his cheroot and smiled as he blew a stream of smoke toward the tin ceiling. "This would be the worse part?"

O'Brien cocked a brow and leaned his shoulder against the wall. "Larson hauled me in at half past nine last night an' forced me to spend two friggin' hours in his sparklin' company. Had a lot of questions for me, he did."

Larson and O'Brien. Not a good combination. If blood hadn't spilled it would have been one of their tamer sessions together. "Questions about what?"

"Where you are, mostly," his man replied. "He's not believin' you're in Paris like your da's sayin' you are. That dead bastard in your rear yard has Larson turnin' over every rock he can find as fast as he can lay eyes on 'em. He's figurin' two murders makes you the meanest dog in London an' that his bosses'll have his head if he doesn't serve yours up first."

No real surprise in all of that, Barrett decided. "I'm assuming that in your usual efficient fashion, you've been turning over a few rocks yourself. Tell me about the dead man."

"I figured like you. That he was bein' paid for his brawn. Can't tell you for sure that the coins in his pocket was from the Lemon Girls or from Prancer though. I've had the boys watchin' all three of 'em since they turned 'em up an' no one's seen a meetin' with anyone that looked like a hire-lin'. Don't know how the word's being passed down on what they want done."

O'Brien might not be able to see it, but he could. Some-one in Nickel's was a conduit, passing instructions from the conspirators to their henchmen. Caribe or the sisters went to purchase candy and deliver their wishes. Someone else went in after them and was handed their marching or-ders, sweetened with chocolate and peppermint. As a strat-egy, it was well designed; Caribe and the sisters remained neatly and safely removed from direct, overt involvement.

"Don't know who killed the one in your yard, either."

"But you're working on it," Barrett ventured.

The man nodded and took another pull on the cheroot before answering. "It was a clean shot from what Larson let slip in demandin' information outa me. Someone will be awantin' the credit for it. I'm waitin', listenin' for the cock to crow. Also have a man lookin' for the wake an' plannin' to be there when the talk flows like a river of whisky."

Barrett counted the hours back. A little more than eight hours ago. An eternity considering all that had transpired since then. In another eight the word of the wake would be passed. And whoever had pulled the trigger would be near-ing the end of their restraint. "All in all," Barrett observed, "it's not terrible news. I was expecting worse."

"Well, I was just workin' my way along," O'Brien coun-tered dryly. "Larson's got the docks covered, boss. You ain't gonna make a dash for Paris now without havin' to slip past his men. Got the rail stations buzzin', too. An' it's not just Larson an' his bloody beagles you got to worry 'bout. You're front page of the early edition of today's frig-gin' *Times*. With a hundred pounds over your head."

"Well, that does meet my standards for worse," he con-fessed with a wince. Knowing that there wasn't anything to be done about the unexpected turn of events, he set it aside. "Did Larson ask you any questions about Belle?"

"Who?"

"Isabella Dandaneau."

O'Brien flicked another ash while slowly shaking his head. "Only skirt he mentioned was the one found dead in the alleyway. That Mignon Richard woman."

"What did he want to know about her?"

"If I knew her or anything 'bout her an' you. Gave ol' Larson honest answers on those. Figured it couldn't hurt you none an' might even help a bit for him to hear your story one more time."

"Did he ask about the de Granvieux sisters or Emil Caribe?"

"Nope. Them I held close to the vest, figurin' it was up to you what's to be done 'bout 'em."

O'Brien, Barrett mused—not for the first time—might lack social graces, but he more than made up for the shortcoming in his ability to think fast and on his feet. He had an uncanny, innate sense of what to say, when, and to whom. Not once in all the years of their association had the man blundered.

"Boss?" he asked, intruding on Barrett's silent appreciation. "What do you want me to do next? Keep lookin' for the ones we haven't found yet? Or just watch real close the ones we have?"

It was, Barrett realized, only one of several decisions that had to be made. Larson was on the hunt; it was only a matter of time before he found them. When he did . . . Barrett frowned up into the cloud of smoke. He didn't want Belle to see him taken into custody. He'd humiliated Larson and his men in making them run all over London in search of him and they'd return the favor tenfold the first chance they had. He could endure the rough treatment, but he wasn't at all sure that Belle could watch it happen without trying to intervene. If she entered the fray with a weapon . . .

No, he couldn't let Larson find him. Better to find Larson himself. There were now enough pieces of the puzzle to present. He had the story of Mignon's past and the roles the de Granvieux sisters and Emil Caribe had played then and the parts they were likely playing now. He had the story of Lafitte's treasure. He could hand Larson a beautifully wrapped package of motive and opportunity. If Larson was willing to hear him out with an open mind, he stood a reasonable chance of walking out of his office an absolved man.

But if Larson's mind wasn't open . . . Barrett chewed on the end of the cheroot and considered the possibilities and his options.

"Boss?"

The decision made, Barrett blew another stream of smoke toward the ceiling and replied, "I assume that you still have the boys working to find the others?"

"I do."

"Then let them continue with their task. For the moment, I want you to stay here and keep watch over Belle. She's sleeping upstairs. If I'm lucky, I should be back well before she wakes."

O'Brien's chin went down as his brow went up. "Where are you goin'?"

"Lord Lansdown's Haven House is first," Barrett explained. "He's going to accompany me to Larson's office."

"The son of a bitch will arrest you, boss."

A distinct possibility, he had to admit. But it was a risk he'd already weighed and deemed an acceptable one. "Even if he does, he'll have to ask me some questions sooner or later. Most likely sooner since Carden—my friend and a well-regarded, influential peer—will be there to see that he exercises both restraint and common sense. Once he hears the stories I have to tell, he'll have no choice but to focus his suspicions where they properly belong."

His man shifted between his feet and glanced toward the back door. "Are you sure 'bout this? It's damn risky."

Barrett shrugged. "It involves considerably less risk than any other course I have at the moment."

"What do you want me to tell the lady if your luck turns to shit?"

Barrett made a mental note to write Belle a quick missive before he left. Just to tell her O'Brien was there and to warn her about the man's rougher edges. "Give her nothing more than my basic plan and keep your doubts to yourself," he instructed, knocking the fire out of the cheroot and handing the remnant of it to the other man. "If I'm not back here by mid-morning, take her to Haven House and deliver her into Lady Lansdown's care. Seraphina will manage matters from there."

"Boss, I—"

"Stow the reservations, O'Brien," he interrupted, his mind clicking through the tasks, large and small, that lay in the hours ahead. "I appreciate your concerns, but they're groundless. Everything will come right in the end."

The hair on the back of his neck prickled again, harder, and Barrett stilled in the deep shadows of Carden's carriage house. The east side of his friend's home loomed ahead, dark and silently slumbering in the cold gray predawn mist. Nothing moved. The only sounds were those in the distance, those typical of a city that never truly retired for the night. Watching, listening, he slowly reached behind himself and drew his revolver from the small of his back. His gaze and the muzzle sweeping over the ground between himself and the house again, he lifted his left hand to press it against the breast of his coat, making sure that the land grant was still safely tucked inside.

Reassured, he took a cautious step forward, straining to

hear, to see. The sound was fast, the blow even faster. He heard the bone snap a full heartbeat before the pain blasted into his brain, a full two heartbeats before he saw the gun tumble from his useless hand. Instinctively, he whirled toward his right, his left arm up in defense. A dirt-streaked face. Two. Three. A blur of motion, an explosion of pain. His left leg crumpled beneath him. His stomach heaved. Sparks danced before his eyes and then there was nothing at all.

Chapter Seventeen

It was a good thing Barrett had thought to scribble her a note, Isabella thought as she accepted the cup of steaming coffee from the wiry Irishman. If he hadn't, she'd have shot Patrick O'Brien dead in the parlor doorway. Between his ratty, ill-fitting clothing and the distinct odor of whisky that wafted around him . . . Well, Barrett had warned her that he wasn't exactly the most reputable-looking sort. And the way his eyes unexpectedly darted toward the slightest noise . . . She gave him a strained but hopefully polite-looking smile, and lifted her mug to him in salute to the new day.

"I figure ten to be mid-morning," he said. "If 'n the boss ain't back by then, I'll haul you over to Lady Lansdown like he told me to."

To her ears O'Brien sounded rather excited about the prospect. Hopefully he didn't mean to literally haul her. Being dumped in Lady Lansdown's foyer like a sack of potatoes was utterly unacceptable. If ten o'clock arrived before Barrett did, she'd have to tussle control of the situation from his man. While smiling sweetly, of course. And letting him think that he'd surrendered it of his own accord.

But judging by the pale light coming through the kitchen windows, ten o'clock was at least a good two hours away. Waking to find Barrett gone had been disconcerting, but it was nothing compared to the prospect of passing two hours with a very nervous stranger. Having decided on reading Barrett's note that the rules of basic hospitality applied, she'd climbed into a dress and put up her hair before coming down the stairs to meet her temporary protector. And once begun, there was no going back. Retreating to her room now would be unconscionably rude. She would simply have to find some subject on which they could pleasantly converse and pass the time.

"So," she said, smiling politely, "do you happen to know where Barrett went?"

"He was going first to Lord Lansdown's an' then the two of them was headin' over to Larson's office."

Her heart slammed up into her throat. "Larson's?" she managed to croak out around it.

O'Brien nodded and took a long, slow sip of his coffee. "I'm supposed to tell you—in case you miss it—that Mr. Stanbridge has the land paper. He took it with him so he could lay it down in front of the inspector. Proof of motive and all, ya know."

Her mind reeled between all the points of information she so unexpectedly needed. "Barrett wouldn't have gone to see Larson without having a suspect to hand him. Who is it?"

O'Brien's gaze darted out the window. Pointing with his coffee mug, he said, "You can ask him yourself. Carriage just pulled up an' . . ." He leaned forward and tilted his head to presumably get a better view. "Yep," he declared, coming back to center and taking another sip of coffee, "it's Lord Lansdown comin' through the gate."

Belle stepped to the window. Carden was already halfway to the back door. The carriage sat in the alleyway, the driver still in the box and clearly waiting for his return. But the gate was closed and Carden was alone. "I don't see Barrett with him," she said, moving to the door and pulling it open.

"Must have hit a rough patch at Larson's," O'Brien said morosely from behind her. "I warned him not to go."

"Carden," she offered in greeting as he gave her a tight smile and stepped past her into the kitchen. "Where's Barrett?"

He looked at her, at O'Brien, and then back at her. The thinness of his lips, the hard light in his eyes set her pulse skittering. "Where's Barrett?" she repeated, unable to keep the notes of burgeoning panic out of her voice. "Has something happened to him?"

Barrett's friend visibly squared his shoulders and widened his stance. "I presume that he was on his way to Haven House for some reason?"

The shudder that ripped through her was instant and cold and soul deep.

"He was thinkin'," she heard O'Brien supply, "to take you with 'im to Inspector Larson's office. He didn't get that far, did he?"

From his pocket Carden drew a crumpled bit of paper that had been folded into quarters. "This was wrapped around a rock and pitched through my parlor window not thirty minutes ago."

Belle took the paper from him with one hand while blindly setting her coffee aside with the other. Her hands trembling, her breathing shallow and painful, she opened the note. The script was feminine, but the gentle lines didn't mask the harshness of the message.

We have Stanbridge and the land grant. We'll trade him for a legal transfer of the grant to the bearer. Tonight at six on the steps of the West Portico of St. Paul's. Isabella comes alone. If she's late or brings the police, Stanbridge will be killed.

Belle locked her knees and closed her eyes, trying desperately to keep herself upright as the world spun around her and her heart tore in two. Barrett. Oh, dear God in heaven. They had Barrett. She had to get him back. Whatever they wanted, she'd give them. Where they wanted, when they wanted. If they hurt him . . .

Fear evaporated in a sudden, red-hot anger. If they'd hurt him, she'd make them pay. She'd track them through hell and back and she'd make them pay.

The dull drone of quiet conversation drifted past the edge of her awareness and she focused on it, letting it ground her. Her pulse wouldn't slow, but her mind calmed just enough for her to grasp a bit of reason from the rubble of her existence.

"Who is 'we'?" she demanded, lifting the note and looking between the two men. "Do either of you know?"

Carden shook his head. O'Brien nodded, though, and crisply replied, "Odds are it's the de Granvieux women and Emil Caribe."

She blinked, stunned. "Rose and Emma?"

"I gather you know them?" Carden asked, his brow cocked in the same way Barrett cocked his when surprised and trying to appear still in control.

"Their father was having an affair with Mignon when he died," she explained. "He left a sizable portion of his estate to her. Rose and Emma and their mother were furious and fought the will in court."

"But they lost," Carden finished for her.

She nodded, her mind leaping forward to the implications. "That they'd want Lafitte's treasure and be involved in Mignon's murder makes a perfect, if sick and demented, sense. Recompense and revenge."

"And this Emil Caribe?" Carden pressed.

"He was Mignon's lover when the news came of our inheritance. All of his money is through his wife's family and she's the sort to never let him forget it. He claims to have served with Lafitte for years. He could have known that the treasure was in London and been the one to send Mignon after it."

"To follow her and take it from her once she found it," Carden suggested. "To have wealth his wife didn't control."

Belle nodded, her mind still racing. "But why involve Emma and Rose?" she wondered aloud. "He didn't need them to carry through his plan. With them in league, he has to share the treasure. Why would he do that? Why wouldn't he want to keep it all for himself?"

O'Brien snorted. "He's sweet on one of 'em."

"The only person Emil Caribe cares about is Emil Caribe," Belle countered with absolute certainty. "If he's courting one of the sisters, then there's something to be had from it. The question is what that might be."

"Some folks," the Irishman said, "call it earthly delight."

The tone of his voice suggested that he thought her naïve about such matters. Why his presumption irritated her, she didn't know, but she was determined to put an end to his illusions. "He could have rented his delights locally, Mr. O'Brien. And for considerably less than it's costing him to support and squire the de Granvieux sisters. Why bring them with him all the way from New Orleans? I know Emma and I know Rose. They wouldn't tolerate being kept in lowly quarters. Why would Emil willingly agree to that kind of expense?"

O'Brien was too busy studying her through narrowed eyes to say anything. Carden, however, replied, "You're assuming that he's doing it willingly. Perhaps the sisters have a bit of leverage on him and used it to force their way into his plan."

No wonder Carden was Barrett's good friend; the two of them thought so very much alike. Talking with Carden, thinking aloud with him, was so very much like working through matters with Barrett. But he wasn't Barrett. Not at all. "It's possible, I suppose," she admitted, tilting her chin up and furiously blinking back the hot, welling tears. "But I don't have the slightest idea of what that leverage might be."

"If'n that's the case," O'Brien contributed, his manner a bit more subdued than previously, "and if'n Caribe's as greedy and selfish as you say he is, then they stand a good chance of windin' up dead for all their schemin' with 'im."

Even as she was deciding that he could very well be right, Carden added, "As could Barrett. Simply for being in the wrong place at the wrong time."

Simply for having the misfortune of being in Mignon's path that night at the theater. Simply because his secretary had let her into his office so that she could trap him into helping her. The tears welled again and again she blinked them back. "Not if I can prevent it," she declared, shifting her gaze back to the ransom letter crumpled in her fist. Six o'clock at St. Paul's.

"You'll sign over the grant?" Carden asked, sounding, she thought, a bit uncertain.

"Without hesitation," she assured him while telling herself that he hadn't meant to question either her integrity or her devotion to his friend. He didn't know her, didn't know the special kind of relationship she and Barrett had.

"How large a grant is it, Belle? I'm assuming it must be of considerable size to make all this effort worth the bother."

"Half a million acres in the American West."

O'Brien made an appreciative whistling sound. Carden Reeves simply blinked in a refined sort of way before finding the wherewithal to inquire, "Would Caribe have known that?"

"I don't know," she answered honestly and not much caring whether she ever knew the truth of it. It didn't matter. "He could have assumed—as I did—that the treasure was the more traditional kind one thinks of with pirates. Jewels and such." She shrugged. "But half a million acres will buy him all the jewels he or the de Granvieux girls might want."

Six o'clock. A good ten hours away. Why such a long span of time? Why such a public place? Why not as soon as possible and on a deserted country road or in some abandoned dockside warehouse where the transaction wasn't likely to be witnessed by a hundred casual passersby? She could sense the answer hovering just out of her grasp and knew that she had to find it, that it was vitally important.

"You're not going to the exchange alone, you know."

"Wouldn't be safe," O'Brien chimed in.

Of course it wouldn't. And Emil knew her well enough to realize that she wouldn't jeopardize her own safety and thus the chances of getting Barrett back alive. So why had he bothered to make the demand in the—

The answer to her questions bloomed suddenly large and full and certain. The time and place didn't matter to Emil Caribe; he had no intention of trading Barrett, no intention of letting her get to St. Paul's either alone or with reinforcements at her back. He hadn't taken Barrett to trade him, he'd taken him knowing that she'd have the transfer drawn and then search heaven and hell for Barrett while she awaited the appointed hour. Emil would be waiting; not at St. Paul's, but to step out of the shadows of some alleyway or dark corner. To that end, he'd keep Barrett alive; dead men didn't make for good bait. Emil had learned from war. Just as she had.

Belle looked between Carden Reeves and Patrick O'Brien as she tucked the note into the pocket of her skirt. "Actually, I'm of a mind to set my own terms for the trade."

O'Brien again considered her through narrowed eyes. Carden frowned for a moment and then sighed, shook his head and said, "I don't know—"

"I do," she assured him. "Do you have a key to Barrett's house?"

"No," he replied hesitantly, "but I know where the spare is kept."

"Good enough," she declared, her mind racing through the course that lay ahead. "That's our first stop. I'll need a more respectable dress than this one."

"To do what?"

"Barrett's right. It's time to work with Inspector Larson instead of against him."

O'Brien contributed another of his seemingly characteristic snorts. "An' you're thinkin' a dress matters? Missy, Larson's made of stone. You could walk in there bare arse naked an' he wouldn't get so much as a twitch in his—"

Carden pointedly and loudly cleared his throat while casting the man a warning look.

O'Brien snorted yet again and took a long, noisy, obviously disgusted slurp of what had to be ice-cold coffee.

"A dress matters," she clarified for him, "only to the degree that it adds to the impression of respectability and credibility. Please wait right here, gentlemen," she asked, turning and walking toward the front of the house. "I'll be down shortly and we'll be on our way."

She didn't wait for their assent or give either of them time to protest. Yes, she admitted as she made her way up the stairs, she was being presumptive and perhaps a bit high-handed, but . . . But it was fully her fault Barrett was in danger. Mignon had used him, certainly, and that had ended with Barrett being an innocent suspect in her murder. It wasn't until *she'd* walked into his office that his life had been well and truly turned upside down and inside out. She'd placed Barrett in danger and it was her moral and ethical responsibility to extract him from it.

Drawing her skirts in, she passed through the bedroom door and made her way to the island of pillows Barrett had fashioned for them before the hearth. The dishes from their last decent meal sat neatly stacked to the side of the cold hearth. Their wine glasses were still on the mantel where Barrett had placed them out of harm's way. And on the little table lay the maps of London Barrett had asked Carden to bring them.

Belle dropped to her knees before it and snatched up the candle. Placing the wick between her fingertips, she held the divining tool a scant distance over the vellum and began to slowly search for a beginning point.

And found none.

Because he was— Panic shot through her heart and tears filled her eyes. No, she sternly commanded herself, lifting her chin and swiping her eyes with her sleeve. She couldn't fall apart. She couldn't give up hope. Barrett was out there and she'd find him. He needed her. She wouldn't, couldn't fail him.

Telling herself that it was a matter of calming and focusing her mind to a sufficient degree for the magic to work, Belle laid down the candle. Sitting back on her heels, she laid her hands on her thighs, closed her eyes, and drew a long, slow, settling breath.

A memory slowly drifted through the chaotic whirl of her thoughts. Barrett as they'd stood in the kitchen of his house the first night they'd been together. The mischievous light in his eyes, the deliciously wicked taunt of his smile as he'd lifted his arms and offered her a choice between stepping into them or sliding the apron over them and onto his shoulders. Regret twisted through her soul; she should have thrown the apron away.

Another memory drifted over the first. *"You're perfect just the way you are, Belle. Absolutely, stunningly perfect."*

The sound of his voice, so clear, so rich and vibrant . . . Her heart aching, she wrapped her arms around her midriff and rocked slowly back and forth as she desperately pushed away the possibility that she might never hear it again.

"Kiss me, Belle."

"Love me."

Realization came, not as a lightning bolt, but as a brilliant, breathtaking dawn. She did love him. She'd loved him from the very beginning. And hadn't known it. God, how could she have been so blind? How could she have not seen the most wondrous and certain truth of her life when it had been standing right in front of her with open arms?

Her heart shattered and a soul-wrenching sob tore past her lips as tears filled her eyes and spilled hotly down her cheeks. "Please, Barrett," she sobbed into her hands. "Don't let it be too late. Please."

Regret and fear overwhelmed her, battering her body and her mind. Quaking, she struggled to breathe, to find the strength she needed to go on, to do what had to be done.

From deep within her soul came a slow swell of resistance and burgeoning resolve. They deserved a chance to be together. To be happy. Barrett was worth all she had, all she could give. He was her life. She'd pay any price, take any risk.

Dragging a shuddering breath into her lungs, Isabella scrubbed the palms of her hands over her eyes and cheeks, and then lifted her chin and squared her shoulders. *I will find you,* she vowed, picking up the candle and setting to work again.

She saw the quick look the two passed between themselves as she entered the kitchen. Unwilling to give them a chance to comment on her tear-swollen eyes, Belle dropped her valise to the floor, tossed aside her redingote, unrolled the map, tapped her fingertip on the spot she'd circled, and met the Irishman's gaze. "Do you know this area?"

He leaned close, squinted for a moment, and then straightened. "It's near the center of Cheapside," he said, his expression hard. "It's a part of London mostly known for cutthroats, whores, tumbledown tenements, an' big rats. Ain't no place for a lady to even think about goin'."

All of which made Cheapside the perfectly logical place to look. There was no thinking to be done. She tapped the map again. "Barrett's somewhere in this general vicinity."

O'Brien managed not to snort; he rolled his eyes instead. Carden tilted his head and gave her a look that she suspected he usually reserved for possible lunatics. "How do you know that, Belle?"

The hope that they wouldn't ask had been tiny, but she felt its deflation in the most acute sort of way. "Divining," she supplied simply. "And before you dismiss it as desperate, empty magic, understand that it's the means by which we successfully narrowed the search for Lafitte's treasure. It does work. If Barrett were here, he wouldn't bat an eye."

Carden cleared his throat and stared down at the map, a brow raised in obvious skepticism.

"Even if'n he is in there," O'Brien all but snarled, "findin' him'd be like comin' up with the needle in the hayloft. He could be in any one of thousands of holes. Damn place is like a rabbit's warren."

"Well," Belle countered, her hands on her hips, her resolve strengthening by the heartbeat, "I can guarantee you that Barrett didn't walk into it willingly or under his own power. He was either dragged or carried in. And regardless of the hour at which he was, someone is likely to have been a witness. It's a matter of finding them and getting them to point in the proper direction."

"Haulin' an' forcin' people about ain't nothin' noteworthy in Cheapside, miss. It'd take us a week an' a small friggin' fortune to track down what was seen just this mornin'. It's a fool's task."

"And if," she posed coolly, "Barrett dies in there because you think it would be too much trouble to look for him?"

Carden's gaze snapped up from the map to openly appraise her. O'Brien heaved a sigh and stared down at the floor, the muscles in his jaw clenching and unclenching.

"I don't care what you think of it, Mr. O'Brien," Belle went on, deliberately keeping her tone firm but gentle. "The task is yours because you have the skills necessary to see it properly done. I'm going to go see Inspector Larson because I alone have the information necessary to enlist his assistance. As soon as possible after that, Carden and I will join you in the search for Barrett. He's there and we're going to find him."

In O'Brien's glowering silence, Carden drawled, "I gather that you're not intending to follow any of the instructions in the note."

"Emil doesn't intend to. Why should I?" she countered. Looking between the two men, she added, "A little lesson I learned in our bloody war, gentlemen. The best defense is an unexpected offense."

Carden nodded ever so slightly. O'Brien looked decidedly doubtful. "Mr. O'Brien," she went on, taking a scrap of paper from her pocket and handing it to him. "On your way to marshaling what manpower you can for the search, I'd appreciate it if you would gather together the things on this list and have them for me by the time Carden and I join you in Cheapside."

His right hand occupied with the coffee cup, he flipped open the once folded paper with his left. Belle watched as his gaze traveled down the list and his eyes widened.

"Jesus friggin' Christ!" he exclaimed, his head snapping up so fast that he had to shift his feet to keep his balance. "What are you thinkin', lady?"

"That Emil Caribe isn't expecting me to take so bold an offensive."

He swallowed, twice, before he managed to choke out, "I can't. The boss'll have my balls."

Carden sighed and mercifully intervened. "Do as she asks, O'Brien," he said evenly. "If Barrett trusts her, so can we. Get her what she wants and start the search. I'll stand between you and Barrett if something goes wrong."

Shaking his head, Patrick O'Brien stuffed the note in his trousers pocket and set his coffee cup aside. "When you head that way," he ground out, clearly more resigned than committed to doing as he was told, "I'll be at the Hen an' Chick."

"Thank you," Belle offered, reaching into her other pocket and extracting the two bundled stacks of currency Barrett had taken from the wall safe the morning they'd fled his house. "In case it does cost a small fortune," she explained, handing them to the Irishman.

Tucking them inside his coat, he moved off toward the door, muttering obscenities under his breath. She and Carden stood side by side in silence, watching him go, wincing together as the door slammed hard in his wake.

"Belle," he ventured quietly, staring out the window and into the rear yard, "are you sure of the course?"

It occurred to her that he knew very little of what she

intended to do. But the fact that he'd been willing to go
blindly along so far suggested that he didn't plan to directly challenge her. "Yes," she assured him, knowing
even as she did that it wasn't entirely true. There were so
many things that could go wrong, so many guesses and
hunches that might not play out as she thought they
would. She was trusting her instincts and hoping for a
solid measure of good luck.

"I'd feel much better about it all," Carden said, interrupting her thoughts, "if you'd stay at Haven House and let
me pursue it alone. I've sent for John Aiden. He'd be a stalwart, able guard and you'd be quite safe. Which we both
know has always been Barrett's primary concern."

She nodded, silently accepting the truth of his state-
ments.

"I also know Larson," he went on, apparently taking her
silence as a sign that she was giving the notion serious
consideration. "And O'Brien relayed his report to me. I
can deliver it to the inspector quite capably. And then
there's the fact that Cheapside is far less dangerous for a
man than it is a woman. Barrett wouldn't want you there."

They were, she had to admit, all very sound, very logical reasons for her to step back and let Carden take responsibility for finding Barrett. "Tell me something," she
began, taking up her redingote. "Do you love Barrett?"

He started, his movement to take the coat from her faltering as he blinked and drew a quick breath. He recovered
quickly, though, and as he assisted her into the garment, he
somberly replied, "He's more a brother to me than either
of my real ones ever were."

"Would you wait at home and let John Aiden go off to
search for him?"

"Of course not."

She turned and faced him. "You can't ask something of
me that you wouldn't consider doing yourself."

It took a moment and an obvious battle between his sense of chivalry and his sense of fair play, but, eventually, his shoulders slumped ever so slightly. "Against my better judgment, I'll allow the truth of that."

Feeling more relieved than victorious, she offered him a sincere, "Thank you," and then moved toward the door, announcing, "I'm ready to go if you are."

Dashing ahead, he pulled it open for her. It was as she passed him that he knitted his brows. "Just out of curiosity," he drawled as he followed her out and down the steps, "What sort of things is O'Brien gathering up for you?"

"Six feet of small-diameter rope, two feet of stiff wire, a small pair of snips, a box of waterproofed matches, and two sticks of dynamite."

She heard him make a gurgling sound, but before he could gather his wits to a sufficient degree to press her for specifics, she jauntily asked, "I assume that you have a solicitor? I want the transfer of the land grant to be absolutely, perfectly legal. And I think I should probably have a will made while I'm at it."

"Belle," he began.

Hearing the doubt and reservation in his voice, she continued on toward his carriage, looking back over her shoulder to smile at him and say breezily, "Oh, and did O'Brien tell you where Emma and Rose and Emil are staying? That's information we're most definitely going to need to give Inspector Larson."

Chapter Eighteen

It frigging hurt to open his eyes. Or rather eye, Barrett decided, trying one and then the other and finding his left one nearly swollen shut. And breathing was even worse. If a couple of the ribs on his left side weren't broken, they'd at the very least been pounded well out of place. As for the rest of his body . . .

Gingerly, painfully, he lifted his head. His right arm lay across his midriff, an unnatural bend in it midway between the elbow and the wrist. The part of him sticking out of his coat sleeve didn't look much like a hand anymore. Actually, if pressed, he'd have to say it more resembled a small ham than anything else.

Ham. He lay back and swallowed. God, he was hungry. And thirsty. And cold to the damn marrow of his battered and broken bones. The latter probably, he allowed, because he was lying on a damp dirt floor. Carefully angling his head, he gazed at the small rectangle of light in the upper corner of the room. Considering the layer of grime hazing the rippled glass, the sunlight passing through was fairly bright. Which suggested that he'd been unconscious for at least three, maybe four, hours. Which explained why he was hungry and thirsty.

He sighed, grimacing and growling through the painful consequence. It took a moment for the sharpest edge to fade and to permit his brain to consider anything beyond the abuse he'd endured. But when it did, it clicked through a series of hideous realizations, his heart starting with each and every one.

The blood pounding through his veins deepened the pain and he clenched his teeth, forcing himself to ignore it, to keep his mind focused on what mattered. The land grant . . . Left inside pocket. Sucking a shallow breath through his teeth, he slowly shifted his shoulder and deliberately pressed his good hand against the outside of his coat. And heard nothing, felt nothing.

Sagging into the dirt at his back, he swallowed his anger and willed his mind to work past it. Caribe and the sisters had the land grant. But it was worthless to them. It had been issued to Lafitte and Lafitte had bequeathed it to Belle and Mignon. Mignon was dead. Which made it Belle's alone. Unless she signed it over . . .

"Christ," he growled as all the ugly pieces of the plan tumbled into place. Three or four hours . . . It was likely that Carden would be the one to receive the ransom note. It had been outside his house that Caribe's vicious little mob had been waiting for him. If O'Brien had done as he'd been instructed and taken Belle to Haven House . . . Oh, God! Into the same snare that had been waiting for him!

He couldn't breathe. He couldn't control the shudders tearing through his body. *Think!* he commanded himself. *Use your bloody brain!*

What did he know for certain? he asked, trying to bring the panic under control. Only one thing, he realized. That he was still alive. If they had Belle, if they'd already forced her to sign over the grant, they'd have dispatched him.

They wouldn't take the chance that he'd live to hunt them down. He was alive because they needed him that way for the time being. They needed to use him to bring Belle to heel. But once they did that, once they had what they wanted from her . . . Neither one of them was going to be allowed to live.

Belle was with Carden, he hastily assured himself. And Aiden. O'Brien was likely there, as well. The Irishman knew the players, the game. He'd relay the information to the others and they'd all see that Belle was well protected. They wouldn't let Caribe past them. She was safe.

But only, he realized, for as long they could keep her shoved behind them. That task would be all but impossible once the ransom note arrived.

Belle would agree in an instant to do whatever Caribe demanded. She'd act out of obligation, out of compassion, out of honor. As for whether she loved him or not . . . A memory came gently into focus before his mind's eye. Belle, standing in the kitchen, looking up at him and confessing the aching hollowness that had come with finding the treasure, the joy that had lit her smile when he'd offered his arms in solace, the yearning in her eyes as he'd gazed down at her and tried to find the right way to tell her that he loved her. How gently, unconditionally she'd accepted his failure. How thoroughly she'd poured herself into his heart and given him all that she was.

She loved him. He knew it. And the truth that he'd so hoped for now frightened him to the very center of his soul.

Belle liked risk, liked the way it made her feel. That attraction, blinded by love . . . She'd see the danger inherent in meeting Caribe's terms, he assured himself, his blood pounding, his throat tight and prickling with tears. Belle had good instincts. She was intelligent, field-wise, and quick.

But even as he considered her strengths, he knew that if her instincts warned her to step back, she'd listen not to them, but to her heart. There would be no flinching. No waffling and trying to work her way around it. No passing it off to Carden or Aiden or O'Brien—no matter how logical they tried to be, no matter how assertive they got. How she'd go around them depended on the kind of resistance they offered in the face of her determination and the exact terms Caribe and the sisters set for the exchange.

He had to count on his friends to stay close to her, to intervene if she tried to take a risk too large. They had to know what she meant to him. Carden had lied to him about his feelings for Seraphina. Aiden had done the same about his feelings for Alexandra. Surely they had recognized his own lies about loving Isabella. But if they didn't . . .

His stomach clenching, Barrett closed his eyes, knowing that all the worry in the world wasn't going to change the outcome. He had to think, to figure out what was likely to happen and how to get between Caribe and Belle.

The land grant needed to be legally transferred. Otherwise, Belle would simply have to present Lafitte's will to the proper authorities and reclaim it. To demand that she put the transfer in the name of either of the de Granvieux women or Emil Caribe would be tantamount to taking out an advertisement in the *Times* and publicly proclaiming themselves murderers, kidnappers, and thieves. And so the transfer would be simply to the bearer of the grant. There was a single, certain consequence in that: Caribe wouldn't send a minion to make the trade, he'd do it himself. But the exact hour and the place where Caribe wanted to make the transaction . . .

God Almighty, that could be anyone's guess. London was a huge city with millions of dark corners. They'd give Belle the time necessary to have a barrister draw up a legal title transfer, but, beyond those few hours, they had no obvious reason to delay.

Barrett eased his head back to consider the window again. Fairly close to noon, he guessed. Perhaps a little after. He moved his head back to center and then to his right. The door out was at the top of four rickety steps. Whether it was locked and what—and who—might lie on the other side of it were discoveries that could be made only when he got there.

His right arm useless, he eased onto his left hip, planted his left elbow in the dirt floor, and began to push himself up. The pain shot through him, white and hot. The shaft of sunlight jerked and danced and then winked out.

It was all moving very quickly. And the pace was only going to accelerate as the day went on. She could feel it in her bones. As Carden helped her out of his carriage, Isabella smiled in thanks and tamped down the hard, twisting stab of regret. He was a most competent man and she was certainly glad for his company and assistance. But, despite their physical similarities, he wasn't at all like Barrett. Carden Reeves's edges were ever so much smoother, his manner considerably more polished and refined. He was, she supposed, a man of his social status; a bit elevated and removed from the grubbiness of the real world.

She wished with all her heart that it was Barrett holding her elbow as they made their way toward the knot of constables on the walkway. Not that that would have been wise at this particular moment, she reminded herself. Larson believed him responsible for two murders already. Three if she'd properly interpreted what the constable at the precinct desk had told them. Still . . .

Belle swallowed and banished the ever-present threat of

tears. She would give Inspector Larson her explanation and the evidence to support it. Calmly, rationally. She would make him understand that he'd been pursuing an innocent man. And when that realization dawned on him, she'd enlist his help. No officer of the law could refuse to admit a mistake. Not when offered the chance to pursue—and apprehend—a clearly identified and obviously guilty suspect.

The group of uniformed constables stood at the base of a set of stone steps that led from the public walkway to the door of what looked to be a fashionable inn. As they neared the men, Carden said softly, "I'll negotiate our way past."

She nodded, grateful that he was willing to take the lead and allow her time to organize her approach to Larson. She'd met him only once—the morning he'd questioned her about Mignon's murder. Directed there by Mignon's landlady, he'd arrived at the door of her rented room, perfunctorily introduced himself, and then bluntly informed her that her cousin had been beaten to death in an alleyway the night before.

In hindsight, she could see that she'd reacted just as he'd intended. She'd stared up at him, stunned and yet not wholly surprised, and answered all of his questions without giving her responses even the slightest consideration. She'd been honest, telling him why she and Mignon were in London. She'd suggested that someone from New Orleans might well be responsible for her cousin's fate, but when she hadn't been able to supply a name with any certainty, he'd smiled thinly and begun to ask her questions about Barrett Stanbridge. The name that had meant nothing to her that morning, she realized, now meant everything.

Carden drew her to a halt before the group of officers, introduced himself as Lord Lansdown, her as Mrs. Henri

Dandaneau, and then informed the gathering that they had important information to relay to Inspector Larson regarding the murder he was presently investigating. At his name the men visibly straightened, at hers they slid a glance in her direction. At Carden's request to be allowed entrance, they all looked at one of their own, a short, lean, dark-eyed man with a jagged scar that ran from just beneath his right eye, over the bridge of his nose, across and down his left cheek to disappear into a dark beard.

Something about him seemed vaguely familiar. Belle met his assessing gaze and gave him a tightly polite smile as her mind tried to put him in a place she'd been or among a group of people she'd met. At his crisp nod and motion to follow him up the stairs, she reluctantly put the conundrum away and focused her thoughts on how to best approach the inspector.

Without a word, the man led them inside the door and up the carpeted stairs to the second floor. Halfway down the hall, he motioned for them to stop and then disappeared through an open doorway. Carden's hand still cupping her elbow, they moved into the doorway before obeying his silent command. The possibility that he might be a mute was squelched as Belle watched him step to Larson's side. While she couldn't hear his voice, she could plainly see that Larson did.

Tall, white haired, and seemingly dressed in the same black suit he'd been wearing the last time she'd seen him, Larson stiffened and let his gaze shift toward the doorway. His bushy white brows knitted over the bridge of his nose to become one as he scowled down at his subordinate and offered what looked to be a single-word response. The man with the scar nodded rather emphatically and said something else. Whatever it was, it clearly surprised Larson. His brows went up and the thin line of his lips shifted to the side.

The exchange continued, but Belle abandoned it, focusing instead on the larger world of the room in which it was taking place. There were two other men there, both considerably younger than Larson, both in black suits, both scribbling notes in small brown leather books as they moved around the badly rumpled bed. Or more accurately, she realized, the body on the floor beside the bed.

Only the lower limbs stuck out from beneath the bloody, crumpled coverlet. Belle considered them, carefully noting the particulars. The dead person was a woman who had, in life, considered the fashionability of footwear more important than the comfort they afforded. They were new shoes; the soles were barely scuffed. Belle looked past them, higher. The legs were oddly bent and at a slight angle off the floor. Death had visited some hours ago.

Isabella glanced up the body, noting the blood pattern on the cover, and then back down. Death had come from behind as the woman had stood beside the bed. The knife had slashed across her throat and she'd crumpled, grabbing the bedding with desperate, dying hands. Whoever had cut her hadn't let her fall uncontrolled, though. Otherwise, the body would be more contorted. No, they'd lowered her down, placing her on her back and half-arranging her as though providing for her comfort at that point could make up for having so brutally killed her.

"Belle," Carden whispered. "Perhaps you should step back."

"I've seen death before," she said, drawing her elbow from his considerate grasp. "Far too many times to be overly distressed by it," she added, moving forward into the room.

Larson gave the scarred man a quick nod at her approach and he scampered past her and out the door. His gait again triggered the sense of familiarity, but Belle deliberately set it aside, knowing that she needed to direct her full attention on Larson.

"Lord Lansdown, Mrs. Dandaneau," he offered with a most abbreviated bow in each of their directions as they came to a halt in front of him. "The sergeant tells me that you believe you have information concerning the murder of this unfortunate woman."

Belle nodded, took a steadying breath, and began. "The coverlet hiding her face prevents a positive identification, but I can guess that she's either Emma or Rose de Granvieux."

He motioned to one of the younger men and the coverlet was discreetly drawn back. Belle's stomach heaved, but she looked away quickly and forced herself to speak. "It's Rose. The older of the two sisters."

"And how is it that you know her?" Larson asked, as the coverlet was dropped and the younger men scribbled in their notebooks. "Was she also your cousin?"

"We grew up together in New Orleans."

"It would seem that something about American women invites a gruesome fate. Was she also in search of a pirate's treasure, Mrs. Dandaneau?"

"I have reason to believe so," Belle replied, deliberately ignoring his insult. "She and her sister, Emma, and Mignon's last lover, Emil Caribe, all came to London in our wake."

He hummed in a dismissive sort of way and then looked past her to Carden. "Might I ask you, sir, just where your friend Barrett Stanbridge might be?"

"We don't know precisely. Not at the current moment, anyway."

"We?" Larson repeated, his gaze snapping to Belle's, his brow cocked. "Am I to presume that you have made the acquaintance of Mr. Stanbridge since last we met?"

She wasn't going to provide him the details of their relationship. Not now, not ever. They were none of his business, none of his concern. Instead, she reached into her skirt pocket and withdrew the ransom note. As she handed it to him, Carden supplied, "That was wrapped around a rock and tossed through the window of my home early this morning. Apparently Barrett was on his way to collect me before finding you and he was taken captive along the way."

Larson didn't reply, but skimmed over the note. "Land grant?" he asked, finally looking up to meet Belle's gaze.

"That's the treasure Lafitte left us—Mignon and me, through our grandmama," she explained. "A grant from President Madison of a half million acres in the Western territories."

"Presumably worth a considerable sum," the inspector ventured dryly.

"It would be especially attractive to people who have survived the ravages of war and emerged with nothing but memories of a far grander time. The desire to live well and comfortably again can be quite overwhelming."

"Would you count yourself among those overwhelmed people, Mrs. Dandaneau?"

"My only desperation, Inspector, concerns Barrett," she provided, anger thrumming through her veins. "I've been to the solicitor this morning and had the transfer drawn as demanded. The treasure means nothing to me compared to Barrett's life."

He gave her a smile that suggested he found her declaration decidedly boring. Again his gaze shifted to Carden. "And why was Mr. Stanbridge on his way to see me? Perhaps to surrender himself and unburden his conscience?"

"According to his man," Carden replied evenly, crisply, "he intended to tell you about the presence of the de Granvieux sisters and Emil Caribe."

"Being in London is no crime," Larson countered. "People are free to come and go at will. There is nothing about this woman's presence in our city to suggest it was motivated by sinister intentions."

"As far as you know at the present moment," Belle pointed out. "According to the officer at your precinct desk, Lord Lansdown and I missed you by only minutes this morning. Since we came directly here in your wake, we can logically infer that you haven't had time to ask anyone anything."

"I think it might be the acerbic tongue that draws mayhem to American women."

Fire shot through her veins and flared behind her eyes. Before she could think better of it, she retorted, "We have a very low tolerance for groundless senses of superiority. Would you care—in the interests of justice—to stow yours and listen to what I have to tell you? With something that approximates an open mind?"

Behind her, Carden sucked a hard breath between his teeth. Larson glowered at her in silence. She didn't wait for Carden to intervene or Larson to grant her permission. And, knowing that there was nothing to be gained from holding back any of the significant details, she told him everything—about Mignon's life and how it had connected to the desperations and desires of the de Granvieux sisters and Emil Caribe. She told him why Mignon had left the theater with Barrett, the bits of the map she'd hidden around his home and property, their return to find the last two missing pieces and the murder of the man in the yard. She told him about the chocolates she'd found in Mignon's things and the peppermint wrappers that had been in the dead man's pockets and how it hadn't made any sense until O'Brien had provided his report. Of how Barrett had taken the land grant with him when he'd left early that morning and how he'd intended to present it as proof of motive.

And then—withholding the fact that the information from O'Brien was thirdhand—she told him that they'd known the minute the precinct clerk had told them of the murder on Queen's Way that the conspirators had turned against each other just as O'Brien had so casually predicted. Meeting Larson's carefully guarded gaze, she listened to her instincts and took a chance.

"I can't tell you for certain what happened this morning, Inspector," she began, "but I can make a reasoned guess or two. Barrett walked into a trap that had been laid for him outside Lord Lansdown's home. There was probably one laid outside his own, that of Mr. John Aiden Terrell, and that of his parents, too, just to make sure they didn't miss him.

"The intent was to take him hostage and exchange him for either the map or the treasure itself. When they found the land grant on him, they realized that the treasure wasn't the immediately convertible reward they'd hoped it to be. But they were resourceful and determined enough to think of a way to make it so. They demanded a transfer to the bearer and allowed me the time necessary to have it legally prepared."

Larson said nothing; he simply considered her, his ice-blue eyes appraising but otherwise expressionless. "It was after the ransom note was written that Rose was murdered," she went on. "She'd served her purpose in writing it. And her death was meant to serve as her last one by consuming your time and efforts in investigating her murder, by trying to make Barrett accountable for it instead of looking at her sister and her lover."

Belle pointed to the desk in the corner of the room. "I'll wager your monthly wages that in the drawer you'll find paper matching the one on which the ransom note was written. I'll wager you two months' that the top sheet, when angled into the light, will be an indented copy of the text you're holding in your hand."

Larson blinked, slid his mouth to the side and then made a sharp motion with his left hand. One of the young detectives instantly moved across the room and pulled open the center drawer. Belle barely kept herself from sagging in relief when he withdrew several sheets of paper the exact color and size of the one Larson held between his right thumb and fingertip. The senior investigator cocked a brow and his assistant tilted the paper into the afternoon light. And read aloud from the blank sheet the ransom demand, word for word.

Larson's gaze came back to her. "I find your knowledge to be a cause of grave suspicion, Mrs. Dandaneau."

The blind bastard. She bit her tongue and searched for a response that might be considered diplomatic. Finding none, she gambled again. "Emma's dead, too," she offered. "Three months' salary says that you'll find her body somewhere near Emil's lodgings on Shaftesbury. How he killed her, I can't say, but it doesn't really matter a great deal. She served her purpose, as well."

"And that was?" Larson asked coolly.

"Emil didn't have money on which to travel and live," she explained, straining to keep the impatience from her voice. "Emma and Rose did. From what their father left them. They were his purses and his message couriers. When you finally get around to questioning the clerks at Nickel's Sweet Shop, you're going to discover that it was Rose and Emma who frequented the establishment. No one there has ever seen Emil Caribe. He used them to finance his hunt for the treasure. Used them as shields. They carried the instructions to his hirelings. The ransom note is in Rose's hand."

"So," Larson drawled, "there is no evidence to tie him to any criminal activity of any sort."

"Precisely," she snapped. "By deliberate design."

"It seems to me," Carden offered ever so breezily from behind her, "that it's a brilliant enough plan and one quite likely to succeed. Based on the assumption, of course, that the constabulary isn't sharp enough to see past the surface of things."

She'd only thought Larson had been glowering before. The look he fastened on Carden was positively lethal. She was scrambling to think of a way to diffuse the tension and get back to bringing Larson into their camp when Carden took her by the elbow and drew her around.

"We have reason to believe that Barrett's being held somewhere in Cheapside," he said as they moved toward the door. "When you've decided that it makes more sense to work with us than against us, ask for our whereabouts at the Hen and Chick."

She held her breath and moved quickly, afraid that Larson would call out and his minions would dash forward to detain them.

"They don't dare," Carden whispered, easing her pace. "Larson doesn't know whether you're right or wrong and he can't afford to make a mistake. He'll send someone to Shaftesbury and Nickel's before he makes a decision."

"Even if I'm right, he still won't know on which side of the fence to fall," she allowed as her heart hammered and they sedately moved down the stairs. "He could just as well suspect me of the murders as he could Emil."

"He won't. Caribe will be his choice."

"How can you be so sure?"

He chuckled dryly and led her down the outside stairs and toward the carriage, saying, "Larson is one of those men who considers complicated murders to be beyond the capabilities of the female brain."

She snorted in unladylike fashion and utter disdain. "I should think that I just proved that notion wrong."

"By the time he's through mulling it over," Carden offered, handing her up, "and collecting the evidence you sent him after, he'll truly believe that the solution was born of his own deductive efforts."

"I really don't care, you know," Belle assured him as he dropped into the rear-facing seat. "All that matters is that he knows that Barrett had nothing to do with the murders."

And none of that mattered to her as much as having Barrett back alive. She gazed out the window and considered the sunlight. Hours down, hours to go. Too many hours to go. Too many hours in which she had nothing to do but desperately search a rabbit's warren and keep the dread from growing and paralyzing her mind.

"You were wonderful, Belle," Carden offered, pulling her from her worries. His smile was soft and easy. "Such poise and careful logic. No one could have done it better. Barrett will be so disappointed that he missed the performance."

Barrett . . . That he might never know . . . That it might be too late . . . The tears came in a sudden, heated, unstoppable torrent. "I'm sorry," she sobbed, burying her face in her hands and desperately wanting to be alone with her grief and fear.

He slipped across the carriage to sit beside her, to gather her into his arms. Strong arms, arms that she knew he meant to be comforting. But they weren't, not like Barrett's.

"It will be all right, Belle," he assured her softly, holding her close as the emptiness inside her deepened. "Barrett's made of steel."

"No he isn't," she hiccuped against his chest. "He's flesh and blood. As mortal as any other man."

She felt him sigh, felt him draw a deep breath. "Yes, I'll allow that he is," Carden countered gently. "But he loves you, Belle. And he wants to live as he never has before. You have to believe in him just as much and as deeply as he believes in you."

Isabella nodded and closed her eyes. It took resolve and a thousand heartbeats, but the tide of fear and dread slowly ebbed away. In the void, she pretended that the strong arms wrapped around her shoulders were Barrett's. And for the first time since she'd been a very little girl, she said a silent prayer and offered heaven a bargain.

Chapter Nineteen

It was mid-afternoon on the streets of London, but the hour of the day was irrelevant in the world of the Hen and Chick tavern. Belle couldn't say that Carden hadn't warned her. Neither could she say that she'd never been in a place as dingy, as dark, and as sordid as this. Actually, it was a full cut above Frank Lazro's tavern on the outskirts of New Orleans. She couldn't count the number of nights she'd spent in the back room of that place, studying maps and formulating strategies.

But the Hen and Chick was different in one important aspect: the air was thick with smoke. No one in Lazro's had been allowed to strike a match, much less smoke their various weeds of choice. There had been enough gunpowder stored beneath the floorboards to blow the building and everyone in it halfway to the moon. Smoking had been done outside and some considerable distance away.

Her eyes having adjusted to the near absence of light and the haze, Belle searched the farthest corners of the single room, looking for a familiar face. She squinted, not quite sure, and turned to whisper over her shoulder, "Carden? Is that John Aiden at the back right?"

He chuckled and pressed his hand into the small of her back, urging her forward as he replied, "He has some experience in living at such a low-water mark. Although it's been a while, it's obvious that he hasn't forgotten how to do it."

She had to give John Aiden Terrell credit for managing to look as though he belonged in a place like the Hen and Chick, as though he were not one whit different from the half-dozen or so other patrons. His clothes were ratty and ill-fitting and definitely the kind worn by working men. Unlike her, she silently groused, reaching back to snatch a handful of skirt and pull it and her hoops through the narrow space between the scarred tables. God, she'd never gone to Lazro's dressed like a lady, never had to try to disappear in the shadows wearing a fashionable burgundy and plum and gold–striped dress.

What had been appropriate for the meeting with Inspector Larson wasn't the least bit so for the Hen and Chick. Or Cheapside. Or for what she suspected would happen in the hours ahead. Belle thought of the valise Carden carried for her, pleased that she'd thought ahead.

But, she reminded herself, there were things to be done, information to be gathered and plans to be made before she could take time for her more personal concerns. Aiden wasn't alone at the table. Another man sat with him, the two of them engaged in a conversation that seemed to be more about polite smiles than actual words. The stranger was a smallish man with a lean face and narrow shoulders that rolled forward and in as though he'd spent every day of his life hunched over account ledgers.

As she and Carden neared, they both rose to their feet, Aiden casting a quick look down as he did so.

"I'm so glad to see you, John Aiden," she offered sincerely as Carden placed her valise in an empty chair.

Aiden gave her a quick smile and wasted no time with pleasantries or formalities. "Belle, Carden, this is Dr. William George. He's a surgeon. I thought it best to be prepared for the worst."

The worst possibility wouldn't require the skills of a surgeon, she knew, but rather the skills of a mortician. She quickly and roughly shoved away the morose thought. "Thank you for coming, Doctor," she said, extending her hand. As he cradled it in his own and bent over it, she added, "I sincerely hope that we won't have need of your expertise."

"No one ever does," he replied, releasing her hand to extend his own to Carden. "They are, however, genuinely pleased to see me when they do."

"As we will be," Carden offered with a smile that struck Belle as being a little forced and slightly shadowed by worry.

There was no comfort at all in knowing that she wasn't the only one considering horrible possibilities. Determined to distract herself, to keep her mind occupied with anything other than dreadful imaginings, she ignored all of her mother's instruction on the requirements of genteel conversation. "Have you seen O'Brien?" she asked without preamble.

Aiden nodded. "He was briefly through here about an hour ago," he supplied as he bent down and retrieved a small wooden crate and a burlap bag from the floor. Placing both carefully on the table in front of her, he explained, "He left these things for you, Belle, saying that there'd be hell to pay if I played with fire or kicked the box."

"He's right," she allowed, gently lifting the hinged lid of the crate. "But since you're still very much in one piece," she added, carefully moving the packing straw aside just enough to examine the contents, "I can see that you took his words to heart."

"What's in there?"

"Dynamite." Both Aiden and the good doctor took a half-step back. "Not to worry, gentlemen," she assured them as she pushed the straw padding back into place. "It's well packed. It's as stable and safe as it gets, as long as none of us do anything rash."

Carden reached past her for the bag, asking ever so nonchalantly, "What are you going to do with it, Belle?"

"I'm going to rig a trip wire," she supplied, lowering the lid. "And hope Emil gives me sufficient time to explain how it works."

Dr. George, a good three shades paler than he had been a few minutes earlier, cleared his throat. "Do you make a habit of playing with explosives?"

His voice was at least an octave higher, too. For the first time since early that morning, Belle felt fully in control, capable of dealing with whatever came her way. "Yes, Doctor, I do," she replied, smiling as she glanced into the bag Carden held open for her inspection. Everything she'd asked for was there.

"Dynamite is a very new development," she went on, meeting the physician's shocked gaze. "It has its drawbacks, of course. All things new do. But it's ever so much easier to transport and conceal than a keg of powder. Not to mention that, ounce for ounce, it provides a much more impressive effect."

"You are," Aiden laughed, his green eyes bright, "without doubt, the most perfect woman in the world for Barrett. You're two sides to the same coin."

She wanted to thank him for the compliment, for the assurance. She wanted to tell him that Barrett was the only man she had ever loved, could ever love. But the tickling low in her throat warned her that the words would come on a flood of tears. She swallowed hard. "Did O'Brien say anything at all about finding him?"

"Aside from the warning about handling the box," he answered, his amusement dimming just the slightest bit, "the only other thing he said was that he hated it when uppity women proved to be right."

Barrett was in Cheapside! She locked her knees as a brilliant, sparkling hope enveloped her. They were close. It could be only a matter of minutes before they found him. Her heart racing, Belle resisted the impulse to lunge across the table and grab John Aiden Terrell by the lapels of his battered jacket. "Did he say when we could expect him to return?" she asked, too excited to care that she sounded every bit as breathless as she was. "Or is he simply going to send word and have us go to him?"

Aiden's smile faded as he shook his head. "I'm sorry, Belle. All he said beyond what I've already relayed was that we were to wait here."

Hope evaporated just as quickly and completely as it had swelled over her. "Well," she said, taking up the handle of her valise and giving them all a weak smile, "if you gentlemen will excuse me for a few moments, I need to speak with the barkeeper."

She felt their gazes following her as she made her way across the room, heard the low sounds of their hushed voices. No doubt they were discussing how completely out of control her emotions had become. At some point one of them would have to suggest that perhaps a woman bordering on lunacy shouldn't be allowed to play with fuses and explosives. And she couldn't really find fault with the logic. As shaky as her hands were . . . And Lord knew that the only thing predictable about her thoughts was how quickly and easily they could produce a river of tears.

The room to which the keep directed her was more the size of a closet. Or a very large hatbox. But since it was the

only private space in the Hen and Chick, Isabella made do
as best she could and hoped that none of the patrons—
those other than the gentlemanly Carden and Aiden and
Dr. George—were trying to peek around the edges of the
skimpy curtain serving as the door. Not that there was
much chance of it, she knew. Not with her hoops swinging
and swaying as she climbed out of them. The curtain bil-
lowed out and fell back into place one last time as she
lifted it all above her head and shoved it into the rear corner and atop a short stack of ale kegs. With a sigh of relief
to be done with them, Belle yanked open her valise and
happily dug out her boots and night clothes. She was
perched on the edge of a wooden crate and pulling on her
boots when the chairs started scraping over the tavern
floor. First one, then a couple more, then a seeming chorus
of them, followed by something of a stampede toward the
door.

Belle peeked out between the curtain and the door
frame. As she blindly fished about in her valise for her hat
and jacket, she watched Inspector Larson saunter toward
the rear corner of the establishment. The two younger detectives were nowhere in sight. Only the sergeant with the
badly scarred face accompanied him.

Deciding to give the men time for their introductions
and the exchange of thinly veiled insults, she separated her
dress from her hoops, abandoning the latter and stuffing
the former unceremoniously into her traveling bag. With
the handle in one hand and her hat and coat in the other,
Belle took a deep breath, squared her shoulders, lifted her
chin, and boldly marched out into the main room.

"Inspector Larson," she said pleasantly as he and his
subordinate turned at her approach. "How good of you to
join us. Do you owe me three months' salary?"

Larson's—and the sergeant's—gaze skimmed down the
length of her and back up. She had dropped her valise and

coat on the seat of the empty chair and tossed the hat onto the table by the time he recovered enough to reply, "You weren't completely correct in your predictions, madam."

"Oh? Where did I err?" she asked, her arms akimbo. "Did Emil actually set foot inside Nickel's Sweet Shop?"

"Not that we have been able to ascertain."

"Emma's still alive?"

He managed a tight, thin smile. "You were correct in both your prediction of her fate and the location of the body. Her throat had been cut in the same manner as her sister's."

Oh, it had practically choked him to admit that. And she wasn't feeling benevolent enough to let him off the hook. "Then where did I err, Inspector?"

"You failed," he announced regally, one brow cocked at a decidedly superior angle, "to predict that we would find the murderer dead, as well."

"Emil's been killed?" she asked, stunned and disbelieving.

"My men tell me that he was a contract man from Southwark whose apparent specialties were knee breaking and strategic stabbings—of the permanently hobbling variety," Larson supplied, his manner undaunted by her challenge. "Adam Gray was his name. And he was a suicide, actually. A single shot to the left temple. Apparently, given the proximity of his body to that of the younger Miss de Granvieux, he was overcome by his conscience immediately after having killed her. We found both the knife and the revolver with the bodies."

She frowned and knitted her brows, remembering. Did the man really think no deeper than that? Good God Almighty, how had he risen to the rank of inspector?

"What is it, Belle?" Carden asked.

"I saw Rose's body, how her throat had been slit," she answered, boldly meeting the policeman's gaze. "Whoever killed her was right-handed. Aside from the fact that mercenary killers don't have consciences to be troubled, much less overwhelmed, why would Adam Gray kill Emma, drop his knife, take out a gun, and then shoot himself with his left hand? For the challenge of it? No," she said firmly, shaking her head. "Once he'd served his full range of purposes, Emil killed him. He's tying up the loose ends. Eliminating anyone who can testify to his involvement in the murders."

"You have to admit that he really is very good," Carden offered, the notes of amusement in his voice earning him a quick glare from Larson. "In a completely evil and twisted sort of way."

"On the off chance," the older man said testily, "that you might be correct regarding the involvement of this Emil Caribe person, I have ordered a contingent of my men to take up positions around St. Paul's. Discreetly, of course."

"You might as well pull them back, Inspector," Belle said, taking up the wooden box containing the dynamite. "Emil has no intention whatsoever of conducting an aboveboard, public exchange. Detailing one was simply his attempt to divert attention and effort elsewhere. When we find Barrett, Emil Caribe will be standing in the doorway."

"And how do you know that?" Larson demanded.

Belle set the box down on a nearby table, shrugged, and returned for the bag of supplies, saying, "I know Emil. I know what he wants and how he thinks."

She was aware that all five men were watching her with acute interest, three of them knowing what she was about, the other two having no idea at all. She wondered how long it would take Larson to inquire. To his credit, he resisted for far longer than she expected. She'd already wired together two ignition devices, wired each in turn to each of the four corners of the folded grant transfer, laid it all aside, and was removing the sticks of dynamite from the box when he finally broke down.

"Might I ask what you're doing?"

She thought it should have been obvious to even the most casual, inexperienced observer, and it crossed her mind to tell him that she was baking a cake, but decided that he wasn't the sort to let sarcasm roll off his back. "I'm building an explosive device."

"A what!"

"A bomb," she clarified, using her knife to shorten the fuses to the barest possible length. "With which I intend to bring Emil to heel and secure Barrett's release."

The sergeant slowly backed away a good six feet. Larson remained where he was, blinking furiously and seemingly unable to get the words spat off the end of his tongue. While he worked at it, Belle dug in her valise for her dress, sliced off a strip of fabric and divided it into two segments. Placing one over each of the ignition bundles, she settled the dynamite into position and began the careful task of final wiring.

"It is illegal to make," Larson finally sputtered, "possess, or employ explosives without permission from the proper civil and military authorities."

"I'm sure it is," she allowed, nodding ever so slightly, "but arresting me for it at this particular moment might be something of a dangerous proposition. If, however, you feel the compunction to tempt fate in the name of public safety, I suppose you could give it a try."

He didn't move. Her work completed, Belle eased back, dropped the snips into her pocket, and considered her creation. Heaven only knew if it would work as she'd designed it to. She'd built in all the margins for safety the materials allowed. It could be transported without undue concern. And she certainly wouldn't arm it unless she absolutely had no other choice. Not that Emil had to know any of that.

The door of the Hen and Chick swung wide and all of them turned as one to see O'Brien scramble breathlessly across the threshold. And come to dead stop, his gaze riveted on the sergeant.

"Patrick," the man said icily.

"Joseph."

Belle looked back and forth between them, suddenly realizing why the constable had seemed so familiar. If they weren't brothers, they were most definitely first cousins.

"Have you found Barrett?" Carden asked, breaking the strained silence and setting Belle into motion.

"Got it narrowed to a single building," O'Brien supplied as she picked up the length of rope and the bomb. "Have the boys watchin' front an' back. Figured the more shoulders we have to throw against doors, the better."

A discussion of sorts ensued, but Belle paid it only vague attention. Centering the device on her midsection, she laid the rope across it and then held it in place with one hand as she passed the binding around her body and brought it back to the front. She tied an overhand knot and then tucked the ends of the rope into the pocket of her trousers.

"I'm ready," she announced, taking her coat from the chair.

Patrick O'Brien snorted and snipped over his shoulder, "Ain't no job for a—"

His eyes went as wide as saucers. Belle nodded. "One doesn't argue with a person who has dynamite tied to their body."

"Jesus, Belle!" Aiden exclaimed, scrubbing his hand through his copper-colored hair.

Carden visibly forced himself to swallow before he ventured, "Are you sure you know what you're doing?"

"Absolutely," she assured them, sliding her arms into

the sleeves. "The strips of fabric prevent an accidental ignition. I have to remove them before the spark can reach the fuse."

"Wouldn't carrying it work just as well?" Aiden asked, looking, she thought, as though he might retch at any moment. "Must it be strapped to you? Barrett will kill us if something happens to you."

Barrett would probably want to kill her himself once he found out. His wrath was a price she was perfectly willing to pay, though. A thousand times over. "In terms of damage, yes," she admitted, "it would work just as well—probably better—to have it away from the body. Unfortunately, I don't think Emil would let me get close enough for it to be a true threat if he were to see me carting it up to him. Concealed," she added, drawing her coat over it all, "is another matter entirely."

"You're insane," Larson said on a whisper that almost seemed awed.

"Sometimes," she assured him as she moved past, her heart pounding furiously and her palms damp. "But at the moment, just enough to be sufficiently, effectively dangerous. Lead us on, Mr. O'Brien. Let's get this done."

She wouldn't have held it against any of them if they'd insisted she ride in a separate, rented hack. Or, at the very least, either on the boot or up in the box with Carden's poor unsuspecting driver. But they hadn't. O'Brien had claimed the driver's box saying that he had to point the way. Carden had handed her up into his carriage and he and John Aiden had settled on the opposite seat. Their attempts at reassuring conversation had been diligent if nothing else and their expressions had frozen only slightly whenever the wheels had rolled through a hole in the roadway. And somehow they'd managed to keep from sighing in utter relief when the carriage had rolled to a stop and O'Brien yanked open the door.

Belle stood on the deteriorating pavers of the roadway, looking at the steps of a five-story ramshackle building. At one time it had probably been a fairly nice place to live. But that had been before the plaster had begun to fall off the exterior in huge chunks, the stone stairs from the street had tilted and pulled away, the majority of the window glass had been shattered, and the roof had half rotted.

"He's likely to be in the lower part of it," Aiden observed quietly from her right side as Larson's coach rolled to a stop behind them. "He's too big to haul up stairs any distance."

"I'll bet he's in the cellar," Carden added from her left. "It'd be much more difficult to escape. The windows are high and small. Do you think Caribe is expecting us, Belle? Or will we have the element of surprise on our side?"

"I honestly can't say," she admitted. "My mind has been down the paths of so many possibilities in the last eight hours that I can't think straight anymore. This morning I thought he might actually try to catch me by surprise."

"You've been moving about the city all day and hard to find," Aiden pointed out, checking the load of a pistol and then tucking it in the pocket of his coat. "And he's been a bit busy with other tasks."

"Then I'll hazard a guess that he's going to be thinking fast in just a few moments. Not that I much care one way or the other," she confessed. "All I want is to find Barrett and go home."

"Then let's see it done, shall we?" Carden proposed.

They'd barely taken a step forward when Larson called from behind them, "Now see here, gentlemen, Mrs. Dandaneau. I am in charge of this inves—"

"No," Belle interrupted, turning back to face him. "Inspector, I appreciate your devotion to duty, but your murder investigation isn't our primary concern. Getting Barrett out of there as quickly and as neatly as possible is. Once we've accomplished that, you may do whatever you like regarding Emil Caribe and without our interference or comment."

His gaze flickered past her to light first on Carden and then Aiden. Their expressions must have been unbrookable because the constable glowered and growled, "I will be exceedingly unhappy if he's allowed to escape."

She didn't care one whit what happened to Emil in the long run. As long as he gave her Barrett and let them be, he could go anywhere, do anything he wanted. "We'll do what we can," Belle promised vaguely, turning back and falling in between Barrett's friends, grateful to have them at her side.

They stopped just inside the front door, Belle staring up the stairs, amazed by the apparent fact that there were people still living in the tumbledown building. She could hear a woman singing, several babies were crying, and somewhere—on one of the upper floors—a man and woman were bellowing at each other over his lack of a job. She couldn't arm the device, she realized, her heart tripping. No matter how she might need to. Innocents could be injured in the blast.

"The cellar stairs are likely to be at the other end of the hall," Aiden said quietly.

She nodded and started down the narrow corridor, doorless, empty apartments on her right, the stairwall on her left, Barrett's friends closely flanking her back. If Emil was even half expecting them, her mind chattered, he could step out from any one of the rooms or from the shadows at the end of the stairwell.

They were halfway along the hall when his choice was revealed.

"That's far enough," he decreed, sauntering out from the last room, his arm extended, the butt of a Colt revolver clutched in his hand and the muzzle aimed at the center of her chest.

Her heart hammering, Belle did as he instructed. So did Carden and Aiden. "Hello, Emil," she said breezily. "Fancy finding you here."

"Isabella," he replied with the barest dip of his chin. His gaze raked her from head to toe and back again. "Your mother would be appalled."

"Wouldn't she? Although I doubt that she'd be terribly surprised."

"I distinctly remember instructing you to come alone."

He was surprised and had at least a dozen questions he didn't dare ask; not while trying to pretend that he wasn't ruffled by her having upended his plan. "I was to come alone to the south portico of St. Paul's Cathedral," she countered coolly. "This isn't St. Paul's."

"Tell them to go."

She shook her head. "They're honorable men. If we can strike a bargain, they'll accept it and let you pass unhindered and unharmed. Shall we begin the dance now and get it done?"

"It will have to be a short one," he countered, the gun unwavering. "I have a ship to catch."

Not for a while, though, she reasoned. They were a good two hours ahead of the schedule he'd set that morning. "Of course," she agreed serenely. "One doesn't tarry when there's a fortune to be claimed. Or four murder charges to be evaded."

One dark brow shot up and his dark eyes glittered. "Did you bring the transfer, Isabella?"

She shrugged and countered, "Where's Barrett?"

"I'll tell you when I have the document."

"Oh, please, Emil," she scoffed. "Do you honestly think I'm that stupid?"

The corners of his mouth curled upward and he waved

the muzzle of the gun slightly to draw her attention to it. "I have the gun, my dear. I have the power to set the terms. The document, please. Now."

Belle gave him the heavy sigh he expected and while Carden and Aiden drew long slow breaths, she opened the front of her coat. Emil Caribe actually rocked slightly back on his heels as his Adam's apple bobbed up and down.

"I do believe that two sticks of dynamite trump a Colt repeater, Emil. Especially when they're rigged to the all-important piece of paper." She took a step forward, adding, "Let me explain the mechanism for you. I consider it one of my better pieces of work."

He checked a backward step and waved the muzzle again. "You're a crazy bitch. You always have been."

And she'd let him go on thinking just that. "As you can see—" She paused and made a production of looking around her. "Well, perhaps you can't, the light is rather dim in here. I suppose you'll have to take my word on it. The fuses are extremely short, Emil. The merest fraction of an inch. The time between spark and detonation would be shorter than a blink.

"And the spark . . . This is the beautiful part of it all, Emil. The transfer document is wired to bundles of matches. The bundles are lying hard between strike papers and the fuses. If the document is moved so much as a fraction of an inch in any direction . . ." She smiled at him. "Boom."

"You'd die."

She had him. He didn't know a damn thing about explosives, didn't know in looking that she'd just manipulated him with a whopping lie. It was only a matter of time. Rolling her eyes, Belle snorted. "*I'm* not going to set it off, Emil. I'm just telling you what would happen and how fast *you'd* die should you be thinking about shooting me and taking it off my body. At that point, being blown to bloody bits along with you wouldn't really matter to me, now would it?"

She saw his lips move, read the silent curse that passed over them. "Oh, and one other thing for you to consider, Emil," she went on as Aiden carefully shifted his stance behind her. "While I was at the solicitor's office this morning having the transfer drawn for the land grant . . . I had him write a last will and testament for me. It's in his office, safe under lock and key. In it I leave everything I own—including the land grant—to Barrett Stanbridge.

"Even if you somehow manage to disarm the ignition mechanisms, Barrett gets Lafitte's treasure. I had the will drawn and witnessed *after* the grant transfer was drafted. My will indicates that it was given under duress and legally supersedes it."

His gaze darted to the shadows at the back of the stairwell, telling her that Carden had been right. "He'd better be alive, Emil," she warned.

"He was ten minutes ago."

"Ten minutes ago doesn't count for much right this moment." He licked his lower lip and she could see the sheen of moisture forming along his upper lip and across his forehead. "I have a proposal, Emil," she offered while his mind was still reeling from the repeated shocks. "Out of it we both get what we want and walk away."

He swallowed and took two deep breaths before he asked, "And that would be?"

Behind her, Carden softly cleared his throat and Aiden shifted his stance again. "You allow Barrett to be carried out of here and I'll defuse the bomb and give you the transfer document. It's been drafted just as you demanded in the ransom note. To the bearer. I won't challenge your claim and I'll destroy the will. You can have the grant free and clear."

He measured the distance between them, his eyes narrowing in calculation.

"Oh, Emil, please," she scoffed. "I'm not about to get close enough to actually hand it to you. That would be incredibly foolhardy. Once Barrett's past, I'll back toward the front door and lay it on the newel post as I go by. It'll be there for the taking once we're gone."

"And if you try to bolt with it?" he countered angrily.

"Then you can shoot me in the back," she proposed blithely, "blow me and the paper to kingdom come, and then try to get past Barrett's friends." She allowed him only a second to appreciate the corner into which he'd been backed. "Do we have a bargain or not, Emil?"

"Don't move," he commanded, brandishing the pistol yet again. "You two," he snapped, looking past her to Aiden and Carden. "He's in a room to the right at the bottom of the stairs. Be quick about it."

"Barrett's all that matters," she whispered as they moved around her. She watched them cover the remaining hallway, keeping their shoulders close to the stairwall and their attention on the muzzle of the gun.

As they rounded the corner and disappeared from sight, Emil quickly swept the sleeve of his coat across his mouth and said, "Now disarm it."

"I'll get the snips," she explained, reaching into her pocket and drawing them out. Holding them up so that he could see, she added, "But I'm not cutting any wires until Barrett's safely outside."

His teeth clearly clenched, he studied her. In the relative silence, Belle could hear the low rumble of Carden's and Aiden's voices. Strain as she did, though, she couldn't hear Barrett's. Her heartbeat quickened and her throat tightened with dread. Determined not to succumb, she forced her thoughts in another direction.

"Just out of curiosity, Emil . . . Was it you Mignon saw at the theater that night?"

"Most unfortunately, with Emma. If she hadn't been

there, I would have been able to spin a believable tale for your cousin and it all would have been ever so much simpler."

"I don't see how," Belle observed. "You would still have had to dispose of Rose and Emma. And Mignon, as well."

"And you, too, Isabella. But when Mignon left the theater with Stanbridge, everything became ever so much more complicated than it should have been. Cursed bad luck that he turned out to be an investigator and that implicating him in Mignon's death drew the police attention it did. But I managed to compensate for it all quite well, if I do say so myself."

Listening to the sounds coming up the stairwell beside her, Belle decided that wisdom lay in not challenging his perceptions. Anyone who had murdered four people had to be mentally unbalanced; insulting him unnecessarily wasn't a good idea. Not when the end of the ordeal was within momentary reach.

Aiden emerged from around the corner first, holding what appeared to be a door firmly in his hands. A door that had been made into a litter, she realized, her heart twisting with full realization. Barrett lay motionless on it, his head at Aiden's end. Her knees buckled and she grabbed the stairwall for support. Her teeth clenched, she focused on the promise in the rise and fall of his chest, and fought the impulse to draw her own Colt.

"He'll be all right," Aiden said, his expression grim as he backed past her. "He'll mend, Belle. Honestly."

Carden's eyes were blazing with outrage as he met her gaze while moving past. "Get yourself out of here," he commanded quietly. "Now."

"Two trills when you get to the road," she said just as quietly, easing backward in their wake, her gaze fastened on Emil's. Blindly, not trusting him, not quite trusting herself, either, she took one of the ignition bundles in hand

and snipped the wires that connected it to the explosive. Dropping the wire to the floor, she carefully backed toward the door and removed the second one in the same manner. Emil inched forward, matching her step for step, always keeping the distance between them constant, always keeping the gun pointed at her chest.

The trills came, high-pitched and emphatic, just as she reached the base of the stairs that led upward. Cutting the wires that bound the land grant transfer to the dynamite, Belle removed the paper and laid it on the newel as she'd promised she would.

"Leave the dynamite," Emil demanded as she started to move back again. "I won't have you tossing it in through the doorway once you're outside."

He didn't know how to properly, safely handle it; leaving it for him could have deadly consequences. So could not leaving it, she realized as he waved the pistol menacingly. "You're a deeply suspicious man, Emil Caribe," she observed, holding the bundle against her flesh with her left hand while pulling loose the knot with her right.

"I intend to be a wealthy man," he countered brightly, as she bent down and gently laid the two bound sticks on the scarred wood floor.

"Be careful if you decide to handle it," she felt compelled to warn him as she regained her feet and moved toward the door behind her. "If you jar it with any force at all, it'll go off. Spark or no spark."

He nodded, his gaze shifting to the newel post and his strides lengthening. In his distraction, Belle turned and bolted out the door and onto the top, tilted step. She didn't bother with trying to hit the other ones, but simply vaulted over them and onto the street below. Darting out of the line of Emil's potential fire, she headed toward Carden's carriage and the too still, battered man lying on the ground beside it.

"He has the dynamite," she called to Inspector Larson as she passed him. "I wouldn't be in any great hurry to—"

The explosion was sudden, deafening, and enormous. Instinctively, Belle dove forward, wrapping her head in her arms. Debris rained down on her back, on the pavers around her. She counted five seconds and then rolled to her knees, casting a quick look back over her shoulder. The doorway and most of the front wall were gone. So were the steps, the little entry area, and half the stairs. All of it reduced to splinters. Two sticks of dynamite had effected as much damage as a twelve-pound keg of black powder. The next time she thought to strap a bomb to her midriff, she'd use only one. It would be more than enough.

"Are you all right, Belle?"

Carden, she realized as he hauled her to her feet and back to her senses. "Instability is one of dynamite's more noteworthy drawbacks," she said, absently brushing off her clothes as she resumed her course toward Barrett. "I'm sure they'll work on that over time."

"How is he?" she asked, dropping to her knees and taking his left hand in hers and desperately willing him to open his eyes for her, to give her even the tiniest smile and tell her that he'd be just as right as Aiden said he would be.

"He has a badly broken arm," Dr. George answered crisply. "At least three ribs that, if not broken as well, are at the very least fractured. His facial injuries appear to be superficial. However, there's swelling on the back of his head that would suggest that he has suffered a concussion. How severe it might be remains to be seen. We need to get him to my surgery as soon as possible."

Yes, that made perfect sense. The surgery. Where his bones could be set and casted and he could begin to get better. She nodded and held his hand tighter and silently promised him the most wondrous meals when he woke. Chicken soup with sweet vegetables and tender noodles until his stomach could handle heartier fare. Apple dumplings and whipped cream. He loved apple dumplings. They both loved the possibilities of whipped cream. God, he had to be all right. He had to be. If he died . . .

No. No, no. She couldn't think of the worst. Fear would paralyze her, make her useless. Barrett needed her now every bit as much as he'd needed her to think around Emil. She had to keep her head squarely on her shoulders, to focus on the moment and not look for the abyss that might lie beyond it.

Tomorrow would bring what it would bring. Now was now and fleeting. But it was all she had and she'd live in it fully, hoping for the best, for happiness. And to do that, she had to stop sniffling, dammit. Had to stop shaking like a leaf in a storm.

Again Carden took her by the arm and drew her to her feet, forcing her to release her desperate hold on Barrett's hand. And then he left her standing there feeling oddly adrift and with nothing to do but hold her breath as he and Aiden lifted Barrett off the door and maneuvered him into the carriage. As gently as they could, she assured herself, as mindful of his injuries as they could be. And Dr. George was helping, guiding them.

"Mrs. Dandaneau!"

She blinked and numbly turned toward the sound. "Inspector," she said, dragging air into her lungs and realizing that she'd been holding her breath.

"It would seem on a most cursory survey that the explosion was quite thorough and initiated in the hand of Mr. Caribe. There are only small portions of him remaining." He handed her a scrap of paper. "My men found this in the carnage. No doubt a portion of the land grant that Mr. Caribe was carrying on his person. I regret to say that I believe it is likely to be the largest piece that we recover."

Small portions. She shuddered and looked down at the

bloody bit of paper in her hand, at the mostly whole signature of James Madison. All that was left of what some people would consider a valuable treasure. "I appreciate your effort to find it for me, but there's no need to collect any more of it. I don't want it. I don't need it." She handed it back to him. "Perhaps you should keep this as evidence."

"I was right," he drawled, shaking his head and tucking the paper into his notebook. "You are an insane woman."

No, there were different kinds of treasures. The most valuable couldn't be measured in acres or in dollars and cents. "You'll be dropping all the charges against Barrett?" she asked, looking up at him.

"Of course."

"And I trust that, being a decent and honorable man, you'll see that the newspapers print a prominently featured story that fully removes all tarnish from his good name?"

He cocked a bushy, white brow. "It wasn't unblemished before this debacle."

"Either you see it done, Inspector," she said sweetly, "or I will."

Considering her with narrowed eyes, he half-smiled. "How soon do you plan to leave London, Mrs. Dandaneau?"

"Not nearly as soon as you're hoping," she countered as she walked off toward the carriage. "Maybe," she whispered, tears welling in her eyes, "if there's a God, not ever."

Isabella added more coal to the fire, then straightened and turned her back on it. They had all finally, mercifully gone to their own homes. Carden and Aiden. Mr. and Mrs. Stanbridge. Now, at last, the house around her sat silent and still as the night deepened over London. Barrett lay just as silent in his bed, the covers drawn up and tucked neatly around him, his newly casted arm cradled by a pillow. She watched the rise and fall of his chest, counting the slow measure of his breathing, and recalled the instructions Dr. George had given her as he'd tucked his stethoscope into his bag and prepared to depart.

She was to keep Barrett sedated, to spoon laudanum between his lips when he began to murmur and thrash. For the better part of the next two weeks, Dr. George had suggested. And she was to summon help at the first signs of fever or a stupor that was deeper than could be attributed to the tincture. Not that the good doctor expected to be summoned back for any such emergency. He was convinced that Barrett, if allowed to rest in a peacefully drugged slumber, would fully and completely mend.

Belle swallowed around the lump in her throat. If only surgeons were God. If only she hadn't, with her own eyes, seen Death take souls that every mortal had considered beyond its reach. A sudden catch in the breathing, a quick start, or sometimes just a long, slow sigh in their sleep. And then nothing more; the body that had been laughing, talking, eating, and mending perfectly well was a corpse. No one could see it coming. No one could ward it off. It came from nowhere, snuffing life, crushing hope, and making a mockery of medicine.

If it was Barrett's time, there was nothing she could do to lengthen the number of his days. Wanting and needing and praying didn't make any difference. She'd learned that truth the hard way. Everyone she'd ever cared about was gone. All of her family, so, so very many of her friends. She hadn't been able to save them, hadn't been able to change the course of events or the twists of Fate that had swept them into dark and cold and lonely graves.

The price of surviving, of living with that failure, had been to accept it. She'd made the decision ever so consciously, ever so firmly, as she'd laid Reny and Nigel and Bart to their rests. She'd stood there, watching as the tombs were sealed, and resolved not to care anymore, to keep a distance between herself and the people who crossed her path. It was easier to let them go if she'd never held them in her heart.

And she'd maintained her vow. Through the rest of the war and into the year after it ended. It had kept her sane and strong when others around her were crumpling in despair and inconsolable grief. It had brought her to England and seen her through the terrible news of Mignon's horrible death. It had given her the resolve she'd needed to keep going, to find Barrett Stanbridge and ask him for his help.

In looking back now, she could see that in the asking, in the accepting, her vow had begun to crack. She had allowed herself to come to know him. Guilt and need had slipped to easy companionship. Companionship to heated, hungry desire. And somewhere along the course of tumbling into bed with him, she'd also tumbled into love. The survivor's vow had been somehow forgotten. Or perhaps, she mused, it simply hadn't been strong enough to hold back the power of love. Of life.

There was no undoing it; no walking away from him, no letting him go. The grief would be unbearable and unrelenting, deeper than any she'd ever known.

Gathering her wrapper and nightrail into her hands, Belle crossed to the bed and then hiked the hems high to gently climb up beside him. "I imagine that you're thirsty," she said quietly, taking the bowl of water from the night table. Barely wringing out the cloth, she trickled precious liquid past his lips. He swallowed and faintly smiled.

"I'm willing to offer some concessions, Barrett," she said, continuing. "I promise that I'll never, ever complain about the cold and damp again. I can learn to live with it. I'll knit myself some wool stockings. And some wool gloves too."

He settled deeper into his pillow and sighed—with what

seemed like contentment. When he didn't open his lips for more water, she wrung the cloth drier and gently laid it over his swollen eye. "And I'll store the trousers away," she promised, putting the bowl back on the table. "I'll try very hard to be a proper lady. At least when out in public. And especially around your parents."

Deciding it was best not to share with him the details of the evening's unfortunate episode in the foyer, she lay down at his side. Trailing a fingertip over the fullness of his lower lip, she went on, saying, "I could help with your investigations. I think we work very well together, don't you?"

She took a steadying breath and summoned her courage. "I want to stay with you, Barrett. I love you. Please, please love me. Just a little would be enough."

In his daze, he brought his lips together as though to kiss her fingertip. Belle closed her eyes and told herself that—for a while—there was no harm in pretending that it was a promise.

Chapter Twenty

Barrett struggled through the last thick wisps of sleep, struggled to obey the urgent command of his mind to rouse. Bits of dream jumbled with bits of reality and wafted past his awareness. Carden was telling him he had to wake up because Belle had a bomb. It smelled like apples and cinnamon to him. The bookish-looking man and the white wall of pain . . . Which wasn't as bad, he vaguely realized. And he wasn't cold anymore. And the ground wasn't hard under his back either. Maybe he was dead.

The tendrils of sleep evaporated in an instant. No, he wasn't dead, he assured himself. Dead men's hearts didn't pound at the possibility. He dragged a shallow breath into his lungs and when it didn't hurt as badly or deeply as he thought it would, he took a deeper one and opened his eyes. A flat, white ceiling, he noted. Realization slowly clicked in his brain. He closed his eyes again, then opened one, closed it, and opened the other. It wasn't swollen shut anymore. It wasn't quite perfect, but it was much better than the last time he'd tried to look at the world through it.

God, where was he? The ceiling didn't tell him a

blessed thing; they were all alike. He turned his head slowly to the right. Home. His home. He recognized the armoire. How had he gotten here? How long had it been? He shifted his shoulders and turned his head to the left.

Belle lay beside him on the bed, curled on her side, her hair tumbling in an inviting, golden riot over her shoulders and across the pillow. Thick dark lashes smudged the high arches of her delicate cheekbones and her luscious lips were sweetly parted as she softly breathed in her sleep. No, he wasn't dead. Not in the least.

"Belle," he whispered, reaching out to take a warm satin curl between his fingers. Her eyes flew open and the instant wonder and joy in them sent his heart soaring. "Isabella Stanbridge," he murmured, trying the sound of it, the feel of it. And loving it as much as he did her, as much as he loved waking to find her at his side.

She didn't appear to feel the same way, though. Her brows knitted, her dark eyes clouded, she pushed herself up onto her elbow and peered deeply into his gaze. He tried to cock his right brow, but it didn't seem to move as effectively as he wanted. He cocked his left instead and asked, "What's wrong, Belle?"

"Dr. George told me to watch for confusion."

Dr. George? "I'm not confused," he assured her. "A bit stiff and sore, yes, but not the least confused, angel."

"What's my name?"

"Isabella Dandaneau." She wasn't impressed. "Destroyer of bridges and lumber mills," he said softly, reaching up to curl his hand around her neck and draw her closer. "Ravager of public peace and order. Daring angel of my heart."

"Oh, Barrett," she murmured, tears welling in her eyes as she leaned down and brushed a gentle kiss over his lips.

He smiled and slid his arm over her shoulder, drawing her closer still and laying hungry claim to her mouth. So welcoming, so lusciously heated. She was all he needed to live, all that he could ever want. She snuggled her hip against his, drew a leg across his own, and desire shot through every fiber of his body, gathering tight and hard in his loins. He was naked beneath the sheets, his brain supplied. A wrapper was all she had on. It and the sheets had to go.

His right arm didn't, though. At least not with any mind of its own. It weighed a ton and he couldn't control it, couldn't keep it from falling against her shoulder.

"Ow," she laughingly said against his lips. Drawing back ever so slightly, she gazed down at him, her eyes sparkling.

"That didn't go as I'd planned," he admitted, bringing his arm down across his chest. "The work of Dr. George, I presume?" he asked, lifting his head to look at the thick plaster encasing his arm from just above the elbow all the way down to his knuckles.

"He said it would be at least six weeks before you can hope to have the cast removed. But since you've been sleeping for the better part of a fortnight, it's not as long as it sounds."

A fortnight? God, no wonder he felt oddly thick around the edges. He rolled the shoulder of his casted arm and felt better for the stretching of the muscles and the popping of the joint.

"Dr. George wants you drugged for another four days, at least, so when he comes in this afternoon, you'll have to pretend that you are."

He wasn't going to pretend for any doctor. He was alive and mending and he had the most beautiful, decadently inviting nurse at his side. Not that he was content with her at that distance. No, as soon as he could manage it, he was going . . . He glanced down at the bend of his casted arm and accepted that they were going to have to make some adjustments for a few weeks. Which wasn't all that bad, he decided. Belle atop and astride him was actually a rather delightful prospect. And the sooner he got her there, the better.

"Baths are certainly going to be interesting," he ventured.

"I'll bathe you," she offered, trailing her fingertips along the rough stubble of his jaw.

Oh, having a broken right arm wasn't going to slow them down the least little bit. "I could hurt myself getting a fork to my mouth."

"I'll feed you, too."

Oh, yes, this was going to be the best convalescence in the history of mangled men. "What else might you do for me, Belle?"

"Anything you want."

"Angel, as I've warned you before, when it comes to you, I want a lot."

"Whatever your heart desires, Barrett. Name it and it's yours."

"You," he said, reaching down to undo the sash that held her wrapper closed. Pushing the silk aside, he slowly brushed the palm of his hand over the heated, satin skin of her hip.

A sultry smile tipped up the corners of her mouth. "Dr. George suggested that your ribs might not be up to robust exercise for yet another week or two. He didn't come right out and ban lovemaking, of course. But he made it clear that that's what he meant."

What did doctors know? "I'll let you know when the hurt outweighs the pleasure," he promised, shifting, thinking to draw her across him. "Which would be," he gasped, abandoning the attempt as his bones and muscles screamed in protest, "right now."

"Do you want some laudanum?"

"No," he breathed, trying to focus beyond the pain. "I'll be all right."

"That's what everyone kept telling me," she said, smoothing his hair. "I was so afraid that we wouldn't find you in time. So afraid that you'd never wake up. That I'd never get to hear your voice again."

Belle had been afraid he might die? His heart swelled. " 'We' being you, Carden, and John Aiden?"

She nodded, sat up, the edges of her open wrapper lying provocatively over the curves of her breasts and pooling around her thighs as she ever so deliberately began to push the bed coverings down. "And O'Brien and Inspector Larson, too. Although, in all honesty, Larson wasn't as concerned about finding you as he was catching Emil."

Lifting his arm to make the task easier for her, Barrett decided that he probably needed to know what had happened during his forced absence. While he still had the ability to think at all. "Did Larson succeed?"

"In a manner of speaking, I suppose."

"Oh?" he pressed, sensing that she really didn't want to tell him the story.

"There were only little bits of him left to sweep up."

Ice shot through his veins. "Jesus, Belle," he gasped. "What did you do?"

"You're assuming I did something to Emil."

Oh, such innocence. Such utterly feigned innocence. He grinned. "Angel, 'little bits' implies an explosion and you're the only one I know who plays with that kind of fire."

"Actually," she said sweetly, sliding a leg slowly across his own, "he blew himself up." The friction was exquisite, a prelude that shimmered through every fiber of his body.

"I warned him not to jar the dynamite," she went on, settling herself low on his abdomen, "that it could detonate without a spark. He didn't take me seriously."

Lord Almighty, she was so good, so distractingly wanton.

Hardening in anticipation, he promised himself that some-day he'd ask her for the details of how she'd come to have dynamite in the first place. He'd ask Carden and John Aiden, too. And when he finally pieced it all together, he and Belle would likely have a set-to that would make the front page of the *Times*. But for the moment, he was less concerned with the past than he was with enjoying the full wonder and joy of their having survived it.

"You could have gotten yourself killed, Belle," he observed, shifting beneath her so that his desire lightly caressed her backside.

She smiled down at him appreciatively for a long second and then seemed to consciously move the sensations to the edges of her awareness. His heart skipped a beat when she nodded. "Yes, I could have. I'll admit that I played hard," she assured him, languidly trailing a finger-tip around his nipple. "But I played as safely as I could."

Belle's idea of safe . . . His heart was pounding so hard his ribs ached. He reached out and caught her hand in his, determined to keep her advance under control until all that needed to be said had been. He'd put it off too many times already. She had to know how much her life meant to him. How deeply he loved her, how forever he would mourn her loss.

"I know that you like dancing on the edge, Belle," he said gently. "I understand the attraction in it. I honestly do. And God knows I find your fascination with it far more stimulating than I should. But please promise me that you'll never again put yourself in true danger."

She shrugged and smiled serenely. "I wouldn't worry about the risks, Barrett. Nothing horrific is going to happen to me. Madame Tanay says that I'm destined to live long."

"Madame Tanay?"

"She's something of a priestess. She's the one who taught me how to divine for missing things."

"And you believe her?" he asked, incredulous. "Enough to risk life and limb on her word for it?" He didn't give her a chance to reply. "Belle, you're a keenly intelligent woman. For God's sake, use some reason in this. Divining is one thing; courting death is quite another."

"I can't make you promises I have no intention of keeping, Barrett," she whispered, looking genuinely regretful. "I could never put my life before yours. Never. I love you too much."

It didn't matter that he couldn't breathe. Or that his heart was hammering on his smashed ribs. Belle loved him. They'd have the rest of their lives to battle over her penchant for risk. "And that makes you sad?" he asked, his soul singing.

"It scares me."

"I understand that, too," he assured her, drinking in the wonder his life had so unexpectedly become.

"You do?"

Oh, Lord, that she'd always look at him with such trust and hope in her eyes. "It rather opens up the heavens," he explained softly, "and demands that you face tomorrow with some firm decisions in hand."

"That's the perfect way of describing it."

"So have you made any decisions while I've been sleeping?"

She grinned wickedly. "Aside from the one to ravage you as thoroughly but as gently as possible in the next few minutes? No, not really."

Barrett smiled, absolutely certain of his course and the rightness of it. She was everything he'd ever desired in a woman. All that he needed now and ever would. She was perfect for him.

"Would you like to know which ones I've made?" he asked.

"While you were drifting in a laudanum haze?"

"No, Belle. Before I left you that morning. As I lay on that dirt floor and realized that I couldn't get to you, couldn't help you or protect you."

"I didn't—"

"I know," he said, gently cutting her off, "that you didn't need to be protected. *I* needed to be there for you. And when I knew that I couldn't . . ."

Her gaze was tender, filled with acceptance, with understanding. Had there been even the slightest bit of doubt in his mind . . . "I'm going to marry you, Belle. And if it takes an eternity to talk you into it, it takes an eternity. I'm going to spend every day of the rest of my life loving you. I'm going to spend every single moment making sure that you never regret loving me."

"Isabella Stanbridge," she murmured, her eyes shining.

"It sounds good, doesn't it?"

She nodded and leaned down. Planting her hands in the feather pillow on either side of his head, she kissed him slowly, deeply, with soul-melting thoroughness.

"Is that a yes, Belle?" he asked when she drew back to gaze down at him adoringly.

She started to answer, then hesitated and sat back. Touching her tongue to her lower lip, she took a deep breath. "What about your parents? They—"

"To hell with my parents," he broke in, grinning. "You're marrying *me*, not them."

The light in her eyes was troubled. "They were waiting here when we brought you from the surgery. Inspector Larson had told them about everything that happened." She sighed and absently plucked at the lace edge of her wrapper. "I was still wearing my trousers. Your mother sputtered for a second and then fainted."

"Ow," he gasped through his laughter. Bringing his arm down to press it against his side didn't help at all. "Oh, God, angel. Ow."

"It's not funny, Barrett," she protested. "Your father was still too shocked, stunned, and outraged to catch her."

He could see it so clearly. "Stop," he begged, laughing and pressing his arm closer.

"Her hoops flipped up over her head."

"Belle!" he squeaked, unable to breathe, unable to stem his laughter. "Mercy!"

Relenting, she shifted her hips, nipping his amusement in an instant, but doing nothing to help him regain his breath. "It's going to take her a while to forgive me for that," she said softly when he could finally fill his lungs.

"I'm glad that you can see some hope."

"Well, it's not so much my hope as it is hers."

"Her only hope in life is grandchildren." He started, remembering. "And that's not a worry, Belle," he promised. "On my heart, it's not. If you want children, we'll have them. There are thousands of children out there who need a home, who need to be loved. We'll haul them in here by the wagonload."

"I don't think that's going to be necessary."

He blinked and knitted his brows. "For you or for my mother?"

With the barest shrug, she answered, "For either of us."

Possibility bloomed in his heart and in his soul. God, he didn't want to presume. It would be so hurtful for both of them if he were wrong. "Belle?" he began warily, desperately hoping he was right. "Are you telling me that you're pregnant?"

There was a most adorable little shadow to her smile. Part caution, part certainty, part wicked happiness. "It will be another week before we know for sure. But my course is late and Dr. George says that I'm showing all the signs. He spoke with me about it at your mother's request. You have no idea how incredibly awkward that was."

And she'd undoubtedly handled it with aplomb. Nothing

rattled his Belle for long. Nothing. He wanted to laugh and shout to heaven. Just as much as he wanted to sob with relief. "You have to marry me, Belle," he said, his heart and soul overflowing. "If you don't, the scandal will kill my mother. You don't want that on your conscience."

"To hell with your mother, Barrett," she countered, chuckling. "To hell with scandal, too." She looked down at him, her eyes bright, her smile wide and adoring and sure. "I'm marrying you because I love you. Because I can't bear the thought of living a single moment without you."

And he without her. "Kiss me, Belle," he whispered, slipping his hand beneath the edge of her wrapper to skim his fingertips up the inside of her thigh.

Her smile sparkled with boundless, wanton joy. "Is that all you want?"

"Actually, it's the very least of what I want," he admitted, his fingers slipping through her moist curls. "But it's the traditional place to start."

"Really," she drawled, lifting her hips, easing his access. As he caressed her, she closed her eyes and dreamily smiled. "I've never been terribly bound by tradition, you know."

So beautiful in pleasure . . . "I have noticed that a time or two. I'm not, either. Which, to my thinking, doesn't bode well for our public reputations."

She laughed, the soft and throaty sound thrumming over his senses and overfilling his heart and soul with certainty. Forever and always, they were one.